### Prai

"An entertainin[g]
characters with[...]
delivered an ever-intensifying level of danger and
suspense."

—*Goodreads* on *Guarding Jess*

"This mistaken-identity caper is a gem... Readers
looking for excitement and action will definitely be
left satisfied."

—*RT Book Reviews* on *Viper's Kiss*

"A fast-paced storyline that's entertaining from
start to finish."

—*RT Book Reviews* on *Wolf Undaunted*

### Praise for Deborah LeBlanc

"*The Wolven* seamlessly weaves a remarkably
well-detailed mythology into the recent history of
New Orleans. LeBlanc's dialogue sparkles and the
sexual chemistry between Shauna and Danyon is
delicious."

—*RT Book Reviews* on *The Wolven*,
4.5 stars, Top Pick

"An interesting new mythology and non-stop action
make LeBlanc's story a fun read. Her descriptions
are vivid and the chemistry between Viv and Nikoli
is hot."

—*RT Book Reviews* on *Witch's Hunger*

"Exciting from start to finish... LeBlanc's lush
descriptions will help readers envision the magical
beings at work in this story. The attraction between
Evee and Lucien sparkles."

—*RT Book Reviews* on *The Witch's Thirst*

# WOLF UNDAUNTED

# &

# WITCH'S FURY

## SHANNON CURTIS

### AND

## DEBORAH LeBLANC

**H HARLEQUIN**® NOCTURNE™

Recycling programs
for this product may
not exist in your area.

ISBN-13: 978-1-335-83217-7

Wolf Undaunted & Witch's Fury

Copyright © 2018 by Harlequin Books S.A.

The publisher acknowledges the copyright holders
of the individual works as follows:

Wolf Undaunted
Copyright © 2018 by Shannon Curtis

Witch's Fury
Copyright © 2018 by Deborah LeBlanc

This edition published by arrangement with Harlequin Books S.A.

For questions and comments about the quality of this book,
please contact us at CustomerService@Harlequin.com.

® and TM are trademarks of the publisher. Trademarks indicated with ® are registered in the United States Patent and Trademark Office, the Canadian Intellectual Property Office and in other countries.

Printed in U.S.A.

# CONTENTS

WOLF UNDAUNTED                                    7
Shannon Curtis

WITCH'S FURY                                      275
Deborah LeBlanc

**Shannon Curtis** grew up picnicking in graveyards (long story) and reading by torchlight, and has worked in various roles, such as office admin manager, logistics supervisor and betting agent, to mention a few. Her first love—after reading, and her husband—is writing, and she writes romantic suspense, paranormal and contemporary romance. From faeries to cowboys, military men to business tycoons, she loves crafting stories of thrills, chills, kills and kisses. She divides her time between being an office administrator for the Romance Writers of Australia and creating spellbinding tales of mischief, mayhem and the occasional murder. She lives in Sydney, Australia, with her best-friend husband, three children, a woolly dog and a very disdainful cat. Shannon can be found lurking on Twitter, @2bshannoncurtis, and Facebook, or you can email her at contactme@shannoncurtis.com— she loves hearing from readers. Like...LOVES it. Disturbingly so.

### Books by Shannon Curtis

#### Harlequin Nocturne

*Lycan Unleashed*
*Warrior Untamed*
*Vampire Undone*
*Wolf Undaunted*

# WOLF UNDAUNTED

## Shannon Curtis

This story is dedicated to Vivianne Sidhom,
the friend who first introduced me to the "racier"
Mills & Boon novels in the back of the classroom.

You now have a sexy hero of your own.

# Chapter 1

Vivianne Marchetta forced herself to listen as her Southern district manager gave his report. Her first week back
at work, and her days had been full of meetings, reports,
brain-draining budgets…

Something dark flitted at the corner of her eye, and she
brushed her hair away from her forehead. Damn it, not
now, not here. It was important that she came back from
her "rest" fully charged and healthy. Strong. She had to be,
otherwise it would be a bloodbath for her vampire colony if
there was even a hint of weakness in the Nightwing Vampire Prime. She couldn't afford to weird out her followers.

"Explain to me again why we can't use the river to transport these goods?" she interrupted in a cool tone. She didn't
miss the fact he'd glossed over that detail.

Mike Falcone halted, lifting his eyes from his laptop
to meet hers. He seemed a little hesitant, and Vivianne
frowned. Mike was rarely hesitant. It was one of the rea-

sons he was usually so good at his job. Yet he looked reluctant to share some critical information with her. She arched an eyebrow, and he sighed as he leaned back in his chair.

"Things have changed since…" He frowned, trying to find the right word. She couldn't blame him. What did you call an eight-month coma that was magically induced after what should have been a lethal werewolf bite?

"My break?" she supplied.

A breathy chuckle whispered past her ear, and she turned. Who the hell was that? The area behind her was empty, with just a few yards between her seat and the wall—just the way she liked it in the boardroom, so she could see whoever was coming for her, no sneak attacks…figuratively or literally.

She frowned as she turned back to the table, then quickly composed her features when she realized her six directors were watching her warily. "I'm waiting," she prodded primly, ignoring her interruption.

Mike nodded. "Your break. Woodland Pack and River Pack formed an alliance—"

"How is that possible? Woodland are fighting with everyone."

"Not since Rafe Woodland was cast out of the pack and Matthias Marshall became Woodland Alpha Prime."

Vivianne's lips tightened at the mention of the former alpha prime's name. Rafe Woodland was the reason she'd been lying in a coma for eight months. Still, apparently there had been quite a shift since that late afternoon when the black mutt had bounded out of the shadows and attacked her. Her eyebrows rose. "Marshall is now Woodland?"

Mike nodded.

She leaned back in her chair. Rafe Woodland had been wild and erratic. Matthias Marshall would be a steadying influence in controlling the Woodland Pack and its territory. Damn it. It was so much nicer when things were a little chaotic. She'd managed to creep their border forward when Woodland was distracted with its petty squabbles with River Pack.

"Why did River Pack shut down our access to the river?" She'd asked a direct question, she'd better get a direct answer. Forcing their goods to be delivered overland was costing them a small fortune. "And please, let's not make this a breadcrumb trail. Tell me everything."

Mike sighed. "When you were attacked by Rafe Woodland, your brother found your body. He then attacked Woodland—"

"Of course," she responded, dipping her head. It was the obvious course of action.

"He killed some dog, and they teamed up with River against us."

"Well, you know my view—the only good werewolf is a dead one. My brother did the right thing. But are you telling me we've lost river access to Irondell, all because my brother killed some mangy mutt?" Vivianne shook her head. And in all this time, none of her guardians had successfully rectified the problem. What had they all been doing while she was in her coma? Watching the lycans ride rough-pad over the Nightwing empire?

"This was an across-kind crime. We can bring this to Reform Court and demand retribution." She jotted a reminder to speak with her legal counsel, but paused as Mike shook his head.

"The original crime occurred in Nightwing territory, but Rafe Woodland had already been banished from his pack and was technically a stray, with no affiliation to any pack at the time of his attack on you. Your brother trespassed on Woodland territory and killed a lycan. If we requested a transfer to Reform jurisdiction, Nightwing would have been penalized."

"And all because some measly little mongrel was put down—"

The notepad she'd been jotting notes on flipped up from the table, startling everyone, and Vivianne rose sharply from her seat.

"Stop it," she ordered, glancing wildly about. As Vampire Prime of the Nightwing colony, she sat at the head of the table, and neither of her closest neighbors were within reach. She bent to check under the table, then whirled as she sensed someone behind her.

Only, nobody was there. She turned back to the table, and something dark shifted in her peripheral vision. She twisted again, only to see her PR director's puzzled expression as he, too, peered over his shoulder.

"Did you see that?" she demanded.

He shook his head, wary and confused. She glanced down the table. "Did any of you see that?"

They all shook their heads, and Mike rose slowly from his seat. "Are you all right, Vivianne?"

It was the quiet concern that gave her pause, and she glanced at her guardians. They were all looking at her as though she was either having a medical episode or just slightly unhinged.

This was not the impression she needed to make in her first week back at work after surviving a werewolf bite.

"I'm fine," she muttered, as she stepped back a little from the table, although she glanced vigilantly around the room.

"Do you need a break?" John, the PR director queried, although his lips curved in the smallest of smirks. "Maybe you've come back too soon."

Vivianne forced a smile as she strolled around the sleek curve of the glass and chrome board table. She had her suspicions about John. He was good at what he did. Always on message. Particularly if it was his own message, like a leadership gambit. She also suspected he'd had something to do with tipping off the lycans and allowing them access into Nightwing in order to abduct a murder suspect—one who turned out to be innocent of the charge. Either way, her border had been compromised by the wolves, but only with inside help. Not that she could prove her suspicions. Still, he was challenging her, in a very subtle way, one that she couldn't let slide if she was to restore control and calm to her colony.

"You know, I think you're right, John. I think I do need a break," she sighed as she patted him on the shoulder. Quick as a flash, she grasped his chin and shoulder, then twisted, hearing the satisfying crack of bone. Her momentarily dead PR director slumped over in his chair, his forehead landing with a distinct crack on the glass table, his neck bent at an unnatural angle. When he revived once again, he'd have a hell of a headache.

"Anyone else think I need break?" she inquired calmly and glanced at each district guardian in turn around the table. All of them quietly shook their heads. She nodded with satisfaction. She was older than most of them. Stronger, too. Hopefully that killed any suggestion that she was not fit to work, or to hold the position of Vampire Prime for the Nightwing Colony. "Then let's stop wasting time. I want that river access reopened by the end of the month. Now, Jimmy, what's happening over on the west coast?"

She resumed her seat, crossed her legs, and continued to chair the meeting.

Zane Wilder bared his teeth as the Marchetta prime held court. That little—she'd called him a mangy mutt. A measly little mongrel. He held up his fisted hands. He felt so damn ineffectual. Nobody could see him. Nobody could hear him. He didn't know what the hell was going on, but he didn't like it. He certainly didn't like being attached to the stone-cold heartless head of the Nightwing vampire colony.

Everyone knew of Vivianne Marchetta, heiress to the vast Marchetta Empire. Ruthless, relentless and strategic, the daughter of a Reform senator, Vivianne's reputation was widely known, and in some cases, feared.

Not by him, of course. No. She was a vamp. She was walking worm food, just like that vicious, feral brother of hers. Zane rubbed his neck. He couldn't feel any markings, but there was still a shadow of pain from where he'd been bitten by Lucien Marchetta. After that, he had no recollection, not until he awoke, along with the Marchetta prime, in an underground clinic. Since then he drifted around with this stone-hearted corporate crocodile, an invisible, silent shadow. He'd watched her rule over her colony. He'd watched her hunt. He grimaced. She always gave them a fighting chance, no sneak attacks, but every single one of them seemed mesmerized by the little pocket-sized beauty and would succumb without much of a struggle at all. Surprisingly, though, it was always men, no women, no children—no easy prey.

He eyed her as she concluded the meeting. Every now and then, he thought he was getting through…like just before. She'd heard him laugh. He was sure of it. She tried to ignore him, but every now and then she'd crack. Her eyelids would flicker when he spoke, or…she'd peer under the table for him. He chuckled. That had been a good one, he had to admit.

Vivianne glanced about, then rose from the table, effectively dismissing her minions. She collected her bag and notepad—she'd occasionally surprised him with her old-school practices. Most everyone else was using a device, but she used the old-fashioned method of notetaking—pen and paper.

One of the guardians waited for her at the door, stepping aside as the others filed out. Zane couldn't help noticing that nobody moved the guy with the broken neck. He shook his head. Vampires were nasty. So little regard for life. Still, the guy was annoying, and Vivianne had been quite effective in silencing him. He liked effective. Not that he liked Vivianne. *Hell, no.*

Zane's gaze dropped to Vivianne's hips as she halted at the doorway, and he folded his arms, leaning against the jamb. Much as he'd like to get the hell out of Vamp Central, he'd discovered he couldn't range far from Vivianne. The voluptuous little vampire was exhausting. Constantly on the go, from one meeting to another, although how she managed to do it in those killer heels all day, he had no idea. He eyed her legs. Her slender, golden-skinned legs…the top of her head barely grazed his shoulder, but she had the figure of a pocket Venus, all curves and hollows and smooth skin, dark chocolate eyes and lips that were full and pouty. He frowned. If you were into that sort of thing.

"Uh, look, I realize you're probably busy, getting back into the swing of things, and all," the guardian began. Zane noticed it was the one who told her about his death. *Death.* But not…quite. He didn't feel dead. He didn't know what death was supposed to feel like, though, but he didn't think it was this. He was…*aware.* He always thought death was supposed to be peaceful. Being somehow anchored to Vivianne Marchetta was not peaceful. His eyes widened. Maybe he was in hell. Yeah. A werewolf being stuck with a vampire for all of eternity sure sounded like hell to him, especially if that vampire was Vivianne. The woman brought a whole new level to the world "cool". Arctic, maybe.

"I'm fine, Mike. Really," she said, her tone confident.

"Yeah, I can see that," Mike said, lifting his chin to indicate the slumped-over vamp. "I just thought, with everything that's happened while you were on your 'break,'" he said meaningfully, "that maybe, if you needed to be quietly brought up to speed, I could help."

"Oh, puh-leeze," Zane muttered. He could see the thinly-masked appreciation in the guy's eyes.

Vivianne stiffened next to him, and he saw her eyes shift, just a little. She tilted her head, and her dark hair slid across her back to brush Zane's arm. He glanced down. She had dark, wavy curls that he'd learned were all natural. Pretty. He frowned and moved to create a little more distance. He didn't need no sexy, alluring vamp to rub herself up against him, with her tempting hair and—he inhaled—damn it, not even her scent was soft or comfortably, florally, feminine. No, it was zesty and spicy and sexy all at once and was becoming part of his natural breathing, no matter how hard he fought it…

"What are you suggesting?" Vivianne asked, her voice low and husky.

Zane frowned. "You're not falling for this, are you?"

Vivianne tilted her head forward, her expression hidden behind that ebony, wavy curtain of hair.

"Perhaps dinner?" Mike suggested. His voice had lowered, and there was a definite glint in the guy's eyes.

"I think I'm going to puke," Zane muttered. "Get me out of here." Watching vamps flirt was about as much fun as being skinned alive, he was sure of it.

"I think dinner could be a good option," Vivianne agreed evenly. "You can fill me in on anything else I've missed."

"I'd be happy to fill you in," Mike said, winking. Zane made a gagging noise. The guy was not subtle at all. "I'll pick you up—seven?"

Vivianne nodded, then watched as Mike left the room, whistling. At least, Zane thought that's what he was trying to do. It came out like a little wheezy whine.

"This is definitely hell," Zane said, nodding. Watching these two vamps tap dance around a flirty little power play was beyond tedious.

Vivianne frowned, and Zane's eyes narrowed. "Can you hear me, darlin'?" he asked, straightening up from the doorjamb to face her, excitement and hope flaring within him.

Vivianne stepped toward the door, her chin lifting as she flicked her hair over her shoulder—and into his face.

Zane flinched as a tendril caught him in the eye, his lips tightening, then he followed the vamp. "Your taste in men sucks. He can't even whistle properly."

Vivianne walked away faster. Zane was content to hang back and watch the swing of her curvy hips.

# Chapter 2

"How is everything else going, then?"

Vivianne finished applying the cinnamon-red lipstick and smacked her lips before turning back to her phone. She had her sister-in-law, Natalie, on an interactive call, and Natalie was cleaning a—Vivianne frowned.

"What *is* that?"

"It's a sword," Natalie answered. "I dug it up from a Peruvian ruin. How awesome is it?" Her sister-in-law displayed it proudly, balancing it on her palms and holding it up to the camera.

"How dirty is it?" Vivianne responded, grimacing.

Natalie shrugged. "Now, yes, but once I've finished with it, she'll look good as new."

"Speaking of good as new," Vivianne said, "Everything is going fine."

"Uh-huh. Did you visit the doctor?"

Vivianne averted her eyes. "I haven't had time," she murmured.

Natalie put the dirt-caked sword off to the side, and leaned closer to the screen. "You have to. You're just putting it off."

Vivianne frowned. She wasn't used to someone speaking so plainly with her. Natalie was the only person, apart from her brother, Lucien, and her father, Vincent, who didn't seem to cower or simper around her. No, the woman was incredibly genuine and caring, and she could totally see why her brother had fallen so completely, sickeningly in love with her. Still, it was annoying when not everybody swallowed the line you fed them. "I'm fine."

"Do you still have shadowy vision?"

Vivianne had mentioned her issue with shadows in her peripheral vision to Natalie before her brother and sister-in-law had left Marchetta Manor. Natalie and her father did not get along. She couldn't blame her. Vincent Marchetta had kidnapped Natalie for her strange blood—the same blood that had proven to be the vampiric cure against a werewolf bite, and what had ultimately saved Vivianne's own life, neutralizing the lycan toxin that had slowly spread through her body and would have killed her. Vivianne's father, Vincent, would have consigned Natalie to a lifetime of captivity as a blood donor if Natalie hadn't busted free and Lucien hadn't fought his father on it. To say the Marchettas weren't playing happy family at the moment would be an understatement.

"No," Vivianne lied. "All good."

Natalie's eyes narrowed. "Vivianne…"

"Natalie…" Vivianne responded in the same low, firm tone.

Natalie frowned as she gazed behind her, and Vivianne whirled. "What? Do you see something?"

"I'm not sure... I thought I saw..."

Vivianne turned back to the phone warily. "What do you see?" Natalie had a...gift. She could see ghosts, and Vivianne had been in awe when Natalie had told her some stories about spirits she'd spoken with. It would have been easy to chalk it up to her sister-in-law being a bit of a loon, but she'd seen Natalie morph into a cross-breed; part-vampire, part-werewolf, part-human—something that wasn't supposed to exist, so she'd decided to have a little faith in her sister-in-law's ghostly abilities.

Natalie squinted, then shrugged. "I get nothing."

"A ghost?" Could that explain the sense of being watched, of not being alone...? Could it explain the deep, almost gruff voice she occasionally heard in her head and desperately tried to ignore?

Natalie shook her head. "I don't think so," she said, then smiled in reassurance. "Don't mind me, I'm just tired. So, tell me about this date!"

Vivianne pasted a smile on her face to hide her disappointment. If Natalie couldn't see a ghost, then...it was all in her head. The visions, the voice... She swallowed. Maybe there was some permanent damage from the lycan toxin?

A werewolf's bite was lethal to a vampire, and she'd been brutally attacked by Rafe Woodland, a stray, angry wolf. She should have died, if it wasn't for her brother's efforts to find a miraculous cure and the aid of an unusual witch. A vampire had never survived a lycan's bite before. Nobody knew if there were any side effects to what she'd experienced. Maybe the toxin was coming back? She remembered the early stages: the agonizing, searing pain, the burning of her blood vessels as the corrosive throbbed its way through her body with every beat of her heart... The terrifying, petrifying hallucinations... Her fingers clenched at the torturous memories. She'd never given voice to that experience, hadn't told anyone, not even her brother, how scared and alone she'd felt, trapped inside a decaying body. No, because that would be a weakness she could ill-afford as she reestablished herself as the reigning Marchetta Prime. She forced herself to concentrate on the conversation with Natalie.

"Uh, he's one of the district guardians—"

"Do you like him?"

"Sure, he's nice enough."

"Nice enough?" Natalie rolled her eyes. "A shiraz is 'nice enough.' You're talking about a guy. Is he gorgeous?"

Vivianne nodded. "He's good-looking," she admitted. Then she smiled. "He surprised me."

"Why? You're gorgeous, he's gorgeous, you already have so much in common."

She shrugged as she played with her foundation brush. "It's just—it's been a while since I've been out with a guy."

"You were in a supernatural coma for eight months, Vivianne. That will put a dent in anyone's social life."

Vivianne chuckled. "No, I mean—I'm a Prime, Natalie. Not many guys are willing to ask a Prime out on a date."

"Ooh, so this is a *date*. You said it was business meeting when I first called."

"Well, I'm not sure. Maybe it's both."

"Do you want it to be?"

Vivianne hesitated, her teeth sinking into her bottom lip as she thought about her response. "Dating is…hard. When I was younger, I couldn't tell if the guys were asking me out for me, or because it gave them access to my father." She'd learned that, the hard way. She shrugged. "I don't get…too involved."

"You're playing it safe," Natalie commented. This time it was her sister-in-law who shrugged. "That's smart. I get it. But every now and then, a risk can pay off."

"I take enough risks in business," Vivianne said.

"I'm just saying, maybe you can trust this one a little more?"

And let him find out that either the toxin was back, or she was going crazy? Yeah, no. Some of her worry must have shown on her face, because Natalie's expression grew serious.

"Do you want me to come back, Viv?"

Only Natalie and Lucien called her Viv. Only they had the audacity to do so. She was touched by Natalie's offer. It would mean returning to the very place she'd been held captive, and facing the man who had orchestrated it… Vivianne's father. That Natalie was prepared to do that just made her care for her sister-in-law all the more. Not that she'd ever admit that to anyone. She sucked in a breath and shook her head.

"No, thanks so much for the offer, but I'm fine. Really." She'd figure it out on her own, just like she always did, and she'd sort it out. One way or another. The phone chimed, and Vivianne grimaced. "Dad's trying to get through."

Natalie made a face. "That's my cue to leave. I'd say give him my best, but we both know I don't mean it."

Vivianne was still chuckling when her sister-in-law disappeared. She fidgeted with her robe, making sure she was modestly presentable, then accepted the call from her father.

Vincent Marchetta's face peered back at her. His expression was cool, remote, and she quickly adopted the same.

"Hello, Dad."

"Vivianne, I need to talk with you." Vivianne kept her features calm. There was never any greeting from her father.

"I'm about to go out—" she began, but he shook his head.

"No. I won't do this over the phone. I'll meet with you tomorrow night, seven o'clock, at home."

She knew her father expected a quick acquiescence, a

display of obedience, but she'd been his daughter for hundreds of years, and disappointment came with the role. "I'll see if I'm free." She quickly pressed a few buttons on her phone, and scanned her calendar. Sure enough, she had a meeting scheduled.

"Push it to eight and I can make it."

His lips pressed together. "I'm fairly busy—"

"So am I, Dad," she interrupted. It was the family business she was working at, after all. Besides, she'd learned that if you didn't push back a little with her father, he could be a steamroller, crushing everything in his path.

He sighed noisily, clearly communicating his disappointment, before finally nodding—once. "Fine. Eight."

"Can you give me any idea what this is about?" She could try to guess, but she'd learned she could never figure out how her father thought.

"A campaign," her father stated shortly. "I'll see you then."

The phone screen went black. Vivianne's shoulders sagged. "Good talk, Dad. Yeah, love you, too." She stared at the blank screen for a moment. Just once, she wondered what it would be like to have a genuine conversation that didn't revolve around business, or what he wanted her to do for him, or what he expected her to do for family.

But that kind of wondering led to wishes, and wishes were a waste of time. She was a centuries-old working woman. She wasn't some simpering little girl with pointless dreams. She grabbed up the remote to her stereo and switched it on. Rock and roll music from the 1950's era, before The Troubles. She shimmied her shoulders to the beat, singing out "tequila!" She never got tired of this music, and used it to unwind from the stresses of the day—like talking to her dad.

She rose from her dressing table and danced barefoot

across the charcoal-colored plush carpet to the wardrobe. She had about twenty minutes before Mike was due to pick her up. She was so surprised and yes, flattered, that he'd invited her out. She'd seen that glint of desire in his eyes, the attraction…she wasn't a novice when it came to men. It was just rare that guys acted on that attraction. She was the head of the Nightwing colony, she also ran a multimillion-dollar empire. And she knew she wasn't the easiest woman to get to know. All that was enough to intimidate most men. But apparently not Mike Falcone. She started to do the twist, swinging her hips with her hands swaying. God, she remembered dancing to this music in the dance halls. But then, she remembered dancing the Charleston, too.

Vivianne flicked through the hangars, head bopping along as Chuck Berry told Beethoven to roll over. Her lips quirked. She'd met Ludwig, once. Weird little guy. She pulled two dresses out: one red, one black. She held the red one up to her body, turning a little. It was a figure-hugging dress with a deep V neckline. Sexy and feminine. She hung it on the hook near the mirror, and held up the black dress. This one was also slim-fitting, but with a bateau neckline. Demure and feminine.

"Go with the black—you don't want to look desperate."

She whirled, glancing wildly about her room. "Who's there? Show yourself!"

The music blared across the room. Her breath hitched as she strode over to the crimson curtains that covered the floor-to-ceiling window of her penthouse apartment that looked out over the city of Irondell, and she twitched the fabric, checking to see if someone was hiding behind it.

Nobody was. She strode over to the dressing table, and switched the music off, listening intently. Nothing.

She dropped to her knees and peered under the king-size bed. Nobody there, either. She covered her face, rocking on her knees for a moment. "I'm not crazy, I'm not crazy," she whispered to herself, until she could calm her racing heart. She took a deep, shuddering breath. Okay. Get dressed. Go out. Pretend everything is just hunky-dory.

She rose to her feet, and padded over to the mirror where she'd dropped the dress. Black, huh? She reached for the red dress, in an open act of rebellion, and untied the silken belt around her waist. The silk robe parted, and she slipped it off her shoulders, revealing her black, lacy, unlined uplift bra and matching lacy panties.

She heard a low whistle. "Better yet, don't wear a dress at all."

Her wide-eyed gaze lifted to the mirror. In its reflection she saw the figure of a man behind her. He was tall—huge, really—and broad-shouldered, his muscled arms and chest revealed by a white singlet. He wore khakis that flattered the long, muscled length of his legs, and his brown hair was scruffy, matching the stubble on his face. A weird light glowed through the dark tendrils of fog or smoke gently swirling around him.

Vivianne screamed.

Zane winced at the ear-piercing shriek. God, that woman could break glass, if she put in just a little more effort.

She backed away from him, her head slowly shaking in denial, and then it hit him.

"You can see me," he breathed.

"Get out!" she screamed again, then raced to her dressing table. "Get out, you pervert." She picked up a container of moisturizer, turned, and hurled it to him. He ducked.

"Hey, if I could get out of here, princess, I would," he snarled back at her.

"Get. Out. Of my. House!" She picked up another bottle, then another, and threw them in quick succession at him.

He dodged the first, but he wasn't quite fast enough to get out of the way of the second missile. He froze as it sailed through his chest and smashed against the wall behind him. Er. *Yeesh*. That felt weird. Like fuzzy electrical shocks.

Vivianne's eyes grew even rounder, if that was possible, and she picked up the vase off the end of the table and hurled it. He shifted, but it still caught him in the shoulder. Or rather, through it. More fuzzy tingling, like he'd cut off the circulation, and the numbness was about to wear off, right before the pins and needles.

She stalked up to him, her eyes glowing red like cigarettes, incisors lengthening, dark hair streaming behind her, silken robe flapping around her, and that curvaceous body quivering with rage. She fisted her hand and punched him—right through the face. He felt a nice little frisson, but that was about it.

He arched his eyebrow. "I can keep this up for hours. You?" He looked around the room. "There's a crystal lampshade over there that looks handy."

This time both of her hands clenched into fists. Her chest rose and fell in furious pants, and for a moment he just followed the movement: in, out, in…he blinked. She was… magnificent. He frowned. And she was not happy.

"Who—or what—the hell are you?" she rasped, her eyes bright with anger.

# Chapter 3

"You don't—you don't know me?" His jaw dropped, and then he raised both hands in exasperation. "Oh, come *on*. That is so unfair." He'd been stuck as this vamp's sidekick for—hell, he didn't even know how long, but it felt like an eternity. She had become his guide, his anchor... Everything he saw was around her, bound to her.

And she had no idea who he was. Well, that sucked. He pursed his lips. His ego would recover, but he'd need a minute.

Her hand shot out to grasp his throat and passed through him. His lips quirked. So far the only good thing about this was watching her try to hit him and fail. Again, and again. He liked sharing the frustration. He folded his arms, waiting patiently as she tried to move, shove, punch, kick, bite... in scraps of lace that barely covered her.

"This reminds me of a movie I once saw, but I think there was jelly involved."

She halted, glaring at him through a curtain of dark curls. He waggled his eyebrows and mouthed the word *jelly*.

"What the hell is going on here?" she snarled as she pulled her robe tight around her, concealing her golden-skinned curves framed in black lingerie. She was such a contradiction. All soft curves and femininity from the neck down. From the neck up—well, she was all sharpness and frost with a hint of homicide. At least her eyes weren't glowing anymore, but had returned to their normal brown. Well, kind of normal. She had these cool little splinters of dark among the brown, and every now and then there was a fleck of gold. Fascinating. Damn it.

"I'm as confused as you are," he answered truthfully.

She folded her arms, her lips pursing in a tight, tempting little pout. "Who are you?"

He inclined his head. "Zane Wilder, Alpine Pack Guardian," he said formally.

She sneered. "A mutt? How dare you come into my home."

He held up a hand. "Trust me, princess, this is the last place, and you are the last woman, I'd ever want to hang with." He shuddered. Ugh. Vamps. So full of themselves. They carried the stench of death with them. Usually. Vivianne, though, had quite a pleasing scent. And again, he was not going to focus on that tempting, seductive, sassy little fragrance.

"I find myself...stuck."

*"Stuck?"* Vivianne's eyebrows rose as she grappled with the word.

"On you."

"On me."

"Stuck on you," he clarified.

"Stuck on—"

"This conversation is going to be a long one if you're just going to repeat everything I say," he muttered.

Her brows drew together, and her eyes flashed. "Forgive me, I'm trying to understand how a dog got *stuck* on me."

Zane narrowed his eyes. He was getting tired of her dog and mutt references. "And I'm trying to figure out how I got hitched to a soulless bloodsucker."

She lifted her chin. "When?"

"When what?"

"When did you get stuck to me?"

He shrugged, frowning. "I don't know. I woke up inside some hospital room, and then all hell broke loose."

"And?"

"And what?"

She rubbed her forehead, as though an ache had started behind her eyes. Good. He hoped he made her head ache. His head pounded from trying to piece together the puzzle, particularly when he only had half the pieces.

"And what happened after that?"

He gestured around the room. "This happened. Where you go, I go. I've tried to walk away. Hell, I've tried to run away, and it's like a revolving door, I'm running away, the world tilts, and I'm right back where I started."

"With me."

He nodded. "With you."

She crossed her arms, then raised her hand to her face, nibbling on her thumbnail. It was an unconscious gesture, and possibly one of the most vulnerable he'd ever seen her do. She turned, took a couple of steps, hesitated.

"So…you've been with me for…a while."

He nodded.

"Since I woke up?"

He shrugged. "I guess so."

"The hospital room—what can you remember of it?"

He frowned. His memory was a little fuzzy. He was pretty sure there was a massive hole in it, somewhere. "You were lying in a box, your douche of a brother was there, some cute chick, and a guy in motorcycle leathers."

She nodded. "Yeah, that's pretty much when I came out of a coma."

He frowned. "Why were you in a coma? You're a vamp." Vampires, like werewolves and other shifters, had the ability to self-heal. He'd never heard of vamps succumbing to a coma.

She started pacing again. "It wasn't a normal coma," she murmured. He rolled his eyes.

"I gathered that. I don't *normally* float around coma patients."

She shot him an annoyed glance. "I was put in a coma by a witch because I was attacked—by one of your kind." She said the last words with bitter animosity.

Fleetingly, the thought of her being attacked, of being hurt by another, bothered him. But fortunately he was able to tamp that down, squish it into a dark place where nobody would know a werewolf briefly cared about what happened to a bloodsucker.

"Rafe Woodland," he said quietly, a fragment of memory surfacing among the murk of his brain.

Her eyes narrowed. "How did you know?"

"Your douchebag of a brother brought you to our camp, looking for revenge."

"I was attacked on Nightwing land," she said, frowning. "He had every right."

"He had no right," Zane corrected her harshly. "Rafe had been cast out of Woodland. Whatever he did, he did on his own. Woodland wasn't to blame."

"He practically killed me," she exclaimed. "He *bit* me."

"And your brother bit *me*," Zane snarled. "What should his punishment be?"

Vivianne's eyes widened, and he watched as realization crept in. He nodded. "Yes, I'm that mangy mutt, that measly little mongrel who cost you your river access," he snapped in disgust.

Her mouth opened, but no words came out as she struggled to process his words. Her doorbell rang downstairs, and she clapped her hand over her mouth. "Uh-oh."

She whirled and ran over to scoop up the red dress, stepping into it quickly and dragging it up over her body, slipping the robe off her shoulders as she did so. There was a tantalizing glimpse of golden skin, and then she turned, contorting as she pulled the zipper up and slipped into her shoes at the same time.

Zane frowned. "What are you doing?"

"I'm going out," she muttered, checking her reflection in the mirror, spritzing herself with some fragrance, then plucking up the clutch purse she'd placed on the bed.

"You're going out?" he repeated, incredulous.

"Yes, I'm going out. I'm going to have dinner with a good-looking man, have some conversation that doesn't involve—" she waved her hand in his general direction "—weird, freaky stuff, and I'm going to have a nice evening that I'm going to enjoy like a normal woman."

She hurried over to her bedroom door as the doorbell pealed again from the floor below. She hesitated, then turned back to him.

"Wait a minute, were you stuck with me *all* of the time?" Her gaze darted toward her en suite bathroom.

His lips quirked. "Yep."

Her cheeks bloomed with heat, and her mouth parted,

then she snapped her lips together. "That wasn't gentlemanly," she hissed as she backed out of the room.

He chuckled. "That's because I'm no gentleman."


Vivianne forced her gaze to Mike's. "So, it sounds like a lot happened when I was…away?" She sat for a moment, digesting the information. Woodland had a new alpha prime, light warriors had been discovered after hundreds of years of folks believing they'd been completely wiped out, and one of the most prominent men in Irondell society, Arthur Armstrong, was now dead.

"It's great gossip, isn't it?" Zane chirped, his hands cupping his chin as he leaned on the table between her and Mike.

She glared at him. He'd appeared in the car—God, what an awkward trip that had been, with him chattering away in the back seat. She tried to ignore the lycan—a difficult task seeing as he was six foot three, built and ripped, and mildly gorgeous. For a lycan.

"Who is managing the Armstrong interests?" Arthur Armstrong had been a wily competitor. She'd tangled with him on a few occasions. Sometimes he'd won, sometimes she'd won. She wanted to know who Nightwing were up against now.

Mike grimaced. "Armstrong Enterprises is no more. His sons discarded his name and wiped it out of the family tree. Everything is now Galen Inc."

"As in, Ryder Galen? Doesn't his wife work in our legal department?"

Mike shook his head as he chewed on a morsel of steak. "She left when your father stepped in to run the business. She now works as Galen's legal counsel."

"Darn," Vivianne muttered. "She was good."

"Good for Ryder," Zane said, nodding.

He knew this Galen? Vivianne didn't know if that was

good or bad. If the lycans were in any way affiliated with Galen, then that was probably bad news for vampires.

Zane twisted in her direction.

"How is the wine?" he inquired, then frowned. "Please tell me that's wine, and not blood." He made a gagging sound, and she pursed her lips.

"What's it going to take to re-open the river channel to market?" she asked, determinedly focusing on the handsome vampire in front of her, and not the annoying werewolf at her side.

Mike shrugged. "Not sure. It's difficult to get them to the table. They're very eager to strengthen the relationship with Woodland, and apparently that lycan your brother killed was well liked."

"Aw, now that's sweet," Zane said, sniffing as he dabbed at his eye. "They did that for me? That warms the cockles of my dead little heart."

Vivianne's gaze dropped to the fork in her hand. It was so tempting…

"Go on, you know you want to," Zane said, indicating the fork with a lift of his chin. "I'm sure Wheezy Whistler here would love to see you go batcrap crazy on empty space. They can't see me, remember?" He blew a kiss at Mike, who smiled, oblivious, at Vivianne. "See?"

Vivianne forced herself to place the fork gently on the plate. "Find out what they want. Then make sure we get it."

Mike nodded, then glanced down at the fork. "You don't like your meal?"

"It's fine." It was the company she had issues with. Oh, not Mike, he seemed nice enough. She smiled brightly.

He reached over and covered her hand with his. "I'm glad you're still with us," he told her softly. She was surprised by the contact and instinctively pulled away. She wasn't the touchy-feely type.

Zane dropped his forehead to the table. "I really wish I could puke."

"Me, too," she said. "Glad I'm still here," she clarified, when Zane lifted his head to look at her in surprise. No, she didn't mean she wanted to throw up with him.

"Like, hurl until I get this sick all out of my system. But I can't," Zane elaborated, his fist tapping his flat stomach. "Can't pee, can't poop. Can't puke. Must be a dead thing. Hey, you're dead. Well, undead. But you pee and poop. How does that work?"

She closed her eyes as warmth bloomed in her cheeks. Had he been stuck with her when she did *that*? And just like that, he'd obliterated any hope for an intimate evening with Mike.

"Is everything okay, Vivianne?" Mike asked, and she opened her eyes to see his concerned expression.

She nodded. "I'm fine. I just remembered I have some work to finish at home before a meeting tomorrow," she lied. "I'm sorry, can we do this another time?"

"Sure," Mike said, smiling in understanding. "I figure it's going to take some time for you to adjust to your normal routine." He signaled for the waiter, and in moments she was back in his car, her date ending earlier than she'd expected. Earlier than she suspected Mike expected.

She turned in the foyer that led from the elevator to the front door of her penthouse. Mike stood there, his expression curious, tinged with anticipation.

And right next to him stood a hulk of a werewolf, muscular arms folded as he glared at her.

"Do *not* invite him in," Zane warned her. "You and I need to talk."

She arched an eyebrow and looked at Mike. There was no way in hell she would let a wolf order her about. "Would you like to—"

Zane snarled, and in a flash, her clutch flew out of her grasp.

Mike's head reared back to avoid the missile, his expression clearly surprised.

Vivianne covered her mouth. "Oh, I'm so sorry," she gasped. She'd nearly smacked her date in the head with her bag. Her eyes narrowed as she glared at Zane. No, *he'd* nearly smacked her date in the head with her bag.

"Uh, that's...fine," Mike said as he bent to retrieve her purse. He handed it to her. "You were about to say?" he prodded her.

This wasn't going to work. Not tonight. She had a furious, impatient werewolf ghost, or spirit, or phantom, or hallucination, or whatever the hell he was, effectively blocking any attempt she made at communicating with this man. Frankly, the effort to ignore him and pretend everything was normal was exhausting.

"Would you like to do this again sometime?" she finished gently.

Mike's disappointment was quickly replaced with a smile and a nod. "Sure."

He leaned down to kiss her, and Zane's nose blocked her view of her date for a moment.

"I swear, if this turns into some sort of twisted voyeur experience, you're going to need to make me some popcorn. Just saying."

Vivianne tilted her head away from Zane, and Mike's lips landed on her cheek. "Uh, thanks for a great evening," she said, then turned and unlocked her door, stepped inside and gave him a shaky wave. She closed the door, then leaned back against it, shutting her eyes.

That had to be the most embarrassing, weird and frustrating—

"Can we talk now?"

She opened her eyes to glare at the six-foot-three-inch wall of infuriating male. He arched an eyebrow, and with his scruffy brown hair, and a short beard that framed his jaw and—wow, he had really nice lips. The bottom one was slightly fuller, and a mental image of her sinking her teeth into it surprised her. Mainly because it wasn't an image of her ripping him to shreds like she tried to convince herself she wanted to, but because the image was playful and sexy and all kinds of wrong.

His brown gaze met hers, and for the first time she realized he had hazel flecks, green and gold shards the gradually lightened the longer they stood there, staring at each other.

She frowned. This…man, if she could call him that—was he even real? She reached out, swiping her arm across his body, and he closed his eyes as her arm swept through his body. She felt…nothing. No, maybe there was a slight change in air temperature. Or was she desperately clutching at any detail to justify what was going on?

Was he just a hallucination? But she didn't really know him… She'd never heard his name before today. Would she hallucinate about a guy she never knew existed?

"We need to talk," he told her quietly.

She shook her head. "No. You need to go away."

She moved away from the door and walked right through him, hearing his swift inhalation as she passed. She strode up the stairs.

"I can't," he exclaimed as he followed her. Damn, he was so big. Even as some insubstantial existence, he seemed to swallow up her awareness, and she found it was hard to focus on anything else. Just like it had been hard to focus on Mike with this large, attention-consuming presence next to her.

Normally she was repulsed by the werewolves. They were animals, reverting to their inner beast with ease and frequency, their civility only a thin veneer, and their fragrance quite odious. Zane, though, smelled of something different. His scent was earthy, woodsy, with notes of myrtle, cedarwood and almond. How was that even possible? How could find a lycan's scent be almost attractive? She slammed the door shut on him, hearing him growl in frustration before he floated through the timber.

The fact that she was having these reactions to him was what freaked her out the most. She could see something that wasn't there. She could hear his deep, smooth voice in her head, but if he really was a lycan, she would never, ever find him attractive. And she did.

Which meant she really was going crazy.

"You're not here," she muttered, as she crossed to her bed and picked up the nightgown that one of her staff had placed at the end of the bed before they'd left for the day. Unlike her father, she didn't like to be surrounded by servants, and wanted them gone by the time she came home. This was her space, the only place she could be by herself. She didn't want to worry about who was watching her for whom, and as a Prime, that happened.

"Oh, I'm here," Zane told her.

She wasn't going to argue with him—because that would make him, or the hallucination that was him, all the more real.

She kicked off her shoes and didn't bother to put them away. Instead, she marched into her en suite and closed the door. She looked into the mirror over the vanity for a moment. She looked...spooked.

Her shoulders sagged. It was a good thing she hadn't invited Mike in. She couldn't afford to let anyone see her like this, or guess at what was going on with her—whatever that turned out to be. Her vision blurred for a moment, and she blinked, tilting her head back. Marchettas didn't cry. That's what her father had said, the night he'd turned her.

Marchettas were the strongest of their kind, he'd said. It was why they'd become so successful, so powerful. Tears were a weakness. Feelings were a weakness. If someone in the Nightwing colony guessed that she was losing her mind, that she was mentally deteriorating, it would be a bloodbath within the colony until a new Prime was selected. And that was the internal strife.

If the other vampire colonies scented blood, a scandal or a weakness, they would pounce. If a shifter breed, like the lycans or the bears, suspected the Nightwing colony was weakening, there would be territory wars. Whichever way she looked at it, if she gave in to these hallucinations, if she let herself indulge in an annoying, frustrating, rude companion that nobody else could see, feel or hear, she was leading her people down a path to bloodshed and death. Despite what everyone thought, she really did care for Nightwing, for her colony. They were as close to a family she was ever going to get. She needed to protect them, if only from herself.

Tomorrow, she'd visit Ryder Galen. His family were shadow breed healers, and maybe he could figure out what was wrong with her. She just hoped she could trust him.

She got ready for bed, removing her makeup and brushing her hair. For once, Zane didn't make an appearance.

Maybe she could control him, after all? Maybe he only appeared when she was tired? Or distracted?

She opened the drawer under the counter to put her brush away and paused when she saw the small bottle rolling around inside. The pills the doctor had prescribed for her recuperation postcoma. She'd had nightmares, horrendous nightmares about the attack, and these pills were supposed to help her sleep. They had worked—sometimes. If they'd blocked her nightmares, they might be able to block these auditory hallucinations…

She shook two out of the bottle and took them with a glass of water, then brushed her teeth. By the time she stepped out of the bathroom, she was already feeling relaxed.

"*Now* can we talk?" Zane muttered.

She kept her eyes resolutely forward as she crossed to her bed and pulled back the bed covers. *Ignore him.*

"You can't ignore me forever, princess," Zane said as he stood at the end of her bed, frowning. Her eyelids flickered. Could he read her thoughts now?

She climbed into bed, her lips firmly pressed together to prevent any response to him.

"We need to figure out what's going on here," he stated.

She brushed her hair off her forehead and lay back. *Just ignore him.* Her eyelids began to droop, and he stalked around the bed to stand by her hip. He really was a gorgeous man, all beautiful muscles, tanned skin, and she thought the close-cropped beard was growing on her. It gave him a rough, dangerous look that was very attractive.

Her eyes widened, but only briefly. Wow, these tranqs were good. They had to be if she thought Zane Wilder was kind of sexy.

"Speak to me, damn it," he demanded.

She smiled. He was cute when he was angry. His eyes narrowed, and he leaned down to look closely at her eyes, his gaze shifting from one to the other and back again.

"Damn it, you took a tranq, didn't you?" His lips tightened, and although it took a great deal of effort, she raised her fingers to his lips to smooth them out again.

"Shh," she said soothingly.

He swore under his breath, his hands momentarily clenching, and then that smoky, inky fog swirled around him, and he was gone.

Her eyelids drooped shut, and her mouth dipped at the corners, and she could barely retain her last thought.

*Don't go...*

# Chapter 4

Zane sat in the wingback chair next to Vivianne's bed, his feet on the covers, and he watched her sleep. He didn't have anything else to do. Her chest rose rhythmically, her breathing deep and even. She looked like a dark angel, her hair fanned out on the pillow, her features so relaxed, so damn composed.

She'd donned a white nightgown, the satin and lace concoction contrasted against her olive complexion, making her skin look warm and silken in the dim light that filtered through a crack in her curtains. He swallowed. He always gave her privacy when she was in the bathroom, despite the impression he'd given her earlier, but he hadn't expected her to take sleeping pills to avoid talking with him. That didn't seem like Vivianne's normal style. He'd seen her in action. She was direct, decisive, and hadn't shied away from anything, whether it was chairing a meeting with a bunch of seasoned vampire guardians, or negotiating with a strategic business partner.

If he was going to be honest—and in the middle of the night, in a darkened room, with the only other occupant knocked out by sleeping tablets, he could afford to be honest—the Marchetta Vampire Prime had surprised him. She'd faced every decision she'd had to make with a calm confidence. She had a reputation for being ruthless, especially with her enemies, but he'd also seen her be fair. She was a hard taskmistress, but she never demanded of her staff anything she wasn't prepared to do herself. And he'd been with her since the moment she'd awoken in that nutty little clinic under her father's home, and she'd been hurt. She'd been tired, and yet she'd never let anyone see it, not even her brother, and most especially not the senator.

She'd swung into action immediately, taking control of everything in a seamless, effortless maneuver that had been almost genius. In a pack, if the alpha prime became ill, there was usually a leadership challenge. Only the strong could lead, and Vivianne had given that impression immediately—only he knew how much it had cost her.

Those moments she'd hidden behind closed doors, trying to catch her breath, or those long nights where she was plagued by nightmares.

Her hand twitched on the cover, drawing his gaze. There it was again, a flinch. He looked at her face.

Her brows were pulled in a faint V, and her head moved slightly in denial, her lips forming soundless words. He sat up. She was dreaming again. No, not dreaming... She flinched, and this time the movement was sharp, almost violent, and her hand rose as though to ward off something.

Her head rolled from side to side. "No," she whimpered.

Zane frowned as he leaned forward. "Shh," he whispered and reached for her hand.

His head spun, and he heard a loud, rushing sound, like a thunderous waterfall. He stumbled, falling to the ground, dizzy.

His knees were on concrete, and he felt the burn in his palms, as though he'd skidded along the surface. A driveway. *What?* Zane shook his head, then looked up when he heard a scream.

Vivianne was struggling against a black wolf beside a dark car and tripped over the body of her dead guardian. The large black wolf stood over her, teeth bared. Her skirt was ripped, and he could see the mangled wound on her thigh, the bloom of dark red on her side.

Vivianne's eyes blazed, her fangs lengthening, and she bared them at the beast, hissing as the wolf growled.

The lycan lowered his head, his jaws snapping, and Vivianne dodged those razor-sharp teeth, pushing against the powerful chest. The lycan fell back, and Vivianne managed to regain her feet before the black wolf launched himself at her, and Zane winced as he heard the dull thud of her body hitting the car door behind her, and Vivianne's cry of pain as those teeth sank into her shoulder.

"No," Zane yelled, his voice emerging as a deep roar.

The black wolf turned, and Zane glared at him, his head dipped low as he let a low, dangerous rumble emerge from his throat. The black wolf turned tail and ran. Vivianne stared at him, her hand pressed to her shoulder, but even now, Zane could see the crimson blood turning black as the lycan toxin started to act on her vampire blood.

Her face was pale, and he saw the stark realization in her eyes, the awareness of the death sentence she'd just been handed as she slowly slid down the side of the car. He raced toward her, catching her before she hit the ground.

She shook her head, her brown eyes tearing up. "I let him down," she choked.

"Shh," he whispered, smoothing her hair off her face.

"I've let them all down," she said, and he could feel her trembling in his arms. He laid her gently down on the driveway and drew his singlet off over his head. He ripped the garment into shreds and pressed the rags to her wounds. She frowned, then gazed down, fingers tugging at the cloth.

"No, leave it—"

"Let me see," she whispered frantically, surprisingly strong as she struggled against him. She peeled his fingers back, and they both looked down. Zane frowned. Her clothes were torn, but her wounds were closed. Healed.

He sat back on his heels, confused, and he saw the same confusion in Vivianne's eyes as she sat up. She ripped her blouse open, twisting to look at the wound that had been on her side. Nothing. No marks, no scars, not even a smear of blood. Zane reached out, stunned, and slid his hand over the skin, trying to find the wound he'd seen.

Her skin was flawless, smooth and golden. Warm. She wore a lacy sage-green bra, her breasts swelling above the decorative cups. Her breath hitched, and he raised his gaze to hers. He stroked her again, watching her eyes darken with awareness. She didn't brush his hand away. She didn't move away from his touch. She did tremble, though, and this time, it wasn't from shock, judging by the heat in her eyes, and the rapid rise and fall of her chest.

He leaned forward, tilting his head to the side, his eyes on hers, until he could gently press his lips to the silky smooth skin of her shoulder. She swallowed, a soft gulp drawing his lips up in a smile as he kissed her again, this time closer to her collarbone. She moved her head to the side, her hair sliding back over her shoulder.

Her scent hit him, low in his groin, tugging at him, hardening him. Cinnamon, musk and a zing of ginger. His lycan nose peeled back the layers of her natural fragrance, delighting in the full body and spicy tones, and his body throbbed. He slid one arm around her slender waist, the other sliding up the creamy column of her throat to delve into the dark curls that had tempted him for so long.

He lifted his gaze to her eyes. She was watching him, and she raised a dark eyebrow.

"What are you waiting for?" her voice was low, husky, and his beast inside perked up, a sensation he hadn't felt since he'd regained awareness in that hospital room.

His lips curved. "Patience, princess." He lowered his mouth to hers.

Vivianne closed her eyes as his lips touched hers, giving herself up to the sensation. His tongue slid inside her mouth, and her breath caught in her chest. She could feel her breasts swelling, rising for his attention. His arm tightened around her waist, drawing her closer, and she sighed when her breasts met the muscular wall of his chest.

He growled, his torso vibrating against hers, and she moaned at the exquisite sensation, her arms sliding up over his broad shoulders to twine around his neck. He leaned closer, and her mouth opened further as his tongue and lips played with hers.

Her heart thudded in her chest, her nipples tightening, and she scraped her nails lightly down his neck. He made a deep, low rumble of pleasure, his hand tugging her head back, and she arched her back. Her nipples were hard little nubs beneath the lace of her bra, a delicious friction sensitizing them further as his chest moved against hers. He slanted his mouth at a different angle, and the kiss got even better.

His hands roamed over her back, smoothing, scraping, smoothing, and she writhed to his rhythm, her own hands skimming the defined rope of muscles across his shoulders, delving into his hair. It was long enough for her to curl her fingers in and pull, and she decided she liked scruffy, after all, especially when his head tilted back, and she could trail her lips down his neck, feel his pulse on her tongue, smell that enticing male fragrance that was cedarwood and spice.

He dipped his head again, and it became a playful tussle of nip and lick between them.

His hands slid around her ribs to cup her breasts, and Vivianne's eyelids flew open.

She was flat on her back, the bedcovers twisted, and Zane hovered above her, panting. His eyes mirrored her shock, and she swallowed.

"You shouldn't be here," she whispered.

Something dark and battered flared in his eyes, and suddenly he was gone, the midnight tendrils of inky fog swirling around her.

She sat up in the bed and stared out into her empty bedroom, blinking rapidly in the gloom. Had she—had she just dreamed that? Or had it actually happened?

Zane strolled along the line of shelves, scanning the spines of the several hundred books as though he gave a crap.

Whatever, as long as he didn't have to look directly at Vivianne.

*You shouldn't be here.*

Even the memory of the words still stung. No, he shouldn't be here, watching her sleep, kissing her in her dreams—how the hell had *that* happened?—or just floating along like a shadow in her life.

She hadn't acknowledged his presence, and he was secretly relieved. If they didn't talk about it, they could pretend it didn't happen, right?

"Tell me, what is this about a campaign?" Vivianne asked quietly. He wasn't going to look. He wasn't going to look. Zane glanced over his shoulder. Okay, so he looked. Her expression was remote, cool. He shook his head. She was talking to her father, and they both sat there as though facing off against adversaries. Vampire families were about as warm and cuddly as a porcupine on crack. His gaze drifted over her.

Today she wore her hair in a single braid that twisted from one temple, around the back of her head and over the opposite shoulder. Pretty. She wore a gray silk blouse that billowed and rippled with her movements, and a slim-line skirt that followed the shape of those sexy hips of hers. He frowned. He should be strung up. He should rip his fangs from his jaw and hand them in, skin that pelt of his and burn it, because after what he'd done last night he should resign from the lycan breed before he shamed them any further.

Kissing a damn vampire, even in a dream, was not the done thing.

"Well, it's more of a bill, and you must keep this confidential," Vincent Marchetta stated, his expression just as stern as Vivianne's. Zane wrinkled his nose. The older man wore the stink of death, his dark eyes cold and soulless. A true vampire who made Zane's skin crawl.

Vivianne sighed. "Dad, of course—"

"Don't 'of course' me," Vincent snapped. "I don't take anything for granted anymore, not since your brother's defection."

Vivianne frowned. "Lucien didn't 'defect.' You kidnapped his wife—"

"She wasn't his wife at the time," her father corrected, his tone harsh. "And don't you dare defend him—or that woman. We kept you alive, Vivianne. The only reason you're here is because of the trouble and risk your family went to in order to save your life."

Zane's eyebrows rose. Wow, that was harsh, coming from your old man. He could see what the patriarch was doing. He was trying to guilt his daughter into doing what he wanted. He glanced at Vivianne. It was like looking at a mask. No emotion. Strange. He guessed you could only guilt someone into doing something if they had the capacity to feel...guilt. He'd only ever seen her completely shut down her reactions with this man, but right at this moment, he wondered just exactly what Vivianne was capable of feeling. The woman sitting in the chair, her legs crossed, hands folded in her lap, was nothing like the warm, vibrant, voluptuous vixen he'd held in his arms—or dreamed he'd held in his arms. He tilted his head. Had he dreamed it? Or had it happened for real? Like, as real as it could get with a ghost? If it was just a dream, had he dreamed it, or had she? He shook his head from the never-ending round of questions bombarding his mind, and focused on the not-so-subtle power play.

Vivianne didn't bother to address her father's remark.

"I'll ask you again," she said, and her gaze was direct. "What is this campaign—bill," she corrected, "and what do you want from me?"

"I want you to purchase that parcel of land on the western border of Summercliffe."

"Why?"

"I'm your father. I don't need to explain myself to you. Just do it."

"And I'm your Prime," she snapped, and Zane's eyebrows rose. This was more than your average daddy-daughter issues, he suspected. "You're a Reform Senator. You don't control Nightwing anymore, Dad. I do."

Zane folded his arms and sat on the corner of Vincent's mahogany desk inside the expansive den of the cold and draughty Marchetta Manor. His gaze darted between the two vampires. Things were getting interesting. Reform senators had to renounce any familial or tribal associations, to avoid conflicts of interest. Vincent Marchetta had once been the Nightwing Vampire Prime, but had had to cede his position in order to run for politics.

Vincent's gaze lowered, and Zane saw the old man's fist clench. "I want to purchase that tract of land."

"Why? It's virtually bear country."

"It's also a thoroughfare for wolves between Woodland and Alpine."

Zane frowned at the mention of those packs. *His* packs.

Vivianne sighed. "What do you plan to do? Shut down the thoroughfare to get back at the lycans?"

"Oh, no," Vincent said, smiling. "In fact, I want the opposite. I want it used. A lot."

Vivianne straightened in her chair, suspicion bright in her brown gaze. "Why?"

"Because I'm proposing a change to the territorial rights bill," Vincent told her. "I want to adjust the jurisdiction for trespass."

"Why?" she asked, frowning.

"Because I want the crime reclassified as a Class 1A crime."

Vivianne's frown deepened, and Zane saw her confusion creep through her mask.

"*Why*, Dad?"

Yeah, why? Currently trespassing was a Class 2 crime. When a trespasser was caught, there were two options. If it was interbreed, say, a werewolf trespassing on another pack's land, there was the escort to the boundary. If it was crossbreed, say, a vampire trespassing on a pack's land, then either hostage and negotiation for release, usually resulting in a boon for those being trespassed against, or an outright kill. Upgrading to a Class 1A crime meant the prime owner of the land could kill or imprison the trespasser indefinitely.

"Because I want to set up a new clinic on that parcel of land, and send any lycan trespassers over for testing."

Zane gaped. That sounded…wrong. Like, weird wrong.

"Testing? Don't you meant *torturing*?"

Vincent shrugged. "Semantics."

Zane's head whipped around to face Vivianne. "You *can't* be serious," he roared.

# *Chapter 5*

He'd overheard some of what that underground clinic had been used for, and it turned his stomach.

Vivianne flinched slightly, but masked the move by skimming her hands over her skirt, as though straightening the fabric over her curves. Yeah, she'd heard him. She could try to ignore him all she liked, but he was going to make sure she heard him, on this topic at least.

"I know you want to resume your project—" she began, but halted when her father leaned forward in his chair.

"My project?" he repeated in a low voice. "Don't you mean *our* project?" Zane's eyes widened, and he glared in accusation at Vivianne. She'd been part of it? Had she condoned what her father had done at that clinic? He'd heard the whispers, the stories of those who'd been abused, but who'd escaped just before the clinic was destroyed. He'd also heard the cries of pain, the moans and screams of the other "patients," just before her brother, Lucien, had unleashed on his father. He folded his arms as he glared down at the senator. The man was a monster.

Vivianne's father tapped the top of his desk with his forefinger. "Those experiments are designed to create weapons we can use against the werewolves." Vincent Marchetta shook his head. "We were so close, with that Segova woman—"

"You mean Natalie, your daughter-in-law," Vivianne interrupted. "She's family now, Dad. And there was no 'we'—neither Lucien nor I knew anything about this clinic of yours."

Her eyes met Zane's briefly, and he relaxed a little at her pointed message. She hadn't been involved in that madness, and she wanted him to know that.

Vincent nodded. "And that was my mistake. That's why I want you involved, from the ground up, this time, Vivianne. After what they've done to our family—what they did to *you*—I think you'd jump at the chance to eradicate the wolves."

Zane watched as Vivianne's eyes rounded, just a little. "You—you want us to work together?" She was blinking, as though trying to hide her shock, her...was that *hope* he saw flare in her eyes? His brows drew into a deeper V. Did she want to hurt the wolves? Him?

"Think about it, Vivianne. The only advantage lycans have over vampires is that their bite is lethal. Otherwise, strength, speed, agility, etc.—we're evenly matched." Vincent's eyes sparked with anticipation. "If we could create some sort of inoculation, some defense that would render a lycan's bite harmless—imagine what that would mean for us?"

"It would definitely give us an advantage," Vivianne admitted, and Zane's heart sank at her words. He could almost see the wheels turning in her head. He'd learned she was quick to assess the benefits and pitfalls of a project, to think several jumps ahead of those around her, and in this situation, she didn't disappoint. "It would also position us as the strongest colony among the vampires. Maybe open up some trade potential."

"You're talking about conducting mad science experiments on werewolves," Zane hissed at her. Her eyes glinted with steely determination before she looked at the man sitting on the other side of the desk.

"It's not legal," she told her father gently.

"It's not ethical! It's not right!" Zane exclaimed.

"We can get around it," Vincent told her, "once this bill is passed. But I want that tract of land for when it does."

"I'll think about it," Vivianne said, then rose from her seat and gathered her handbag.

"Tell him no," Zane said forcefully.

"You do that." Vincent watched as his daughter prepared to leave.

Zane glared between the two, then shook his fist in the senator's face. "If you come anywhere near my pack, old man, I will rip you limb from limb." The old man didn't even blink. Zane twisted to face Vivianne, not trying to hide his anger as he clenched both hands into tight fists. He wanted to yell, he wanted to punch—he wanted to stop Vincent's plan, but most of all, he wanted Vivianne to stop it, and he was so damn useless. The fact that she seemed to entertain the idea infuriated him, disappointed him… hurt him. He growled, and the fog whirled up around him, blocking her from his view.

Vivianne hesitated briefly as Zane disappeared in a virulent mist, then adjusted the strap of her bag on her shoulder and left the room.

Vivianne looked out of her car window, her gaze resolutely fixed forward as her driver turned onto the ramp lead-

ing to an underground car park. Rock music was thumping
through the earbuds in her ears. She'd had to resort to that
tactic to drown out the six-foot-three werewolf who had
argued with her ever since her father had dropped his little
bomb back at the family home that evening. Even now, with
the moon rising, she could see him out of the corner of her
eye, sitting next to her on the back seat, hands gesticulat-
ing wildly, his expression dark and fierce as he protested
her family's plans.

As if he thought she could stop Vincent Marchetta.

Vivianne looked up at the building to the left of her. It
was an architectural masterpiece, with glass corridors leading off to the left and the right, allowing plenty of moonlight into the interior of the building. There were two wings
leading off the central block, with an abundance of balco-
nies that suggested access to the outside, but also privacy
from each other. Each window, though, and each balcony
door, held the same darker glass she had at her own home
and office building, as well as her vehicle. Tempered glass.
It allowed in light, but blocked UV rays, so that vampires
could function in daylight hours without burning to a crisp.

All except for one end of the building that was completely constructed of glass—but this glass was designed to
let in the sunlight. Probably to feed the light warriors who
had now revealed their existence to the world. She shook
her head, not bothering to hide her amazement. She'd had
no idea Arthur Armstrong and his sons were light warriors.
Everyone thought they'd died out during the time of The
Troubles. Her eyes narrowed. They'd managed to hide their
existence for centuries. That showed a shrewd calculation
and patience that she'd do well to remember when dealing
with the Galen brothers.

The Galen brothers, who were apparently doing very
well, going by the new state-of-the-art clinic they'd set up.

She leaned back into her seat as the car entered the dim car park. The Galens seemed to think of everything, providing not only a discrete entrance for those who didn't want to be seen visiting them, but also a UV-free access for vampires.

Her car pulled up at the portico and a tall man with dark hair emerged from the doorway, his arms folded.

Ryder Galen.

Vivianne's driver hurried around to open her door, and she gave him an intent look. Harris had been her driver for several years, and she trusted him implicitly. She hoped nothing had changed during her coma. She didn't want word of this visit to get back to anyone in her colony, and especially not her father.

Harris winked, and she gave him a small smile. She hoped some things never changed, namely his ability to keep her secrets. "I'll wait in the car," he said quietly.

"Thanks, Harris." She saw Zane also emerge from the car, and sighed. He looked furious, but the curiosity at their location was winning over as he glanced around, and his features relaxed when he saw Ryder.

She strode up to the doorway, and met Ryder's gaze directly. The man eyed her, his bright blue eyes keen with interest.

"Do you personally greet all of the patients for this clinic?" she asked, slowly removing her earbuds.

He raised an eyebrow at the rock music that could still be heard blaring from the earbuds, and she switched the music off on her phone app.

"Only the interesting ones," he responded, his brow dipping slightly in curiosity. "I was surprised to see your name pop up on my schedule." He gestured to the doorway, and she preceded him into the clinic.

"Thank you for seeing me so quickly."

"You didn't really give me much choice," he told her dryly as he guided her toward the lifts. She gazed around with interest. Instead of the linoleum she'd come to expect in hospitals, the hallway was lined with timber floors. Clean, crisp, but with a warmer, softer tone than she'd expected. The walls were tastefully painted in a soft gray that was both calming and restful, and not in the least depressing.

Zane let out a low whistle as they stepped into the elevator. "Things are looking good for the Galens."

"You've made quite a few changes since your father died," Vivianne said, looking over at Ryder. "Do you miss him?" She knew there'd been a rift between them, but she couldn't imagine what it would be like to lose someone who was such a key part of your life for so long...

Ryder dipped his head for a moment. "Like a migraine. We can choose our friends, but we can't choose our family, can we? How is your father?" He looked at her just as closely.

"Oh, he's peachy," Zane muttered. "Happily plotting the extermination of the werewolf breed at this very moment."

"He's fine," Vivianne said, keeping her gaze on Ryder. "How is Vassi?" Her voice softened unintentionally, and she cleared her throat. She would never admit it, but she'd come to admire and respect his wife, Vassiliki Verity. As a lawyer, she was exceptional at her work. As a person, she'd be challenged to find someone with a stronger code of personal ethics, and a love for truth and honor. They'd had several arguments about the direction of the Marchetta businesses, and certain decisions that Vivianne considered "gray," whereas Vassi deemed them "downright dodgy." Vivianne had enjoyed their heated debates. She would have to see what she could do to tempt the lady lawyer back. First, she'd have to find out why Vassi had left in the first place.

What had occurred between Vassi and her father to make her leave the company?

"Vassi is good," Ryder said, his face softening into a smile, and there was no hiding the warm pride in his eyes. "We're setting up a second clinic location, and she's working on the permits and negotiating access."

Zane tilted his head. "I don't think I've met Vassi," he said. "She worked for you, right?"

Vivianne stared at Ryder for a moment, trying to ignore Zane's presence. Ryder's respect and delight in his partner was almost tangible. When had anyone spoken about her like that? Certainly not her father. She and her brother were working on their relationship, but they argued, just like any normal siblings. She smiled briefly, dropping her gaze. She was a Vampire Prime, she reminded herself. She didn't need anyone to be proud of her. She didn't need those other softer emotions. She needed to ensure her colony were safe and thriving. Period.

The doors opened, and she followed Ryder out into a hallway. This one had carpet, with tasteful art lining the warmer-colored cream walls. Wall sconces with—wow, with real candles—were sporadically placed, creating a soft ambience as Ryder led her to a door with his name on it.

He stepped inside, then halted. "Dude, that's my desk!"

Vivianne peered around him. A man with dark hair and dark eyes peered with annoyance over his shoulder. The stunning redhead in his arms hastily rearranged her top into a more presentable appearance, and she slid off the desk.

"I was just saying hi to my wife," the man said, then grinned. "Besides, you know that saying, never let a good desk go to waste," the man said, as he reluctantly let the redhead step away from him.

"That's not a saying," the woman said, trying to hide her smile. She faltered when she saw Vivianne.

"A vamp?" Her nose wrinkled with distaste, and her fingers curled. Sparks of lightning arced between her fingertips.

Vivianne's eyes narrowed as Zane chuckled next to her. "A witch?" Her tone was just as frosty.

"A vamp, a witch and a light warrior walked into a bar," the man at the desk quipped, then placed his hands over the redhead's fists. "Easy, Mel. Remember, we're being more accepting…" He gave her a quick peck on the cheek.

The red-haired witch curled her fingers into a fist, extinguishing the arcs of power. "Acceptance sucks," she muttered, then pasted a bright smile on her face as she strode toward the door. "Besides, I have a client to see." She paused next to Vivianne, her green eyes brittle. "Something about a silver glove," she said nonchalantly. She looked over her shoulder at the man with the dark hair. "See you tonight."

Vivianne's lips pursed as the witch left the room. Silver. She hated silver. Every vamp hated silver. Lycans, silver, witches, were all at the top of her "things to despise" list. Zane shuddered next to her. Silver was just as toxic to werewolves as it was to vampires.

"Feisty," he muttered.

Ryder sighed as he turned to Vivianne. "I'm not sure if you've had the pleasure, yet, but this is my brother, Hunter. Hunter, this is Vivianne Marchetta."

Hunter strolled forward, his brown gaze touring over her. "So, you're the vampire prime that gave my father so much trouble." He frowned. "You're shorter than I thought you'd be."

"Don't be deceived," Zane muttered. "She might be short, but she can be vicious."

Vivianne's gaze slid briefly to glare at the werewolf by her side, then she smiled at Hunter. "I prefer to avoid making assumptions," she told him sweetly.

Ryder closed the office door, then gestured to a comfortable-looking wingback chair. "Please take a seat. As you can see, we've delivered on your special requests."

"Demands," interjected Hunter as he leaned against the bookcase lining one wall.

"I'm sure you can appreciate my need for discretion," she said quietly as she sank into the chair.

"Why are we here?" Zane asked, and leaned an arm along the ridge of the wingback above her head. She glanced up briefly. He was close, leaning his hip against the side of her chair as his brown enquiring gaze found hers.

She turned back to the Galen brothers, both of whom were watching her closely. "You've probably heard of my recent…break."

Ryder's eyebrow rose. "Break? I was there, Vivianne, when Lucien brought you into Woodland. I saw your injuries with my own eyes." He shook his head. "The fact that you're sitting here, talking, it's nothing short of miraculous."

Hunter snorted. "I don't believe in miracles. But, if it was so miraculous, Ms. Marchetta wouldn't be here visiting us. So, what gives?"

"Anything I say here is treated as confidential, correct?"

"Of course," Ryder responded. "All our patients' records are confidential."

"I want your word," she insisted. She'd known Ryder long enough to know that he was an honorable man, and this was too important to not get his personal guarantee.

He nodded. "You have it." She turned her gaze at Hunter.

Hunter sighed, rolling his eyes as he held up his little finger. "Pinkie swear."

She pursed her lips. She guessed that was about as good as she'd get from this brother.

"I need your help. Since I woke up, I've been…seeing

things." She rubbed her forehead. "Not just seeing things, but hearing things, too."

"You left out the part about the dreams," Zane pointed out, his lips quirking. She ignored him. Again. But she couldn't stop the warm bloom of color that swept across her cheeks.

"What kind of things?" Ryder asked. At least he wasn't looking at her as though she was going mad. *Yet.*

"Well, one thing, really," she said, glancing quickly up at Zane, who raised an eyebrow.

"What thing?" Hunter asked, and she was surprised by the patience in his tone.

"Uh, a—" She swallowed. Putting it into actual words was a lot harder than she thought it would be. "A, uh, were-wolf."

Ryder leaned back in his chair. "Well, I guess that's not surprising," he commented. "You were attacked by a were-wolf."

"It could be a form of PTSD," Hunter suggested, and straightened away from the bookcase. "Having visions or memories of the wolf who attacked you...do you have night-mares?"

Her cheeks heated. "Uh, at first, yes, but that seems to be lessening."

Ryder nodded. "Over time, the nightmares become less frequent as your mind starts to heal from the trauma. It's PTSD if the nightmares keep recurring after a significant period, along with a few other symptoms."

"No, it's not like that," she said, shaking her head. "I'm not talking about Rafe Woodland—although I have had nightmares about him, about the attack. The werewolf I see is—" She hesitated. God, how did she explain this without sounding like an absolute nutter?

"Gorgeous?" Zane suggested. "Sexy? A downright fox?"

"Annoying," Vivianne stated, frowning.

Hunter's eyebrows rose. "Annoying?"

"Yes, annoying. At first he was just a shadow out of the corner of my eye, and every now and then I heard him laugh, or mutter—"

"I don't mutter," Zane muttered.

"Yes, you do," she snapped at him. She turned back to the Galens. "But now—" She swallowed again. "Now I can *see* him. Hear him."

"And he's…annoying?" Hunter said, walking slowly toward her, his head tilted as he watched her keenly.

"Yes. Distracting."

"You left out sexy," Zane reminded her.

"Shut up," she hissed, then bit her lip when Hunter halted directly in front of her.

"I beg your pardon?"

"Sorry, I didn't mean you, I meant…" She trailed off, gesturing toward Zane.

"You can see him now?" Hunter narrowed his eyes as he followed the direction she indicated.

"Yes," she said, her lips turning down. "And you can't." She wanted to cover her face, hide from the reality of admitting her condition, her mind's weakness. "I think either the lycan poison is coming back, or I'm going mad," she said in a whisper.

"You think I'm a figment of your imagination?" Zane said, his tone incredulous.

Hunter sank to his heels in front of her so that their gazes were level. "Those would be obvious possibilities," he conceded softly, and her heart sank at his words, and she saw sympathy spark in his eyes.

"I need to figure out what is wrong with me," she said, trying to hide her fear.

"I'm not something 'wrong,'" Zane said as he walked

around the chair to face her, his expression troubled. "This is why we're here? You think I'm driving you crazy?" Surprisingly, there was hurt in his tone, but there was also something else...she'd almost think it was concern. "I hate to break it to you, vamp, but I'm not some latent memory of yours. We never met before—" the muscle in his jaw twitched "—before I died. And I'm not a damn poison."

"I need to fix this," she said, her voice stronger. She was looking at Hunter, but her words were intended for Zane. "I can't lead Nightwing if I'm losing my mind."

"And it's all about position and power with you, isn't it, Vivianne?" Zane said, his deep voice rumbling in a snarl.

"You're worried about your colony?" Ryder asked, and she looked beyond Hunter's shoulder to meet his gaze.

She nodded. "A prime can't hold their position if they're non compos mentis. Only the strong can lead, and mental deficit is a weakness. There will be a leadership stoush, which would weaken Nightwing among our neighbors, and our enemies. Fighting from within, fighting from without—it will be a bloodbath for my people."

"What about Lucien? Can't he take the prime position?" Ryder asked.

Zane's lips curled back at the mention of Vivianne's brother's name.

Vivianne shook her head. "No. He's taken a leave of absence from Nightwing, and so has surrendered any claim to the Nightwing Prime position. He would have to fight for it, just like anyone else, and after what my father did to his wife, I don't see him wanting to be Prime."

"I can't believe your brother and I have something in common," muttered Zane. "We both hate your old man."

She frowned. She was already divulging more information than she was comfortable with. "Can you help me?" she asked Hunter.

He gazed at her for a moment, assessing her. He shrugged. "We can run some tests, and find out what we're dealing with," he told her. She settled back into the chair, relief lessening the strain in her shoulders. She would have preferred a "yes, we can fix you" response, but she appreciated he wasn't prepared to make false promises. She could respect that.

"Okay."

"You agree to the tests?" Hunter asked.

She nodded. "I do. When do you want to schedule them?"

He smiled. "No time like the present," he said, touching her forehead lightly.

Darkness descended across her mind, and the last thing she saw was Zane's concerned face as she slid into unconsciousness.

# Chapter 6

Zane watched as Hunter lifted the unconscious Vivianne onto a gurney that Ryder had wheeled in. He couldn't help but be impressed with how quickly and smoothly Vivianne had been knocked out. Hunter had easily bypassed Vivianne's natural mental defenses, no small feat when dealing with a vampire prime.

"I'll take her to my rooms for a scan," Hunter told his brother. "She's got auditory hallucinations, but what we saw doesn't quite gel with a normal PTSD diagnosis."

"Schizophrenia?"

Hunter shrugged. "I don't think so. She displayed ordered thinking and behavior, apart from the occasional side trip to Crazyville."

Ryder nodded as he reached for the phone. "I'm calling Dave in. He was the one to put her into the stasis. He was also there when she came to. He might have something to offer."

Zane drifted along, watchful carefully as the older Galen brother, Hunter, rolled Vivianne's gurney into a well-lit room. A massive hearth took up almost one entire wall of the room. Hunter snapped his fingers, and a fire flickered to life. Zane's eyebrows rose. Wow. He'd remembered some of the old tales of light warriors, of how they could harness the power of light and fashion it into weapons, or for healing. He never thought he'd see a light warrior in action, though, and settled back to watch.

His gaze slid to Vivianne. She looked relaxed, but he wasn't fooled. She'd wake up spitting venom when she realized she'd been rendered unconscious so easily. His brow dipped when he thought about her words back in Ryder's office.

She thought she was going crazy.

He was driving her nuts. The sentiment should have given him some satisfaction, but for once he felt no triumph in causing pain or discomfort to a vampire. To drive a woman to despair—well, that was just one more hit to his ego around this woman. Still, he never wanted to make a woman feel miserable in his presence. It didn't sit well with him. He shifted. Guilt was not a comfortable coat to wear.

Hunter stood at Vivianne's feet, gently clasping her ankles, then closed his eyes. Zane leaned back against the wall, arms folded, and watched.

Tendrils of light swirled and ebbed from the fire, arcing toward Hunter, as though attracted by a magnetic field. Zane frowned. It was light, though, not flame, that danced across the room to skim and flit across his skin, to eventually snake around his wrists, and flow on to Vivianne's ankles. There was no singeing of hair, or blistering of skin. It was…remarkable.

Her body twitched, and Zane straightened. Was Galen hurting her? He strolled forward, eyeing her face, but her features remained calm, relaxed. The light danced along her legs, up over her hips and across her torso. The tendrils gathered close, and became a glowing orb around her body.

Zane didn't understand how the examination worked, but could only assume Hunter was working his way along Vivianne's body as the light changed in color in a slow wash drifting up over her form. It took several minutes, but eventually the orb positioned around Vivianne's head. Hunter frowned, and released her ankles at the same time that Ryder opened the door and stepped into the room.

A man followed him, and it took Zane a moment to recognize him. The man wore black boots, black motorcycle leathers and a black T-shirt beneath the leather jacket. His eyes were shielded behind a pair of dark sunglasses, his dark sandy hair cropped short, as was the beard dusting his jawline. Dave... Carter. The name came to him through a fog. He had a murky recollection of meeting the man, but the details were a little hazy.

"Dave." Hunter greeted him as he strode along the gurney to Vivianne's head. He gently threaded his fingers through her hair, and for the briefest moment, jealousy flared within Zane at his familiarity with the woman on the table.

"Hunter." Dave nodded. He frowned when he saw the woman on the gurney. "Vivianne Marchetta, huh? What's wrong with her?"

"That's what we're trying to find out," Hunter said quietly, then closed his eyes once more. A golden glow enveloped Vivianne's head, bathing her face in a warm light. She looked...beautiful. Zane frowned. He didn't understand this softening toward her. In the period he'd been with her, he'd seen her feed—and hunt. He'd seen her rule the boardroom with glacial control, and hatch plans for the annihilation of the werewolf breed. Everything a vampire did—the cold, emotionless, self-serving nature of the breed—was repellant to the loyal, family-bonded lycan, and yet every now and then he was caught by an unexpected, inexplicable thawing toward her, a…concern for her that was about as comfortable as mange skin scrapings. Maybe it was a side effect of death. Did death have side effects? Could one of them be abandoning your principles in favor of a pretty face? Well, okay, she had a beautiful face. Damn it, did death result in falling for seductive, destructive charm?

"What the…?" Hunter frowned, and tilted his head. He raised a hand, and a tendril of undulating light stretched between Vivianne and Zane.

"What is it? Did you find something?" Ryder asked, leaning forward, his expression curious.

"Not sure." Hunter opened his eyes, gazing blankly at his brother. "I can feel something in her mind, but I can't get past the darkness."

Zane's eyebrows rose. "I'm 'the darkness'?" Could they not see the ribbon of light? He'd hoped he would be illuminated also, but the two light warriors were oblivious to his presence.

"Is it a tumor?" Ryder asked.

Zane rolled his eyes. "I am not a tumor."

Hunter shook his head. "It doesn't feel like a tumor."

"That's because I am not a tumor."

Ryder turned to Dave. "Could this have something to do with your spell?"

Dave's lips twisted. "My spells are not carcinogenic."

Zane glanced at the man. Spells? Dave was a witch?

Ryder shot the biker an exasperated look. "Seriously, Dave. What do you think?"

Dave shrugged. "Beats me."

"It was your spell," Ryder pointed out.

"Believe it or not, I've never actually prevented a lycan's

bite from killing a vampire, before," Dave muttered. "This
is new territory for all of us." He stepped closer to the gurney, and Zane approached from the other side. "So, she said
she was having hallucinations?"

"I'm not a hallucination, damn it," Zane growled. It was
so damn frustrating, watching them try to figure him out.
He wished they could see him, hear him. Maybe even help
him. Did he need to pass on? Is that what the problem was?
He'd had to accept that he no longer had a tangible form, that
he was no longer…living. That sucked. Big-time. What he
wouldn't give to offer Vivianne's brother a little payback.
But if he had to pass on, why wasn't it happening? Why
was he still hanging around?

And although it was every werewolf's ultimate fantasy
to drive a vampire nuts, the notion that Vivianne thought
she was going a little batcrap crazy because she could see
him when nobody else could—well, it made him feel a little guilty. He wasn't a figment of her imagination. He was
real. Well, as real as a ghost could be. Vivianne was a strong
woman, vivacious, clever, confident. Regardless of whether
she was vamp or lycan, no guy wanted any woman in his
orbit to feel "less" because of her dealings with him. That
didn't make you a man, it made you a bully. Sure, he'd take
on a vamp, male or female. But he'd do it face on, in a fair
fight. He'd seen Vivianne in action enough times to know
she was nobody's "girl," that she could defend herself in a
fistfight just as well as a war of words. Hell, his own alpha
prime was a woman. One of the attributes of a vampire was
their physical strength, and he'd fought against a number
of them. But he was always brought up to respect women,
and to protect those around you. Making a woman doubt
herself, or scared to tell the truth because of how it might
make her look, or fearing she'd lose her position because

of her association with you didn't make you a legend, it made you a douche.

And damn it, it was just one more thing to hate Lucien Marchetta for.

Dave reached for her hand, and Zane saw the tendril of light stretching between himself and Vivianne glow. Warmth encompassed him, and his frown matched Dave's when he glanced up.

"Well, I'll be…" Dave murmured.

"What?" Hunter asked.

"Who are you?"

Zane's eyes widened as he realized Dave was speaking to *him*. "You can see me?" The witch's lips quirked, and Zane wished he could see behind the dark lenses of his sunglasses.

"I see a lot of things…" Dave responded. He lifted his hand, and the tendril of light dimmed. Dave frowned, then touched Vivianne again, and the light ribbon glowed. "Interesting."

"Who are you talking to?" Ryder asked, and Hunter squinted as he glanced around the room.

"Vivianne's not hallucinating."

Zane nodded. "Thank you. I've been trying to tell that to anyone who can hear me."

"If it's not hallucinations, or delusions, or a very creative imagination, then what are we dealing with?" Hunter asked, and folded his arms. The light in the room ebbed.

"She's picked up a passenger."

"What?" Ryder asked, perplexed.

"She's haunted," Dave explained.

Hunter started to stroll away from the gurney, looking into every shadow of the room. "As in a ghost?"

Dave tilted his head as he gazed at Zane. "I'm not sure…"

"Can you help me?" Zane asked Dave.

Dave shrugged, his own expression puzzled.

"So what do we do with a ghost?" Ryder asked.

"An exorcism?" Hunter asked.

Ryder turned to his brother. "Since when do we do exorcisms?"

"Hey, there's a first time for everything. I've never had a patient haunted by a ghost before."

"You want to experiment?" Ryder asked in disbelief.

"No," Zane said, shaking his head.

"Hell, yeah," Hunter said.

"And how do you think you'll sell that to Vivianne Marchetta?" Ryder asked, gesturing to the still-unconscious woman.

Hunter grimaced. "Good point. She's already going to be pissed when she wakes up…" He brightened. "So why not give her something she can be really pissed about?"

"No," Zane repeated, louder.

"Exorcisms work on demons, not ghosts," Dave interjected, then shrugged. "I think."

"How do we know this is really a ghost, and not a demon?" Hunter asked.

Zane put his hands on his hips. "Oh, come on. First I'm a hallucination, then a tumor, and now I'm a demon? I take offence to that."

Dave's lips quirked, then he met Hunter's gaze. "He's not a demon. He's offended by the suggestion."

"He? Who's he?" Ryder asked.

"Good question," Dave said, and arched an eyebrow. "Who are you?"

Zane sighed. "My name is Zane Wilder."

"Zane Wilder?" Dave repeated. "Why does that name sound familiar?"

"The Alpine guardian?" Ryder asked. "Wasn't that the name of the guardian Lucien Marchetta killed?"

Dave glanced between Vivianne and Zane. "Interesting."

"Stop saying that," Zane muttered.

"A lycan?" Hunter asked, then chuckled. "Oh, man, a lycan haunting a vampire. That's gold."

"How does that happen?" Ryder asked. He frowned as he turned to the witch. "Dave?"

Dave tilted his head as he thought about it, then shrugged. "Yeah, I'm drawing a blank." He glanced over at Zane. "Did you have a thing for Vivianne?"

Zane frowned. "No."

"I mean, before you died?"

"No."

"Were you both in some sort of relationship?"

"Hell, no. I'd never even met her. She's a vamp, for crying out loud."

"Huh."

"What's he saying?" Ryder asked.

"Uh, no," Dave told them. His frown deepened. "Does she have something of yours? Maybe it's not the woman you've attached to, but an object that she holds...?"

"Nope."

"Then, how are you attached?"

"If I knew that, I would be able to unattach and get out of here."

Dave sighed gruffly, then nodded to Hunter. "Wake her up."

Hunter grimaced, and gently pressed his fingers to her temples.

Zane watched as Vivianne's eyelids fluttered, then her eyes opened. He saw confusion, perhaps tinged with a little fear, and then the anger flared.

She was on her back, staring up at a group of men, with no recollection of how she got in this position.

And it freaked the crap out of her.

Eyes sparking red, she bared her teeth, and she welcomed the sharp sting of her incisors lengthening.

She swung her legs off the gurney, landing lightly on her feet. She glared at Hunter, then Ryder, and she hissed when she noticed the tall, muscular man with the dark sunglasses.

Zane braced his hand against the gurney, and shot her an expectant look. Damn it, she could still see him. Yet, the reason she was here, the current bane of her life, was not a face that caused her fear. In fact, seeing Zane came with a soft dose of reassurance. God, wasn't that all kinds of sad.

"What the hell did you do to me?" She rasped at Hunter, her fists clenched as she started to slowly advance on him. The last thing she remembered was him asking her if she was ready for tests, and then boom—blackout.

Hunter Galen held up his hands, but didn't retreat from her. "Whoa, lady prime, relax. I had to get you to completely relax so I could scan your mind."

Her eyes rounded. "You knocked me out?"

Hunter shrugged, and she couldn't help but notice he was not remorseful in the slightest. How the hell did some-one—anyone—knock out a vampire prime so quickly, and so damn easily?

She was nine hundred years old. She'd honed the com-pulsion skills to a fine art, and had built her defenses so strongly that not even her older father could crack her men-tal barriers.

And this light warrior had tapped her on the forehead, and she was out like a light.

What had he seen in her mind? What secrets had she revealed to him, exposed to him? Damn it, she felt com-promised. Violated. Her eyes narrowed, and her lips pulled back to reveal her teeth.

He arched an eyebrow and held out his palm. A ball of liquid fire rolled and flared, hovering over his skin.

Vivianne flinched, springing away before she could control her reaction. Fire. One of nature's weapons that a vampire couldn't fight. And something that she feared beyond a reasonable self-preservation. Zane shifted in front of her, and the golden light dimmed a little.

"Hunter!" Ryder snapped. He flicked a spark that hit Hunter on his earlobe, and the light warrior jolted. The ball of fire dancing in his hand winked out.

Hunter frowned at his brother as he rubbed his ear. "Party pooper."

Ryder shot him an exasperated glare, then turned to face Vivianne. "I know you're pissed, but you want us to treat you, and this is the only way we can do it. Vampires, especially vampire primes, have natural shields that can prevent us from scanning, or even treating. You want to know why you're seeing and hearing a lycan, this is how we figure it out."

His words, uttered so calmly, so earnestly, gave her pause as the meaning sank in. "Did you?" she asked as she peered around Zane's broad shoulders. "Figure it out?"

Ryder held up his hand, palm down, and dipped it side to side. "Sort of."

Her shoulders sagged with disappointment. She could still see Zane. Hell, she was hiding behind the big lycan. She straightened her shoulders at that realization and stepped out to his side. She'd hoped Ryder would snap his fingers with an "Ah-hah!" and then follow it up with a temporary prescription to kill off her hallucinations. But now that there were two light warriors looking at her warily, a werewolf phantom who was still very much present, and a guy wearing motorcycle leathers and sunglasses—she frowned.

"Who are you?" she asked him. She'd seen him before, but couldn't quite place him.

He pursed his lips. "Really? I've saved your life twice now."

She arched an eyebrow.

"My name is Dave Carter, I'm the witch who put you under the suspension spell to stop the lycan toxin spreading your system. I'm also the witch who was there when you woke up, and fought with your brother to defend you against your father's men."

"You're the one who put me in the coma?"

Dave gave her a courtly bow. "You're welcome."

"Then how do you explain him? Can you see him?" she asked, jerking her thumb in Zane's direction. Zane frowned.

Dave shook his head. "I can only see him if I'm linked with you."

Vivianne frowned. "Linked? What does that mean?"

"If I touch you, I can see him, hear him. If I'm not touching you, he's gone."

"He's right here and can hear every damned word," Zane growled.

Vivianne swallowed. He'd been touching her when she was unconscious. Her hands curled into fists, and Dave held up a finger.

"Don't. I'm not a sleaze. For this, think of me like you would a doctor."

"You're not a doctor," Ryder and Hunter chorused.

"A magical doctor. Whatever. What do you remember of the night you were bitten?"

The change of topic caught Vivianne off guard, and she blinked. "Uh, pain," she said instinctively. Zane looked at her, an understanding in his eyes. He'd "visited" her last nightmare. He'd seen her memory on replay—although there were some bits that were more of a fantasy than a memory.

Oh, God, no. Not a fantasy. That would imply she'd wanted him to kiss her, that she'd been harboring some secret desire for the damn werewolf. Ugh. No. Not that.

Although, he was a good kisser. In her dreams, anyway. Better than good, actually. Pretty damn fantastic—damn it, there was that word again. She was not crushing on the lycan. Her father would disown her. Her colony would spurn her.

"It was pretty sudden." She hurried on, hoping that Hunter didn't still have some backdoor access to her mind and see her mentally fumbling about over Zane. "Black wolf, bounding out of the darkness, fangs. Pain. Then pretty much nothing."

Dave folded his arms, and his leather jacket creaked with the movement. "Do you remember anything about visiting the Woodland pack?"

"That wasn't a damn visit," Zane muttered. "There were no tea and scones and civilized conversation."

She shot him a quick glance, then shook her head. "No, not really. I vaguely remember my brother finding me, but then it's all a bit black until I woke up in my father's clinic."

"You don't remember the bonfire?"

She shook her head. "No, I don't."

"You don't remember your brother attacking Zane Wilder?"

She shook her head. "I didn't even know who he was until last night."

She heard Zane mutter, but couldn't quite make out the words. Something about ego, and sucks.

Dave rubbed his chin. "You two are definitely connected somehow."

"Ask him how we disconnect," Zane said, elbowing her

gently to catch her attention. His elbow passed through her arm, and she felt a warm tingle. Not painful, just…stimulating. For a moment she was surprised by the contact. Then she realized Zane wanted to get gone from her about as much as she wanted him gone. That realization brought with it just a tinge of…what? Hurt? Dejection?

Oh, crap, there was no way she was going to feel *sad* about that. No. *Way*.

"We want a separation."

Zane turned to her, and their gazes met. Sadness, confusion—she didn't quite understand it, but they seemed to mirror each other.

"I can't separate them," Hunter said, shaking his head. "Whatever is linking them, it's a really strong bond that I can't break."

Dave's head whipped around and he stared at Hunter. "What?"

Hunter gestured to Vivianne casually. "I can't fix her, it's not really a physical problem."

"No, what did you say? About the link?"

Hunter shrugged. "I said it's a strong bond."

Dave rubbed his chin. "A bond…" he repeated. He snapped his fingers. "Of course. A bond. It's so obvious."

"Care to share?" Ryder asked patiently.

"It's a bond. A blood bond," Dave said, and Vivianne frowned.

"What?" she asked.

Dave stepped out from behind the gurney. "Your brother carries you in to Woodland," he explained, his arms out as though carrying an imaginary Vivianne. "You're covered in your blood—you were pretty gross, actually," Dave admitted, then continued. "He hands you off to one of his bloodsucking cronies, goes to attack Matthias Marshall, only Zane Wilder jumps to his alpha prime's defense and takes the bite instead."

Vivianne's eyes widened, and she turned back to Zane. He'd stepped between her brother and his prime? That was such an act of loyalty, of protectiveness...of supreme sacrifice. She wasn't quite sure what to do with the little flare of respect, of admiration, that sparked inside her.

Zane nodded when he saw her assessing look. "Yeah, I know. I'm awesome."

And there went the spark. She rolled her eyes. "If you were that awesome, you would have been faster."

"If I was faster, both you and your brother would have been dead."

She sobered at the remark, seeing the truth in it. Her brother had faced down a pack of werewolves in their home territory. If he'd been bitten...

Hunter shook his head. "This is so weird."

Vivianne realized she'd lapsed again, acknowledging Zane and responding to him in front of others.

"So Zane is bitten and drained by Lucien—how does that result in Zane haunting Vivianne?"

Haunting. It was the perfect word to describe Zane and hers relationship. Wait, relationship? No, this wasn't a relationship. It couldn't be. More like—an association. Yes, much better.

"Lucien, covered in Vivianne's blood," Dave says, gesturing all over his form, "bites Zane—and there's a blood exchange between Vivianne and Zane. Then, because Lucien now has Zane's blood on him, he carries Vivianne, and bam—another blood exchange, this time from Zane to Vivianne, completing a blood bond, and then—" Dave snapped his fingers "—suspension spell, Vivianne goes into a coma and Zane is unable to pass on to—" the witch rolled his wrist "—that great werewolf farm in the sky."

"So it's his fault," Zane said, glaring at the witch.

"Well, if that's the case, why didn't Zane 'pass on' when I came out of the coma?" Vivianne asked.

Dave nodded. "Yeah, that's a good question. A ghost's spirit leaves a body at the time of death, but here Zane attached to you instead. You have to take him back to his body."

"And then he'll pass on?" Vivianne asked, and even Zane leaned forward, keen to hear the witch's response.

Dave grinned. "If you return Zane's spirit to his physical form, he will no longer haunt you in the metaphysical plane."

Zane closed his eyes in relief. Vivianne smiled. "Great. So, where is Zane's body?" Finally! Some good news, a plan of action. All they had to do was reunite Zane with his body, and poof, haunting problem solved.

Ryder dipped his head to look at his shoes. "Alpine," he said quietly.

Vivianne's smile fell. "Oh."

# Chapter 7

"Why doesn't your pack put a road in?"

Zane turned at Vivianne's question. Her annoyance was clear in her tone as she trudged through the knee-deep snow. She was wearing a red ski jacket and black ski pants that made her curvy legs look slim and strong. Sexy.

The snow reflected the silvery light of the waning moon, creating a glowing landscape that brought back so many memories for him, of midnight hunts and teenage trysts. He eyed the woman who was shaking the snow off of her boot before sinking it back into the powder. He hated to admit it, but she made moonlight look good. Her dark hair was a stark contrast against the pale snow, her cheeks flushed. She looked remarkably vibrant for a deathwalker.

"Because we prefer to watch visitors hike," he told her, his lips quirking as Dave waded behind her. The man still wore his sunglasses and stern expression, but every now and then the guy would bend over, pick up a fistful of snow, pack it and then hurl it, his lips curving into a grin. Zane got the impression the witch didn't get to play in snow very often.

Vivianne paused, panting. "I don't know if this is such a good idea," she said, looking between Zane and Dave. "I'm walking into a werewolf den, for crying out loud. That's vampire suicide."

"It's this or hang out with your lycan shadow for all eternity," Dave pointed out.

Vivianne nodded. "Den, it is, then. Lead on," she said to Zane, gesturing with her hand.

Zane grimaced. "Actually, at this point, you're going to have to be blindfolded."

Vivianne frowned. "What?"

"This is as much as we let strangers see," Zane told her. "Dave will have to blindfold you, and guide you along."

"How is Dave going to know where to go if he can't see or hear you?" she asked impatiently.

"He'll hold your hand, and he'll be able to see me."

"Why does he get to see, and I don't?"

Zane frowned. "Because you're a vampire, Vivianne, and like any good werewolf pack with a healthy dose of self-preservation, we don't let vampires know where our den is."

"You don't trust me?"

His eyes rounded. "I saw you talk with your father about setting up a permanent torture chamber for werewolves. No, I don't trust you."

The den was the central home of the pack. Elders, pups, juveniles—they were all located in the den, and werewolves took the care and protection of their elderly and the young very, very seriously. He may be dead, but he still considered himself an Alpine guardian, and it was his duty to ensure the safety of his pack. That meant not trusting the Nightwing Vampire Prime with the location of the heart of the pack.

Her gaze skittered away from his for a moment. "I haven't agreed, yet."

"Yet." Zane shook his head. "You didn't say no, either."

"What do you expect, Zane? He's my father, and I'm a vampire. This is what we do. You can't tell me that lycans aren't also looking for ways to ruin us vampires."

Zane pressed his lips together. She had a point. Vampires and werewolves were natural enemies, and were always conspiring against each other. "Well, as long as we're clear—neither of us trusts the other."

"Crystal."

"What's going on?" Dave asked, stopping by Vivianne's side. "Why have we stopped?"

Vivianne relayed to Dave what Zane had said, and Zane noted her impatience. For the first time since he'd awoken in that dim little hospital room, he was calling the shots. They were on his turf now, and Vivianne would have to follow his cue if she didn't want to wind up dead.

Dave pulled a black bandanna out of the back pocket of his jeans, and lifted it toward Vivianne's head.

She held up a hand. "Please tell me that's clean."

Dave sighed. "It's clean. Now let me do this. You might be a vampire and accustomed to this cold, but I'm not, so let's hurry."

He tied the bandanna around her head, masking her eyes. "I'm going to reach for your hand, now, so don't hit me."

Her lips pursed as she raised her hand, and the witch clasped it. Once again, the tendril of light that stretched between Zane and Vivianne became visible, and Dave followed it until his gaze met Zane's.

"Where to?"

Zane pointed toward a rock face. "This way."

Two hours later, Vivianne braced herself against the rock

wall, and paused to catch her breath. Zane glanced up to the niche he knew so well.

"Get ready," he told her.

She frowned behind the blindfold. "What? Get ready for what?"

A wolf launched from its hiding place, landing on the snow less than a foot away from her, growling low and deep. Zane recognized him immediately, and smiled. Nate Baxter.

Dave held up both hands. "Whoa, easy."

Vivianne stumbled, arms out, and her hand went to the blindfold. The wolf snapped at her, and she pressed herself back against the rock wall, blindfold in place.

"Parlay," she said abruptly. "I am Vivianne Marchetta, Vampire Prime of the Nightwing Colony, and I demand parlay with the Alpine Alpha Prime." She drew herself up to her full five feet five inches of glacial contempt. Zane had to admit, he was impressed. Not many people could wear a blindfold and convey disdain quite like Vivianne could.

The wolf crept closer, and Zane watched as the Alpine guardian inspected both the vampire and the witch.

Dave held up a hand and waved. "She's with me," he said. "We're here about Zane."

The wolf stared at Dave for a moment and then Zane watched as his friend morphed from wolf to man.

"Whoa, dude, give a guy some warning before you flash all that," Dave muttered to the now-naked man.

"Flash what?" Vivianne asked, tense.

"Never mind, just keep that blindfold on," Zane said. He eyed Nate. He wanted to go up to his friend, shake his hand, hell, give him a hug. It was so good to see him, so good to see not just a familiar face, but a lycan one at that. He couldn't help but notice some changes with his friend, though. There were grooves around the corners of his mouth and eyes that hadn't been there before, and they didn't look like laugh lines. His friend had lost some of his good humor.

Nate's face was stony as he stepped closer to the vampire. "I should kill you here and now for daring to show your face, here, vamp." His voice was low and harsh. Zane shifted closer, not sure if he was wanting to protect his friend from the vamp, or Vivianne from Alpine's guardian prime.

Vivianne's eyebrow arched, and she smiled coolly. "That's Vampire Prime Marchetta, thank you very much."

"What the hell do you want with Samantha?"

"That's between her and me," Vivianne stated calmly. Zane watched her closely. She was blindfolded, at a distinct disadvantage, yet not at all rattled by his friend's imposing presence.

Nate smiled grimly. "I'm the Alpine Guardian Prime. Any business you have with Samantha Alpine also involves me, so if you want to get anywhere near my alpha prime, I suggest you tell me exactly what it is you want, otherwise you're not seeing anyone."

Vivianne tilted her head for a moment, as though assessing her options. "I have invoked parlay. By Reform Law, you can't kill me, and you have to allow me access to your prime." She shrugged, her hands out at her sides. "I'm here alone. I'm no threat."

Nate snorted. "You've got teeth. You're a threat."

"I'll stow mine if you'll stow yours."

Nate looked over at Dave. "What's this about Zane?"

Dave took a deep breath. "We need to see where he's buried."

"Why?"

Dave hesitated.

"I want to pay my respects," Vivianne said, and Zane was surprised at her tone. She sounded almost sincere.

Nate shook his head. "You're the reason my friend is dead. That's a no-go."

"It's like talking to a brick wall," Vivianne muttered, and both Nate and Zane smiled. That's exactly what a guardian was supposed to do, guard access and protect the pack. She put her hands on her hips. "Look, your friend is haunting me, and this witch thinks if we can reunite Zane's ghost with his body, he'll finally be able to get some peace."

Nate blinked. He looked between Dave and Vivianne. "Is she for real?" he asked, gesturing to the vampire.

Dave nodded. "Yep."

"Zane is haunting her?"

"Yep."

Nate started to laugh, and it took a while for him to get his mirth under control. He cleared his throat, and shook his head. "I'm surprised, Dave, that you could be fooled by the vamp—although it's a novel approach, I'll admit." Nate folded his arms, expression turning serious. "Not happening."

Zane rolled his eyes. Nate was always a stickler for the rules. Nobody got through on their first pass. Deter, deter, deter. Unfortunately, he didn't have the patience to wait for Vivianne to jump through all the hoops his friend usually laid out. "Tell him if he doesn't give you access, you'll tell."

Vivianne frowned beneath her blindfold, but it was the only indication she gave she'd heard him. "If you don't let me pass, I'll tell."

Nate arched an eyebrow. "Tell what?"

"Tell him you'll tell the Thompson twins."

Her mouth opened a little, then she lifted her chin. "I'll tell the Thompson twins."

Zane grinned when he saw his friend straighten, saw the shock bloom on his face. Nate looked beyond Vivianne to Dave, who shot Vivianne a glance.

"Really? You can tell me," the witch suggested.

Nate's lips firmed. "Follow me."

The blindfold was removed, and Vivianne blinked in the dimness. It didn't take her eyes long to adjust, though, or to see Dave's set expression as well as the group of werewolves surrounding her, their features harsh as they stared at the vampire who dared enter their den. Dave still wore his sunglasses, even inside this dim cave.

She took her time to stare at each face. Men, women, they all stared at her warily, suspiciously. Not a friendly face among them. She couldn't blame them. She was a vampire. They were werewolves. There was no love lost between the breeds. She maintained eye contact, though, and didn't dip her gaze. She would not show any submission in this place. She took a slow, steadying breath.

She was surrounded by werewolves.

That's okay. She could handle this. Led into a small cavern, outnumbered, with the only tunnel leading from the rock-walled room blocked by somber, intense and fit individuals who all looked like they wanted to sink their teeth into their unwelcome guest. Yeah, she could handle this. The memory of the dark wolf bounding out of the darkness hit her, made goose bumps rise on her skin. A wash of coolness cascaded over her, from her hair follicles to her snow boot–covered toes. This room was full of shadows, ink on black, with only a low light filtering down the tunnel and into the room. She wasn't afraid of the dark—hell, she lived in the dark—but this was damn creepy.

"Calm down," Zane murmured, shifting into her line of sight. "They'll hear your heart pounding in the main hall, at this rate."

She swallowed, consciously relaxing the tense muscles in her shoulders. She had to focus a little to unclench her fists. "Is this the normal way you greet a guest?" She asked calmly, lifting her chin as she addressed the group.

"You're not a guest."

It was the voice of the lycan who'd led her into the den. She looked at him carefully. Golden haired, green-eyed, he was tall. Although, at five foot five, everyone seemed tall. He wore a pair of jeans, the top button undone, as though they were hastily donned. He was barefoot and shirtless, despite the cool temperature, yet didn't seem to feel the chill in the air. She didn't normally feel the cold, but she couldn't help but notice she did now, feel it in a way she hadn't since—her eyes rounded. Since before she'd turned vamp. The air in the den was cool, but the air smelled fresh, as though it was drawn in directly from the mountainside and circulated. She glanced around the cavern, and it took her a moment to locate the vents, small holes cut in the wall close to the rock ceiling. Very clever.

But she wasn't here to admire innovative thermal management.

"I need to speak with Samantha Alpine," she stated, glancing at the group. "Which one of you is she?" Samantha Alpine had never attended any of the Reform society's scion balls, and Vivianne had no idea what the woman looked like.

"She's not here. You need to pass us to get anywhere near her, so start talking."

Vivianne sighed brusquely. She wanted to get this over with. Find Zane's body, transfer his ghost and then get the hell out of there. Without any of her colony knowing what she'd done, or why.

But she wasn't willing to talk about this with all of the damned Alpine pack listening in and thinking Nightwing's leader was a loon.

"Just you," she said to the guardian prime.

He shook his head.

She glanced at the small expectant crowd, and blinked the second time she saw the same face. Twins.

"Are you the Thompson twins?" she asked. Light brown hair, green eyes, tall and lithe, they were reasonably attractive, by lycan standards, she guessed.

The guardian prime frowned. "Clear the room." The werewolves paused for a moment, and glared at Vivianne, as though collectively warning her against trying anything before they shuffled out of the room.

Dave chuckled softly. "I so need to hear that story."

"What is your name?" she asked the man.

"Nate Baxter, Alpine Guardian Prime." Nate folded his arms. "This better be good," he muttered, "because I'm not known for my patience."

"Actually, he is known for his patience," Zane commented. "He's very zen." Zane shifted to look at her directly. "He's also fair. Take your time," he told her, his voice low and soothing. She wouldn't admit it, but right here and now, she was comforted by his presence. Again.

"Your packmate, Zane, has not…passed on," she said. Was that the best way to describe it? Did ghosts "pass on"? She had no idea of the technical term for having your life and spirit extinguished from this world.

"Explain." The Alpine Guardian Prime's comment was just as clipped as hers.

"I don't know how to explain," she admitted, then glanced at Dave, who shrugged. Great. The witch was willing to let her make a fool of herself. "I can…see him."

The guardian prime's eyebrow rose. "What?"

"I see him, I hear him, he's right here."

"Here…?" Nate looked at her as though he doubted her sanity.

She sighed. "I know it sounds crazy. Believe me, I thought I was—" She paused. She couldn't just spill her experience to this guardian prime. Once she left here she would still be the vampire prime of a rival colony. "It took a little getting used to," she said. "Apparently when we were bitten, there was a blood mix-up," she said, waving her hand, "and Zane passed on to me instead of the hereafter." She pointed to Dave. "He can explain it. It's his fault."

Dave pursed his lips and frowned at her. She frowned right back. The man still wore his sunglasses, even inside this dim cave. And yes, it was his fault. This blood link business wouldn't have happened if he hadn't done his witchy-winks stuff. Of course, she'd be dead if he hadn't done his witchy-winks stuff, and it was darned annoying having this mental conflict of frustration counter-balanced with relief.

Dave described the details of the blood bond, and Nate listened with the same what-the-hell expression she assumed she'd worn when she'd first heard the theory.

"So you think that by putting the vamp into the coma, she prevented Zane from resting in peace?" Nate asked.

Vivianne frowned at Nate's comment. "I don't know if I'd say it quite like that…" she muttered.

Nate shook his head. "This sounds like you drank a bad batch of blood," he told her.

Zane braced an arm against the rock wall. "Ask him to test you."

Vivianne frowned at him, and Zane sighed. "He won't hurt you. Just ask him questions only I'd know the answer to. Otherwise this will take ages, and I'm getting itchy. Let's get this thing moving."

"Fine," Vivianne said, then smiled at Nate. "Why don't you ask me something that only Zane would know?"

"Ask you to tell him about the Thompson twins," Dave suggested.

"How did we first meet?" Nate asked instead.

"Too easy. Paw Patrol."

"Paw Patrol," Vivianne repeated.

Nate shrugged. "Anyone could have guessed that."

Vivianne shook her head. "I have no idea what Paw Patrol is. Personally, I've never heard of it."

"Well, I could assume you're telling the truth…but I won't," Nate said. "When was Zane's first time, where, and with who?"

Vivianne blushed as she glanced at Zane. Did she really want to know the details of Zane losing his virginity?

"I was four, behind the kitchen, with Jared."

Vivianne's eyes widened. "*What? Four? With Jared?*" She didn't know where to start with that one. There was so much wrong in that. *Four.* As to it being with Jared Grey… well, she wasn't one to judge, but she was surprised. Zane was such a great kisser—in her dreams, at least. Maybe he swung both ways. But Jared—she'd met him, and she'd never guessed he was that way inclined. But so *young.* "You know, there are laws against that sort of stuff," she said.

Zane frowned at her, then his eyes widened as comprehension dawned. "He meant when I *shifted*," he exclaimed. He shuddered. "No, gross—how twisted are you vamps?"

"Well, you need to explain these things to me," she protested, her cheeks warming. "Vampires don't shift, how am I supposed to know that's what he meant?" She turned to face Nate. "It was when he was four, behind the kitchen, and he was with Jared."

Nate stared at her for a moment.

"I've heard enough." The woman's voice was soft, yet firm. Vivianne turned as a woman entered the cave. She was…well, interesting. Her hair was long, tawny and thick, and her blue eyes were bright in the dimly illuminated room. She was tall, athletically built, and had an air of power around her that Vivianne recognized easily.

"She's had the baby," Zane whispered, smiling. "God,

I'd love to see Jared's son." Jared Grey had been the Alpine Alpha Prime, but was killed in a bizarre plot orchestrated by her old nemesis, Arthur Armstrong. Which would make this woman the current Alpine Alpha Prime.

"Samantha Alpine, I presume?" Vivianne didn't hide her curiosity. She'd heard about the woman, but this was their first meeting. Once the life partner of Jared Grey, Alpine Alpha Prime, their relationship was legendary, as was the woman's desire to avenge her husband's death. Vivianne had heard she was tough, fair and just as lethal as her husband.

Samantha nodded, then halted, her feet planted shoulder-width apart, her hands on her hips. "Why are you here?"

"You heard. Zane Wilder hasn't passed on, so I'm hoping to facilitate that."

Samantha's lips quirked. "Yes, but why?"

Vivianne frowned. "To reunite his ghost with his body."

"But why?"

"So he can pass on." Vivianne's frown deepened. She thought it was all fairly obvious by now.

"But why?"

She glanced at Zane, then shrugged. "So both he and I can get some peace," she said.

"But why?"

"Because he's annoying me," she told the alpha prime.

"Yeah, well, you're just as annoying," Zane told her.

"He's annoying, and he needs to find his peace." Vivianne glared at him.

"Why is a vampire so concerned about a lycan finding his peace?" Samantha enquired, her eyebrow arching. "Seems to me a vamp would delight in any discomfort caused to a werewolf."

"Unfortunately, his peace is tied to mine—as is his discomfort. That's why I want him…" She stopped short of saying "gone"—it sounded harsh—but Zane folded his arms, as though he knew what she meant. "To find his peace," she finished lamely.

Samantha stepped closer, her gaze narrowed as she stared at Vivianne directly for a moment. Then she shifted that cool blue gaze to Dave. "You believe her."

Dave nodded. "I've seen him, through her."

Samantha's shoulders relaxed, and she dipped her head. "Jared told me that story," she said quietly, gaze on the stone floor. "He was a little older than Zane, and said it was one of the funniest things, watching a cub shift for the first time."

"Every cub has to go through it at some point," Zane grumbled as he shifted to lean against a rock wall.

"What made this so...funny?" Vivianne asked, curious. She wasn't sure if the curiosity was about the humor, or learning more about the lycan she'd carried with her since waking up.

"He was busted with his hand in the cookie jar. Literally," Samantha said, and her lips curved. "He and Jared were looking for a snack when Zane's dad found them."

"Scared the bejeebus out of us," Zane said, his own lips pulling up in a reminiscent smile.

"Zane shifted. Apparently it was his attempt to disappear. The cookie jar toppled over on top of him, and his head got stuck. They had to use soap to get the jar off his head."

"We lost a lot of good cookies that day," Nate commented. Vivianne couldn't help but notice the softness in his tone, the humor that brightened the lycan's eyes, if only for a moment. Or how Samantha's smile warmed.

"You liked him," she said.

Zane chuckled. "Don't be so surprised."

Samantha shook her head. "No. We *loved* him."

Zane blinked, then looked away, swallowing.

"I heard he died...protecting his guardian prime." Her tone lifted at the end, questioning. She couldn't help it. She wanted to know more about Zane Wilder, about what he was like—before he became her annoying shadow. She turned to Nate. "I heard what happened. For what it's worth, I actually respect Matthias, and I didn't blame him for Rafe Woodland's attack." Matthias was now the Woodland Alpha Prime, but when he'd been Alpine pack's guardian prime he'd negotiated access for his wolves to pass through Nightwing while they pursued Rafe, the man who'd organized the poisoning death of Alpine's alpha prime—Samantha's husband. Matthias had struck her as decent, shrewd, but fair, despite being a werewolf.

Nate straightened his shoulders. "It's a pity you didn't say that to your brother."

Vivianne's eyes narrowed. "I didn't have a chance. One of *your* kind came into my territory and attacked me. That was not the deal I had with Matthias. Of course there should be retribution. Admittedly, I would have preferred the lycan responsible for the attack to have been punished instead of Zane."

Zane glanced at her for a moment, surprised. "Thank you for that," he said solemnly.

Footsteps echoed down the tunnel, and Samantha turned as a young woman tentatively peered into the cavern. "I'm sorry to bother you, Samantha, but J.J. needs you."

Samantha nodded, then glanced back over her shoulder to meet Vivianne's gaze. Vivianne got the impression she was being measured. Assessed, weighed and found moderately acceptable when Samantha beckoned. "Walk with me."

# Chapter 8

Zane followed closely behind the two women. Part of him felt such joy. He was home with his people. His alpha prime was right in front of him, strong and healthy. His closest friend strode along behind him, talking quietly with the sunglasses-wearing witch. He did a little skip and a jig. He was home.

He'd always loved pack. The unity, the loyalty, the friendship… He'd always wanted to be his own alpha, and had realized that would probably require him leaving Alpine. He wouldn't displace Nate or Samantha—he had too much respect for both of them. Now he realized he'd never have his own pack, never have his own family… There was sadness with that realization, but right now, surrounded by Alpine werewolves, it was a bittersweet moment. He may not establish his own pack, but if he could just spend one more day with his family, then he'd be happy.

Just one more day.

He stumbled over that thought. What would happen next? When Vivianne found his body and Dave did whatever witches did, what would happen? Would he pass on? What would that feel like? Would he just die for good? Disappear into the ether…? What happened to the dead? Like, the normal dead? Did they follow the light to a place of happy-ever-after? Or was it just a void, with no sense of time, space or self?

For just the briefest moment, trepidation flared within him. What if there was nothing? What if this was all there was to life? And he'd had his run at it, game over? He swallowed. Well, if that was the case, he would make damn sure he made the most of what little haunting time he had left.

They turned a corner in the tunnel and entered the main hall, and he plowed right through Vivianne as she halted, the fuzzy tingling thrumming through his body.

He turned to face her, exasperated that she'd stopped so suddenly and then saw the look on her face. It was fleeting, immediately covered by an impassive calm, but he'd seen it, seen the shock, the momentary terror. He glanced around, and it took him a moment to shift perspective, and see the scene through Vivianne's eyes.

His packmates lined the walls of the main hall. Sofas and armchairs were clustered in small groups for the benefit of discussions, meetings and general conversation, and a large number of those seats were occupied. A hush fell over the hall, save for the fretting and occasional cry of a baby, and the pack watched Vivianne warily. Many of the guardians stepped forward.

What was a natural protective instinct in the werewolf would be seen as an intimidating move to the single vampire in the den. She again was surrounded, but this time by far more lycans.

The memory of her dream—the scary part, not the sexy

part—replayed in his mind. He'd seen the event from her mind, and it had felt like Rafe had attacked *him*. Rafe had bitten *him*. The pain, the terror, the realization that death would claim her... For the first time he truly understood the cost to Vivianne to come here. And she was here alone. She hadn't told her father or brother where she was going, and had left her usual bodyguard snoozing in the parking lot at the Galen medical center.

She was here so that he could "find his peace." Sure, she had as much to gain from that as he did, and he didn't delude himself that she was here from the goodness of her cold dead heart. When she found his body, she would no longer be haunted by a lycan in what must be a constant nightmarish reminder of the attack that very nearly killed her. But no vampire would want to run the gauntlet of a werewolf den.

Ever.

Vivianne lifted her chin and followed Samantha through the hall, a baby's cries the only sound to register in the space.

It wasn't surprising. Only one vampire had ever walked the tunnels of Alpine's den, and even then she'd been a half-breed looking into Jared Grey's murder. Any meetings with vampires occurred off-site, preferably in a neutral zone, and only when it was absolutely necessary. A vampire in these halls was a rarer occurrence than an eclipse.

Samantha walked up to the dais, and Zane gaped as she held her arms out for the babe one of the elders was rocking. Samantha's face softened into a smile as she cradled her son and sat down in the large chair on the platform. The elder handed Samantha a soft, fluffy, baby blue blanket, and his alpha prime tickled her son's nose with it. Marjorie, the elder, handed her a teething rusk, and Samantha gave it to her son as she settled them in the alpha prime's seat.

Jared's son.

Samantha had been pregnant with the babe when Jared had been murdered. She'd still been pregnant the last time he'd seen her. This babe looked to be about six months old. God, he'd lost so much time. He glanced at Vivianne.

She was staring at Samantha up on the dais with an emotion that was just as fleeting as her fear, before she put that well-rehearsed cool mask back in place. Was that— was that envy?

He blinked. Surely not. A vampire being envious of a werewolf was about as logical as a fish nesting in the trees. And yet, there was this spark, this curiosity mixed with that something that looked so much like envy, but couldn't be, that made it difficult for him to look away.

"How is this process supposed to work?" Samantha asked as she looked over at Vivianne and Dave.

Dave winced. "We need to see his body. She'll need to—" Dave made a gesture with his hand "—touch it."

"No," an older voice exclaimed, and Zane turned to see Dietrich, one of the elders, rise to his feet. "That's obscene. Not just her being here, among us, but to give her access to our *dead*. Samantha…" His voice came out low, chiding.

Samantha lifted her chin. "I understand, Dietrich. But we know Zane is not at peace. She is the key to giving him that."

Vivianne frowned. "How do you know he's not at peace?"

Zane walked closer to the dais. Had his pack noticed something? Had they sensed something wasn't quite right?

Dietrich shifted on his feet, frowning. "This is wrong, Samantha."

Samantha's smile was brittle. "My son growing up without knowing his father is wrong, Dietrich. Zane—our loyal, funny, full-of-life guardian—being killed by a vamp is wrong. His body… There are so many things that are wrong, Dietrich, this is just going to have to get in line as we deal with it."

The baby in her arms fussed, and she dropped her gaze to the wriggling boy she held, and smiled. She adjusted their position, and lifted the baby up to her shoulder and gently rubbed his back, ignoring the mess he was making with the now-soggy biscuit.

"We need to do this. Not for her, but for Zane."

Zane tuned out the rest of the argument as he stepped up onto the platform. The baby lifted his head and blinked, and Zane smiled at his attempt to focus. J.J.—Jared Junior. It was so obvious who had sired him. From the pale hair that looked dusted with gold under the lights from the hall sconces, to the silvery-blue eyes, the little boy looked the image of his father.

The baby gurgled, then smiled up at him, and Zane moved, stunned when the baby's gaze followed him. J.J. could see him. He leaned down until his face was level with the baby's and smiled. The baby chuckled, then burped, and a wave of sweet smelling breath wafted over to Zane.

He scrunched his nose up and poked out his tongue, and the baby laughed again.

He glanced up, hopeful, but disappointment crushed when he realized only the babe saw him. Dietrich and Samantha, Nate, the rest of the pack, they were all oblivious to him.

Everyone except Vivianne, who watched him curiously, a faint smile curving her lips.

"Then it's settled," Samantha said as she rose from her seat. She gave J.J. a cuddle and a kiss before handing him back to Marjorie, the elder who stood nearby on the dais.

She strode down the steps to the hall floor. "Nate, bring two guardians, the witch and the vamp." She turned to Dietrich. "We'll make sure Zane is treated respectfully."

Dietrich nodded, but Zane could see the man wasn't pleased. Zane was touched. He hadn't expected anyone, let alone one of the elders, to be so defensive, so protective of his... Wait. He frowned. He realized Samantha hadn't answered Vivianne's question.

"Ask her what's wrong with my body," he said as he leaped from the dais and strode over to Vivianne.

She frowned, shaking her head slightly in confusion.

"Ask her what is wrong with my body? Why am I not buried?"

Vivianne gaped for a moment, then turned as Samantha approached her. "Is Zane buried?"

Samantha strode past her, and beckoned Vivianne with a flick of her fingers. "No."

"Why not?" Zane asked as Vivianne turned and followed Samantha, Nate and Dave close behind, with two more guardians in their wake.

"Why isn't Zane buried?" Vivianne repeated, then shrugged as she looked at Zane. She clearly had no idea what was going on. They entered a tunnel, and Zane shook his head. He knew this tunnel. A little ways down it housed the mortuary and then there was an exit, the mouth of the cave that lead out to the icy graveyard.

Samantha didn't reply, and just kept walking.

"I don't understand," Vivianne whispered. "They said they knew you weren't at rest. How?"

Zane shook his head. "I don't know. Lycan custom is to place the body in a viewing coffin, and three days later we take the bodies out and either bury them, or cremate them so their ashes can be scattered. Depends on the time of year, and if the ground is too frozen for burial. Either way, we're supposed to return to feed the earth."

"And you think you haven't been buried? Or..." Vivianne hesitated.

"Burned," he supplied. "Buried or burned." He was surprised to see her flinch, and gave her an odd look. He'd never expect a vampire to be squeamish over death.

"Do they do this a lot?" Nate asked Dave.

"What, you mean the chitty-chat?" Dave enquired. Nate nodded. Dave nodded. "Yeah."

"Weird."

"Yep."

"You don't know the half of it," Zane muttered.

They rounded a bend and entered the mortuary. Little rock shelves lined the walls, and Zane paused when he saw a body on a shelf. "Damn, Patrick died? How?"

Vivianne sighed as she glanced over her shoulder at Nate. "How did Patrick die?"

Nate's eyebrows rose, and he glanced between her and the shelf. "How did you—" He held up a hand. "No, don't tell me. Tell Zane it was Patrick's time. He passed away in his sleep."

Zane nodded. Patrick had been a tracker, and had taught pretty much all of the pups for the last three generations how to track and move through their territory.

Samantha picked up a lantern from the floor, and paused long enough to light it, then stood to the side as the guardians stepped forward to shift a large boulder that looked like part of the wall.

Zane's trepidation grew. What the hell was wrong with him? This was one of the rooms they reserved for bodies that could be contagious and pose a health risk to the rest of the pack. In effect, the quarantine room.

"What the hell is going on?"

Vivianne turned to Samantha. "You didn't answer my question, before. If you can't see or hear his ghost, how did you know Zane wasn't at rest?"

Samantha stared at her for a moment, then spoke slowly,

as though carefully choosing her words. "Our custom is to let everyone come and pay their respects to a dead lycan. Three days later, when certain…changes start to occur, we bury or burn."

Again, Zane noticed Vivianne tense up at that.

"The problem is, with Zane, those changes were…missing."

"Missing?" Vivianne repeated.

Samantha gave her the lantern and gestured to the now darkened doorway into the smaller cave. "See for yourself."

Vivianne grimaced, then took a step toward the opening.

"Wait," Zane called out, bounding in front of her. "Wait."

Vivianne halted, frowning. "What?"

"Once you go in there, and see my body, I will pass on. At least, that's the plan."

"Then why are we waiting?" Vivianne asked, and Zane noticed Samantha's eyebrows rising as she watched Vivianne talk with thin air.

"This is the last chance I'll get to talk with…my pack." *You.* Talking with her was his first thought, and the realization that this would be their last moment together seemed to hit them both at the same time. Why it should seem quite so important and meaningful, he couldn't, shouldn't try to fathom.

"Oh." Vivianne nodded, then tucked a dark curl behind her ear. "Did you—did you want to say something? To your pack?" she ended hurriedly.

"Yeah," he said, his voice rough. "Tell Samantha— Tell her congratulations on J.J. He looks like he's thriving. Tell her I'll miss not being around to see him grow, but I know she's going to be a phenomenal mother. It was an honor to serve her."

Vivianne nodded and turned to repeat the words to Samantha. The alpha prime blinked, her eyes glistening as tears formed, and she nodded, smiling sadly.

Zane turned to Nate. "Tell him I'll see him on the other side, but not too soon. Tell him he needs to find his smile again. Oh, and that Emma Thompson has a freckle above her left eyebrow."

Nate smiled when Vivianne told him what Zane had said. "You brat. You knew all along."

Zane grinned, then turned to face Vivianne. She swallowed.

"I guess this is it, then..." he said to her.

She nodded. "I guess so."

He took a deep breath, then stepped a little closer. "You work too hard." If this was the last he'd ever see her, he felt the need to share something meaningful with her. He'd been her shadow for so long, had seen and heard so much... He understood her. Sort of. As well as any lycan could understand a bloodsucker.

Vivianne blinked. "What?"

"I know the great Vivianne Marchetta would kill anyone who implied she was a people-pleaser, but I'm already dead, so you can't. You look after your colony, all the business interests, you try to please that lifeless father of yours—God only knows why. You should take some time for yourself."

"Are you seriously giving me lifestyle tips right now?"

Zane grinned. "I know your secret."

Vivianne paled, and glanced at the others around her. "And what is that?" she asked coolly.

He leaned down so that their gazes were level. "You're nowhere near as scary as you like people to think."

Her lips pursed, and he chuckled softly at her show of annoyance, before his gaze dropped to her mouth. He was tempted to kiss her, to press his lips to hers. So tempted. He cleared his throat. But he was a lycan, she was a vamp.

Oh, and there was that minor detail where he was…dead. He didn't think kissing Vivianne would lead to him finding peace. No. He suspected that one kiss wouldn't be enough, though, and he didn't want to spend his eternity wanting more of what he couldn't have. Besides, under normal circumstances, there would be no way in hell he'd be entertaining fantasies of kissing the Nightwing vampire prime.

"Let's do this," he said gruffly, and stepped into the cave.

Vivianne followed him inside and held up the lantern. The soft glow illuminated the waist-high ledge that cut across the middle of the room. On that ledge lay…him.

Zane gaped as he stepped closer. Wow, this was… weird. He looked down at himself. His beard was the same length, as was his hair. Zane frowned. He hadn't quite known what to expect, but he was thinking more of a zombie kind of look, or skeletal, but no. He looked… like he was sleeping.

"That's not normal," Vivianne stated, setting the lamp on the ledge next to his shoulder. She turned to Dave, Nate and Samantha who clustered around the opening. "He hasn't decomposed."

Samantha shook her head. "No, he hasn't. When we realized, we held off moving him, waiting for the decomp to start, but it didn't. So we kept him."

"That's sweet," Zane said. He took a deep breath, let it out and then reached out toward his body. "Okay, here goes."

He closed his eyes as he touched his hand, waiting for the whoosh. Or the poof. Or whatever it was that signaled passing on.

It didn't happen. He opened one eye, and Vivianne stared at him in confusion. "Why are you still here?" She turned to Dave. "Why is he still here? Do you need to do some sort of spell or something?"

Dave shook his head. "Nope."

"Then why isn't he moving on?"

Zane opened both of his eyes to glare at the witch. "Did he screw this up, too?"

Dave stepped closer to the doorway. "He's attached to you. You're the one who has to move him on."

"How do I do that?" Vivianne asked.

Dave's lips quirked. "You have to connect with him."

Vivianne reached over and picked up the corpse-Zane's hand. Zane closed his eyes again, waiting for the whoosh.

Still nothing. His shoulders sagged and he opened his eyes. "Oh, come *on*."

Vivianne dropped his hand and picked it up again. Squeezed it. She looked up at Zane, her face crestfallen. "I'm so sorry," she whispered.

Zane frowned. "Why are you sorry?"

"I wanted to help you, but I can't. You're stuck."

He was stunned. Her desire to help him was genuine. She'd done this—for him. Braved a werewolves' den, at the risk of not only her life, but her professional reputation—if his pack spread the word that the Nightwing vampire prime thought she could talk with ghosts, well, she wouldn't be prime for long. Warmth bloomed in his chest, as did a need to assuage some of her obvious guilt.

"This isn't your fault, Vivianne. You're just as much a victim of this mess as I am."

Dave sighed. "He's not stuck." He stepped inside the cave. Even in the darkness, he didn't remove his sunglasses. "Zane's essence is currently with you. You need to give it back to his body."

"How?" Vivianne exclaimed.

Dave folded his arms and grinned. "The way to return a spirit to a vessel is to breathe his essence into him."

Vivianne's nose scrunched up. "As in, CPR?"

Dave rubbed his chin. "No, as in a kiss."

\* \* \*

Vivianne gaped, then took a deep breath. "I think you're going to have to repeat that," she said, "because I think I misheard you." She thought she'd heard the witch say "kiss."

"Kiss," Dave repeated. "As in smooch. Snog. Tonsil hockey. Tongue—"

"Whoa, easy there. I get it." Vivianne held up a hand to stop the barrage of words.

"I don't know about this," Samantha said from the doorway, her expression wary.

"Oh, I know about this—I know it's not happening," Vivianne said, shaking her head. Nate ran his hand over his face.

"A kiss. That's all it takes."

"This isn't some fairy tale," Vivianne cried in protest. She gestured to Zane, lying so darn peacefully on the slab, his ghost looking just as confused as she felt. "He's no sleeping beauty."

Zane folded his arms. "Hey. I take exception to that."

"You know what I mean," she muttered to him. Truthfully, he was a beautiful man, and he so didn't look dead. He looked like he'd wake up any minute. She reached out and prodded him, surprised his skin could still feel so warm, so solid, after all this time.

He still wore khaki pants and a white singlet, and he looked…ripped.

Not rotting.

She swallowed. "I can't do this."

Dave shrugged. "Okay. As long as you're okay with Zane haunting you every minute of the rest of your eternity."

She thought of all the meetings Zane would rant about, all the dates he'd ruin. She'd never get anything done, never have a meaningful relationship with another man as long as this particular werewolf was around to distract and annoy her. She looked up at him.

"What do you think?"

"I think this sucks," he told her frankly. "But I don't think either of us wants this," he said, gesturing between the two of them, "to go on forever."

She nodded. "True." She glanced down at the Zane lying on the rock shelf. "This is ridiculous."

"I think I'm going to puke," Nate muttered, and turned away.

She closed her eyes, her hands gently lowering to the ledge. "I can do this. I can. It'll be like that story, where the girl kisses the frog."

Zane arched an eyebrow. "Are you calling me a frog?"

"Shh," Vivianne hissed. "Stop distracting me." She had to mentally prepare herself. She would lean down, brush her lips against his and then back away without disgracing herself by wanting more. Or acting out that fantasy from yesterday. No, she needed control. Control and calm, soothing vibes. She took a deep breath, counted to four, then exhaled.

"Are you—are you working yourself up to this?" Zane exclaimed.

"Shh," she hissed at him again.

She reached out to hesitantly touch resting Zane's face, and leaned forward.

"Yeah, I don't think I can watch this, either," Samantha said from the doorway.

Dave chuckled, and leaned back against the cave wall. "I'm fine with it." Nate reached in and tugged the witch outside.

"Just get it over and done with. I don't think my ego can take much more of this," Zane muttered.

Over and done with? Is that how he felt about this? About her kissing him? Well, how did she expect him to feel?

She still wasn't sure what had happened yesterday, whether she'd just dreamed the moment, or whether she'd somehow dragged him into her fantasy. Regardless, all she had to do was kiss him and then this would all be over.

She leaned down and gave him a quick peck on the lips, and straightened. She glanced up, and frowned when she saw his ghostly presence next to her, his hands on his hips, an exasperated look on his face.

"You're still here."

"You call that a kiss?"

She gave him a narrowed-eyed glare and then leaned forward again, pressing her lips against his. It was weird, kissing a nonresponsive man. Even though his lips were soft and pliant, it still felt odd not getting any kind of reac—

Her eyes widened when the lips beneath hers moved, and a hand slid into her hair.

# Chapter 9

His lips were soft and gentle, his kiss tender as his hand delved into her hair. A soft light glowed around them, between them, and she had to close her eyes as the light grew in intensity.

She braced her hands against his chest to push him away. *Oh, wow.* For the first time her hands didn't go right through him, but came into contact with warm, solid muscle. She smoothed her hands over him, feeling the soft cotton fabric of his singlet, the smooth glide of skin that was taught over muscle.

So much strength.

The muscles beneath her hand bunched as he raised his other hand to slide it around her waist and pull her closer. She sighed, and the kiss changed.

His tongue slid into her mouth, his hand tightening in her hair as he angled her head. His other hand slid up her back to cup her cheek. His thumb pressed lightly at the corner of her mouth, and she opened her mouth wider.

Heat. So much heat. From him, from the light enveloping them…

His tongue rubbed against hers as his hand slid through her hair, until both of his hands held on to her curls, and he controlled the kiss. Over and over, his lips moved against hers, his tongue delving deep inside.

God, he was such a fantastic kisser. Damp heat bloomed between her thighs, and her breasts swelled. She leaned into him, pressing her breasts against his chest.

He growled, a sound that was so deep in his throat it made his chest rumble against her breasts, and she shuddered. He slowly rose to a sitting position, and she had to tilt her head back to follow the movement. He dropped one hand down to her shoulder, and she held her breath as he then slid that hand down to the front zipper of her ski jacket.

The noise was so loud in the quiet rock chamber, the soft hiss as the zipper lowered an erotic counterpart to their heavy breathing. Her heart pounded in her chest, as though she was sprinting a one-mile race.

The garment relaxed around her shoulders as the jacket parted.

All the while, he kept kissing her, as though he was a starving man, and only she could satisfy his hunger. She could relate. She couldn't get enough of him, either.

She moaned as his hand slid inside her jacket, and her nipples tightened into peaks as his hand cupped her breast. Wicked heat spread up from her core to flood her body, her breasts so sensitized she craved his touch.

"Uh, did it work?" Dave called out, and Vivianne jerked her head back, eyes wide.

Zane stared at her with a heavy-lidded gaze. It was him.

Like, real, solid-mass him. She glanced around the cave to be certain. No more ghostly Zane.

A slight flash of something—disappointment—burst through her. He was gone. The man who had haunted her dreams and flitted on her periphery for so long, was gone. The man who had reluctantly kept her company, whose voice had pierced her mental shields to tease, chide and tempt, was now gone.

And yet, not.

She stared at the man who sat on the rock ledge in front of her. He was so familiar, yet so…different. Her gaze swept from the top of his head to the high forehead, the warm brown eyes that even now had hot shards of golden-green desire in his irises. His high cheekbones, and a jawline that looked strong beneath the dusting of a brown beard. His lips…oh, those lips. She swallowed. This was Zane, but he wasn't an annoying ghost who could disappear in an inky black puff of wispy fog. He wasn't the intangible vision who couldn't be touched and who couldn't touch her. No, this Zane was flesh and blood, muscle and mass, and sexy sensation. And she was still plastered to him. She withdrew her hands from his chest. Slowly. God, he felt good. She took a deep breath to calm her racing heart.

He stirred something primal within her, something that was unfamiliar, yet so instinctive. It felt like—like something was awakening deep within her, something powerful and primal, and perhaps just a little out of her control.

"Vivianne? Did it work?"

"Uh, I'm not sure." She glanced at Zane, who continued to meet her gaze with a calm curiosity. Wasn't he supposed to pass on? Was he now going to die for real, right in front of her? That thought sent a hot arrow of pain in the vicinity she'd normally associate with her heart, but it had been so long since something had stirred there, she couldn't be sure.

"You think—" Dave sighed brusquely and stepped inside the cave.

Vivianne tucked a strand of hair behind her ear, then frowned when she felt the tangled locks at the back of her head. She hurriedly tried to smooth the hair down. Zane's lips quirked when he noticed her unobtrusive attempts, and she shot him a quick frown.

He winked.

She blushed.

Oh. My. *God.* She turned to face Dave. She didn't blush, yet the warmth flooded her cheeks, all the same. What the hell? She was a vampire. A nine-hundred-year-old vampire who had seen enough in her lifetime to make the devil blush, not her.

She lifted her chin. "He's not passing on."

Samantha and Nate stepped inside the cave, and both of them looked at her oddly before turning to Zane. She'd forgotten they were there. Had they seen…? She looked momentarily to the ceiling as more warmth—damn it— flooded her face.

"Zane," Samantha breathed and crossed the floor of the cave to hug him. Nate also approached and pulled Zane into what could only be called a bear hug, thumping him on the back so hard Vivianne was surprised a rib didn't break, and then just held him.

"It's good to see you, bro."

Vivianne looked away. Bro. They weren't brothers by blood, but they obviously considered themselves close enough that blood didn't matter. There was heartfelt relief in Nate's face, along with something that went deeper than honest affection.

These lycans displayed emotions without fear of consequences, without the fear of being considered vulnerable. As though it wasn't a weakness.

"He hasn't passed on yet," Vivianne said in a low voice to Dave. Something itchy burned in her eyes, and she had to rub it away. What, tears? Hell, when was the last time she'd cried?

There must be something in the Alpine den's air. Blushing, weeping. *Ugh.* She didn't do this touchy, weepy, huggy stuff. She had to fight hard not to let her eyes stray back to the man she'd gotten all touchy-huggy with. All those rippling muscles…

He seemed so alive, damn it. It would be painful to watch him die again.

"Is he—is he going to…?" Die. *Just say the word, Viv. Die.* Is Zane going to die now? Her mouth opened, but the word got stuck in her throat.

Dave shook his head. "No."

Her eyebrows dipped as she stared at him, perplexed. "But you said this was how he would pass on."

Dave grinned and shook his head. "No, I said that if you did this, he wouldn't be haunting you as your ghostly sidekick for eternity."

"What are you saying?" Zane asked, and she watched as he held up his hands and stared at them. "That I'm…alive?"

Dave leaned forward and slugged him in the arm.

"Ow," Zane exclaimed, rubbing his arm.

Dave nodded. "Yep. You're alive."

"I don't understand. Zane…died." None of this made sense.

"We all saw that," Nate said, his voice tinged with pain. He jerked his chin toward Vivianne. "Her brother drained him."

Dave rubbed his bottom lip with his thumb. "I'm thinking he wasn't quite dead. When I did that suspension spell on Vivianne, it must have suspended the last moment of

Zane's life, and Vivianne's carried that last spark of life and has now given it back to him."

"What, so he's pressed reset?" Nate asked.

Dave nodded. "Yeah, that sounds good."

"Sounds good?" Samantha repeated. "You're a witch, don't you know for sure?"

Dave's head tilted back, as though he was rolling his eyes behind the dark lenses of his sunglasses. "I'm a witch, not God. I'm not all knowing. Sometimes I guess."

She heard the rustle of clothing as Zane swung his legs down from the ledge, and she turned to face him as he rose to his feet. His knees shook, and his face showed surprise. Vivianne was by his side in a flash, ducking under his arm to catch him as he started to drop.

"Whoa," Zane said, blinking. He tightened his arm around Vivianne.

Nate shot him an exasperated look. "Dude, you've been dead for almost a year. Take it easy."

"I don't want to take it easy."

"Yeah, well, patience was never your strong suit."

"Do you think you can walk back to the hall? I think there are a lot of people who'd like to welcome you back to the land of the living."

"Is that lycan code for party time?" Dave enquired.

Nate grinned. "It is now." He ducked under Zane's other arm to give his friend some support. He looked around Zane's shoulder to give Vivianne an enquiring gaze, and she tried to step away, now that Zane had a lycan's help.

Zane's arm was unrelenting, though, and he pulled her closer.

"Thank you," he whispered into her ear. She trembled at the warm gust of breath against her skin.

"Don't mention it." She smiled briefly, then met his gaze. "Like, seriously, this did not happen. It would be hard to explain why I resurrected a lycan." Her father would freak. John, her P.R. manager, would have whatever ammunition he needed to try and usurp her. Her colony would never forgive her for helping a werewolf.

"'Cause I'm awesome."

"Just because you keep saying it, doesn't make it so," she told him, but couldn't help the smile that curved her lips.

Zane was alive.

Zane watched from across the hall as Samantha and Vivianne sat talking quietly in a dim corner. Samantha and Nate had insisted he go shower and change before meeting folks in the hall, so he was refreshed, if still just the slightest bit shaky on his feet—but that was slowly dissipating. He'd returned to the hall to find Samantha and Vivianne deep in conversation, and Dave Carter in a corner painting some of his intricate tattoo designs on the young women who didn't seem to mind the fact he was a witch. Then he'd almost been swallowed up by his packmates—shaking hands, hugs, sharing greetings, stories and jokes. Nearly two hours later, he'd finally managed to dodge the spotlight and sit in a dim little alcove of the hall, just to get his bearings, take a breath, and generally get used to being alive again and the shock that came with that.

He was *alive*. His hands grasped the armrest of the sofa he was sitting on. No more fuzzy little electric shocks, he could touch, feel, smell, taste…*everything*.

He eyed the two women. Okay, Vivianne. He was eyeing Vivianne, and Samantha just also happened to be in his line of sight. They'd started off sitting with straight backs, but three shots of Dietrich's moonshine later and they both leaned forward, elbows on the table between them, fingers waving as they spoke to each other. But it wasn't a finger-wagging discussion of blame. No, it looked like…chatting.

The two women had to lean closer occasionally, to hear each other over the impromptu band that had set up when he'd walked into the main hall.

"What the hell do you think those two have in common?" Nate came up beside him, his gaze on his alpha prime. Nate had stationed three guardians a respectable distance away from Samantha. Respectable in that the women had enough space for a private discussion, but close enough that they could rip the vamp to shreds if she so much as flashed her fangs.

"No idea."

Nate tugged the mug of beer out of Zane's hand. "You're recuperating. You shouldn't be drinking this."

Zane's lips quirked as his friend drained the glass, but didn't argue. He'd have to do some conditioning to build up his strength and stamina, and alcohol wouldn't help.

Nate wiped the beer from his lips with the back of his hand. "The things I do for you."

"I appreciate your sacrifice," Zane said. Honestly, he wasn't that interested in beer. Sure, he wanted to celebrate. Hell, he wanted to climb to the top of Mount Clawface and yell at the top of his lungs while he beat his chest. But no, at the moment he felt a little unsettled. Maybe it was waking up alive after so long feeling like a shadow. Maybe it just took time to adjust. Whatever it was, there was a gnawing in the pit of his stomach that he couldn't quite figure out. He'd eaten so damn much—and yet still didn't quite feel satiated. He supposed it would take a little time to fuel the hole left by almost a year in—what? A coma? That didn't sound right. Suspension? Whatever.

Nate sat on the arm of the sofa and let himself slide down into the cushions. Zane shook his head as he shifted to make room for his friend. It was a habit that Nate had developed as a kid. For some reason, he liked sitting on the end, right next to the armrest, and would wriggle his way in every time, no matter who was sitting where. If it was a sofa, the space near the armrest had Nate's name on it.

"Matthias appreciated your sacrifice," Nate said quietly.

Zane's gaze dropped to the floor. "I did my job."

"You did it spectacularly." Nate closed his eyes and pinched the bridge of his nose. "When you died—or whatever the hell it was that you did—God, we all went through hell."

"Funny. I didn't see you there."

Nate grinned and dug his elbow in Zane's ribs. "You know what I mean."

Zane nodded. "I do. I went through the same thing. Not being anywhere near you guys, not being able to communicate with anyone except Vivianne…"

"Damn, that must have been torture."

Zane smiled. "It was…interesting."

"What was it like? Really?" Nate asked, his head lolling along the back of the sofa until he could meet Zane's gaze.

"It was a version of hell," Zane admitted. "I could see things, hear things, but when I talked—yelled, screamed, whatever—nobody could hear me."

"Nobody except Vivianne Marchetta. And she didn't mention it to a soul." Nate's lips twisted as he returned his gaze to the spot where Vivianne sat talking with Samantha.

"She had no idea, at first," Zane told him. "It wasn't like she was trying to hide me. Every now and then, she'd hear me, or see a shadow. She thought she was going crazy."

"Really?" Nate said, eyeing the vampire prime with new interest.

Zane understood what his friend was doing. He was assessing the enemy, looking for vulnerability, a pressure point. Zane knew he should be doing the same, but for some reason, he just couldn't see Vivianne as his enemy. She'd risked so much for him.

"She's not as bad as they say." From what he'd seen, she knowingly cultivated her reputation, but he'd seen the woman who wanted the best for her colony, the daughter who tried to please her father...

"Are you defending a vamp?"

Zane frowned. *No, not...really.* "I'm just saying there's more to her than her reputation," he said simply.

"Well, you were getting to know her pretty damn well in the mortuary."

Zane shrugged. "I woke up to a beautiful woman kissing me. I'm not going to apologize for going along with it. You know my motto—if it feels good, go with it."

"Dude. It's Vivianne Marchetta," Nate groaned.

"Trust me, I know."

Nate looked at him intently. "I'm getting the sense that there are feelings there."

Zane glanced about, relieved nobody was close enough to hear them. "Oh, there are feelings. She can be damn infuriating."

"Yeah, I don't think it was fury that I saw in that cave."

Zane looked away. He wasn't going to think about it. He wasn't going to dwell on how damn good she'd felt in his arms, how alive he'd felt with her lips on his, her hands touching him, or how he'd wanted more.

"She's a vamp." Period. Even thinking about it was so... weird. He'd lost sight of Vivianne the vampire prime and had focused on Vivianne, the voluptuous woman. But he was back in reality, now, and vampires and werewolves didn't mix. Didn't date. Didn't kiss or do anything more. Ever.

"I don't know how you managed to survive being hitched to a vamp for so long without losing your sanity."

Zane snagged a footstool that stood in front of a nearby armchair with his toe and dragged it closer, then rested his feet on it. "It was touch and go, for a while. I remember screaming so long, hoping someone—anyone—would hear me. *See* me. I kept thinking about you, and Samantha, wondering about the baby...the rest of the pack. I almost went stray."

"Damn," Nate said and took a swig of beer.

Strays were werewolves without a pack. Homeless, no association or loyalty to any pack, they drifted, constantly looking for shelter, food and companionship...a home. Sadly, though, without the connection to pack, strays eventually went feral. They had a shorter life expectancy than most, as without a pack, the lonely wolf was preyed upon, or starved—either from lack of food or lack of love. Going feral was the beginning of the end.

"I'm glad you're back," Nate said quietly.

"I'm glad to be back." *Glad* was actually a pretty pathetic word choice. He was ecstatic. Thrilled.

Samantha laughed, a long, vibrant chuckle, and Zane looked over in time to see Samantha high-five Vivianne. His eyebrows rose. That was unexpected. His curiosity got the better of him, and he rose, tugging the now-empty mug of beer out of Nate's hand.

"I'm getting a refill." He drifted slowly toward the spot where the women were seated. Along the way members of his pack stopped him to give him a hug, or slap him on the back, or just greet him. The guardians saw him and smiled, then turned back to watching the visiting vampire like a hawk.

"...I'm their alpha. They don't see me as a woman." Zane arrived in time to hear Samantha's comment.

"You've just had a baby—how can they not see you as a woman?" Vivianne's tone was curious, with more than a hint of awe as she gazed down at the sleeping baby in her arms, despite the raucous revelry in the hall. Zane occupied himself with filling his mug with beer he had no inclination to drink. He was hungry—starving, actually, yet nothing here seemed to appetize him. He shifted his focus back to the conversation he was trying to appear oblivious to.

"Well, I figure vamps do this differently, but in a pack, there is a form of succession for the alpha. The closest relative, or even scions, if they're old enough, can lobby for alpha prime position, but they have to defeat any challengers in order to ascend to the position."

"But you were only just pregnant with your son at the time of Jared's death—how does that work?"

Samantha smiled sadly. "It was because I was pregnant that I couldn't be challenged. Now, everyone just accepts it. I have the support of my guardian prime, and his loyalty and acceptance have influenced the pack."

"You're the first female alpha prime I know of," Vivianne said and turned to look out at the crowd. "None of them seem to want to challenge you."

"Not yet," Samantha acceded. "But later...who knows. What about you?"

Zane glanced about, and then neatly turned to lean against an indent in the wall, hiding himself from view from most of the room—and the two women.

He shouldn't be eavesdropping. Not on his alpha prime, not on Vivianne...but he couldn't deny the desire to know more about Vivianne. He'd gotten to know her very well during the time he'd been 'stuck' with her. He'd seen her in action with her underlings, with various members of her colony, with her father... The only person she came anywhere near opening up to was the sister-in-law, and even then she was guarded. Right now, though, it seemed her guard was down with Samantha in a way he'd never seen before.

"My father was our prime for so long...but he didn't die, he stepped down from the position in order to enter the senate. He nominated me as his successor."

"Did you have to prove your worth?"

Zane peered around the outcropping in time to see Vivianne's features tighten.

"Yes," she said quietly. "My father's guardian prime thought I was too young, too inexperienced, for the position. And a female."

"What has that got to do with anything?" Samantha exclaimed.

Vivianne smiled. "It's a little different for us, Samantha. We vampires have lived for generations, and many of the older vamps come from a time when women were treated as less valuable as the men—weaker. We have to learn to live with that attitude."

Zane frowned. Did Vivianne subscribe to that point of view? His gaze wandered around the room. Alpine had many women in the position of guardian, and recognized strength and power in all of its forms, included the feminine one. All you had to do was watch a she-wolf defend her young, and you never again made the assumption that the female lycan was weaker than a male. At least, not if you wanted to keep your gonads.

"You won."

"Yeah, I won."

The baby snuffled, and Vivianne's head tilted as she eyed the child. "He's beautiful."

Samantha looked at her for a moment. "Would you like to hold him?"

Zane almost laughed at the stunned look on Vivianne's face. "Oh, no," she said, shaking her head. "I couldn't—"

"Sure you could," Samantha said and stood to lean over the table, handing the baby to Vivianne.

Vivianne received the baby awkwardly. "Uh, I don't know how to—"

"Support his head with your arm," Samantha told her gently, positioning them both with care. "See, nothing to it." Samantha waved away the guardians, who'd all stepped forward.

Zane couldn't look away. Vivianne's face was full of wonder, full of something so warm, so gentle—the expression was completely alien on the vampire prime's face. Tender. That's it. Like she was cherishing the moment, cherishing holding a babe.

"Oh, my God," Vivianne whispered, "I'm holding a baby."

Samantha nodded. "Yeah, you are."

Vivianne swallowed. "Is he—is he okay?"

Zane almost looked away, so unsure, so vulnerable did Vivianne sound, it was almost an intrusion to witness it.

"He's fine." Samantha's brow dipped with curiosity. "Have you ever wanted one of your own?"

Vivianne's lips rubbed inward as she shook her head, her focus on J.J. asleep in her arms. "It's impossible," she said in a whisper. "You can't create life out of death."

"That's not what I asked," Samantha pointed out.

Vivianne glanced up at the woman, and Zane saw her eyes go luminous with what he almost thought were unshed tears, before she blinked furiously. "Uh, I was turned before—before I gave it any real thought. Now, it's not possible."

This time Zane looked away. He didn't think she realized how much raw pain she'd revealed, the wistfulness, the regret… That was when he noticed the hush that had fallen over the hall, as the pack warily watched the vampire holding the Alpine scion in her arms.

As though finally realizing they were the center of attention, Vivianne glanced about, then leaned over to hand the baby back to his mother. "Thank you," she whispered. She stood up and picked up her red ski jacket that she'd draped over the arm of the chair. "I, uh, have to be getting back," she said, jerking a thumb over her shoulder.

Samantha eyed her intently. "We won't forget this, Vivianne."

Vivianne opened her mouth. Hesitated. Then shook her head. "I wish you would." She cleared her throat. "I, uh, have to go. I trust someone can escort me to your boundary?"

"Yes, but it's nearly daylight," Samantha said, glancing at her watch.

"Then I'll need to hurry," Vivianne said. Samantha eyed her for a moment, then nodded. She glanced over to one of the guardians nearby.

"Warwick, please escort the Marchetta Prime to the Nightwing boundary."

The guardian nodded and proceeded to lead Vivianne from the hall. Vivianne waved casually to Dave, who raised his mug of beer before taking a swig. The witch grinned beneath his sunglasses. He was happy to stay a little longer. Vivianne nodded, then left the hall.

Zane frowned. That was it? She was leaving without even saying goodbye?

Hell, no. He jogged after her.

# Chapter 10

"Vivianne, wait."

Vivianne glanced over her shoulder. Zane bounded up to her. He'd showered and changed before joining the party in the hall. Now he wore jeans with a dark gray T-shirt. And he looked great. Tall, fit...not dead. Who knew undead could look so damn sexy? He nodded to the tall werewolf charged with seeing her out of Alpine territory.

"I'll take her from here, Warwick."

The lycan frowned. "Are you sure you're up for it? Maybe you should take it ea—"

"I'll take her," Zane repeated, his voice firm.

Warwick shrugged. "Fine by me." He shot her a brief look, and he wore an expression of thinly veiled distaste.

"I have to go," she told Zane, turning to walk farther down the tunnel. Samantha had been decent, and Nate, too, although she got the impression he would still smile politely at her as he ripped her throat out if she so much as blinked wrong at his alpha prime, or her baby. Everyone else, though, had made their wariness, their antipathy, quite clear. She glanced about. Tunnels intersected the main channel regularly, going off in all directions. No wonder they escorted visitors to and from. This place was a rabbit warren inside the mountain. She started to walk briskly. It wouldn't be dark outside for much longer, and she needed to get off the mountain before the sun rose. "I need to get down to shelter before sun up."

And she had to get out of here. Out of this pack den, where the sense of family was enough to nauseate any self-respecting vampire.

Or make them writhe in envy.

"Without saying goodbye?" Zane asked quietly.

Vivianne glanced up at him, surprised. "I would have thought you'd be happy to see the back of me." It wasn't long after they'd left the mortuary cave that Nate and Samantha had insisted he go to his quarters to "refresh." He'd returned to the main hall, but had largely avoided going anywhere near her during the celebrations.

Not that she'd cared. Not really. She expected that—he'd made it abundantly clear how torturous, frustrating, annoying, hellish, etc., it was being trapped with her. It made sense he'd tried to stay away. She wasn't offended. Much. She frowned at the little shard of hurt that lanced her.

"Well, I have to say, I'm relieved to be back in my own skin, instead of yours."

Her frown deepened. Why? Was her "skin" so repulsive?

Zane looked at her for a moment, and his brow dipped. "I mean, it's nice having others see me, hear me."

And not be stuck with just her. *Double ouch.* She lifted a hand.

"I get it, Zane, you're happy to be rid of me. Just show

me the quickest way out of here, and we can pretend this didn't happen."

Zane pulled her to a stop. "That's not what I meant, Vivianne."

She glanced down at his hand on her arm. He was touching her, again. Really touching her. His skin was golden brown, his grasp warm, strong. Tempting. All this time he'd been a shadow on the edge of her vision, a voice inside her head, and more recently, an apparition who made her doubt her sanity. Now, though, she could *feel* him. And he felt surprisingly good.

She glanced up at him. Everything about him seemed so much more vibrant, so much warmer. His skin, his brown eyes with shards of green that had glowed so beautifully when they'd kissed earlier...the dark dusting of beard that seemed to enhance his jawline rather than hide it...

What the hell was it about this guy that so caught her? He was a werewolf. The natural enemy of the vampire. She should be repelled by him, not drawn to him. And yet, here she was, supremely conscious that she was alone with this sexy man in a dim tunnel, and wanted to—what? Touch him? Kiss him? Hang on to the man before he disappeared from her life forever?

"What *did* you mean?" She tried to remain calm, poised, like the head of the wealthiest, most successful vampire colony in Irondell she was, and not be the eager, starry-eyed woman she was fearing she was turning into.

"I wanted to say that I'm relieved I'm alive, and I have you to thank for that. What you did for me, Vivianne..." Zane shook his head. "I know it wasn't easy, coming here—alone—to return me to my pack. Especially after what happened with Rafe." He dipped his head and seemed to realize he was still holding on to her. He rubbed his thumb over her arm, and her heart beat just that little bit faster. Was it getting warm in here?

"I guess what I'm trying to say is, thank you." The words were uttered so simply, so sincerely, it took her a moment to recover. "Why don't you stay a little longer? As you said, the sun will be up soon, and you're really going to have to race to beat it. You're welcome to stay here for the day, and I'll make sure you get back down the mountain this evening."

She stared at him for a moment, shocked. Stay? Here? In a den? With him?

She was stunned by the invitation. Tempted. So very tempted… More time with Zane.

Samantha was nice, too—surprisingly. As an alpha prime of a pack and a vampire prime of a colony, they'd discovered a few things in common when it came to asserting their leadership position, about ensuring their people were provided for and the challenges they faced as women in their positions. She'd never had that before. She was the only lady prime in Irondell, and her issues were vastly different to her male counterparts. Sure, there were female coven leaders, but she dealt with the witches only when it was absolutely necessary, and only as adversaries. Samantha was a werewolf, but Vivianne got the sense that if but for that one key, critical difference, they could have been friends.

And then there was J.J. She swallowed. He was cute. *Too cute.* Holding his warm, cuddly little body had stirred something deep and long forgotten inside her. She knew she gave the impression of being cold and ruthless—and she had that reputation for good reason. She'd shoved aside any inclination, any desire or yearning for a family centuries ago, when she'd learned that being a vampire meant one couldn't bring forth life from a dead shell. She'd learned to deal with it, to get over it and move on, but for the briefest of moments, when she'd seen the baby suckle at his mother's breast, when she'd held the sleeping babe in her arms, she'd had a painful, agonizing need awaken inside her.

She shook her head. "No, I have to go." If she stayed, she'd want things she'd never, ever have, a fruitless exercise in self-torture and frustration. She had to get back to her own kind, reconnect with her colony and put all these silly little fantasies to bed. She'd left Harris snoozing in the parking lot back at the Galen clinic. Nobody knew she was here. Not only was that incredibly risky—what if one of these lycans decided to act against the conditions of parlay, and bite her, or kill her outright? Nobody would know, her colony would lose its prime and have no idea how, why or who. She shouldn't have trusted these people. She shouldn't have trusted Zane. How could she explain this brief excursion with the lycans to her people? To her *father*?

"I have to get back home."

Zane's grip loosened, and he withdrew his hand. "Back to your father."

She nodded. Back to where she wasn't plagued by a desire for family and babies and a brown-eyed lycan who knew her too well.

"Help me put a stop to his project."

It wasn't a question. Vivianne frowned. "No." She started to walk through the tunnel. "How can you even ask me that?"

"How can I ask you that? Vivianne, he intends to pass a bill through the senate that will allow vampires to bag and tag werewolves, to kill them…"

She shook her head. "You do realize that is pretty much already in effect? If I had not invoked parlay, what do you think Nate would have done with me when he found me at the cliff?"

"You would have been trespassing."

"Exactly. You don't think you werewolves have killed vampires before for trespassing? Every breed has some sovereign rights over the territory within their borders."

"Killing trespassers is one thing, but abducting them, holding them against their will for God-only-knows how long and subjecting them to torturous experiments is not permitted."

Vivianne's lips tightened. "You sound so high-and-mighty, Zane, as if you and your kind have never done anything heinous against vampires, or any of the other breeds."

"Hey, we'll fight, and we'll kill, but those fights are fair."

She turned on him, her eyes glowing with anger. "Don't kid yourself, Zane," she snapped. "You lycans have done plenty to hurt us vampires. You think this hate," she said, gesturing between them, "just grew in a vacuum?"

His chin jutted forward. "What your father is proposing is wrong."

She started walking again. The tunnel was descending, and she could see an opening where the background was slightly lighter than the walls surrounding it. Alpine didn't light their entrances. No wonder it was so difficult locating the pack. Their caves were black holes against dark walls.

"What do you expect me to do, Zane?"

"Stop him."

She shot him an incredulous look. "You want me to go against my father?" She shook her head in disbelief.

Zane frowned. "Of course."

She paused at the lip of the cave and looked out. The stars were slowly disappearing from the night sky, and she could see a band of indigo light against the midnight black of the horizon. There was a hush over the landscape, and despite the darkness, the snow grabbed at any light it could and reflected it, creating a quiet, wintery scene of white carpet and capped mountains. If she wasn't so annoyed, so irritated, she'd take a moment to appreciate the view. Alpine had constant snow. Down in Irondell spring had...sprung. But not here. It was a testament to the Alpine's pack strength and determination to survive in such an inhospitable area. They could even defy death, apparently.

She turned to the lycan who had done just that. Did he have any idea how amazing that was? How incredible? And he wanted her to now turn on her family. "Believe it or not, Zane, werewolves don't have an exclusive claim on loyalty, or family, or honor. We vampires live for centuries, and we take our oaths of allegiance very seriously."

Zane's eyes narrowed. "I've seen how you and your 'loyal subjects' treat your oaths. You're always having to prove yourself. After all these years, you have men who want your role, who want that prime position, and you are constantly fending them off, defending your right to be there."

She slid her arms into her jacket and pulled the zipper up, her movements tight and jerky. "You think your own pack doesn't have its power play moments?"

She smiled tightly. "You forget one thing, Zane. Nightwing is one of the few vampire colonies that is ruled by a family. We haven't just drifted toward each other and decided to forge a colony. We are *family*. We may not have the perfect relationship, we might bicker among ourselves, but when it comes down to it, we are family, and we have each other's backs. I will not betray my father, so don't ask me to do it again."

"Even if what he's doing is so wrong it makes you sick to your stomach?"

She smiled tightly. "What makes you think I'm sickened by his plan?"

Zane's hands were on her arms, her back against the rock wall before she could blink. Her eyes brightened, and her incisors lengthened instinctively.

"You might think you've fooled everyone, Vivianne, but I've lived with you for months," he told her, his voice low. "I know how you like to relax by dancing in your bedroom with the curtains closed, that you always go for men when you hunt because going after a human woman isn't a fair fight in your eyes, that you'll see an opportunity in business and seize it, but when it comes to dealing with your own kind you're tough, but fair, and that you are turning yourself inside out trying to please everyone, especially your father." She shook her head, but he continued.

"I know that when you woke up in that clinic, you fought against your father to free the woman who saved your life, and I know that for just the briefest of moments, there in your father's office when he told you his plans, you were as horrified as I was. You're a fair person, Vivianne, and you know that what your father is proposing is anything but fair."

She stared at him for a moment. She'd never felt so naked, so vulnerable, in all of her life—not even when Rafe Woodland attacked her. For the first time she realized just how much Zane Wilder had seen and heard, how much he'd witnessed, and how much of a threat he was to her. He knew too much. Nobody knew that much about her. She was supposed to be tough, ruthless, and he knew it was a facade. He'd seen her worry and double-guess her sanity. He'd seen her afraid of losing her mind. He'd seen her do the twist. She had to claw back some of that dignity, some of that power.

She shoved him, panic giving her strength, and he flew across the mouth of the cave to crash into the rock wall. He landed on his feet, though, poised and balanced. Almost as though he'd expected the move.

She flashed her eyes and revealed her fangs. "You think you know me, Zane, but you have no idea how much your breed has cost me and my family, or what I think is fair when it comes to dealing with the lycans." She held up a finger. "From now on, you look after your kind, and I'll look after mine."

She took a running jump out of the mouth of the cave, arms out by her side as she landed in the snow thirty feet below. She glanced up at the cave. Zane walked to the edge and gazed down the cliff face to where she now stood.

His lips were moving, and she had to strain to hear him.

"You are my kind."

She shook her head. His kind—his kind had babies and referred to non-bloodkin as family, and made her heart ache with a glimpse into a forbidden desire for something she could never have and shouldn't want.

She took off running, gritting her teeth as she plowed through the deep snow, her eyes on the horizon. She was a vampire, and she belonged in the night.

Zane rubbed his stomach. Damn. Despite the big meal he'd finished less than an hour ago, he felt like there was nothing in there, and the stomach acid was eating through his gut lining. On top of that, he could hear his pulse in his ears. It had taken him a while to figure out what the noise was, but in the four days since he'd awoken in that mortuary cave, the sound had become quite intrusive.

"Are you sure about this, Zane?"

Zane glanced up at his guardian prime. Nate and the small team of elite guardians stood peering over a massive map rolled out onto a desk. Samantha was putting J.J. down for his nap inside a cot, and she looked over her shoulder at him. Dietrich and Marjorie glanced up from their spot by the fireplace. They were all in the alpha prime's private den.

Zane nodded. "I'm sure."

"It's bear territory." Nate folded his arms, frowning.

"Why would they sell?" All breeds valued territory, and it was very rare to relinquish land, particularly across breed. It made more sense to charge a toll if people needed to cross it, or to lease it, and have an ongoing income.

"I don't know if they are," Samantha said as she stepped back to the table. "At least, not publicly."

"It borders Alpine, some of Woodland and it even shares a common border down there in the southwest corner with ClawRunners." Nate traced the area with his finger.

Dietrich snorted. "I hate panthers."

"My point is," Nate said, tapping the surface of the map, "apart from the tiniest section here, where it meets Nightwing in that point, there are no other vampire colonies—no neighboring allies, they're all shifter breeds. There is limited water, it's not exactly hospitable and it leads nowhere. Why does he want it?"

"It's close to the East-West Trail," Zane said, pointing. "From what he said, Marchetta believes there's enough wolf movement through this area for this purchase to make sense." He glanced up at Nate. "We have to stop him. My earliest memories of waking up in that clinic is hearing the screams of the others. I don't quite know what sick crap that guy was doing, but it wasn't good. I don't want him doing it to any more lycans."

Nate nodded. "Yeah, Dave mentioned something. He was able to free about a dozen of them, but they scattered. Dave didn't try to stop them, though."

Zane nodded. His memories were getting sharper, clearer. Dave Carter had the reputation for picking his battles, and nobody could quite figure out the rhyme or reason for his selection. He was fairly easygoing, though—until you crossed whatever line it was he'd decided to define. "He probably thought if they wanted to run, let them."

Nate nodded. "That's almost word for word what he said."

Zane scratched his arm. He was itchy. No, maybe not itchy—twitchy, more like. "What the hell is Marchetta's problem with the werewolves, anyway?"

Samantha shrugged. "I'm not sure. I think it was a little before my time."

Dietrich shrugged. "He's a bloodsucker. He'll find any excuse to fight us werewolves."

Zane shook his head, frowning. "No, this is more than just your average hatefest on the lycans. This man is going to considerable expense and effort." His eyes narrowed as Dietrich looked away. "You know."

Dietrich shrugged, and Marjorie sighed.

"It's not like it's a secret, Dietrich," she said.

"There's no use dredging that old news up now," the elder muttered.

Zane glanced at Nate, whose eyebrows rose. "If you have information that could help us understand, perhaps even defend, I'm interested to hear it, Dietrich," the guardian prime stated.

Dietrich scowled, and Marjorie gave him an encouraging nod. "Oh, fine, but nothing was ever proven, so I don't like talking about it."

"I understand," Nate said.

Zane leaned against the wall, waiting. He had to hear this. If it gave him any insight into Vincent Marchetta, to Vivianne, he wanted all the information he could get his hands on.

"Marchetta's wife died in a fire on the pier."

Zane gaped. "The Ballroom Blaze?" It was almost an urban legend, it had happened so long ago. Nate grimaced. "Oh."

"Ballroom Blaze?" Warwick asked, frowning. "Someone want to fill the rest of us in?"

Dietrich leaned back in his chair. "It'd be close to fifty years ago now. There was some fancy-schmancy event for the vamps, they were all doing some sort of fund-raising—can't remember what for. A blaze started in the ballroom. All the ground floor doors were chained shut, so the vampires trapped inside had two choices. They could perish in the fire or jump from one of the upper level windows into Harmony Bay."

"Salt water," Zane said quietly.

Warwick winced. "Damn. I almost feel bad for the bastards."

"They never caught who did it, but ever since then the vampires believed it was lycans who set the fire and blocked the exits."

Zane rubbed his forehead. Vivianne's comments the other night, about lycans costing her and her family too much, and the other remarks she'd made about werewolves and their contribution to the hate between the two breeds, was all beginning to make sense now.

She'd lost her mother—in what could only be described as a horrific situation. He hadn't realized.

That knowledge, though, made him admire her just a little bit more, made him feel a little more humble. Despite what had been done to her mother, and the belief that lycans were responsible, despite what had been done to her by Rafe Woodland, she'd still traveled into werewolf territory—by herself. She'd faced down a pack—by herself, and then she'd reunited his spirit form with his physical form. She was pretty damn amazing.

But was she also prepared to kill werewolves in some twisted plot created by her father?

A tiny little patter caught his attention, and he tilted his head. What was that? He glanced at the others. They didn't seem to be troubled by the sound. He tried to focus on the conversation as the guardians, the elders and their prime discussed alternative options, but that pitter-patter noise kept distracting him.

He drifted away from the table, inclining his head, then ambled across the room, the sound getting slowly louder, more distracting. Almost in syncopation, his own heart started beating along with it, until he found himself gazing down at little J.J., asleep in his crib. Zane's lips lifted as the baby boy's hands relaxed, opening, palm up like a cupped blossom on the crib's mattress. He bent over and placed his finger in the baby's hand, and his smile broadened as the little fingers curled around his. He couldn't help noting the disparity in size. The baby's fingers couldn't close their grip, so tiny was the boy's hands. His gaze drifted up to the boy's face, but halted when he saw the pulse fluttering in J.J.'s collarbone.

There. A swift, strong little pitter-patter as the boy's heart pushed his blood through his body. Zane's mouth went dry, and his vision turned red, as though a blood haze covered his pupils. He blinked, and his vision cleared. Zane frowned. Weird. He went to turn away, but that pulsing flutter at the base of the boy's neck caught his attention again, and this time his gut cramped. His vision turned red, and the scent of life, warmth—it hit him hard in his solar plexus. Who knew vibrancy had a scent.

His teeth ached, and he could feel something shifting in his gums. Oh, God. Pain. Hot, searing pain lanced through his gums as something beneath the skin shifted, pierced it, and he doubled over as his gut clenched again. He wanted— No, he needed— He shook his head.

*No.*

He sucked in a breath, and J.J.'s scent flooded him, enticed him. God, what was happening to him? It was so damned painful...sickening. The things he wanted to do.

He glanced surreptitiously at the group by the table. Marjorie had her gray hair pulled up into a neat bun, and he saw the flesh of her neck. He wanted to bite—no, not bite, *feed*.

*Oh, God.*

"Zane? Are you all right?" Samantha's voice was soft with concern as she called to him gently.

He shielded his face from her gaze, rubbing his temple as though he had a headache. "I think I need a break," he said, then turned and walked for the door.

"Do you want me to come wi—"

"No," Zane interrupted Nate's offer with a bitten off word and hustled his butt out of the room. He jogged down the tunnels, switching back and forth, until he could burst into his own den.

He doubled over in pain and staggered through to his bathroom. He wanted, no, needed something. He scratched at his arms. It felt like fire ants were crawling under his skin, and then he halted when he caught sight of himself in his mirror.

His eyes were bloodred and glowing, and his teeth—his *teeth*. His incisors were longer, sharper... He wasn't supposed to do that unless he transformed into his beast's form, and yet here his teeth were, all pointed and fangy.

Just like he'd seen Vivianne's go when she was on a hunt.

Zane's eyes widened as he twisted his head from side to side, peering closely at his reflection.

*Hell*. He was turning vamp.

## *Chapter 11*

Vivianne signed the contract, and handed it back to Mike with a smile, then turned towards her director guardians. "We now own the North Fork of the Kingfisher River," she told them. "Let's invite River Pack in for a chat and show them the plans for a dam and power station. I'm feeling the need to branch out into capital works."

"They'll think we're bluffing," John informed her. His expression was stony as he glared at her. The man was still upset about her killing him, apparently. She sighed. It wasn't like it was a permanent state. Still, the guy was pissed, and she needed to sell this concept to him so he could sell it to those who mattered.

"Why would they think that?" she asked calmly. She flexed her right hand. Her fingers tingled. She'd had that a lot, recently. A tingling that flared up in random areas of her body. She frowned. She might need to visit the Galen brothers again—but this time she'd be ready for any of Hunter Galen's mind-blanking woo-woo stuff.

"A dam? Come on," John said, frowning. "Those things are damned expensive to build."

Vivianne nodded. "True. But I think it will be worth it."

"It's a little tit for tat, though, don't you think?"

She tilted her head. "Not at all. They control the transport down the river through their section. The fact that we're operating up-river, and that our dam may affect their transport hub is just business. They can't run a river trade if there's no river to trade on."

"But there will be a river to trade on," John pointed out. "Reform won't pass a dam."

Vivianne smiled. "We are looking at creating a public works project that will a, provide a benefit to the people of Irondell, as well as some of the outlying areas, and b, will generate employment for our colony, as well as the community in general, along with an income by way of selling power. It delivers on the criteria required for re-zoning. It fits the default parameters for capital works. This has the potential of netting us millions, if not billions of dollars in the long run. Actually, I'm surprised we haven't looked at doing this before."

She shook her hand. Damn. Pins and needles, all over it.

John slowly nodded. "Okay," he admitted. "I can see the benefits of the arrangement."

She beamed. "Great. Share it with River Pack. I want flyers, posters, etc. I want this everywhere, and I want everyone talking about it."

"It's going to affect a lot of people," John warned. "You'll get pushback from many sources."

Vivianne shrugged. "That's not new."

No. What was new was that she was giving her PR Director a story to run with, without telling him the truth of the matter. She had no intention of building a dam. Are you kidding? Those things cost a fortune to build and manage, and with the Reform Senate making various decisions on spending, there was no way they would approve a major infrastructure investment like this. But John didn't need to know that. Neither did River Pack. But this could get River Pack to open up the river transport to them, again.

"I'll schedule a meeting with River Pack," she said, leaning forward to write a note in her diary. There was a barely audible crack, and her middle finger twitched. No, not twitched. It broke and realigned itself. Her eyes widened as she saw the not-so-normal bend to it.

Perspiration beaded on her brow as her pain receptors reluctantly kicked in.

*Yowch.* What the *hell*? Her lips parted, and it took every ounce of control not to scream in pain. She had to go somewhere, fix this. Damn, it hurt so much.

"Uh, that concludes this meeting—"

*Oh, dear mother of God.* All her fingers cracked, twisting in on themselves, and she hissed at the excruciating pain. John frowned.

"Are you okay, Vivianne?"

Oh, hell, not now. She didn't need weird crap going on in front of this group of people, in front of John, who would use any issue in yet another attempt to cast doubt on her leadership.

"Fine," she said, smiling calmly, praying he wouldn't notice the perspiration dotting her brow and upper lip. God, her hand hurt. "But we all have work to do," she said.

Tingling, like thousands of tiny piranha nibbling at her hand, made her glance down. Her eyes widened when she saw the hair growing out of her skin.

She slapped her book closed around her hand, then stood

abruptly. "Right. You all know what you need to do. See you next week."

She bustled out of the meeting room, then almost ran to the elevators. She dialed up Harris on her cell phone. "Bring the car around," she said, then peered anxiously down at her hand. "Oh, God." Hair, lots of ha—no, *fur* covered the back of her palm, and her fingers were twisted into an unnatural shape, scrunching over in a way that looked unnatural. And painful. Blood drained from her face. Holy heck, what was going on?

The elevator doors opened directly into the parking garage, and Harris was right there, engine running.

"Home," she ordered, then almost dived into the back seat. She pressed the button to engage the screen between the front and back seats, then stared in horror as her hand seemed to fold in on itself, looking suspiciously like—her jaw dropped. A *paw*?

Two nights after the discussion in the alpha's den, Zane eyed the lynx in the moonlight as he hunkered down low behind a boulder in his wolf form. He ignored the snow covering his paws, his attention focused on his prey. He sniffed the air. The lynx was pure animal, not a shifter. A gust of chilled night air blew over him, ruffling the fur on his back. He closed his eyes for a moment, enjoying the sensation of his fur lifting in the breeze, as though someone had combed his coat against the natural fall of hair. His eyes opened again, and this time the snowy landscape had a red glow to it. He loved hunting in the moonlight, but for some reason, tonight was even more enjoyable. His senses were sharper. He could smell more keenly, catching the lynx's scent from a remarkable distance. Hearing, taste—hell, he could almost taste the lynx on his tongue each time he inhaled.

The lynx halted, ears twitching, as though finally sensing the danger stalking him.

Zane's muscles bunched, and he leaped from behind the boulder, snarling as he attacked his prey. The lynx tried to run, tried to fight, but a blood craze swept over Zane, his growls coming out of his throat low and harsh as he ripped with tooth and claw. The lynx struggled, but Zane's jaw snapped over the lynx's throat, and the warm blood burst onto his tongue, the flavor so strong, so thrilling. Almost immediately, the blood hummed through his own veins. Life. This is what it tasted like. He drank it, consumed it, feeling the sensation wash over him, as though someone was taking a static charge of electricity and rolled it over him, his fur standing on end.

When there was no more to drink, Zane lifted his head, and the red haze receded, leaving him to gaze about him in stunned awareness. For the first time since he woke up, he felt satiated.

He looked down at the now-dead lynx, and shifted back to his human form. He'd consumed the blood. His pulse pounded, as though only now had he really awoken from his slumber in death. He covered his mouth, his eyes widening when he felt his fangs. He'd shifted, but still had fangs. He'd hunted, and instead of eating meat, he'd drunk blood. His stomach lurched as he sagged to his knees, staring in shock at the reality of the dead lynx.

He'd fed on blood.

He cradled his head in his hands. Oh, God, what was he becoming? He'd fed like a vampire in his beast's form, and from the sense of satisfaction of the animal within, he'd liked it. What was wrong with him? He wiped the back of his hand against his lips. How was he supposed to return to the den? How could he be trusted in the den? Hadn't he felt the urge to drink while gazing down on a sleeping *baby*?

He rocked on his knees, hugging himself, the cold air enveloping his lonely form, the carpet of snow twinkling as it reflected the light of the stars above, except for the blood-stained kill zone. Self-disgust flooded him, along with mental images of what would probably happen. When his pack learned of his—abnormality, they'd turn on him. Hell, he'd turn on him, if he could. He wanted blood. God, no. He pressed the base of his palms against his temples, and he rocked a little faster. They'd have to kill him. They needed to kill him. What if he attacked one of them? Nate, his best friend? Samantha, his alpha prime, the woman he was sworn to protect as a guardian? He paused. Or worse, little J.J.? He squeezed his eyes shut and lay down in the snow, curling into the fetal position. *Oh, God.* He was acting like a vampire. Of all things, a bloodsucker. He was a horrible human being. Now he understood the soulless aspect of being a vampire. You couldn't have a soul and still want to harm a baby. He didn't want to harm a baby, but could he trust himself?

What the hell kind of monster was he becoming?

The door to her office snapped open, and Vivianne glanced up coolly. She hated interruptions. Her father stepped inside, and shut the door behind him, his expression cold.

Colder than normal, that was.

Vivianne pointed to the chair opposite her desk, and then carried on with the budget forecasting. If they wanted to convince River Pack that Nightwing were ready and determined to make their lives very uncomfortable, she had to find the money somewhere. She frowned. Only, she couldn't quite see the money. Anywhere.

Which was highly unusual. Lucien had looked after the colony's interests, stepping in as Vampire Prime while she was in her coma, and she knew her brother was exceptionally good at creating wealth—he'd started up a West Coast division that was still lucrative, despite him stepping away to spend time with his new wife.

"How dare you," her father hissed.

She didn't look at him, but kept scanning the spreadsheets on her screen. He must have heard about her dam proposal. "How dare I what, Dad?"

"How dare you betray me," he said, thumping the desk with his fist. This time she did look up at him. He was really riled. His lips were tightly pursed, color blooming in his cheeks, his eyes bright with fury. Her brow dipped. This seemed a little much for disapproving of one of her projects, considering all of her projects had made Nightwing very profitable.

She lightly clasped her hands in her lap and relaxed in her chair. Her father still hadn't taken his seat—one of his usual intimidation tactics. Well, she knew all his tactics, and she would not be intimidated. "How, exactly, did I betray you?"

"You told them," he thundered.

She took a deep breath, praying for patience. "What did I tell whom?"

"The werewolves." Her father braced his hands on her desk and leaned over. "I know it was you."

"Me what?" she asked, tilting her head back to lean against her chair's backrest. "I'm sorry, Dad, but I don't know what you're talking about."

He reached into his pocket and pulled out a folded sheath of papers, and held them in front of him. "I went to sign this contract of sale today," he said in an almost casual tone. "Only to learn the land had already been sold." He flung the papers down on the desk.

She frowned as she eyed the mess of papers on her desk.

"Well, Dad, sometimes you miss out on a deal. I still don't understand why you think I had anything to do with this."

"Because, darling daughter, Alpine Pack bought the tract of land."

Vivianne's muscles froze for a moment. "Alpine?" Her mouth dried. No. Please, no. He wouldn't. "I don't know—"

"Don't lie to me!" her father yelled. She flinched. Her father didn't raise his voice often. Damn it, she wasn't going to be berated like one of his underlings. She rose to her feet, eyes narrowed. Tingling started in her feet, and her hands itched.

"I am not lying to you, Father," she said through tight lips. She prayed her body didn't betray her. Over the last few days she'd had hair sprouting from the most unlikely of places, only to recede again, or her bones would do that sickening crunch and rearrange into some new malformation. She'd been darting into restrooms or unoccupied offices to avoid discovery, panting through the pain until she returned to normal. She sure as hell didn't want to break any bones or go all Hairy McNairy in front of her dad.

Her father bared his teeth at her. "Do you think that you can do *anything* without my knowledge?"

Her blood chilled in her veins at her father's contempt. The tingling increased. Then his words sank in, and her father nodded as he saw realization spark.

"That's right. You don't make a decision, you don't take action, you don't note anything down—hell, you don't even *breathe* without me knowing about it. You think I don't know about your little excursion to Alpine?" His hand rose, and his fingers curled over into a tight fist. "You are the only one I told about this, and you scampered off to Alpine at the first opportunity." He'd lowered his voice, but it still trembled with his rage.

"It wasn't like that," she argued.

His eyes widened in fury. "Don't *lie*. I *trusted* you, and what you did—that was worse than your brother."

"I didn't tell them about your plan," she insisted. Anger was rising inside, and she felt the little toe on her right foot flutter.

His smile was brittle. "Then why were you up the mountain?"

Her toe snapped, and she glanced down at the desk, taking a deep, swift breath to stop from screaming. Perspiration broke out on her forehead as she tried to remain calm. She couldn't tell him the real reason—that she'd had to lose the ghost of the lycan who haunted her by delivering him to his resting place, only to wind up rejuvenating him.

After what had happened to her mother, he would see that as the ultimate betrayal, giving a lycan life when they'd stolen his wife's.

"It had nothing to do with your plan," she reiterated. Her fourth toe snapped, and she slapped her hand down on the desk to stop from crying out. Her father frowned at what must have looked like a fit of temper.

He shook his head. "I don't believe you."

"Well, apparently your spies don't know everything," she snapped. He spied on her. Hell. Talk about a breach of trust. *Please, just go*. She didn't want to talk anymore. No. She wanted to curl up under her desk until her bones stopped breaking.

"Then you fully support my project?" he demanded.

Her mouth opened, but the words wouldn't come. Did she? She'd seen what he'd been doing, had heard the screams of the others inside that clinic, before it had been destroyed. Could she support that kind of cruelty?

She understood why her father was so embittered. He'd loved her mother so much, and had been devastated by her death. He'd never remarried in the decades since. Her mother's death had been agonizing. Brutal. She could understand her father's pathological need to ruin the lycan nation—but did she agree with it?

Her father lifted his chin at her hesitation. "Well, I did not expect you to be a dog lover."

She shook her head. "I'm not." She wasn't. They were uncivilized, they were smelly… Zane's image came to mind. Actually, he smelled divine. She shook her head. Nope. Not a dog lover. She hadn't seen him in the week since she'd left Alpine. She would not admit that she missed him. Ha. Loving a lycan. Not likely. But she didn't hate him, either.

Her father sneered at her. "You disgust me."

He turned and left her office, slamming the door behind him. Vivianne's legs snapped, and she collapsed to the floor behind her desk, her mouth open in a silent scream of agony. Hair follicles pushed through her skin, and she ducked her head as she tried to control her breathing. The more she panicked, the worse it got. Oh, God, she hurt. She hurt in her body, all the way down to the tips of her broken toes. Her head hurt, the pressure of hiding what was going on with her building into a migraine of epic proportions, as though her skull also wanted to rearrange its form. Her brain hurt, from trying to second-guess her father, from hiding her secrets, but most of all her heart hurt. Her brain replayed the conversation with her father. He thought she'd betrayed him. He had spies watching her. She realized now that he'd never trusted her. She blinked. She would not cry, damn it.

Because Marchettas didn't cry.

# Chapter 12

Zane growled at the vampire guardian. "I said, let me pass, Harris." They stood in the grand reception area of the executive offices in the Marchetta Tower. After months of haunting Vivianne, he'd learned almost every inch of this building—and how to circumvent the security. He'd managed to bypass the cordon of guards on the ground floor, and had used Vivianne's own security codes to access the private elevator to the executive suite.

Harris flashed his incisors. "No. I don't know who you are, or how you think you know me, but you're not getting past me." Vivianne's bodyguard went for the alarm he wore on a cord around his neck.

Zane reached out and grabbed his hand before he could depress the button and call for reinforcements. "Call Vivianne." He wasn't in the mood to play games. He thought he'd made that pretty clear to the other thirteen vampires he'd rendered unconscious to get to this point.

Harris's eyes flashed red as he shook his head. "No." He tried to twist his hand out of Zane's grip, and the two men wrestled briefly. Zane growled when he felt the vampire's teeth sink into his forearm, and in a well-practiced move he twisted, grasping Harris's chin to expose his neck. Normally a werewolf would go in for the kill strike—bite the vampire in the neck and let the toxin finish the kill. But despite this guy being an annoying jerk, he was just doing his job, and Vivianne trusted the man. Instead, Zane jerked the vampire guardian's chin around and back until he heard the neck snap.

The big guardian slumped in his arms, and Zane caught him. A broken neck would only stop this vampire guardian for as long as the body took to rejuvenate. A few hours at most. Zane grabbed the left hand of the guardian, and pressed his thumb to the security panel that controlled the tempered glass between the elevator and the hallway that led to the executive offices. The sensor scanned the thumb print, and the light above the door turned green. The doors opened. Zane frowned as he let the guardian fall. He had to talk to Vivianne about her security. For a vampire prime, it was ridiculously easy to get to her.

He stalked down the hallway and around the bend to the last door. He could hear voices in the other offices, but all the doors were closed, and there were no windows—heaven forbid a vampire see daylight, despite the expensive tempered glass used everywhere to cut out the UV rays. He tried her door, only to find it was locked. He pounded on the timber. He was tempted to kick the door in—and the old Zane would have done exactly that, but after nearly a year on the sidelines he'd learned the art of patience. Sort of.

"Open up, Vivianne. I know you're in there." He didn't, not for sure, but wherever Vivianne went, her bodyguard, Harris, followed—unless she was visiting enemy werewolf packs. If Harris was guarding the executive entry, it was a safe bet Vivianne was in her office. Anger laced with impatience gave him added strength, and the door shook in its frame. Damn, there was that telltale sensation in his gums again, the teeth sliding forward. "Open up!" He kept his voice low. This level held the elite of Nightwing—such as it was, in the way of director guardians, and their staff. He didn't need to alert them to the fact a werewolf was roaming the halls.

He raised his hand to knock on the door again, but had to pull back when the door whipped open. He met Vivianne's wide-eyed gaze, and she glanced briefly about the hall, before grasping his jacket and yanking him inside, slamming the door shut behind him.

"What the hell are you doing here?" she hissed. She let go of him, and placed her hands on her shapely hips.

Her hair was in a loose, rumpled braid, as though she'd run her fingers through her hair. She had color in her cheeks, and her white silk blouse draped over her chest. He could just see the faint imprint of her lacy bra beneath. The tail of her blouse hung over her skirt.

Tousled looked good on her. Damn good. He wondered briefly if he'd interrupted something, but looking around the office proved her executive suite was empty, and he couldn't sense anybody else hiding in the bathroom or the lounge area. Besides, in all the time he'd known Vivianne, she'd never once dallied with anyone in her office, or in the Marchetta Tower—and if she had, he didn't think she'd try to hide it. Actually, apart from that awkward date with the wheezy whistler, she hadn't done anything with anyone—anywhere. Still, this relaxed, tousled look was…sexy. She should do it more often.

His eyes narrowed. But Vivianne didn't do tousled. Not unless she was in her bedroom with the curtains closed and busting out some dance moves. Otherwise, she preferred the well-groomed corporate crocodile look. "What's wrong?"

She blinked. "What's *wrong*? I have a lycan in my office, that's what's wrong." For a tiny little thing, she had a lot of sass.

She opened the door and peered down the hallway, then closed the door again, frowning. "How did you get up here?"

"Well, your guards and I played this really cool game of Whose Neck Snaps First, and I won." She shot him an exasperated look, and he shrugged. "I know all your access codes."

She closed her eyes briefly, and he realized she hadn't even thought to change them.

"And of course you had to use them," she said, opening her eyes to glare at him.

"You're slipping up, Viv." She hadn't considered him a threat. For a moment he relished the bubble of happiness that thought brought him.

"No, I didn't expect you to abuse my trust." And pop went that bubble.

His eyebrows rose. "You trust me now?" It was a revealing comment. She gaped at him, then shook her head.

"No, I'll never trust you, Zane. I should have known you were a shifty little mutt." She stalked back to her desk and leaned over to lift her phone from its cradle. "But don't worry, I won't make that mistake again."

He stepped up close to her and depressed the phone's lever. He didn't believe her. She'd dragged him into her office before anyone could see him—in what could almost be a protective move. She hadn't screamed, hadn't attacked him. She might claim not to trust him, but her actions said otherwise. And she still hadn't answered his question.

"What's wrong?" he repeated. Her body faced him, but

her eyes were focused on the phone on her desk. Was she avoiding meeting his gaze?

She turned her head, her eyes lifting to his, and he was surprised by the hurt he saw in them. "You told your pack." Her voice was soft, but still accusing. He sighed. He knew exactly what she was referring to.

"Of course I told them. We needed to do something."

"You overheard a conversation that didn't concern you—"

"Didn't concern me?" He frowned, incredulous. "Your father is planning to push through a bill that would make it legal to torture lycans. Of course it concerned me."

"It was discussed in confidence—"

"Did you really expect me to do nothing?" His frown deepened. How could she not know him better than that? "What would you do, if you were in my position?"

"I wouldn't sneak behind your back," she muttered.

He let go of the phone to hold up his finger in protest. "We didn't sneak. We strategized. There's a difference. And that's exactly what you'd do."

Her gaze dropped from his, and he felt relief when she didn't argue. He gently tapped her on the shoulder. "Admit it, you're just pissed we outmaneuvered you."

"You outmaneuvered my dad," she corrected. "Who now seems to think I betrayed him by selling out to Alpine."

Zane scoffed. "Where the hell would he get that idea? Nobody even knows you were there."

Vivianne looked at the door. "He knew."

Zane's eyebrows rose. "I'm surprised you told him."

"I didn't."

Zane frowned, and raised his head to the ceiling as he mulled over her words. If she hadn't told him, and Harris hadn't known she'd left the clinic, then how did Vincent Marchetta find out his daughter was visiting with the werewolves? The realization hit him. "Wow. He's spying on you?" He shook his head. "That's seriously twisted."

She pursed her lips. "So, not only have you killed a deal my father was working on, you've used my codes to access this building." She rubbed her forehead, and he realized there'd be a record of his access—as her. And a lot of vampires with sore heads. After what her father assumed she did, the senator would think she'd given Zane, a lycan, her access codes, too.

He winced. "Sorry. Believe it or not, my aim here was not to add to your grief."

Vivianne frowned. "Why *are* you here?"

He stepped back and folded his arms. Now he was here, facing Vivianne—a very disgruntled Vivianne—he was hesitant to say what he wanted, what he needed. "Oh, I just thought I'd drop in and say hi, see how you were doing…" he prevaricated.

She mimicked him by folding her arms, also. "You're doing a welfare check on me?"

"You don't call, you don't write…" He said it flippantly, but underneath that was a thread of seriousness. He'd missed her. A little. Like a migraine you noticed you didn't have anymore when it dissipated.

She arched an eyebrow. "We're not friends, Zane."

No, they weren't. They were natural foes, but he wanted to be…more. Zane frowned. Sort of. He thought, for a brief moment, that maybe they could be friends, or…something. Could you get friendly with a vampire? Okay, so this train of thought was going down a dangerous path. Time to reel it back in. His gaze ranged over her again. She looked…unsettled. The tousled hair, the slightly disorganized state of her clothes…maybe he wasn't the only one who had something going on?

"Are you okay, Vivianne?"

"Yep. Hunky dory. Thanks for stopping by."

There it was again, that slight shift of the gaze. How the hell had she become such a successful tycoon when it was so easy to tell when she was lying?

"So you're all good? No weird little…episodes?" He didn't know what made him ask that question. He'd come here hoping for some answers, some guidance. He'd never once considered that Vivianne might also be experiencing some differences.

Her gaze flickered. "Nope. Not since you stopped haunting me."

She really sucked at lying. But for whatever reason, she wasn't prepared to trust him. Well, he could only imagine how her father would have reacted when he learned his land grab was deader than a vampire's conscience, so he guessed he couldn't blame her there. He sighed. He'd have to go first. *Ugh.*

"I need your help," he told her quietly.

Her brown gaze immediately zeroed in on him. "What with?"

Well, at least that was better than being told to go jump in a vat of molten silver. "Something—weird—is going on."

Curiosity flared in her eyes, and she didn't even try to pass him off with a placatory shove out of her office. Her gaze warmed with concern. "Weird? How weird?"

He opened his mouth. Hesitated. Wow. This was harder than he'd thought it would be. To put into actual words his worst nightmare. He couldn't. Did he really want to tell Vivianne he was becoming a monster? Did he want to admit his vulnerability? Exposing himself like that, especially with a vampire, was something that went against every lesson he'd ever learned about the breed growing up.

But she was the only vampire he could reach out to. The only *person* he could reach out to, shadow breed or not, who could possibly understand, and maybe even help him.

"Zane?" she prompted him.

He sighed. "I think—I think some of you got stuck on me, or in me, or something."

Vivianne frowned, confused. "I don't understand."

"I do some things…like you do," he said.

Vivianne blinked as she tried to follow the conversation, and he was frustrated with himself for saying it so lamely.

"What? Female things? Like peeing sitting down?"

He gaped at her for a moment. "Uh, no," he said slowly. "Like wanting blood," he clarified.

"You want blood? What do you mean, you want blood?"

He leaned forward. "I crave it," he said in a low voice, his gaze dropping to her throat. He looked away. "I don't like it, but I need it."

She was silent for a moment. "Does your vision go red?"

"Yes."

"Are your senses heightened when it does?"

"Yes."

"Have you fed?"

He opened his mouth, but couldn't quite admit it, so he nodded instead.

"What you're describing sounds like—a vampire."

"Exactly."

"How does that work?"

"I have no idea."

"Does that mean you're—you're changing from were-wolf to vampire?" He didn't miss the momentary hesitation. He shook his head.

"I don't think so. I can still shift."

Her eyebrows rose. "Do you still feel the bloodthirst when you're in your beast form?"

"Yes," he said quietly.

"So, you're like some sort of hybrid breed, then?"

"If that's what you'd call a monster, then yes."

"Interesting."

His eyes narrowed. He'd just basically told her he was a freak of nature, a veritable monster, and she found that interesting. Why wasn't she backing away from him, or calling for help?

"What's your story?" he asked her.

She shrugged. "I don't have a story."

He stepped closer. "I tell you I'm turning into a monster, and you find it 'interesting' instead of running for the hills. Why?"

She eyed him intently. "You think you're turning into a monster?"

"Don't you?"

She thought about it for a moment. "I think that you're changing…but that doesn't necessarily make you a monster. It just makes you different. Special."

He wanted to hug her. He'd been freaking out and trying to act normal with his packmates. He'd been trying to limit his time with J.J. He'd been hunting solo, trying to fight off the craving for blood, the compulsion to feed, and hated himself for all of it. But she didn't act as though he was some repulsive abomination. No, to her, he was special, and hearing that was like a calming wave washing over him. He wasn't about to let her see how much her words, her opinion, mattered to him, though.

He tilted his head. "That's very open-minded of you, and forgive me for saying this, but when I think of you, Viv, open-minded isn't what comes to mind."

"Well, maybe you don't know me as well as you think you do," she said, her voice soft with challenge.

He smiled. "I know you well enough to know when you're lying. Are you 'changing', Vivianne?" Suspicion was building inside him. It was too easy, she was too damn accepting. Something was going on.

Her mouth opened, and he pressed his finger to her lips.

"Remember, I know when you're lying." Her breath gusted across his finger, and his body tightened with reaction. Apparently his body didn't change in some ways.

She met his gaze, and he could see the wheels grinding in that clever little brain of hers. She was assessing her options; tell him the truth, or lie her butt off.

"I'm a walking hairball," she blurted out.

He blinked. "What?" He hadn't seen that one coming.

"I'm growing hair. Everywhere. It's gross—and *so* unsexy," she said, the words falling over themselves as though a dam had broken.

His eyebrows rose. "You're growing...hair." He looked at her dark braid. It didn't look that much longer than the last time he'd seen her. The rest of her still seemed...hairless. Her skin was that warm, golden color, and smooth. He resisted the urge to reach out and touch her, caress her, to prove himself right.

Vivianne nodded earnestly. "And my bones." Her eyes closed. "Oh, my goodness, my bones. Cracking, breaking, fusing back together, but wrong..." She looked up at him. "It's disgusting."

He gaped at her. "Your bones are breaking?"

"Yes, and it is so. Very. Painful." Her words came out in succinct, short bursts.

"Are you morphing?"

"I don't know what I'm doing, but whatever it is, I'm doing it really badly," she admitted.

He checked her over. "You don't look hairy." No, she looked gorgeous. Sexy.

"Well, see, that's the other weird thing. Everything goes back to normal. Excruciating pain, gross hair growth, and then bam, everything reverts to normal."

"You're shifting," he said in awe.

"I'm what?"

"You're shifting. Is it your whole body?"

"No. Just a little bit at a time."

"Oh, man, partial shifts are the worst."

"I can't be shifting. Vampires don't shift."

"And yet, you're changing form," he pointed out. He leaned his hip against her desk. "What the hell is going on with us?" He was turning part-vamp, and Vivianne was shifting. That went against the natural order of the breeds. "How do we stop it?"

Vivianne shook her head. "Once you've fed on blood, you complete your transition. I've never heard of someone turning back the clock on vampirism."

Zane's eyes widened. "You mean I'm stuck like this? I can't be stuck like this. How am I supposed to return to my pack as some sort of hybrid vamp-wolf? How can I lead a pack, if I'm like this?" Every guardian wanted to one day run their own pack, if they could prove alpha status. But with him like this, no werewolf would follow him. "I don't want to become a monster." His pack would disown him— if they didn't kill him for the threat he posed. Vivianne flinched, and her expression became closed.

"Yeah, well, turning into some sort of disgusting, hairy, bone-crunching mutt isn't a picnic in the park, either."

They stared at each other for a moment. He realized that each of them were turning into what they considered a grotesque aberration—which was vaguely insulting to the other.

"Help me," he said quietly. "I can't do this—I need to control this."

"I think I've helped you enough," she told him, leaning back against the desk, hands braced by her hips. "I've entered a wolf's den for you. My father thinks I'm untrustworthy, and now I'm turning wolf myself. Helping you seems to work out badly for me."

Zane stared at her. He couldn't go back to his pack, not when he could harm them, or worse, kill them in some blood haze. He needed to learn to control the bloodthirst, and who better to teach him than the most controlled person he knew.

Vivianne.

He stepped up close to her, and braced his hands on the desk, on either side of hers. She arched an eyebrow at his move.

"Help me," he demanded softly.

She gave him a cool look. "We seem to bring out the worst in each other," she said, her tone carrying a hint of frost. Then her gaze drifted to his lips, and her throat moved as she swallowed.

He smiled. She wasn't as cold and detached as she'd like him to think. He leaned even closer, feeling her warmth, and her scent, that sassy little unique fragrance, teased at him. He could feel his body tighten, his beast awakening inside him, as though recognizing a stimulant.

"Help me, and I'll help you."

She lifted her chin. God, did she realize her lips were so close? She met his gaze with equanimity. "I don't need your help," she told him tartly.

He grinned. "You do realize we're coming up to a full moon? These little 'episodes' are going to occur more often, and they'll be stronger. Then you'll do a full-body shift on the night of the full moon. It's unavoidable."

There. Her eyes widened a fraction, her lips parted. "F-full moon?"

He nodded. "Yep. We're talking running in the moonlight. Hunting. It's wild, it's liberating—you'll be the strongest you've ever been. Faster. There is nothing quite like shifting on a full moon."

Her gaze was glued to his, her brown eyes showing both curiosity and a faint thread of horror.

"I can teach you to control it—so you don't attack your

own vamps," he whispered, leaning in close. "If you will help me learn to control my bloodthirst."

She leaned back to meet his gaze, and he took advantage of her position, moving to occupy that space, until she was half sitting on the desk, their hips so damn close—and yet not close enough, not for his liking. He could feel the heat in her, and it was so damn seductive. He wanted to clear that desk, lay her down on the surface and kiss away her resistance. He wanted to tousle her up some more, until she was writhing and panting beneath his mouth.

He wanted her.

As though sensing his attraction for her, her eyes brightened, just a little, and she tilted her head, her hair sliding back over her shoulder, exposing the slender line of her neck.

"And just how do you think you can help me?" Her question came out husky. Flirty. He lowered his head to her neck and breathed in her scent. Cinnamon. Musk. Ginger. Sexy spice. His heart thudded strong and regular in his chest, and he could feel himself lengthening, thickening. Every breath of hers brushed her breasts ever so gently against his chest. Heat built within him, and it seemed like there was some playback field between them, with the heat his body was creating coming back to him in spades—from her.

"I can teach you to run in the moonlight." His voice came out low, raspy.

Her lips curved. Damn, when she played the vixen, she played it well. "I'm a vampire. I'm already a child of the night," she pointed out to him.

He chuckled, and he sensed her tremble as his chest moved against hers. "Oh, princess, there is nothing childish about the games we can play in the moonlight."

He finally gave in to temptation, and let his body press gently against hers. Her head tilted back, and he heard her sigh, felt the soft exhalation brush past his ear. She arched her back a little, and her breasts pressed, just a little firmer, against his chest.

He closed his eyes, giving himself over to the sensation of her body, her soft curves, gently writhing against his with a slow undulation designed to drive him crazy with lust.

It was working.

He brushed his chin against her neck, enjoying the soft shudder that racked her body.

"I can help you shift, Viv. I can show you how to ride the pain until you conquer it, and how to live with your beast, and love it." He nipped at the sensitive indent where her neck and shoulder met, smiling when he heard her gasp, then moan. "I can help you get in touch with your warm and fuzzy side."

She pulled back a little so that she could meet his gaze. "I don't do warm and fuzzy," she told him. She gave him an arch look. "More like sharp and deadly." She flashed him her sharp teeth in a smile that should have looked scary, but had enough sass and spunk that it looked sexy instead. It was one advantage the vampires had over werewolves. They didn't need to go full vamp to expose their fangs, whereas werewolves had to shift.

"Sharp and deadly doesn't scare me," he told her softly, and the teasing light disappeared from her eyes, to be replaced by a swirling cloud of emotion. Desire. Surprise. Interest. Caution.

He wanted to show her he understood her need for caution. She was a vampire prime, and he was a werewolf. They both had so much to lose…but they were both in a position to help the other.

"I'll keep your secret if you'll keep mine," he said.

She opened her mouth, and he sensed her denial—her cold caution was creeping in again.

"I wanted to feed on J.J.," he told her in a raw whisper, and didn't hide the horror and shame that confession caused him.

Understanding crept over her face, and she nodded slowly. "I'll help."

He tilted his head forward until his forehead touched hers, and closed his eyes in relief. "Thank you."

A strident alarm rang through the building, and he winced as he lifted his head. "Looks like someone found my calling card," he said quietly, and backed away from her.

Her eyes narrowed as she shook her head. "I'm not going to ask. Come on." She pulled him over to the bookcase, and pulled on the spine of the Bible on the second shelf. He heard a faint click, and the door swung inward revealing an elevator.

"You vamps do like your secrets."

"Hurry," Vivianne said, pushing him into the dark space. "This one is off the books, and off surveillance. It will take you to a subbasement. Follow the tunnel—you'll come out near Reform Square."

She started to pull on the shelving to close the door, and he could hear banging on her office door.

"Wait," he said. "Where will we—"

"My place, tomorrow morning, nine o'clock. I'll send Harris out for..." She shrugged. "Something." She pulled the shelving unit closed, and there was a moment when he stood in the darkness, surprised at what had happened. Then it felt like the floor dropped away from him, as the bullet elevator dropped forty-three stories to the sub-basement level, leaving him a little breathless, a little unbalanced, and riding a little adrenalin high.

Pretty much the reaction he normally had to spending time with Vivianne.

# Chapter 13

"Close your eyes, and clear your mind," Vivianne said quietly to Zane. Zane nodded. Her lycan was lying on her sofa, head cushioned, knees bent over the armrest on the other end. The man was huge, and made her furniture look like it was made for a dollhouse.

He shot her a warning look. "No funny business, okay?"

She rolled her eyes. "Just do it, mutt."

He closed his eyes, and she couldn't help but notice his eyelashes resting in half-moon crescents against his tanned skin. The man had long eyelashes. She frowned. But she wasn't here to notice that. No, they had serious work to do. Serious work that didn't involve enjoying his scent, or eyeing his massive lycan frame with an interest her father would not appreciate. Not for a werewolf. She frowned with impatience. She'd been thinking of Zane constantly. Before and after his visit to her office…when he'd brushed up against her. She shook her head. No. *Focus*.

"You need to think of a happy place," she told him as she lifted the cloth off the tray on the coffee table. She checked to make sure he wasn't peeking.

"Are you thinking of your happy place?"

He nodded, his eyes remaining closed. "Uh-huh." His lips parted just a little with those words, all relaxed and full and…sexy. She realized she could look her fill without him being aware of her stare. The man was crazy gorgeous. But she knew a lot of good-looking men—what was it about Zane that fascinated her so?

"Great. Think of the smell of it, the feeling you get from being in there, the happiness and peace…"

She lifted a needle from the tray, and jabbed it into his forearm.

Zane roared, bolting upright, his eyes glowing red, his incisors lengthening.

"What the hell?" he exclaimed. He eyed the needle in her hand in shocked anger.

She shook her head. "You didn't stay in your happy place."

"You stuck me with a needle!"

"And all it took was one tiny prick to get you to go full, raging vamp," Vivianne stated calmly. "How long do you think it would take before you felt that annoying little stab within your pack, and turned on them?"

Zane settled back on the couch. "That's not fair."

She smiled sweetly. "Life's not fair. You need to learn to control your emotions." She wagged her finger at him. "You need to learn patience."

His lips tightened. "I can be patient."

Vivianne's eyebrow rose as she replaced the needle on the tray, pulled out a shaving mirror and covered up her other tools. "That would be interesting to see. Maybe my father has a point. All you lycans revert so easily to your animalism…"

"I don't see anything wrong with that," Zane commented.

"No, your kind wouldn't," she said, shaking her head. "It must be exhausting, swinging from one extreme emotion to another. You really are animals," she surmised, purposely baiting him.

He straightened, frowning. "We have certain traits, just like vamps do—you know, cold-blooded, callous, ruthless."

She kept her expression calm, although his words hurt, just as his words the previous day had hurt. He saw vampirism as something monstrous. Evil. Abhorrent. Was that how he saw her? Cold-blooded? Callous? She shoved the hurt aside. No matter, there was a point to this conversation.

"You mean we think with our heads, and lycans…don't." She tapped her chin. "So I guess it begs the question, what actually makes killing lycans different to killing, say, a pigeon, or a chicken?"

His eyes flashed red, and his fangs lengthened, and she held up the shaving mirror, showing him his reflection. He reared back when he saw the changes in his face, then covered his face with his hands.

"Get rid of it." His voice was low. Angry. Ashamed. She felt a pang at being responsible for creating these emotions in him, but she had to in order for him to learn his triggers—his vulnerabilities—with this new side of him.

"Anger and pain are transformative emotions for us vamps. As is fear," she told him quietly as she placed the mirror face down on the coffee table. "Also, hunger. You will need to feed often, as the longer you leave between feeds, the stronger the cravings, the more difficult it is to control."

He dragged his hands down his face, and she sighed. He looked tired, drained. Despite his enhanced strength, speed and reflexive thinking, he was still a newbie vampire, grappling with bloodthirst.

"Come with me," she told him, and stood. He rose, and followed her to her kitchen. She opened the fridge door. Next to the yoghurt, salad ingredients and milk was a neatly organized tray of blood bags. She removed two and handed one to him.

"When you have this under control," she said, lifting the blood bag, "then you can enjoy that." She indicated the other items in the fridge. "If you haven't fed, then all this will do nothing for you until you do."

His lips tightened. "I don't want to be ruled by a thirst for blood," he said bitterly.

She smiled, but there was a bittersweet tinge to it. He found everything about vampirism repugnant—did he also find her repugnant? "Zane, it's what we need to consume in order to survive. Lycans and vamps are alike in that way. We each have a diet necessary to our survival. You guys hunt animals, feed on blood and meat—"

"Mostly meat," Zane muttered.

"My point is," she said succinctly, "you and I aren't so different. We feed to live." She grinned. "Lycans are just more squeamish when it comes to blood."

"You say squeamish. I say we have a conscience."

"I bet you don't agonize over hunting little squirrels, do you?" She'd seen werewolves on the hunt, and they went after their prey in much the same way vampires did.

"That's the difference, though. Vamps think they're higher in the food chain—you equate people with squirrels when you hunt, but you don't think you're squirrels, do you?"

She thought about it for a moment. "You're right. I don't think I'm a squirrel."

He shot her an exasperated look, and she waved her hand,

acknowledging his point without agreeing with it. The reality for her was that people were her food, and she needed their blood to survive. You didn't have to kill them to feed off them, though, and she hadn't killed a human in many years—not that she let that fact out of the bag with her colony... "Drink up, and let's get on with it. Harris will be back soon, and you've got to be out of here when he returns."

It had been hard enough to explain Zane's intrusion to her guardians when they revived—and why she didn't want him killed for his audacity. She still couldn't believe Zane had managed to get past over a dozen Nightwing guardians, as well as her private guard. That had been a Herculean effort, and unprecedented. She wondered briefly if this new shift gave him an added advantage with speed and strength, more so than the average shadow breed. She gazed at him. He did look strong. He had broad shoulders and lean hips, and the cloth of his T-shirt clung to the breadth of his chest, faintly delineating his pectoral muscles, before draping over what she knew was a flat, muscled abdomen. He was worried about the bloodthirst, she knew, and the threat he posed to his pack—and J.J., but she knew that worry was unfounded. Zane was one of the strongest people she knew.

Zane tilted his head back and drained the blood bag, the strong column of his throat moving with each swallow. She eyed him as she drank her own snack. He looked good today. He wore a khaki green T-shirt and jeans, and a brown jacket that emphasized his physique, his strength. She averted her gaze. Good enough to eat.

Not in a vampire-slaughters-prey way, but in a stay-the-night-and-play way...

She scrunched up her now empty blood bag. When was the last time she'd had a man stay in her home for the night? Long before her attack, she remembered that. She frowned. When had she apparently given up on male company? She'd lived so long, and was so focused on her colony, so guarded with her associations—she'd dodged so many assassination attempts, as well as the sneakier, manipulative, seductive efforts to either harm her or wrest away her control of the colony, that she'd somehow decided relationships were more trouble than they were worth.

Why was it Zane who was waking up that desire for companionship, for frivolity, for…a closeness that wasn't just physical? He'd told her sharp and deadly didn't scare him. Well, the fact that it didn't scare him, scared her. She was able to control most guys with her cool demeanor. She could take her fun, and walk away, and everyone understood it was just temporary. No strings.

But she couldn't control Zane like most guys, and that scared the hell out of her. He wasn't buying any of her distance-building tactics, and the man seemed to have a beacon on any attempt she made to deceive him, to mask her true emotions.

He was also the only person she believed she could trust with her new problems, and didn't that confuse the hell out of her?

Damn. She needed to focus on what they were doing here, and why.

If Zane didn't learn to control his bloodthirst, his pack would realize he was vamping out on them. They'd either cast him out, or kill him.

If she didn't control this annoying habit of randomly shifting into the hairball from hell, her colony would realize she was no longer a pure vampire—and they'd kill her.

And her father would probably be leading the charge.

Just the image of her father discovering what was going on with her was enough to prod her back into reality. This is why she and Zane were spending time together. It wasn't because of some weird, unnatural desire for each other.

He didn't take down thirteen of her guardians because he wanted a date. He hadn't sought her out with a desire to romance her.

No, he needed her help—and she needed his.

She threw the crumpled blood bag into the trash bin near the back door. "Come on, we have work to do."

Zane tossed his empty bag into the sack and stretched his neck. He already looked much more relaxed. It was amazing what a pint of AB negative could do for a vampire's disposition.

"Fine, what are we doing next?"

She was tempted to do more stimulant testing, but now that he'd fed it would be harder to get a reaction from him. So she decided to not fight the blood high, and use it to their advantage.

"Meditation."

Zane's shoulders slumped. "That sounds boring."

"Did I mention you'll be dodging knives?"

Zane tilted his head. "You really are about as warm and fuzzy as a viper, aren't you?"

She smiled. "I told you, sharp and deadly is more my style."

He strolled up to her, eyes keenly assessing her as he braced his hands against the kitchen bench behind her, once again bracketing her within his arms.

"And I told you," he said softly, his gazing dropping to her mouth, "you don't scare me."

Vivianne took a hesitant breath. Just like that, he'd changed the mood from professional to intimate. Anticipation zinged through her, awakening all of her senses. She glanced down at his chest—that massive, muscled torso so damn close to hers...

"Back in your office, I had some thoughts about you...

and me," he told her, his breath whispering against her neck as he grazed his lips down the side of her throat.

Her eyes widened at the tickling, yet carnally seductive sensation. She swallowed. "Really? What thoughts?" she almost gasped the words out as his hands rested briefly on her hips, before sliding up to the indent of her waist. Her breasts swelled in her bra, and heat pooled between her thighs. This man had the most enlivening effect on her body. So much so, he robbed her of her customary caution, dampening any kind of resistance.

"I thought of doing this," he said, lifting her up on to the cool marble of her kitchen counter top. Her nipples tightened at the easy display of strength for him. He stepped between her legs, only getting as close as the taught fabric of her skirt would allow.

"Really?" she asked casually. The splinters of green in his irises started to warm among the honey brown. Damn, the man was gorgeous. She eyed the sexy man standing between her thighs, could feel her center melt at the frank look of desire in his eyes, his attraction—for *her*. That should have made her push him away. He was a werewolf. Forbidden. A man she was supposed to despise, to repudiate… to escape.

And yet, she'd never felt threatened by Zane. She'd never felt the intense dislike she was supposed to for his kind. She'd met him as a trapped man fighting against the yoke of death, and watching him struggle, with dignity and humor, had sparked respect instead of disgust. And now he was so much more than just a werewolf, more than just a man. He was the one she'd turned to when she was desperate for help and not wanting to admit it to anyone. He was the one man she trusted more than her brother, more than any of her guardian protectors. More than Harris…

"What else?" she asked, her eyebrow arching.

His lips curved, slow and sexy, and she caught her lip between teeth as his hands slid up her thighs, lifting the skirt back with it.

"I thought about doing this," he said, lifting her slightly by sliding his hands beneath the cheeks of her bottom and the counter top, taking her garment with him, until the fabric was bunched about her waist. That heated core of hers just turned molten, and her breasts swelled even further, the fabric of her lacey bra tight against her skin. Her heart thumped in her chest.

"And?" This time her voice was just a little husky. Zane grinned as his hands slid to her waist.

"And this." He dragged her hips forward, and leaned down to capture her lips with his.

Zane closed his eyes, totally enthralled by the taste of her. This hadn't been his plan. Not at all. She was a vampire, and a vampire *prime*, at that. She commanded a colony of a breed he'd grown up to hold in contempt and disgust. Yet what he felt for Vivianne was nowhere near contempt, nor disgust.

Her lips softened against his, her mouth opening, and he slid his tongue inside.

The corporate crocodile he'd thought she was turned out to be a very carefully created illusion she nurtured in order to hold her position. A corporate crocodile wouldn't meet with him in secret, keep their relationship from her father, her people, and risk not only her position, but possibly her life, in order to help him.

She sighed against him, and he pulled her even closer, his hands sliding up to her back. Her warm curves had been driving him insane. She'd told him to picture his happy place. Well, from now on, this was his happy place, with her in his arms.

Vivianne entwined her arms around his neck, meeting the slide of his tongue with gentle thrusts of her own, changing the pace, the tension of the kiss. Heat raced through him. Zane was now throbbing, trying to get even closer to the damp heat he could feel between her legs.

She moaned, writhing against him. Vivianne was no shrinking violet, and he relished that she showed him her desire, a desire that matched his in heat and fervor. Her hands clutched at his chest, and for a moment he thought she was going to push him away, and then he felt his jacket slide off his shoulders, her hands reaching around to caress his back. He shuddered at the contact. Her nails raked him gently through the fabric of his T-shirt, and tendrils of arousal snaked down to his groin.

He drew back just enough to kiss her neck, his teeth gliding down the soft skin of her throat. She gasped, and her hips jerked against his. She wrapped her legs around him, crossing her ankles, anchoring him to her.

His beast inside him rumbled with pleasure, and the sound echoed through his chest. He slid his hands to the front of her silk blouse, slipping the buttons through the holes in the fabric, but apparently his patience was not appreciated. Vivianne gave a soft little growl, a sound that was so cute, yet so damned sexy, it had his beast and other parts stand to attention. She pulled at her shirt, and the buttons popped, some hitting him on the chest, others clicking onto the counter and floor around them. He leaned back. She wore a smoky gray bra with black lace panels, and she looked so damn gorgeous, he could only stare.

Her breasts were heaving, swelling over the top of the constraining bra, and her eyes were glowing a warm gold as she reached for him. She yanked his shirt over his head, sent it sailing.

Her movement made something snap inside him, and he

lowered his head, kissing his way from her collarbone to her chest, hands sliding around to easily deal with the bra's clasp at her back. He didn't lift his head as he stripped the clothes from her body. Vivianne cried out softly as she raked her nails up the back of his neck, lightly scoring his scalp. Her touch awakened sensors he wasn't aware of. His scalp felt alive, his skin felt alive, alert, anticipating her touch.

His cock throbbed, and he rubbed himself against her molten heat as he took one of her sweet, rosy nipples into his mouth. She keened in response, her head tilting back as she arched into his embrace. Her hair brushed the backs of his arms as he held her up, it was one of the most sensuous sensations he'd ever experienced.

She was so damn hot, writhing in his arms. He suckled her flesh, rubbing his tongue against her nipple, his heart rate throbbing in his ears, in his groin.

"Please," she gasped, pulling him closer, tighter. He raised his head.

"Please what? Stop?" God, if she wanted him to stop now, it would kill him, but he would. He was wound so tight he felt like he would burst.

# Chapter 14

Vivianne's eyes widened as her gaze met his. He was waiting for her response. The muscles in his neck where tight with restraint. His arms were solid steel bands, entwined around her, his biceps against the sides of her breasts, and his chest was… She gulped. So. Damn. Gorgeous.

"Don't you dare," she rasped, and Zane grinned. She reared up, arms around his neck, and she took his mouth in a hot, passionate kiss. She was so hot for him, so damp, so ready… He was tying her in knots, but she was confident she could do the same to him. She moved, writhing, pressing against him, and he groaned, sliding his tongue inside her mouth, his hands curling against her waist. This was not slow. This was not exploratory. This was hot and fierce and demanding. She felt something unfurl inside her, something that was triumphant and responsive to Zane on a level that went beyond the physical. She would have startled, but Zane, and what he was doing to her body, distracted her.

Her pulse beat strongly in her ears as he dropped one hand to his fly, and lowered his zipper. She could feel the back of his hand pressing against her. He'd be able to feel her liquid heat—he had to. As if in total sync, Zane groaned again, low and deep, as though touching her was like setting a match to tinder. His lips pressed harder, his urgency matching hers as he pulled himself free of his jeans.

Vivianne wriggled up close to him, eager to close any distance. He was so much bigger than she, broader, stronger, just being like this, bodies pressed against each other, was an intoxication all of its own. Zane tugged the panel of her panties to the side, his fingers running along her hot delta. She moaned, in frustration, in satisfaction, in impatience... He wanted to stay and play, but both of them were way past that point. She wanted him.

*Now.*

Again, as though he could read her mind, he slid his length inside her. He hissed with pleasure as he did so. She gasped, her gaze meeting his, and she focused on the sweet, tantalizing sensation of his flesh inside her. He'd seated himself to the hilt. Then he withdrew slightly. He shuddered at the sensation, and her eyes closed in what could only be described as a tidal wave of hot bliss. She trembled with want, with desire, so close to satisfaction, and the realization sent Zane over the edge. He thrust inside her, again and again. She moaned. She gasped. She loved the sound his breath made, that soft little grunt, every time his groin met hers. Over and over, he thrust, and she took him, her muscles clenching, tightening, as something curled inside her, tighter and tighter.

Zane's jaw muscles flexed, and she could feel his fingers digging into the flesh of her hips, and she jolted with each contact of their hips. Hotter, faster, she could feel the heat building inside her, inside him. Her head tilted back, and she cried out as a hot wave of euphoria swept her away, and she heard his shout of exultation as he joined her.

It took them a few moments to climb down to reality, but when she did, she enjoyed the warmth of Zane's embrace. Which was unusual, as she didn't do cuddles.

Panting, Zane tilted his forehead against hers. "Damn. That was…unexpected."

His words brought a cold wave of realization that quickly chased away the heat of their passion. She swallowed, could feel the heartbeat in her chest slowly decrease to a more normal rate. She'd done it. She'd had sex with a werewolf.

A little voice suggested she'd made love to a werewolf, but she shoved it aside. She didn't do love. After nine hundred years, she'd learned love was really just a fleeting phase of a strong affection.

She'd had sex with a werewolf—willingly.

Oh, so willingly.

This could never get out. This could never happen again. Her father wouldn't understand, and the sense of betrayal, of disappointment, he'd felt when he thought she'd told Alpine of his plans would pale into insignificance if he ever found out she'd been intimate with the enemy.

She nodded, then swallowed again. "Whoa." Her voice came out thin and raspy. She looked down at their bodies, chests heaving. His skin showed a slight sheen of perspiration, his abdomen scored with tight muscles, and those muscles rippled as he stepped back. She closed her eyes at the sensation of his body leaving hers. He was…intoxicating. Already, her body was looking forward to the next time.

Only, there could never be a next time. Vivianne stiffened at the intrusion of reality. Feeling strangely vulnerable, she grabbed her silk blouse from the bench beside her, and slid her arms back into the sleeves, holding the front panels closed with her hands.

Zane's gaze dropped to her chest, and her cheeks warmed. Her breasts still felt sensitive, the nipples tight against the silk fabric—and probably plainly visible to him. She refused to look down though, to acknowledge the effect his presence still had on her.

She had to claw back some control, some distance. They were already sharing so much, she was afraid she'd share everything.

And that thought scared the hell out of her, because it made her want to curl up into his chest, to cuddle, and whisper, and share her fears, her desires... Make her comfort and security dependent on another.

No. She'd learned from her father that family could be trusted—but only up to a point. Putting faith in others— not so much. None of her colony, her family, would understand her association with a werewolf. None of them would accept it, either.

She eyed Zane, schooling her expression into something that she hoped looked calm and serene, and hid her turmoil inside. She was very good at hiding her emotions. Another thing she'd learned fast in her nine hundred years. And yet, this time she felt something curl inside her, something that seemed just a little hurt, a little disappointed, at her course of action.

Zane's lips tightened, and he adjusted himself, zipping up his fly.

"We should get back to work," she told him.

He arched an eyebrow. "Work?"

"Yes, work. We have a lot to learn."

Oh, wow. Apparently she wasn't the only one who could wear a mask. Zane's expression grew shuttered, impassive.

"Yeah. We do," he said, his voice low.

Zane walked down the tunnel to his quarters, checking over his shoulder every now and then. He didn't want to be surprised by a member of his pack. He covered the bandage on his upper arm with the sleeve and lapel of his jacket. After their time in the kitchen, Vivianne had become a hard task master—as though wanting to teach him what he needed to know in as short a time as possible. To be rid of him? His lips tightened. He was still trying to figure out what had happened. One moment she'd been crying out with pleasure in his arms, the next she'd shut down on him.

His beast growled sulkily at the memory.

Harris had returned, and she'd sent her guardian on a second, much longer errand. Harris had grumbled, and she'd felt guilty on insisting, but her bodyguard finally left once more. Then she'd train with Zane for hours. She'd been right, though. Her meditation was in no way warm and fuzzy, and very much sharp and deadly. She hadn't been kidding when she'd said he'd be dodging knives. He'd been surprised with her reflexes—and her aim. She'd managed to nick him.

Twice.

His fault. Vivianne was very distracting.

But he'd learned a valuable lesson. The first time it had happened, he'd vamped out on her, the blood haze coming on so fast as his body had reacted with pain and anger.

The second time, he'd flashed his eyes, and his gums had itched, but he'd taken some deep breaths, and practiced her calming techniques. It had worked, he'd been able to tone down the reaction. For the first time, he'd felt that maybe he could control this situation.

"You're out late," a deep voice said from a dark bend in the tunnel. Zane halted, muscles tensing, and he inhaled, held his breath until the count of four, then exhaled. His gums itched for a moment, and then the irritation subsided.

He shook his head. "You shouldn't sneak up on me like that, Nate," he told his friend as the guardian prime emerged from the shadows.

"I didn't. I'm just on my way back from a meeting with Samantha." Nate gestured over his shoulder, then frowned. "Where have you been? We all missed you at supper."

"I went for a run." Zane hated lying to his friend, but he wasn't ready to tell him the truth. He wasn't sure if he'd ever be ready to tell him the truth. "Is everything all right?" It wasn't unusual for the alpha prime and guardian prime to meet regularly throughout the day, but at this time of night, it was generally pretty serious.

"River Pack have reported some missing lycans." Nate shrugged. "We were just trying to figure out what resources we could provide to help locate them." Nate tilted his head. "You've been gone for hours."

Zane frowned. "I wasn't aware I had to account for every minute of my day."

Nate frowned back. "You don't, but, Zane, you're back from the dead. We were worried about you."

Zane ducked his head. He felt like a jerk. He shouldn't have snapped—not to his guardian prime. Nate had every right to want to know where his guardians were, just in case he needed them. Normally he'd advise his friend where he was going. This time, he hadn't. He hadn't wanted to lie, so he'd avoided him all together.

"I'm sorry, Nate. I'm trying to get back into shape, build on my stamina," he told him, which wasn't quite a lie. "I want to make sure I'm strong enough to do my job."

As yet, Nate hadn't given him any boundary drills, or put him on shift for any guardian duties, and Zane wondered if it was to give him a chance to fully recuperate, or if Nate doubted his ability to perform after such a long… break—or whether Nate suspected something was wrong.

Did vampirism make you paranoid? He hated this, the hiding, the lying, the practice of deceit. He'd learned he wasn't a fan of deceit. If he thought Nate wouldn't kill him, he'd rather tell Nate the truth about what was going on—not only because the guy was his guardian prime and as such commanded a certain level of respect, but because Nate was also his friend. Zane wanted to trust him. The problem was, Nate would probably kill him for it. Whether it was turning vamp, or associating with a vamp—his lips twisted. Associating. He and Vivianne had done a whole lot more than "associating"…and he wanted to go back and talk. Okay, make love to her—real love, instead of a snatched, hot quickie in the kitchen.

Ah, hell. He was damned.

Nate eyed him closely for a moment, then nodded. "I appreciate that. Hey, let me know when you're going out next time, and I'll try and come with you and run some drills. We'll get you back on track."

Zane smiled weakly. The thought of Nate being anywhere near him when he was trying to learn to control his bloodlust was something he wanted to avoid at all costs. He'd hate to wig out and attack Nate. He'd also hate for Nate to see him at his worst, and kill him for it. He swallowed. Everything always came back to that. After being "dead" for so long, he didn't want to return to that state any time soon. He'd found a new value for life.

Nate slapped him hard on the shoulder as he passed. "Good to see you out and about, Zane."

Zane sucked in a breath, then nodded at Nate, turning to watch his friend saunter down the tunnel. Zane then hurried to his den, pulling his door closed behind him. He hissed as he removed the jacket, and looked down at the newly stained bandage. Nate had hit him hard on his wound. He winced as walked through to his bathroom, and it wasn't until he was unwinding the bandage that he realized what had just happened.

He'd suffered pain, and had been surprised—but he'd managed to keep his teeth in his gums.

Vivianne's sharp and deadly approach seemed to be working.

\* \* \*

"Imagine you're shifting into your beast," Zane instructed his student. Yep, that's how this "association" was going to go. Teacher and student. Not...hot, sticky lovers. Vivianne had made that perfectly clear.

And he wasn't happy. His beast wasn't happy. But Vivianne needed his help to learn to shift, in order to hide it from her folks, and if protecting her meant giving her the right tools to protect herself, then he could suck up all this unwanted attraction and get on with the job.

Vivianne frowned. "I don't have a beast."

They were in the woods just beyond the small town of Summercliffe. On Nightwing land, but a section that bordered both Alpine and Woodland pack territory. It was an area where few of Vivianne's vampires would venture, and off limits to the werewolves. They'd have space to shift and run away from prying eyes—if Vivianne could manage a shift.

"Everyone's got a beast. That's the source of your shifting."

Vivianne shrugged. "I don't think I've got a beast."

Zane frowned. "So what do you feel, just before you start to transform?"

"Pain," Vivianne said immediately.

Zane nodded. "Yeah, we all get that. But what about before the pain?"

"Uh, tingling—like pins and needles, only a little more painful."

"Do you have an unsettled feeling? Like something moving around inside you?"

Vivianne frowned. "You mean, apart from the bones that are breaking and reforming?"

Zane sighed. "Okay, here, sit." She was fixated on the pain that came with shifting. He'd have to get her past that. Otherwise her first full-body shift could be excruciating.

Vivianne looked at the forest floor, and grimaced. "It's dirty."

"Of course it's dirty. It's…dirt."

"But I don't want to ruin my outfit," she protested. She was wearing a dark trousers and another one of her customary silk blouses. This one was the color of midnight, an inky blue that looked very attractive on her. She'd scheduled an early evening meeting, and had slipped out of her office. She hadn't had a chance to change, and Zane fluctuated between amused and exasperated with her traipsing through the woods in her executive attire. This time, it was exasperation. Zane tilted his head back. Okay. This was going to require some patience. He almost told her that she'd be going through a lot of clothes, as a werewolf, and then decided that was a surprise she could figure out on her own. He shrugged out of his jacket and laid it on the ground, outer layer on the dirt, and made a courtly bow. "Milady, please doth takest this seateth."

She shot him a tight look, and then subsided on his jacket. She curled her legs to the side, and braced herself on her left palm.

"Comfortable?" he asked her. She nodded. "Good. Okay, close your eyes—"

"You're not going to stick me with a needle, are you?"

"It would serve you right if I did. But no, I'm not going to stick you with a needle. I'm not going to hurt you at all."

She stared suspiciously at him for a moment, then closed her eyes. Then he saw her left eyelid crack open a little. "Close them both, Viv. You'll need to concentrate for this."

She sighed primly, but obeyed his instruction.

"Good. Okay, you need to relax."

"I am relaxed."

Zane arched an eyebrow. Today her hair was pulled back into a tight bun at the base of her neck. Her silk blouse had this little silky tie thing at the neckline that was done up in a pretty bow. Her pants were figure hugging, and her ankles were neatly crossed, her feet sheathed in black heeled boots that were hell for hiking, but still managed to make her legs look long and shapely. She looked exactly like she was—a business executive way out of her element.

"Just think, you've got nothing to do, no deadlines—"

"I have heaps to do, and everything is pretty much urgent," she argued. "I can't just sit here and twiddle my thumbs, waiting for my 'beast' to speak to me."

Yep, lots of patience. He rubbed the bridge of his nose, then sighed. For the amount of time he'd known Vivianne, he'd never seen her sit quietly and do nothing. If she sat, she was on her phone, barking orders over her desk, or reviewing some report, and yet she managed to be focused on each task as she performed them. The other day, when they'd started this training program, he got to feel what it was like to be the target of that focus. Vivianne had been incredibly patient with him. Well, aside from that shared moment in the kitchen. Then she'd been deliciously impatient. But with the training, he'd been surprised—and impressed. She'd never once lost her temper with him—which had to be a record. She'd been calm, composed, controlled, and he felt much more capable of wrestling with this nightmare that was becoming a vampire werewolf.

Right now, though, she looked a little too prissy to get in touch with her inner beast. He sat down behind her, his back against a tree, and stretched his legs out either side of her hips. He drew her back against him. Damn, she smelled fantastic. All heat and spice.

"Just relax," he told her.

"Is this really necessary?"

"Hey, you thought throwing knives at me was necessary. This should be a walk in the park. Trust me, I just want to help you."

She sighed impatiently, then shifted until her back was resting on his chest. He closed his eyes. Damn, she felt good. All warm, soft curves.

"Now what?"

His lips quirked. She was so eager to get things moving, to take action. She wasn't the kind of person to sit back against a tree in the middle of the night and watch the stars.

"Look up," he told her. She leaned her head back against his chest and glanced up. "What do you see?"

"Uh, trees. Stars. Clouds. The moon."

"Do you recognize any constellations?"

She twisted to look back at him, her brown eyes confused. "You want to look at the stars?"

"I want you to relax, and give yourself to the moment," he told her. "Being a werewolf, shifting from human to lycan and back again—it's about freedom, Vivianne. Being free to be wild. It's about noticing the little moments, and letting yourself go. Smell the forest. Taste it. Feel it. Surrender to it." He wanted to let go, to lean down and kiss those pouty lips of hers... He indicated the night sky above them. "So tell me, what do you see?"

She settled back against him, and he smiled when he felt her shoulders relax.

"Well, there's the Big Dipper, and Sagittarius..." They talked quietly for the next little while, watching the breeze stir the tree branches above their heads.

Vivianne sighed, and he heard the wistfulness of it. "What?" he asked quietly.

"My mother loved stargazing. When I was a little girl, she used to come kiss me good night, and we'd sit on my bed by the window and name the stars."

Zane stroked Vivianne's arms through the silk blouse.

The night air was cool—it was midspring, but they were still close to the Alpine border, and snow was about a two-hour hike away. Yet Vivianne never seemed bothered by the temperature. Still, it was almost instinctive, this need of his to touch her, warm her.

"You had a childhood, then?" He hadn't considered that she hadn't been a vampire all of her life.

She nodded. "It's pretty rare to be a vamp from birth. Vampire women can't spawn life, so most that are born are a half-breed vampire."

"How did you...turn?" He was curious to understand why this woman, who seemed so vivacious, so vibrant, would prefer immortality as the walking dead, rather than life. He felt her shoulders stiffen, and reflexively he rubbed along her neck and shoulders until he felt the muscles relax again.

"My father turned us."

Zane's eyebrow rose. "How did that conversation go? How does a father convince his family to die with him?"

Vivianne was silent for a long while, and he almost thought she'd fallen asleep, when she finally responded. "We didn't really talk about it."

Zane frowned. "What do you mean? You all just agreed?"

Vivianne leaned forward, separating herself from him as she turned to look at him—or rather, turned to look at his shoulder. She didn't quite meet his gaze. "I mean there was no discussion—at least, not with Lucien or myself. He talked about it with Mom, and she loved him so much, she would have done anything for him."

He straightened away from the tree. "But—you have to die to become a vampire. Did he—did your father kill you, and then...what?"

She grimaced. "Poison. He and Mom made a beautiful dinner, and then Lucien and I died from the poison he slipped into our food."

Zane blanched in horror. "He *poisoned* you? And you had no idea what was coming?" When he was thirteen years old, he'd eaten some toxic berries, and if it hadn't been for his lycan metabolism, he would have died. As it was, it had been a very painful, frightening experience to feel like you were dying.

"Tell me it was at least quick and painless."

Her gaze shifted. "We were dead by morning. He fed us his blood that following night, and then we revived." He noticed she didn't comment on the pain aspect. Dead by morning. That was hours after dinner—which could feel like eons if you were writhing in pain.

Holy crap. He rose to his feet, stunned, and took a few steps away from her. "Your father killed you. That's not love, Vivianne, that's murder."

She rolled to her feet. "You don't understand. He was turned, and when he realized he would live forever—without us—it nearly broke him. He turned us because he loved us."

"But what about you, Vivianne? Did you *want* to be vampire?"

She gave him a dry look. "I'm over nine hundred years old, Zane. What I wanted this is moot."

He shook his head. "It's never *moot*. How old were you when you turned? Twenty-five?"

"Twenty-seven."

"What did you want for you, Vivianne? You had your life stolen away by that prick—"

"That prick happens to be my father, so take care with how you talk about him," she hissed. She shook out her foot, as though she had pins and needles.

"He stopped being your father the day a vampire turned him into a monster."

She gaped at him, and he almost apologized, but the words stuck in his throat. No. What her father did, with her mother's approval, was unconscionable. This was the guy who wanted to conduct medical experiments on lycans. He shouldn't have been surprised by the depths the man would sink to, but to learn he'd killed both of his children, in what seemed like a painful manner, was saddening. He almost felt sympathy for Lucien, too. Almost.

"How is my father different to yours?" Vivianne argued, stepping toward him, her features tight with anger. "You were taught to hunt, to kill—you lycans are so damn self-righteous when it comes to us vampires, and you're really not any better."

His eyebrows rose. "Seriously? My father taught me to hunt, to kill—as a way of survival. He never wanted to change me, turn me into something I wasn't. He never wanted to end my life." He stalked up to her. How could she not see what she was robbed of? How could she defend the man who'd taken her very life, and who now thought nothing of murdering werewolves in an endeavor to wipe them out?

"Did you want to be a vampire? Or did you want something different? Kids? Family?" He remembered how she was with J.J., that tender expression, that hint of envy, and thought he had his answer.

"I have family, regardless of whether you think it meets your definition," Vivianne snapped, then started to stomp down the trail. "I don't see what any of this has to do with learning to shif—"

She cried out in pain, stumbling, as her tibia snapped. He caught her as she fell.

"Easy" he murmured. He winced as he heard the bone crack again, and she whimpered. His heart twisted at the sound of her pain. He lifted her into his arms, cradling her as he sat down on his jacket. She leaned her forehead against his, and he could feel her tremble. He leaned down and unzipped her boot, sliding it off her foot.

"Ohmigod," she wheezed, and she lurched in his arms

as her leg buckled and bent. "Make it stop, make it stop," she chanted. He stroked her cheek.

"It's going to be okay," he said softly, quickly.

"No, no, this is not okay," she said, shaking her head.

"Relax. Breathe through it, you'll need to ride it out."

She shook her head, small, tight movements that showed a rigidity that would hurt her beast trying to free itself.

"You need to relax, Vivianne, let it happen, stop trying to control it."

She closed her eyes, and he saw the sheen of perspiration on her brow as she fought for control.

"Let it free, Vivianne, otherwise you'll both kill each other trying to win."

She flinched when the leg cracked again. She clasped her hands, and he could see the whites of her knuckles as she inwardly battled for control. This wouldn't do. This wasn't a bloodthirst that you had to control, this was a beast you had to set free. She was concentrating so fiercely on containing her beast, he could see the bones crack, form, and crack again as the different facets of her new being fought for dominance. He shook his head. This was excruciating to watch, understanding what her inner self was trying to accomplish, and how imprisoned she would feel. The full moon was tomorrow night, and a full body bone crack would be agonizing if she didn't learn to let go. She had such strong control, though, she needed to be distracted, in order for her inner beast to take center stage.

So he distracted her the best way he knew how.

He dipped his head down, and took her lips with his.

# Chapter 15

Vivianne's eyes sprung wide open at the delicious pressure against her lips. Instinctively she relaxed her jaw, her mouth opening to receive Zane's kiss.

His tongue rubbed against hers, and heat, slow and languorous, unwound within her. It was as though something lived inside her, something that sparked up at the touch of his lips against hers.

Almost immediately, the searing agony in her leg subsided, and she felt a sweet, warm release from the pain. She raised her arm, the one that was closest to Zane's chest, and slid it around his broad shoulders, her other hand sliding across the massive width of his muscular torso. She arched into him, and sighed when her breasts rubbed against his chest.

He moaned softly, his mouth widening against hers, and their kiss deepened. Liquid heat dampened the delta of her thighs, and she sighed as his hands slid around her, his arms bringing her even closer to him, to his heat.

Sensations bombarded her—so much heat. Colors rippled behind her closed eyelids, and all she could feel, all she could sense, was light, heat and him. He tasted delicious, he smelled divine, but amid all of that, he made her feel safe. Cherished.

He lifted his head, panting as he gazed down at her. His brown irises were a mesmerizing blend of greens and golds, ever-changing, ever-fascinating.

"You did great," he said, his hand rising to stroke her hair.

For a moment, she was pleased. He was a damn good kisser, so it was nice to know the appreciation was mutual. Then she realized he was looking down at her body, and she followed his glance. She gasped. Her trousers had split from the knee down.

Her left leg resembled a wolf's.

She should have been repelled. She should have freaked out. Instead, she was taken aback by its beauty. Dark fur, mahogany highlights—she should have screamed in dismay. Instead, she reached down to stroke the fur.

She gasped, feeling the sensation from the inside as well as the outside. Hand gliding through silky fur, feeling the delineation of muscle tone beneath that was so alien, yet all her. Something moved inside her, a release, a relaxation… an acceptance.

Zane was right, she could feel her beast inside her, living within her, sharing her body. But it wasn't like a parasite, or a separate being… No, this was like another part of her personality, a dormant characteristic finally awakened.

"You just morphed a major limb. Your body is getting ready for full metamorphosis."

"Wow," she breathed.

"Do you feel better now?"

She nodded, surprised. "How is that possible? I'm looking at my body, and I know I should be freaking out, because this looks all kind of wrong, and yet…?"

"It feels natural," Zane said, his thumb absently rubbing against the back of her neck. She sighed softly, enjoying his touch on her skin. "Most folks think of us as two separate beings, the human and the werewolf, but we're actually one—like a yin and yang. Two elements contributing to the whole."

"I'm not even sure how I did it," she whispered in awe, then frowned in consternation. "How am I supposed to do this again?"

Zane smiled. "You relax. You let it happen. Nature will do the rest."

A twig cracked in the distance, and both of them stiffened. Vivianne's eyes widened. If any of her vamps saw her like this, they'd want her dead. She'd be an abomination—no matter how right this felt. She frowned at her leg, trying to push the fur back, to break those bones again with the power of her mind.

Her beast was reluctant to let go.

Voices could be heard in the distance. Muffled footsteps thudded along the forest floor.

"Stay here," Zane said softly, shifting her to the ground. He rose to his feet, and even from this angle, she could see the seriousness of his expression, the red glow to his eyes.

"Zane, wait," she whispered. If he vamped out on any of her guardians, there would be hell to pay. He'd start a war between Alpine and Nightwing, and neither of them wanted that.

He held up his hand, his head turning slightly, his bloodred gaze landing on hers. "Sh. Stay."

Her eyes rounded as he ran off. Did he just tell her to stay? She closed her eyes, imagining her leg as the smooth, curvy limb it usually was. This time she managed to assert her control over her beast, and the transition ached, but was not the sharp, searing sting of hell it had been before.

She rose to her feet, and as soon as she knew her limb was working normally, she took off running after Zane. She was a nine-hundred-year-old vampire, and a prime to boot. She didn't sit on the sidelines while others took care of things. No. She was the one who took care of things. She had to pause, sniff the air—God knows why, it was instinctive.

There. She closed her eyes, unpacking the scents of the forest, the musty underlay of wet leaves, the sharp scent of pine, some traces of floral…and that signature scent that for some reason she could sense and identify as a easily as recognizing a face or a voice.

Myrtle. Cedarwood. Almond.

*Zane.*

When she caught up with Zane, she'd tell him exactly what he could do with his stay command.

Zane dropped to his knees, peering through the tree fern fronds. Hikers.

Humans.

Not vampires, not werewolves, but two humans hiking through the forest.

*Prey.*

His vision went red, and his fangs slid from his gums.

He shed his clothing. Quickly, silently, his eyes on the couple. One man, one woman. The man carried the daypack, and something the woman said made him pause to laugh.

Zane morphed, already slinking beneath the fronds to the next tree. He stalked them for a moment, listening. Looking. There was nobody else around. His gums tingled. His heart thudded in his chest. He padded on quiet paws, keeping abreast of them, until the man paused to unsling his backpack and open the zipper to withdraw a bottle of water.

Muscles bunching, Zane launched from his position behind a convenient boulder. He heard the woman's screams, but it was the whites of the man's eyes as Zane pounced on him that momentarily caught him. The man went down, scratching himself on a branch, and Zane smelled blood.

It was a mind-stealing, control-grabbing compulsion. Not a craving, not a desire, but something that was fierce and unstoppable and all-consuming. His teeth sank into the man's neck, cutting off the gargled scream.

He drank, and life's nectar tasted oh-so-sweet. The woman's screaming, the man's feeble attempts to fight him off, all receded under the pressure to satiate a hunger he hadn't realized was so damn acute.

And then something hit him in his shoulder, throwing him off. He turned, growling low in his throat, until he realized Vivianne stood there, panting hard, her hair unbound and falling about her shoulders, her eyes flashing gold in warning, her feet bare of those ridiculous shoes.

"Stop, Zane, you're killing him."

He shook his head, fighting the instinct to lash out, to continue the intoxicating feed. But this was Vivianne, the only person who could help him, and the last person he'd ever want to hurt.

Vivianne shook her head. "No, Zane. You don't want to do this." She held up her hand, palm out in a placatory gesture. "Think. Breathe. Control."

He flattened his ears as he swiveled his gaze between Vivianne, and his prey.

The man stared at him, tears streaming down his cheeks as he covered the wound in his neck with trembling fingers. The woman was on her knees, sobbing, her hands clutched together as though in prayer.

He'd done this.

He'd almost killed a man. Zane dropped to the ground, a soft whimper emerging from his throat as he gazed in horror at the scene he'd created.

Vivianne tore off her silk sleeves, wrapping it around the man's throat in a rudimentary bandage. "Relax," she told the man, maintaining eye contact, her voice low and husky. "You surprised a wild animal, and it attacked you before it ran off. Only to be expected, when you hike through these trails after sunset."

The man nodded, his eyes round as he met her stare. "These trails can be dangerous," he rasped. "My fault, for surprising the animal."

Vivianne nodded, then crossed to the crying woman. She clasped her gently by the elbows, and met her gaze. "You surprised a wild animal. It attacked, but you're okay. Get your man down the mountain, find help, he'll be okay."

The woman nodded. "I have to get him down the mountain and find help," she repeated, as though in a trance, "but he'll be okay."

Vivianne nodded, then watched them as they stumbled back down the track, her body between them and Zane.

Zane morphed, covering his face with his hands. "Oh, my God, what have I done?" He lay down on his side, curling up into a ball. He'd nearly consumed the man. So great had been his hunger, all of Vivianne's lessons on control, on focus and discipline and restraint—none had taken root when he'd needed it. He'd just…reacted.

What if that had been Nate? Or Samantha? Or—his stomach muscles clenched—J.J.?

Vivianne turned to face him, and halted when she saw his naked form. "Oh. Wow." She blinked, shook her head and put her hands in front of her, as though forcing herself to focus on something.

Him.

"It's okay, Zane," Vivianne said, kneeling down by his side. "All of us go there."

"No, you don't get it. If you hadn't stopped me, I would have—" He gagged, repulsed by what he'd very nearly done.

"Don't feel guilty for feeding when you need to in order to survive," Vivianne told him, her voice strong, no-nonsense. No sympathy.

"But—"

"Do feel guilty for feeding when it's not to sustain you, but for enjoyment," she continued. "You haven't fed today. *You need to feed.*" She placed her hand on his shoulder. "You're stronger when you've fed, and you're stronger against the bloodlust." She frowned. "Actually, you run pretty fast. I've chased werewolves before, but it was a real effort to keep up with you. Whatever is happening, it's making you faster than a normal lycan. Stronger."

"I can't. I can't do this," he said, shaking his head as sat up. For the first time, the forest's pine needles felt uncomfortable against his bare skin, as though providing a small punishment for his grotesque actions. "I can't live like this."

Vivianne touched his chin, and he finally met her gaze. There was no shock, no sadness or disappointment. Just a shared sympathy that contained no judgement. "You can," she said softly. "You must. Because if you can't, I can't."

He frowned, and she smiled sadly. "Whether we like it or not, we're in this together. We have to figure out how this new 'us' works. Guess how I found you?" She didn't wait for his response. "I smelled you. How the hell does that work?" She shook her head in confusion. "You're a werewolf hybrid, I'm a vampire hybrid. I have to believe there is a way to get through this."

He stared at her for a moment. "How can you be so optimistic?"

Her smile broadened, and warmth ate away at the sadness. "Because in all I've experienced, I've learned the impossible can happen, if you wait long enough."

She clasped both of his cheeks in her hands, her gaze solemn. "Zane, don't sell yourself short. You can do this. You are the strongest man I know." She gave a low laugh. "You actually died and lived to tell the tale. If anyone can do this, you can. And then you can show me how to do it."

He closed his eyes, dipping his head forehead, and he felt the cool skin of her head against his. Her quiet confidence, her faith in his ability, was both bolstering and daunting. What if he failed? Failed himself, failed Vivianne, failed his pack…? He thought of J.J., of Nate and Samantha. Then he thought of Vivianne. She was right. They were in this together. If he couldn't get his act together, then she would be fumbling in the dark.

They had to do this.

He nodded. "Okay."

The next night, Zane watched as Vivianne's car pulled out of the Marchetta Tower parking lot, Harris at the wheel. He'd hadn't spoken with her since the night before, when he'd gone all hunter-killer on the hiker. Zane glanced briefly up at the sky, still bearing the fiery tangerine streaks of the day, edged by the purple of night creeping in, as he drove his car behind her. Technically, it was Nate's car, he was just 'borrowing' it. All going well, he'd have the vehicle back before Nate even noticed it was missing.

The sun had just set, and it wouldn't be long before the moon started to rise. He'd told Vivianne, just before they'd parted ways the night before, that she should come up to Alpine territory for the full moon.

But she was wary of her father's spies, and didn't want to give them any more fuel for the man's paranoid suspicions with regards to his daughter's loyalty.

Zane shook his head. That was just twisted. Vivianne may be the most calculated, composed and strategic person he knew, and she commanded the wealthiest vampire colony of Irondell, but she still wanted to please her father, damn it. The man had no idea how loyal his daughter was to him.

It seemed Vivianne was always serving her colony, her family, but when she needed personal support, she had no one.

Except for him.

She'd stopped him from stealing a man's life blood, an action that would have made him live forever in a state of self-hatred. For that, he'd make damn sure he was there for her when she needed him—whether she realized it or not.

The only hurdle to her accepting his offer of help tonight was that she didn't want it to look like she was in league with Alpine, or any werewolf pack—apparently that would send her father off the deep end.

He could work with that.

Harris had seven established routes between Marchetta Tower and Vivianne's penthouse apartment, and after spending almost a year accompanying Vivianne everywhere, Zane had a contingency plan for each of them.

As soon as Harris showed the selected route for tonight, Zane turned down a side street, pushing the speed limit to arrive at just the right intersection at just the right time.

He pushed his foot down on the accelerator, racing through the red light just as Harris drove through the intersection from the right.

Harris swerved, and the car ran up onto the sidewalk, colliding into the brick wall of a retail store. Zane screeched to a halt, then bounded out of the car, racing up to Harris's door. The vampire guardian was still for a moment, then jerked awake, sucking in a deep breath. Zane skidded to a stop, then reached in and snapped the man's neck before the vampire had quite got his bearings.

"Back to sleep," he murmured. The vampire guardian would wake up in a few hours.

He opened the rear passenger door, and Vivianne was on the back seat, eyes blazing red, incisors bared as she growled. He grinned.

"Hello, Princess."

He reached in and pulled her out, ignoring her struggles. He jerked back when her teeth snapped awfully close to his jugular. He propped her up against the car, his hand curling into a fist. "Lights out," he said, and then lashed out with his fist.

Her head whipped to the side, and then she sagged against the car. He caught her as she started to slide to the ground, and then heaved her over his shoulder, trotting back to the Alpine vehicle. In moments he'd driven away from the scene.

He grinned in the rearview mirror. "Very good."

"I must admit, I almost tore your throat out before I knew it was you." Her voice was just a little grumpy.

"You played along brilliantly." If there were any witnesses, or any CCTV footage of the accident, it would look like Vivianne had not gone willingly. "Although you did turn your head a little early. I didn't get anywhere near your face."

"That's why it's called acting—it doesn't have to be real to make it look real." Vivianne opened one eye, looking up at him from where he'd dumped her in the back seat. "Can I get up, now?"

"Not yet. Let me get outside the city limits, first."

Almost an hour later, Zane leaned against the driver's door and shoved his hands in his jacket pockets. Vivianne walked around the car to face him, and he felt oddly awkward with her.

The last twenty-four hours had been a period of intense reflection—something he couldn't remember doing before. And he hated it. He now understood why Vivianne didn't do warm and fuzzy. That required embracing vulnerability, and after the episode in the woods, he just didn't want to go there.

He couldn't remember a time when he'd felt so low. So... *ugh*. It wasn't so much the killing—he was a werewolf, he'd killed before—it was just…he'd never *consumed* someone before. He could now understand the draw, the attraction for the vampires. He'd wanted everything from that man, and it was a burning need, a compulsion he couldn't resist. He'd always thought being a werewolf held its own honor, its own innate natural law and order. Fight to survive, animalistic power, etc. He'd always thought vampires were cold, ruthless, cursed, unnatural creatures whose very cunning made them perverse. He was beginning to see, though, with Vivianne's help, that they were just as complex, driven and caring as the werewolves. They just showed it differently.

Vivianne stopped in front of him. Her expression was composed, but he knew her well enough that he could read her. He saw her anxiety in the faint lines bracketing her mouth, the troubled distraction in the line that showed between her brows. Something was bothering her. The shift? It was a full moon tonight, and all werewolves shifted. Most of the time they could control when, where and how they shifted, but on a full moon it didn't matter how strong you were, your beast always won out. Usually. He had no idea how a vampire would handle the shift. This was unchartered territory, for both of them.

He gave her a reassuring smile. Tonight she'd worn dark leggings and a black turtle neck to work. If the woman was trying to be discrete, and blend into the darkness, she failed miserably. The figure-hugging clothes made her petite figure look sexy and curvaceous, and his fists clenched in his pockets. He wanted to kiss her all over.

But that's not what she needed from him, right now. No, she needed his wolf. He didn't think she realized just how much. But she'd learn.

He forced his lips into a friendly smile. "Ready?"

She nodded. "Ready."

"Good. Let's go."

* * *

Vivianne stood in the gully, eyes wide as she peered around her. She was stunned at the beauty of this little spot. "What is this place?" she asked breathlessly. He'd taken her for a hike along the tree line, and had slowly ventured higher into the mountain range. Now they were in what looked like the underside of a frozen waterfall, all ice sheets, stalactites and stalagmites. It was eerily beautiful, a silent, blue-green opalesque cavern that gave them some shelter from the icy winds outside. She didn't know this little pocket of serenity, though. It was quite a way away from the Nightwing border, and it wasn't on any maps—not so unusual, though, as many breeds liked to keep parts of their territory secret. Nightwing did the same, with some uncharted zones that were special, or valuable for whatever operation they were earmarked for.

This, though—this was lovely. Her breath gusted in front of her. There was such serenity, such heavenly peace. She could feel her worries and strain lessen, the longer she stood there and soaked in the quietude. Even her current issue of locating a gap in Nightwing funds of approximately twenty million dollars didn't prey so much upon her.

"I like coming here, when I need space, or when I need time to think."

She looked at Zane. This place was personal to him. And he'd shared it with her.

He smiled, and she was struck by the mischief in his eyes, the lighthearted curve to his lips. With his unruly hair and short-cropped beard, he looked like a dark, devilish, sexy rogue. "You tracked me the other day. I figure we do some more scent work." He shrugged.

"Great, because I am smelling so much more stuff now."

She looked at the frozen wall again, admiring the splintered glow of starlight through the ice. This place was truly beautiful.

"Thank y—" She gasped with pain as her arm twisted, snapping. Oh, God. It was happening again. She sucked in a breath, trying to calm herself against the instinct to scream. She focused on her limb, trying to make it heal itself, and Zane stepped up to her, clasping her face between his hands.

"Let it go, Viv. Let it happen. It hurts the first time, but the less you fight it, the less it hurts. After this first change, it won't hurt anymore."

She shook her head, eyes brimming with unshed tears. He was telling her to let the beast out. To relinquish the control she lived her life by—"Ah!" This time her collar bone snapped, and she tried to brace it with her hand. "I don't want to, Zane. It hurts so much."

He gave her an assessing glance. "I don't think it's the pain that is worrying you. You need to let your beast run. It's losing control you're having a hard time with." He smiled, and she nearly whimpered at the understanding, the sympathy. "From dusk 'til dawn, I will be right here, by your side. I won't let anything happen to you, and I'll make sure you come back." He grinned. "As a vampire, you may think you know the night, but as a werewolf, let me show you how to play in the moonlight. Just...let go."

She gaped at him. The words were uttered so quietly, so implacably, and he'd cut right to the heart of the matter. What if she couldn't turn back? How did her beast think? How did it know to shift back into human form? But Zane was so confident, and so convincing. The day before, in the woods, he'd been right. When she let it happen, it hadn't hurt. After generations of werewolves shifting, maybe they knew a few things about the process that vampires didn't understand.

She closed her eyes and did as he instructed. She let go.

# Chapter 16

Something deep inside her stretched, and she felt warm approval wash over her. Then her body started to shift.

Bone by bone, she snapped, shifted, reformed. Fabric ripped, tore… Her long scream ended in a howl. When she opened her eyes, everything was different. Her clothes hung from her in torn remnants. She could see the frayed cloth, right down to the fibrous strands. Her vision was so much sharper. She could see the different icicles within the wall of ice that cascaded along one side of the cavern, and how the moonlight fractured into crystalized rainbows as it hit the ice.

Smell—oh, wow, so many scents…snow had a scent. Who knew? It was cold, oxidized, with a hint of wintery freshness. And Zane…she turned to face him, and the torn clothing fell to the ground. He'd morphed along with her, and now stood before her in his werewolf form. Brown fur, with gold highlights, he stood proud and patient, waiting to see what she'd do next.

She twisted around to look at herself. She was a full wolf. Her pelt was the darkest brown, and depending on the light, she could see deep red highlights in the fur. Her coat glistened in the muted moonlight. And then she realized the thing she'd feared most was nothing to fear at all. She still had some thoughts, some innate "Vivianne-ness" in her shifting. She didn't become a thoughtless creature driven by base needs. No, she was still herself, only…different. The beast that Zane spoke of, she could feel it, and she lifted her head along with it, and…howled.

She wanted to run. She wanted to test her new form. She bounded along the ice wall, until she found the gap at the end, and she burst through into thick powdered snow. So cold! So invigorating! All of her senses were awake, alert, and taking everything in. She felt so…*alive*.

Zane ploughed into her, and she fell into the snow. She sat up, shook the snow off her head, and glared at Zane. He yipped at her, pranced a little, then nudged her with his shoulder. She rolled in the snow, and the sound that emerged from her throat was laughter, but different. She launched herself at him, and they tumbled in the snow.

Zane prowled through the undergrowth, his senses on high alert. He'd let Vivianne dictate what she wanted to do, and they'd been roaming for hours. They'd hunted, and he'd been truly impressed with how strong and fast Vivianne was, how strong and fast they both were. Her skills with tracking were better than most of the guardians he knew— almost as good as Trinity Woodland, tracker prime for the Woodland pack, and she was the best. He had to concede Vivianne's point—with this change they both seemed to have enhanced strength and speed, more so than the average shadow breed.

He glanced up at the sky. The moon was beginning to set. They'd worked their way through the lower range, and were now in that pocket of land between Summercliffe, Alpine and Woodland. There was no chance of coming across hikers—not tonight. All breeds observed the phases of the moon. There were special dispensations under the law when it came to the full moon. Humans knew better than to venture out when the werewolves were out and about, at their strongest. Vampires knew better, too—unless they were just looking for trouble. No, the chances of bumping into anybody out here tonight, of all nights, were slim to none.

And Vivianne had decided to play hide-and-seek. He paused next to a boulder, using it to shield his body from the main track. Where was sh—

One soft pad of paw on ground was all the warning he had, and she collided into him. Damn, she was fast. And strong. In their mock-wrestles she rated up there with Nate—higher than the other guardians he wrestled with, male or female. They rolled off the trail and along the grass, and he sensed her changing as they did so. She landed beneath him, panting, hair spilling out along the grass, eyes bright with laughter. Zane morphed, holding himself above her in human form. He'd never seen her happier, or more relaxed.

"That was amazing," she exclaimed, lifting her chin to shout it to the night sky.

He grinned. "See? Nothing to worry about. You were a champ." He was being honest. Her first transition had been swifter than any he'd ever seen before. Sometimes a first shift could take hours, with all the excruciating agony that would entail. Vivianne, though, had shifted both suddenly and smoothly. As though she and her beast had been in sync.

Her smile broadened. "If you hadn't been here…"

"You would have been fine," Zane told her. "You did really well."

Her gaze drifted down his body, then she realized she was lying buck naked beneath him. She jolted. "Where the hell are my clothes?"

Zane started to laugh, but stopped himself at her fierce frown. "You shift, but your clothes don't. If you don't strip out of them, they tear. We spend a lot of time naked," he said, maintaining eye contact with her. Werewolves didn't have the usual hang-ups about being bare-assed naked in front of others. It was a natural state for them. He realized, though, that others may not be as comfortable in their naked state.

Vivianne's gaze flickered from his, and then slowly drifted down his body. He let her look. Hell, he didn't want to move in case he ruined this rare moment of intimacy with his vamp.

*His vamp.*

Yeah. That's what she was to him, in his mind. Oh, not from a position of ownership… Vivianne would probably rip him apart if he even tried to assert a claim on her. He couldn't see her being 'claimed' by anyone… No, she was his vamp from the perspective that he couldn't, wouldn't, consider getting this close, this cozy or intimate with another vampire. Ever.

Her eyes slowly rose to meet his, and he sucked his breath in at what he saw.

Vivianne was no shrinking violet. She was confident enough to let a man know when she was interested, and from the look in her eyes…she was interested.

He finally let his gaze drift south. Her body was stunning. Perfect breasts, creamy golden skin with dark rosy nipples. He dipped his head, and lathed one nipple, and he could feel the nipple tighten into a bud against his tongue.

Vivianne arched her back, sighing. Her arms slid up over his biceps to his shoulders, and he transferred his lips to her other breast, earning a gentle raking of nails down his back in reward.

His cock stiffened, rising to attention between them, and he rubbed against her.

She hummed in approval, flexing against him, and he kissed his way down her body. Their first time had been hot, fast, and intensely satisfying. Now, he wanted to take his time, to learn the secrets of her body, and to bring her so much pleasure, to make her his vamp, so that she wouldn't, couldn't think of another man.

The streak of possessiveness rushed through him, and he could feel his beast rising beneath him, surrendering to the man's needs in total agreement. Tonight, he was going to make love to Vivianne.


Vivianne's eyes widened as Zane kissed her. There. Her breath hitched, and her heart pounded as he wrung a response from her she'd been unprepared to give. Her hips rolled against him, her channel growing moist and slick from his attentions. He showed no intention of moving, as though content to continue with a leisurely play. She could feel the tension coiling inside her, tighter, harsher. She tugged on his hair, but he ignored her wordless urging. His fingers joined his lips, and she opened her mouth in a soundless scream as her orgasm swept over her.

Again and again, he played with her, wringing every sensation of bliss from her body that she could give him, until finally he rose above her. His muscled arms bore his weight, his skin taught and smooth, cast in silver by the moonlight. His abdominal muscles rippled as he slid into her, and she gasped as her gaze met his. The sensation of him there, hot and thick, was a delicious torture, and her muscles clenched.

Without breaking eye contact, he slowly withdrew, and then slid inside, smooth as silk. Heat bloomed through her, from her core, up to her chest and down to her toes. She couldn't look away, could only open herself up to the sensation that was building inside her, something that was beyond just the physical.

Arms rising, she embraced him as he made love to her. His hips rolled with a grace and expertise that stole her breath. She arched her back, her breasts pressed against his broad chest as he slowly thrust inside her until she peaked yet again, and this time they were chest to chest, heart to heart, when they each found their fulfillment.

Vivianne stared at Zane in wonder as he lay down on the forest floor next to her. That wasn't just sex. That had gone beyond sex. It had been more than a physical release, a venting of rising tension. No, that had been…indescribable, and something she hadn't encountered in her nine hundred years. She could feel her beast stretch, could feel the warmth flood through her, a soft emotion that went beyond the affections she'd allowed herself in the past.

She could sense him. Sense his satisfaction, his relaxation… He cracked an eyelid, and his brown-green gaze met hers. He was happy. He was proud he'd pleasured her so thoroughly. He felt more than affection for her. He was… Her eyes widened as something snapped, much like her bones did during a shift, only to reform into something stronger, something that connected her to Zane.

She bolted upright. "What did you do?" she gasped.

He arched an eyebrow. "Princess, if you don't know what that was, I'll have to do it again, only better."

Her core melted at his words, and she shook her head, stifling the want, the need...the acceptance. "No, something's different," she rasped, gesturing between him and her. "Something changed."

He frowned as he sat up. "What the he—" His eyes widened, and she could sense his stunned shock.

"I can *feel* you," she hissed. Happiness. Shock. Disbelief—but mainly shock. What. The. Hell?

Zane shook his head. "Uh, no. No." He stood and walked a few steps in the clearing, then halted, his back to her. Despite her confusion, and a sense of climbing panic, she couldn't help admiring his physique. Golden skin, broad back roped with muscle. His firm buttocks clenched as he ran his hand through his scruffy hair. "No."

"No, what?" She, too, rose to her feet, trying to understand what was going on. It took her a moment to realize the rising panic she could sense was his. Which created a similar reaction within her. If Zane was mildly freaking out, it must be pretty bad.

"We should get back," Zane rasped, and turned. He halted when he saw her, his gaze sweeping over her naked form, and she could feel it, the rising hunger in him, in his beast. Her own beast stretched in response, and she could feel a similar need rise within her. Her breasts swelled, and she could feel her core pulse with liquid desire.

As though she'd developed a Pavlovian response for the man. See Zane. Want Zane. She swallowed, trying to fight the urge to mate with him.

Mate.

Her eyes widened as her beast made a sound inside her head that was all acceptance and approval.

"What. The. *Hell?*" she exclaimed.

Zane held up his hands in placatory caution. "I can explain, Vivianne. Just—give me a minute." He dragged his hand over his face, and she saw, felt, his surprise. His shock. He stood for a moment, his hands over the lower half of his face, and then he took a deep breath.

"Okay. It seems we may have…bonded."

"Bonded?" What the hell did that mean? It sounded like a restraint, a hold…a limitation. "Explain." The word came out clipped, harsh. She folded her arms as she waited.

Zane sighed. "I'm assuming vampires can form long-term relationships," he began, his arms gesturing. "I mean, you guys live forever, so I figure there has to be some capacity for deep emotion among you?"

Vivianne frowned. "Yes. Vampires can be together for many years. My parents loved each other until the night my mother was killed, and that was centuries—although it's uncommon for a true commitment to last that long."

Zane frowned right back at her. "Really?"

Vivianne pursed her lips. "We're immortal, Zane. A lifetime romance is…forever. It's difficult for a relationship to last forever."

Zane's eyebrows dipped. "You don't think one can?"

She rolled her eyes. "Come on, Zane. I was around when the fairy tales were created. There is no such thing as a happily ever after—ever is a damned long time. Most of the time, if you can find some friendship, some companionship, for a period of time, that's the best you can hope for."

His expression became composed. "Well, for us werewolves, it's slightly different. Unless you're an alpha, you'll pretty much spend your life in one pack. You forge lifelong friendships and loyalties—"

"You guys don't have the claim on that, you know. Vampires can be friends, and loyal."

"We form binding relationships," Zane continued, as though she hadn't spoken. "In some cases we bond."

"What *does* that mean?" Vivianne asked, tilting her head in exasperation, but she couldn't fight the curiosity.

"It means we bond for life. We live with that person. For life," he enunciated succinctly.

She stared at him for a moment. Bonded. For life. Like, ever. "What did you do?" she rasped.

"Hey, this isn't something we can control," Zane explained hurriedly.

"You can't just go around hitching yourself to people for life," Vivianne exploded. "What if people don't want to be hitched?"

Zane's lips tightened. "Firstly, we don't just 'hitch' to random people. We bond, and it takes two to form a bond. Your beast, my beast, something inside of us connected, whether you want to admit it or not."

Vivianne gaped. No. She did not want to admit it. She did not want to be bonded. She was independent—had been since before she'd turned. She was in charge of her own destiny. She ruled her life. She didn't have to consider the feelings of another as she made her personal life decisions. She got enough grief from her brother and father, she didn't need to add to with—what, a werewolf *husband*? "I'm a vampire prime," she said through gritted teeth. "I don't just bond with anyone."

"Neither do I," Zane snapped.

"Fix it."

"What do you mean, fix it?"

"You bonded us. Unbond us."

Zane took a deep breath, as though seeking patience from somewhere deep within, and his massive chest expanded. Again, something deep inside her responded—responded in an entirely inappropriate way, considering the direction of the conversation.

"Okay, first, *we* bonded. Not just me. *We*," he said, gesturing between them both. "Second, the only way a bond is severed is through death. That's the 'lifetime' part," he said, moving his fingers in the universal air-quote sign. "Otherwise we'd call it bonded for two minutes."

Vivianne paled. "Death?" One of them would have to die to get rid of this thing?

Zane nodded. "Death. I've tried that, though, and I didn't like it."

"So what do we do, then?" Vivianne said, and this time the panic she sensed was all hers. "I can't be bonded to a *werewolf*." She turned away, her hands clutching the hair at her temples. "What am I supposed to say to my father? Hey, Dad, meet my mate for life. He's a werewolf." She shuddered. She wasn't sure who her father would attack first, her or Zane.

"Why don't you try something different? Instead of living your life for your father, why don't you live it for yourself?" Zane's voice was heavily laced with sarcasm, and her eyes narrowed as she turned to face him. He didn't realize just how close to the mark his barb had landed. She'd given up on the idea of a man to spend her life with—when you couldn't have babies, it significantly narrowed the dating pool, and after the fourth request to 'merge' so another family could have carte blanche access to her Reform senator father, and the third assassination attempt in a takeover bid for Nightwing's prime position, she'd barricaded her heart behind a cool wall of defense. What Zane was suggesting sounded like either a lifetime of hell—or a glimpse of heaven—and both scared the crap out of her.

"Oh, it's that easy, is it? Why don't we start with your pack? Yeah. I'd love to see how Nate and Samantha would react if you introduced me as your mate."

Zane's mouth snapped shut, and he placed his hands on his hips. "Well, I guess we have a problem."

She nodded. "I guess we do."

They stood glaring at each other, and Vivianne felt herself curl up inside, trying to ward off hurt. She'd never been attached to anyone. Not since before she turned. Oh, she'd had lovers. She wasn't a saint. But she'd never emotionally committed to another. This—this was like an emotional overload. Whatever feedback was going on between them, Vivianne could feel her own panic and fears, as well as Zane's hurt and anger.

Too much. It was all too much. Too much feeling. Too much—ow, heart. She took a deep breath, burying everything under a calm coolness, and Zane lifted his chin.

"Wow. That's impressive."

Her eyes widened, but only slightly. She could feel him. Did that mean he could feel her?

Zane nodded. "Yep."

Vivianne gaped. "Does this mean you can read my mind?" Oh, hell, no. She hadn't signed up for that.

He shook his head. "No. We can sense each other's emotions. I don't read your mind, I read your heart. Hearts don't lie."

Oh. My. God. That was worse. To not be able to hide what was at her very heart—it seemed like the greatest intrusion.

Zane's features softened, as though he could sense her very real fear. The fear that she should be able to keep to herself, damn it.

"I'm not happy about this," she muttered. "I can't tell my colony that they have to accept a werewolf as my partner—for *ever*." She almost recoiled at the dark hurt she felt, but it seemed Zane could employ control, after all, and the searing hurt was swept away under a curtain of cold calm.

"Yeah, well, I'm thinking I'll have to kiss any hope of

forming my own pack goodbye because I don't know who would follow me, bonded to a vamp."

"So you're not happy, either."

"I didn't say that. I'm just trying to point out that there would be adjustments for both of us."

Her chin lifted. "Perhaps we both need some time to… adjust." She used his word, and this time Zane winced.

He nodded. "Yeah." He ran his hand through his hair. "Come on, I'll take you back home."

An hour later, Zane parked Nate's car at the private entrance to the Alpine den. He was surprised to see Nate closing the rear passenger door on the hummer, and wave casually to Samantha and baby J.J. inside. The guardian prime stood back as the vehicle pulled away, driven by Archie, one of the guardians. The vehicle crested the peak just as the sun's light pierced the horizon.

Zane waved as well, then turned around to face Nate. Darn. He was hoping to return the car without Nate knowing of his little midnight rendezvous. Zane nodded in the direction of the vehicle. "Samantha's going somewhere?"

Nate nodded. "She's going to take J.J. to visit her mom, and then she'll call in with the River Pack alpha prime. They've lost more werewolves."

Zane dipped his head. Samantha was from the Golden Plains pack, originally, and J.J. was old enough for travel. "I see."

He started to walk inside, but Nate shifted to stand in front of him, blocking his way. "Been out for a drive, huh?"

Zane grimaced. "Yeah. Sorry for not asking you. With the full moon, I just wanted to get out, test myself."

Nate nodded, grinning. "I get that. We had a lot of juveniles try a campaign tonight."

Zane smiled. A campaign was a pack hunt, a well-orchestrated maneuver that required excellent coordination and communication. That the juveniles organized one of their own indicated a good, strong generation coming through the ranks. "How did they go?"

Nate chuckled. "Let's just say more than a few retired hungry."

Zane nodded. Yep. It took a few years to learn to coordinate a pack hunt. Normally he'd be one of the guardians running perimeter to use the event as a training exercise. He was sorry he'd missed it. His smile died. He wasn't sure if he'd be able to run in a pack hunt ever again. What if he smelled blood? Would he vamp out on his pack mates?

He indicated the tunnel opening behind Nate. "Uh, I'm beat. I'm going to grab some z's."

Nate stepped in front of him again, and tilted his head. "There's something different about you," the guardian prime commented quietly.

Zane frowned, but tried to hide his worry. "Like what?"

Nate narrowed his eyes. "I don't know. You know you can tell me anything, right?"

*No, I can't. I can't tell you I'm turning vamp.* Zane nodded. "I know."

They stood there quietly for a while, staring at each other. Zane was determined not to crack. Nate smiled and thumped him in the arm. "Okay, well, see you later. Sleep tight."

Zane smiled back, and stepped around him. He'd made it four steps before a force hit him square in the back, and he stumbled to the ground.

He rolled, but Nate pinned his arms, his expression fierce. "You son of a bitch," the guardian prime hissed. "You laid with a vamp."

# Chapter 17

"You need to get off me," Zane said through gritted teeth, feeling the anger rise inside him. He didn't need this. Not tonight. He'd fed, but it had been hours ago, and with Vivianne's comments leaving him hurt and angry, his composure was low, and now was not a good time for his guardian prime to pick a fight.

"You reek of her," Nate growled. His hands fisted in the lapels of Zane's jacket. "I thought I'd caught her scent the last time you came in late, but right now, I can barely stomach being around you."

Zane's chin jutted forward, and he hid how much his friend's words hurt. "Get. Off. Me."

"A vampire, Zane? And the Marchetta Prime, to boot. What the hell are you thinking?"

Zane could feel the anger coiling inside him, feel his gums twitch, and he battled for control. "I think you better get off me. Now."

Nate inhaled, and his eyes rounded. "Holy hell. You've *mated* with her?" His friend's exclamation more than adequately expressed his disbelief—and horror. "You can't mate with a damn vampire!" Nate shook him by his lapels, and Zane wrestled with his anger, with the need to let loose.

"You know I can't control the mating bond," Zane snapped, and he could feel his eyes heating.

Nate's expression froze when he looked into Zane's eyes, then he snarled. "What did she do to you?"

Zane shoved, wanting Nate as far away from him, from danger, as possible. "Get away from me."

Nate fell back, his expression momentarily shocked at the unexpected display of strength. Zane rolled to his feet, breathing in deeply, trying to control the burn—in his eyes, in his gums. He had to calm down.

"What did she do?" Nate roared, as he launched himself at Zane.

Zane caught his friend and used his momentum to throw him off to the side. Nate hit the rock face with a thud, then fell to the ground, a little cloud of dirt rising at the impact.

Zane held up his hand, warding his friend off as Nate rose to his feet, his expression dark and fierce. "Stay away from me, Nate. I don't want to do this. I just want to go home and sleep."

Nate bared his teeth and launched himself once more. This time Zane went down, exhaling with a grunt when Nate's fist connected with his gut. The two men rolled, fists thumping against each other. Zane's heartbeat thudded in his chest. This wasn't a training session with his guardian prime. Nate was furious, and on attack mode, and Zane was the focus of his fury.

Nate's fist connected once again, this time with Zane's jaw, and a haze of red clouded his vision. Zane roared, his fangs extending, and he punched his friend in the shoulder.

Nate fell back with the force of it, then Zane sprang, his fist lashing against Nate's jaw. Nate raised his fist, but Zane caught it, and the struggle for supremacy was short lived as Zane forced his friend's fist back to the ground by the side of his head. Zane snarled, his mouth opening to show his fangs, and he saw his friend hesitate, Nate's green eyes showing a mixture of shock, anger and concern.

It was the last that Zane focused on, consciously slowing his breathing, getting his heart rate down to a normal speed. He forced his incisors to retract, pushed the red haze back, until he was panting, glaring down at his friend.

"Stop being such a dick."

Nate's eyes widened in surprise. "Me? *I'm* being a dick? Who's turning vamp?"

Zane's jaw muscles tightened, and he levered himself off his friend. He curled his hands into fists, if only to hide the trembling.

That had been a close call. "A side-effect of sharing blood with a vampire while putting death on hold for several months, apparently," he muttered.

Nate rose, his expression wary, and Zane folded his arms, trying to ward off the hurt of having his friend be so cautious around him. He knew, if their situations were reversed, that he'd be reacting in a similar way—he'd probably be even more volatile, to be honest, but still—it hurt.

"Explain it to me," Nate said through gritted teeth.

Zane shrugged. "I wish I could. I'm finding out more as I go along."

"So, you're not a werewolf, anymore?"

"Oh, I am. Just…more."

Nate shook his head. "And Vivianne? What the hell?"

"Hey, you and I both know mating bonds can sneak up on you. Remember Matthias and Trinity?" Their friends had been members of warring packs, and it had taken everyone by surprise, including Matthias and Trinity. "If I could, we wouldn't be having this conversation." His gaze dropped. "Maybe." If you'd asked him a few months ago whether he'd mate with a vampire—any vampire—his reaction would have been either a big belly laugh or a fist to the face for even suggesting it. Now, though, after spending time with Vivianne, getting to know her…it was so damn wrong, but the longer he thought about it, the more right it began to feel.

"Nobody here will accept that bond, you realize that, don't you? A werewolf and a vampire? You need to nix it."

Zane's blood ran cold at the suggestion. The only way for a mating bond to be severed was through death or rejection. With rejection, both parties suffered, slowly withering—which is why if Vivianne said she needed time, he'd damn well give it to her if it meant she'd ultimately accept the bond—and he wanted her to *want* to be his mate, not feel like she had no choice.

But if Vivianne was dead, he'd no longer be mated to a vampire, and his pack would accept him—if they could get past the partial vampirism…

"You're asking me to kill my mate?" Zane was incredulous. "I can't. I won't." He wasn't even going to consider it, so repugnant was the idea to him.

Nate drew his hands over his face. "Holy hell." He put his hands on his hips. "You know what she's doing, don't you?"

Zane arched an eyebrow. He knew what she was doing. She was getting her inner werewolf on, but that was her secret, and he didn't intend to reveal that to anyone. But that wasn't what Nate was talking about. "No," he said slowly.

"More werewolves went missing. One of them was the scion for River Pack, and she's not yet twenty."

Zane swore under his breath. Old enough to be classed as an adult, but still too young to be on her own in whatever dangerous situation she might find herself, unless she'd trained as a guardian, and as a scion, that was doubtful.

"What's that got to do with Vivianne?"

"Oh, haven't you heard? We know the Marchetta family purchased a huge chunk of real estate. That's one of the things Samantha is trying to find out—where the location is. It appears the deed has been sealed."

Zane didn't know what to react to first. That Vivianne and her father had gone ahead with their psychotic plan, or that Vivianne hadn't given him a heads-up, that the missing werewolves were in significant danger, or that the Marchettas had engaged the private seal on a land grab. As part of the tribal sovereignty of lands, a clan, colony, pack or coven could mask their interests—if they paid for it. That shroud of secrecy didn't come cheap.

"Vivianne's not involved," he said quietly. She couldn't be. There was no way she'd sign off on this, not when she was now part-werewolf.

"How do you know that? Do you trust her?" Nate asked.

Zane thought about it. Vivianne was a shrewd strategist. She was guarded. She put the colony's needs before her own. But she was also a lot more vulnerable than people knew, and with everything they'd shared so far, he couldn't see her keeping this from him, not even after his pack managed to steal away that real estate purchase from beneath her father's nose.

"I do," he said, surprised. He. Trusted. Vivianne. "This isn't something she'd sign off on."

"Then go to her. Talk to her. Get her to kill it."

"He's a Reform senator," Zane pointed out mildly. "From what I've seen, Vivianne might control Nightwing colony, but nobody controls Vincent Marchetta."

"She kills the program, or we kill him. It's that simple," Nate said matter-of-factly.

Zane nodded. If this was truly happening, and Vincent Marchetta was abducting werewolves in a sealed zone, then werewolves, by tribal law, could exact retribution. "He hasn't taken any Alpine, though, has he? Action will have to be taken by River Pack."

Nate nodded. "Unless you talk to your mate and get her to stop him." Nate indicated toward his vehicle, and the road. "Go. Talk. But you need to leave, because I can't let you inside."

Zane tilted his head to the side. "Nate." His voice came out in a whisper coated with soft urging, but it hid his devastation at his friend's words.

Nate shook his head, his lips drawn tight, his features grim, but tinged with sadness. "I can't," Nate whispered. "And it hurts to do this, Zane. But I can't have you going vamp in there. Not for your safety, not for the pack's."

Zane turned and looked at the car, more so to hide the pain of his pack's rejection. He'd known this would happen if he was found out. He should have expected it, but he thought he could hide it long enough to get a handle on it. And at the very first test, he'd failed.

Which was why Nate was right. He couldn't go in the den. He nodded, then started walking toward Nate's care. He unlocked the car and got in, then sat there for a moment, staring at the steering wheel.

Where could he go? Alpine was his family. Vivianne had made it clear she needed space, and time. He blinked. Most everyone he knew was inside that snow-covered mountain. Anywhere else he could think of, he'd run into the same issue. He was turning part-vamp, and that wasn't welcome in any pack. The realization hit him like an axe to the chest. He was as good as a stray. No pack, no family…and a mate who didn't want to be his mate.

Zane jolted when Nate knocked on the window, and Zane depressed the lever to lower the glass.

"You're not a stray, Zane," Nate said roughly. "You're still family. We just need to sort this," he said, gesturing toward Zane's form, "out. I can't let you in now, but I'm not casting you out, okay?"

Zane nodded grimly. It just felt like it.

Nate sighed. "I'll go down and talk with Samantha— we'll figure something out." He snapped his fingers. "I'll contact Matthias, too. He might have an option for you."

Zane nodded again. Matthias Marshall—no, Woodland, now, was his former guardian prime, and close friend.

"Head back down the mountain, and I'll contact you when I've spoken with Matt."

Zane started the car, and turned the vehicle in the direction that would lead him away from the only home he'd ever known. Momentarily, his attention was caught when he looked in the rearview mirror. His friend stood, framed by the dark entrance to the private tunnel, staring after him with an inscrutable expression. As the physical distance grew between them, Zane sensed the same happening with their friendship, and his beast howled inside him at the loss of pack.

Zane's lips tightened. Every alpha aspired to lead their own pack, one day. Being shunned by your pack, regardless of the length of the shunning, didn't normally result in a loyal following. He could feel the reality of leading his own family, of having his own pack, drift away with each revolution of the tire as he drove away from Alpine.

Who would follow a monster?

"You son of a bitch." Vivianne entered her father's office, cold anger coursing through her veins.

Her father's aide tried to stop her, his hand on her arm.

"Your father's not taking any visi—" His words were cut off when she snapped his neck. She turned to the support staff in her father's outer office. She was seriously not in the mood for any annoying obstacles. She was fighting off a fever—and vampires never had fevers—and any distraction from her thoughts of Zane—sad Zane, happy Zane, mischievous Zane, sexy Zane... Oh, sexy Zane.

Argh. She felt wired, energized and just a little cranky, and if this was a way to work off some steam, she was sure as hell up for it.

"Does anyone else want to try to stop your prime from conducting colony business?" she asked coolly. Each vampire averted their eyes from her gaze, all except one. She heated her eyes at him in warning and slammed the door in his face. She made a mental note of his identity. Handy to know which of the Nightwing vampires she could trust— and which she couldn't. She flipped the lock and faced her father over his large desk.

"You shouldn't speak of your grandmother like that," Vincent Marchetta said mildly as he closed the folder he was working on and slipped his pen in the ornately carved iron pen caddy.

"You stole from Nightwing," she said, ignoring his comment.

His eyebrow rose. "It's hardly stealing if it's my money."

She smiled, but it was brittle and forced. "Wrong, Dad. You have your money, remember? We lost a fortune when we had to separate you from Nightwing for your political pursuits. Every cent that's in the coffers now is money that Lucien and I have brought in—and we've been very careful to keep that income separate from yours. You stole from us. From your family, from your colony." She loosened the silk scarf that she'd tied ever so elegantly around her neck earlier in the evening, but that now felt like a stifling, choking band around her throat.

"No, I've invested the money—for my family, for my colony," her father corrected, his voice hard as steel.

"I had those funds set aside for the Kingfisher Dam project," she told him. She slid her jacket off. Damn, it was warm in here.

He shrugged, and she knew it was a move to purposely inflame her—but she was a master at control, and this was too important to lose her cool with her father. She couldn't afford to let emotion provide a weapon for her father to use against her. Although she had to fight the instinct to jump across the desk and thump his head against the surface— an instinct that shocked her. She could look after herself, but she preferred words to violence.

Normally.

"So we have different views on how colony funds should be spent," her father said noncommittally.

"What have you done?" She knew what he'd done—sort of. She could draw the dotted line.

"Nothing to concern yourself about."

Her lips firmed. "You made it my concern when you spent twenty million dollars' worth of colony funds."

Her father made a dismissive shrug. "Well, I'm sure you and your brother will do very well to refill those coffers. Besides, as I said, this is an investment. I'll repay that deficit, with interest, in good time."

She stared at her father for a moment. Sometimes, like now, she could barely believe they were related. She tried to give him some leeway—he was her father, after all, and former Nightwing Vampire Prime—but it was getting harder and harder to accept some of the things he did, particularly when it showed a distinct lack of respect for her own position as Nightwing Vampire Prime.

"Did you really think you could buy land under a privacy seal and I wouldn't know about it?" she asked quietly.

Her father's brown gaze met hers, and for a moment his surprise was evident, before he quickly schooled his features. "I don't know whether to be offended my own daughter is spying on me, or proud that you can be so Machiavellian."

She kept her expression remote. "You're doing it, aren't you? Rebuilding the clinic."

Her father smiled, and for once, the happiness seemed genuine—chillingly so. "This is to protect us, Vivianne. You'll see. We'll find the cure for lycanthropulism—we were so close, with that woman—"

"Dad, she's your daughter-in-law. And she has a name. Natalie. She's family…"

Her father's lips twisted. "She's not one of us."

Her jaw dropped, but she quickly composed herself. "We disagree."

"Vivianne, you know better than that. We're vampires. We're pure. She's not. We should be using her for our cause. She can't be anything more than…" He hesitated, searching for the right words. "A means to an end."

Vivianne quickly blinked away her reaction. Pure. God, what would her father say to her, about her, if he learned she was no longer a "pure" vampire…?

"Tell me, Dad, exactly what is our 'end'?" she inquired.

His eyebrows rose. "Why, to annihilate the werewolves."

Of course. It seemed so obvious. Yet she'd hoped her father had let go of his objective…his hatred.

"That won't bring Mom back," she said softly.

For a moment the mask slipped and she saw the pain, the heartbreak, her father hid from everyone. "They stole her from us," he whispered.

"She died in a fire, Dad. We suspect the werewolves, but no evidence was ever fou—"

"They did it!" His fist punched the desk, and the timber cracked.

She sighed. She didn't know what to think. For so long, she'd believed as her father did, that the werewolves were responsible for the Ballroom Blaze, all those years ago. Now, though, after spending time with Zane, with Samantha and Nate, she wasn't sure. There was an innate sense of honor, of balance and fairness—especially with Zane—and locking people up in a building and setting it ablaze didn't fit in with that philosophy.

"But this, Dad. This is wrong. You want to propose the abduction of werewolves—"

"The incarceration of trespassers," her father corrected.

"You want to conduct experiments on them. Think about it, Dad. What if Lucien or I were abducted by werewolves, and experimented on? Tortured?"

Her father gave her an incredulous look. "That's different. These are pests, Vivianne. Dogs who seem to think they are our equal. We are their superiors, but for that one pesky advantage they have over us."

The "pesky advantage" was that a lycan's bite could kill a vampire.

"Once we can neutralize that, we won't need to worry about the mutt's bite. We'll be able to inoculate all vampires—surely you can't argue against providing that defense against the dogs? You, of all people?"

Vivianne hesitated. When she'd come so close to dying, she'd been afraid. Vulnerable. Alone. And in such pain that her reality was blurred by horrific images, memories that were twisted so that even now, she had trouble distinguishing fact from fear.

And she'd been the lucky one. The only vampire in known history to have survived a lycan attack.

They'd lost so many friends and relatives to the bite of a werewolf. She could understand the want, the desire to research for a cure, just as humans researched for that still-elusive cure for cancer.

But that wasn't what her father was proposing.

"You're doing this to immunize yourself against a werewolf, so that you can kill them without fear of consequences," she said. "This is not some altruistic endeavor to help your fellow vampire, Father, and you know it. I saw some of the old clinic's reports..."

Her father's eyes narrowed, and she nodded. "Yes, I went looking for them. I wanted to know how there could be a high-tech medical facility underneath my family's home without me knowing about it. I wanted to know how you could siphon the funds out of our central depository without any of us noticing. I wanted to know how you could do this, without a word to any of your family, and I wanted to know what you were doing there."

She folded her arms. "Werewolves are a breed, Dad. If anyone saw those records, you would put all of Nightwing at risk of penalty, if not punishment. Do you understand that?"

Her father rose from his chair. "How dare you lecture me, Vivianne," he hissed. "You are Vampire Prime *only* because I allow it."

She shook her head. "No, I'm Vampire Prime because I care for my colony and our collective interests. I'm not so committed to my own quest for revenge that I will take those funds—funds that could be put to good use for all of the colony—and use them to pursue my own selfish, hateful interests."

He shook his head slowly. "If only your mother could hear you now," he said sadly. "She'd be so disappointed."

The remark hurt, her father bruising her heart so effortlessly once again, but she hid it, straightening her shoulders. Marchettas didn't show weakness, especially to each other. "Really, Dad? Do you think she'd still love this hate-filled, heartless man you've become?"

"She is the very reason I am as I am," he thundered. "She would want her death avenged. She would want those responsible brought to justice and punished for their crimes." He sagged back in his chair. "I want her death avenged." His gaze lifted to meet hers, and she had to hold herself back from walking over to him and hugging him at the sight of the desolation in his eyes.

"You've never felt real love, Vivianne. You don't know how it feels, having that one person who knows you so well that they know how you think…how you feel."

"I think I have an idea," she said quietly. She thought of Zane. Constantly. It went beyond the physical—although just thinking about him made her heart pound, her breasts swell, and her body temperature rise. Zane had this uncanny ability to know what she was thinking, and although there was distance between them, she could still feel echoes of his pain at her words, and an ongoing heartache that made her own heart sore. More than that, though, she'd learned that Zane was a man of honor, and one so committed to protecting his pack, even from himself, that he was determined to struggle with the changes forced upon him on his own, and had sought guidance that must have come at great cost to his pride. She'd learned that his personal strength went beyond the physical, that he had a great heart. He also respected her, despite their differences, despite their arguments, he showed a willingness to listen—even if he didn't agree with what she said.

But she couldn't tell her father that.

Her father shook his head. "No, you can't. Your mother and I—we were true soul mates. Everything she did was for me. Everything I did was for her. To have her taken like that—in such a cruel fashion…" Vincent frowned. "Do you have any idea, what it's like to imagine the person you love being left to burn? To know that she would have panicked, she would have felt real terror and great pain, and there was nothing you could do about it?"

Vivianne blinked back tears. These were the rawest words she'd ever heard from her father, and it revealed the depth of his love for her mother—and his pain. It made her want to ease her father's suffering, something that was unexpected and quite alien to her.

"I dream," he whispered. "I dream of that night. Of your mother screaming in pain, in fright. Of her running from door to door, being shoved around by the horde. I feel her desperation, her loneliness…and I can't stand it."

This time a tear did escape, leaving a warm, wet trail as it rolled down her cheek. God, what the hell was wrong with her? Since when was she so…emotional? All these feelings, these worries… Was she coming down with something? Vampires didn't get sick. Didn't get fevers. Didn't let emotions leach out so easily. Maybe this lycan stuff made her vulnerable to viruses, or something. Whatever. She wasn't used to this emotion from her father, nor the emotion it created as a result within her. Her father fussed with the folder on his desk; opening it, closing it. He pushed it to the side, then met her eyes.

"I know I can't rid the earth of the werewolves, but I can defend us from them. I'm not killing werewolves, Vivianne. They're treated as patients. We care for them, we feed them, but they are trespassing, and I can use that to our advantage—to Nightwing's advantage."

His face softened as his gaze met hers. "Do you have any idea what it did to me, learning you'd been bitten by a lycan?"

Vivianne's mouth opened. No. She hadn't. He'd never given any indication...

"To think that my wife—my life's love—and now my daughter, were to be taken from me by those beasts..." He shook his head, his features harsh and drawn. "You can't fault me for wanting to prevent that from happening again, to any of our colony. That's what we have to do, Vivianne. As leaders, as primes, we are supposed to care for our colony. Protect them. Protect and further their interests... Guard their future. This is what I'm doing."

He gave her a small smile. "I'll make you a deal."

Vivianne's eyebrows rose. Apparently their moment of father-daughter bonding—if it could be called that—was over. Her father, the supreme negotiator, had those warm and fuzzies back under control. "I'm listening."

"I will release every werewolf, once I've got my samples—in the most humane way, although they don't deserve that treatment."

Vivianne hesitated. Her beast rumbled in disagreement, but her vampire brain suggested it could be a good thing for the vampire race, to find a cure for the bite of a lycan. It could be a good thing for Nightwing, too, to find that cure. And if she couldn't get her father to stop, perhaps this was the next best thing.

"I want to see the clinic," she said.

Her father's eyes flickered, just once, then he smiled. "All right. I'll organize a driver for you, say, next week?"

She smiled back. "No. Give the directions to Harris, and we'll drive up. Now."

His smile tightened. "No problem."


Vivianne zipped up her overnight bag, then wiped her forehead. She was so darn warm. Not feverish—she'd checked, although she wasn't sure how reliable a human thermometer was on a vampire. She'd been surprised to find her core temperature had risen. She was perspiring, something she couldn't hide too much longer from her directors and staff. She might have to visit the Galen brothers again, darn it. She was definitely running hot, and it was a battle to switch her thoughts from Zane, from his golden body in the glen, those muscles rippling in the moonlight as he— She shook her head. Damn. She had so many other things that desperately needed her attention. Like recovering twenty million dollars of Nightwing money. Like trying to decide one way or another to let the werewolf trials continue. Like whether she wanted a lifelong werewolf mate to live by her side, and if yes, how could she get her colony to accept him? To accept her? And could she handle having a mate? One that really knew what she was thinking and feeling? One that could impact the decisions she normally made for herself. Could she give up that independence?

Her doorbell rang. She frowned. This better not be some contrived delay from her father. She wouldn't put it past him, though. She knew him too well, could read him better than he thought she could. He was keeping something from her, but after the raw emotion he'd shared with her, she was reluctant to destroy this new rough honesty they had going on. It was probably the most genuine and direct discussion she'd had with her father since... She hesitated on the stairs. Since he'd turned her and Lucien, and she'd raged at him, so furious of ever having a family of her own, or a legendary lifetime of love like her parents had shared, stripped away from her so brutally.

She hurried down the stairs and peered through the door. Her eyes widened when she saw Zane standing in her foyer. She pulled back from the door, heart thumping.

He was here.

Zane was *here*. Warmth spread through her, and rational thought burned away under the awakening desire at the sight of her...mate.

Her beast stretched languorously, and Vivianne shook her head. No. Now was not the time to get all hot and horny over a werewolf. She was about to drive through the night to get to her father's new clinic by morning. A clinic that her mate would not approve of, nor condone, and would try to destroy.

But a clinic that could save vampires from lycans. She closed her eyes. She hated this. She wanted to stop the clinic. She wanted to find the cure for others in her colony, her race.

She wanted Zane.

The knock sounded again. "Open up, Vivianne. I know you're in there."

Vivianne rubbed at the frown line on her forehead—one that she'd only developed since knowing Zane—and straightened her shoulders. She fussed with her hair for a moment, annoyed with herself for that nod to vanity, but still wanting to be just a little presentable, then opened the door, her expression innocent and inquiring.

Zane stared at her for a moment, and she had a brief view of Harris, unconscious, just inside her foyer door. She sighed in exasperation. Harris had been angry the last time Zane had visited her. When he revived, he was going to be truly pissed.

"Zane, you can't—"

Her words were cut off as his lips met hers.

# *Chapter 18*

Zane walked into Vivianne's apartment, his arms wrapping around her as he kicked the door shut behind him. Her waist felt tiny, his hands almost spanning her body, and then she had those curvy hips and breasts. She felt so damn good, all warm and luscious against him. That scent, that musky, spicy scent that was all wicked promise and sass, curled down inside him, and his beast hummed with approval.

Her mouth widened beneath his, her tongue flicking out in a carnal welcome that had his body throbbing in an instant. God, what was it about this woman that she could so tie him in knots?

He grasped her hips, lifting her against him as he walked further into her home. She moaned, grasping at his shoulders as she wrapped her legs around his waist. He groaned as he felt her warmth against his groin.

He found a wall, and pressed her against it. She moaned again, writhing against him, kissing him with a passion that ignited a reciprocal arousal that had him hard and throbbing and ready for more.

She tilted her head back against the wall, gasping for breath. "I don't know what it is you do to me," she gasped, then her breath hitched as he rolled his hips against hers, his length sliding along her crease, separated by clothes.

"Feel what you do to me," he murmured, and watched her eyes widen as he rolled his hips again, this time slower, deeper.

"Wait, there's something wrong with me," she said, but her hands slid up over his shoulders, sliding his jacket down off his arms. He ran his hand down her body over the swell of breast and hip, to find the hem of her skirt.

"No, you're perfect," he assured her, closing his eyes as his hand slipped up underneath her skirt, feeling her toned thighs above the lacy edge of her thigh-high stockings—damn, was she deliberately trying to drive him crazy with need? Then he touched the moist dampness between them. God, he wanted her.

"I'm so hot," she said, then gasped as he pulled down her panties and slid his finger inside her wet sheath.

"Yes, baby, yes you are," he nodded.

"No, I mean I'm hot—constantly. I can't concentrate, I keep thinking of—" she slid her hand between them, until she could cradle his length, pressing against the zipper of his jeans "—this. You."

He sucked in a breath, ready to combust at her touch, and tried to hang on to reason, to thought. She was...he winced as her fingers cleverly opened the tab of his jeans and slid his zipper down. She reached in, and he almost exploded when her fingers pulled down his boxers, releasing him, stroking him. She was...

Oh. Wow. She was *good*. He stared up the wall above her head, trying to hang on to the control that threatened to burn away with each caress of her expert hand. "Uh…" He swallowed. He had to tell her.

"You're—" His words were cut off as she lifted her head, taking his mouth in a hot, wet kiss that had him rolling his hips instinctively against hers. He lifted his head. "You're in heat," he gasped, panting.

She halted, her gaze meeting his, her hand still holding him, and he realized what a delicate position he was in with her.

"I'm…what?" she asked, her chest rising and falling as she tried to catch her breath.

"You're in heat," he told her. "It's part of the mating bond. We've initiated it, and until we both truly accept it, we'll…want."

Her mouth opened, and he could see—and feel—her inner struggle, her surprise, her desire to give in to the "want," and her anger at being caught by an unexpected and unwanted passion.

"I'm in *heat*?" Her cheeks reddened. "That is not cool."

He shook his head. "No." That's why they called it heat, and the way he felt for her right now, rock-hard and ready to explode, was in no way mildly warm, or cool, but definitely hot. She was hot. So warm, so ready in his hands.

"How do we fix this?"

He blinked, trying again to focus on the wall above her head. It was hard to concentrate on the conversation at this point. "Uh, we can stop…and both of us would feel very frustrated—but if that's what you want, I'm fine with that," he spoke quickly. "Uh, we can accept the bond, and then the heat will subside. A little." From what he'd seen, bonded mates shared a certain passionate attraction, ongoing, so he didn't think the heat for each other ever truly went away… "Or we could not accept the bond, and help each other out."

She rested her head back against the wall. "Help each other out?"

He flexed in her hand, and her eyes widened at the movement. He slid his finger out, then home again. "Help each
other...out." He flicked her nubbin with his thumb, and she
shuddered in his arms.

She gulped, then nodded. "Help me, help you." She slid
her hand down his length, and he needed no further urging.
He removed his hand, and lifted her slightly, then slid into
her. She moaned, deep and throaty, and he thrust. Once.
Twice. Thri— Vivianne's back arched, her gaze met his in
shock, and then he felt her convulse around him, her muscles constricting, sending him over the edge into his own
hot release as she cried out in pleasure.

It took them both a few minutes to get their breathing
back under control, and then he withdrew, setting her onto
her feet. She leaned back against the wall to look up at him.

"Better?" he asked, watching her closely.

She blinked, then nodded, her brow wrinkling with surprise. "Yes, actually." She ran the back of her hand across
her forehead. "I don't feel so...hot."

He rubbed his lips together to stop his smile from escap-
ing. Her hair tumbled down her shoulders in relaxed disar-
ray. Her blouse hung from her waistband, and her skirt was
creased, but her eyes sparkled, her cheeks were rosy, and
her features were relaxed, dreamy. She was hot. To him,
she'd always be hot.

She licked her lips, then started to tuck in her blouse.
"Why are you here, Zane?"

He looked at the door, then at her. He'd come over to
talk to her, but as soon as she'd opened that door, his beast
had taken over, and he'd acted on instinctive need, with no
cool logic guiding him whatsoever. No, his other control
center had kicked in.

"Uh..." He tidied himself up, adjusting his fly and tuck-
ing in his shirt. He bent down to scoop up the jacket Vivi-

anne had stripped off him. After what they'd done, he was strangely reluctant to raise the topic he wanted—needed—to discuss with her. No. He wanted to talk about them. About how they could possibly make this mating bond work. But there were pressing issues, and her query suggested she wasn't quite ready to discuss them.

"I came to talk about your father's clinic," he told her, sliding his arms into his jacket.

Her features became wary, and he sensed her caution, her awareness. "What about it?"

His eyes narrowed. She knew.

She. *Knew.*

A ripple of disappointment rolled through him, and she lifted her chin. "How long have you known?" he asked.

Her shoulders sagged. "Not long," she told him. "I had my suspicions, but he confirmed them this sunset."

"We need to stop him, Vivianne. He's taken members of River Pack—one of them is a scion. She's nineteen years old."

Her lips parted for a moment, and he sensed her shock, her slight horror, then that cool wash of control she so loved to use. "She'll be fine," she told him. "She'll be going home, soon."

His eyebrows rose in disbelief. "River Pack members have been missing for nearly a week. How long before they're released?"

She frowned. "I don't know, but I'll look into it."

He gaped at her. "You'll *look into it*? Why won't you stop it?"

This time it was Vivianne who gaped. "You would have me stop a program that could really help vampires? You would have me go against my own father?"

"Yes. I would. This 'program,'" he stated, making air quotes with his fingers, "is at the torture of werewolves. They're abducted—"

"Trespassing," she corrected, and his features tightened with impatience.

"Tell me, if the land is under private seal, how are lycans to know whose territory it is, and whether they're trespassing or not?"

She took a short, deep breath. "They won't be hurt. My father gave his word that they'd be treated well, and let go."

He gave her a frustrated look. "You forget, I was there when you woke up. I *saw* some of what he was doing, before that clinic was destroyed, and they weren't treating folks 'well.' Your brother's *wife* was nearly killed by him. Do you expect the lycans to just sit back and let your father steal us, hurt us, maybe even kill us, for what? For yet another weapon in vampire hands?"

She stepped toward him, her features tightening. "So it's okay for lycans to be able to attack vampires, to kill us, and we are not supposed to protect ourselves?"

"You've been protecting yourselves for thousands of years," he protested. "Is this really necessary?"

She blanched, and he felt her pain, coated in fear, and his brow dipped. "You seem to forget, Zane," she whispered, "I've been there. If it wasn't for some weird witchy-woo-woo stuff, I would be dead." She dug her finger into his chest, and he stepped back.

"Is that what you want? This status quo to remain where all it takes is the snap of a werewolf's teeth, and it's say-onara, baby, for the vamps?" She tapped his chest again, and he took another step back. "What if things were reversed? What if all it took was for a vampire to bite you, and you're dead. No second chances. What happened with us, Zane, it's not normal. We got another go-around. Nobody else gets that."

"You are killing us," he told her quietly. He remembered that dream, that real terror she'd felt, the loneliness. He didn't want that for her. Hell, to be honest, he didn't want it for anyone, but what her father was doing—and what she was now condoning—it was cruel, and... "It's inhumane."

She flinched, and this time the pain felt new, hot. She smiled sadly. "But that shouldn't surprise you, should it Zane? We vamps are, after all, inhuman. What did you call us? Monsters?" Her eyes flickered, and he saw the unshed tears, and realized for the first time how deeply he'd hurt her with his antipathy toward becoming...whatever the hell it was he was becoming.

But this wasn't about them. This was about people being abducted, forced against their will to participate in medical tests, and hurt, maybe worse. She may consider herself a vamp, but she also had some werewolf in her, now. Surely she had to see how bad, how wrong this all was?

"This scion is younger than you when you turned," he said softly. "She's going to be scared. She's not strong enough to fight off your father's men, and you know that. She—and the rest of them, wouldn't want to do this willingly." He pursed his lips. "This is River Pack—you wanted to negotiate with them, remember? You wanted to get your goods through their blockade. Do you think they will ever forgive you for this? That they'll let you increase your trade? Your father just closed that river to you permanently."

Vivianne's lips tightened, and he could feel that coolness, that hurt masked with anger, inside her. She wouldn't change her mind. Not yet.

He dug inside his jacket pocket and pulled out a phone. "This is for you. My number is the first preset. Call me if you need me, or if you just want to talk," he told her quietly, battling his own hurt. She was willing to turn against him, against the werewolves, all for a man who didn't deserve her loyalty. "Your father can't trace it."

He let himself out of her apartment, bitter disappointment scarring his heart.

* * *

Vivianne stared out of the window as Harris drove her up to her father's site. The irony didn't escape her. Her father had managed to sneakily purchase a parcel of land she'd earmarked for the Kingfisher Dam project. Son of a— No, wait. Nonna Marchetta wasn't the bitch here.

She saw her reflection in the tempered glass. The sky showed the pale purple of a sleepy sunrise, but it was still relatively dark, and she could easily see her troubled expression. No, Nonna Marchetta wasn't the bitch, here.

She'd sensed Zane's disappointment, his hurt, his sense of betrayal, and it had nearly crushed her. Was it a mate thing? Did your mate's emotions and well-being really weigh that heavily on you? Did you swing from wanting to ease their pain or discomfort—as she'd sensed from Zane when he'd first arrived and they'd…helped each other out, to feeling their hurt, their pain, and the consequential guilt that followed knowing you'd caused it. Hell. When was the last time she'd actually felt *guilt*? She was a vampire prime, and had made difficult decisions in the past, but with each of those she'd had the confidence and commitment knowing she was doing the best for her colony. With Zane, she'd been truly stuck, and it had been easier to revert to being the Nightwing vampire prime than to deal with an angry and hurt mate.

There had been one moment in her life, when she made her first kill after turning, when she hadn't known what to do. When she'd been torn between contacting the family and offering apology and reparation, or her father's instructions to dispose of the body. He'd told her it would get easier— but it hadn't. She'd hovered on that pointy precipice, and in either direction was a painful, rocky fall.

She felt like she was back up on that pointy precipice, and faced once more with disappointing her father, of abandoning the established "standard" behavior of a vampire, of possibly turning her back on her family, on her kind, or losing a man who understood her, who respected her, and who was willing to give her the space and distance she needed to make her own decision, but who wanted— No, *demanded*, she give more of herself, and required more of her.

Zane's phone felt heavy in her jeans pocket. She'd changed into the dark denim and teamed it with shin-high black boots that would be more suitable to tramping through the Vale. She was going to thoroughly check out this site. She would wait until she could see what her father was really up to, before she made her final decision on the clinic.

Then, maybe, she could figure out what to do about this mating bond thing.

Zane sipped from his coffee mug as he watched the Jeep bounce along the track toward the cabin. Shortly after he'd left Alpine, Nate had called him to advise Matthias had a cabin he could use, far enough away from Woodland pack that he'd be of no danger to them. Zane glanced around the meadow. It was ringed by mountains, with a waterfall filling a natural pool at the base of the western cliff. There was a stunning beauty about the soft grass and wildflowers, the gently lapping pool that flowed into a meandering river, and the harsh, craggy bluffs. Right now, the sky was getting the first fiery blasts of orange as the sun began its climb over the peak of the eastern wall. Matthias's wife, Trinity, though, didn't like to come here, the waterfall where her father was murdered. It didn't bother Zane, though, and he was damned appreciative of having somewhere to stay.

He'd been working on his control, using some of Vivianne's meditation exercises. He'd fed, but he was anything but relaxed. His mind kept going back to his conversation with Vivianne. She knew what her father was doing—they both knew what he'd done when his first clinic was in operation, and that he hadn't stopped of his own volition when he'd kidnapped Lucien's wife and tried to syphon her blood. Natalie Segova's blood had held the key for preventing the lycan poison from spreading through Vivianne and killing her, but after saving Vivianne, Natalie had tainted herself by drinking null blood, so that Vincent couldn't keep her as his own personal blood bag. It had been a ballsy move, he had to admit. There had been others in the clinic at the time, though, people he'd never met but had heard their screams, and he wasn't sure if they were all werewolves, or if there had been a mixture of werewolves, vampires and humans. If he'd heard them, Vivianne had heard them. She knew what her father was capable of.

He struggled with respect and admiration for her loyalty, and frustration and hurt for her lack of action. Anyone would be impressed with how far she was willing to go to support her family, her colony. But this particular situation—he couldn't reconcile that his own mate was prepared to turn a blind eye on the torture of her kind—and they were her kind, whether she realized it or not. He'd seen her changes. She was part-werewolf. He hoped, prayed, that she'd accept that. But he couldn't force her to that decision. She was her own woman, she was a prime, and she had the power and control to do as she saw fit. He would never intrude on that. He just hoped that if he gave her enough time, that she'd come to the same conclusion he had about Vincent Marchetta. The man had to be stopped.

The waiting, though, was killing him. Patience was not his strong suit, but he knew Vivianne well enough that if you tried to push her in one direction, she'd push back twice as hard. His lips tightened. It was probably the first time he'd really taken a step back, to let time work itself out, instead of trying to force the matter to his own end. He eyed the phone on the porch railing.

It remained silent.

Matthias pulled up in front of the cabin, and stepped out of the jeep. The tall, blond werewolf stayed at the jeep, leaving the door open. "You need to come with me," the alpha prime stated succinctly. Zane could see someone else in the car, and the witch, Dave Carter, wound down the window to look at him. Despite the inky gloom here in the valley, where the sun's light hadn't yet pierced, the man still wore sunglasses. His face was grim, unreadable.

"Are you sure you trust me?" If the lycan would only remain with one foot in the vehicle, it didn't really give Zane confidence that Matthias was comfortable, which hurt him more than anything Nate had said to him.

Matthias's face softened. "I don't know what's going on with you, Zane, but you jumped in front of a vampire for me. I would trust you with my life, and that of my wife and son. No, I'm here on business."

Zane straightened, relieved by his friend's words, and also that at last, he was being given the chance to serve a pack, even if it was an ally pack, and not his own.

"What's going on? Why is the witch here?"

"I have a vested interest," Dave replied, his words clipped, inviting no further conversation on the matter.

"Samantha called. Nate's missing," Matthias told him.

Zane swore, then tipped the rest of the coffee out onto the grass and placed the mug on the porch railing, then picked up his phone. He swept up his jacket from where it lay over a rocking chair—it was a lot warmer down here in Woodland than in Alpine territory, and he'd hadn't worn it since he arrived.

"How can I help?" Whatever they needed, he'd give.

"Zane—" Matthias hesitated, then grimaced. "Zane, Nate had J.J. with him."

Zane was inside the jeep in seconds. "Let's go."

# *Chapter 19*

Vivianne strode down the hall behind her father's clinic manager, Jerry O'Hanlon. Harris trailed behind her. O'Hanlon was not one of the Nightwing vampires. He was almost as petite as she was, but without the curves. Kind of reminded her of a leprechaun, all ruddy cheeks and sparkling eyes as he spoke enthusiastically of the wonderful gains they'd already had with the program, how they were very close to a solution, seeing as they had managed to salvage some abbreviated notes from the head doctor of the former clinic. With every step the man took, the large ring of keys attached to the belt loop at his hips jingled.

So far he'd shown her the staff quarters, the cafeteria, a state-of-the-art operating theatre that told her her father had been working on this for some time already. She'd even walked through rooms where vampires lay, hooked up to drips as they read from books or watched big screen movies. A couple were even playing chess by the tempered bay window.

She kept her features impassive. Apart from one wing that she was told was still under construction, her father seemed to have made great gains in a short period of time.

And she hadn't known. She took a moment to send her brother a text. She'd spoken to him briefly during the car ride, and he hadn't known anything about it either, and was absolutely furious—with their father, and with her. Lucien had been stunned when she'd shown him the shadow trail her father had left when he'd withdrawn their funds—a trail he was still unaware existed. It seemed the funds weren't just used for the real estate purchase, and she was now looking at the proof of it. She'd found invoices and contracts in a file her father thought he'd hidden behind an impenetrable firewall. She smiled grimly. Harris wasn't just a driver, he was also a damn good forensic hacker when she needed one.

"And if you come this way, I'll show you the rehabilitation area. We have a gym, a pool…"

Vivianne tuned out O'Hanlon as she turned down the hall in the opposite direction.

"Miss? Oh, Miss! We need to go this way," O'Hanlon called, hurrying along behind her.

She arched her eyebrow. "I'm not a miss. I'm the Nightwing Vampire Prime. My money bought this place, I'll go wherever I please."

The door at the end of the hallway bore the sign "private." "What's behind here?"

O'Hanlon smiled. "Oh, that's just a maintenance storage area. You know, mops, brooms, that sort of thing." He indicated over his shoulder. "But if you'd like to follow me—"

"Open it," Vivianne said, eyeing the door.

"Uh, Miss—"

She caught the man by his throat and walked him back against a wall, slowly raising him up until his feet were dangling two inches off the floor. "For the last time, I'm not your miss. I'm a nine-hundred-year-old prime who is fast losing her patience."

"Your father—" the vampire croaked.

She smiled. "My father isn't here. Now, open. The. Door."

She let him fall to floor, and the man held his throat, coughing. He took his time gaining his feet, and she recognized it for the stalling tactic it was.

"Uh, Prime Marchetta," O'Hanlon said as he turned to look at her. "Your father instructed me to show you all common areas. His name is on the property certificate, and my employment contract, and I take my orders from him." The tiny man drew himself up to his full height—which was only an inch or so taller than Vivianne. "This is still a secure site. I won't take you any farther without your father's—"

Harris stepped forward, and yanked the man's neck at such a speed that even Vivianne flinched when she heard the crack of bone breaking. She raised her eyebrows as Harris let the man fall.

"Harris…?"

Harris shrugged his broad shoulders. "This place gives me the creeps, and this guy was beginning to annoy me." He frowned. "Sooner or later you're going to trust me with whatever the hell's going on." He held up a finger. "And if that boyfriend of yours tries to snap my neck once more, I'm not going to be responsible for my actions."

He rolled O'Hanlon to his side and yanked at the ring of keys, ripping the belt loop off the man's pants. He held up the keys. "Seriously? Keys?" The man shook his head as he stepped toward the door. "Security in this place is circa 1950s, for Pete's sake. There are so many things that could make this place more secure—lasers, encryptions…"

"At the moment, 1950s security is working for us," Vivianne commented as the door swung open. She started to walk through, then paused, turning to look at her body-guard. "Boyfriend?"

Harris tilted his head. "It's kind of obvious, Vivianne. For God's sake, just go out with the wolf. You guys don't need to break my neck every time you're hooking up."

She gaped, her cheeks heating with embarrassment. "We're not—" She paused. Actually, she and Zane had pretty much 'hooked up' each time Harris's neck had been broken. "Uh, it wasn't like—"

Harris held up his hand, closing his eyes briefly. "Please, no details."

She walked into the "private area," and Harris dragged O'Hanlon in by the heel of one boot, smiling at the thump the man's head made as it hit the doorjamb on the way through. "That's for calling you Miss the second time," he said, and she smiled. He dropped the vamp in the corner, and closed the door behind them.

This side of the door, the laminated flooring gave way to concrete, and the temperature was significantly cooler. The hall turned to the right, and they paused in front of another locked door.

"So, you know he's a wolf, huh?" she asked casually as Harris started trying the keys one by one. He slid her a sideways glance and grunted, then tried the next key. "And what do you think about me dating a werewolf?" She tried to keep her tone casual, but knew she'd failed.

Harris smirked. "You guys aren't dating. Dating is dinner. Maybe a movie. The occasional flower or chocolate delivery. Maybe a football game if you're lucky. What you guys are doing—hell, I don't know what you're doing, but it's not dating."

"But—he's a werewolf. What do you think of that? Your prime, having a relationship with a werewolf."

Harris slid another key into the lock, and this time there

was an audible click. "Vivianne, I've worked for you for three hundred and seventy-two years. In all that time, this is the first guy you've seen more than twice. It's going to be a hard sell to the rest of the colony, granted, but as far as I'm concerned, as long as he treats you well, and respects your vampires—and doesn't break my neck ever again—I'm fine."

Vivianne gaped as he pushed the door open a crack. "But that's just me," he whispered as he peered around the door. "You have to sell it to the colony."

He took a moment to check beyond the door, then nodded, beckoning her through. She stepped quietly through, not quite closing the door. "Just in case we need to leave in a hurry," he whispered.

She nodded. They stood in a hallway, and along the cold, concrete corridor, the doors were closed, with what looked like grates that had a slider, as though you could open them to peer inside. Soft moans filled the hallway, interrupted by the occasional cry of pain. Her lips tightened, and she walked quietly up to the first door. She reached up to quietly push the slider across, and Harris had to lift her so she could see through the opening.

A man lay on the concrete floor, his eyes so bruised and puffy he couldn't open them, although he lifted his head at the sound of the grate. His naked body was red, black and blue, bearing the signs of abuse. He wore a silver collar, the metal singeing his skin. He snarled in her direction.

"You can take your damn needles and stick them up your—"

Harris slid the grate closed, muffling the rest of the lycan's comments.

Vivianne's mouth turned down, a disappointment so hot, so painful, it brought tears to her eyes. She indicated a door across the hall. "That one," she whispered to Harris.

He walked across and opened the grate, then lifted her

again so she could see inside. She covered her mouth when she saw the young girl inside. Her hair hung in oily hanks, the color a dark copper, and she was cuffed, naked to the wall, the silver chains rubbing her wrists raw. Her body bore what looked like burns, small round blisters that looked incredibly painful.

She lifted her head, her teeth bared. "Let me go," she growled in a low voice.

Vivianne nodded at Harris, and he lowered her to her feet. This time the tears ran down her face, and her beast howled in distress to see a breed sister treated so poorly. She had to be the scion Zane had mentioned. The young woman still had some spark, some fire, despite all that had been done to her. Her alpha prime father would be proud.

"How many do you think there are?" she asked Harris. She pulled out Zane's phone. She needed to let him know. He was right, about everything, and she needed him. Now. She texted a message, then frowned. Damn it. All the concrete that surrounded them prevented the message from transmitting.

Harris's face was grim. "I count twelve doors here. I don't know if there are more…"

Vivianne brushed the tears from her cheeks. "We have to free them. We can't leave them—"

A baby's wail echoed along the hall, followed closely by the deep roar of an adult male. Vivianne frowned. "A—a baby?" She turned and trotted down the hall, following the noise.

As she went, the captured werewolves yelled and roared from within their cells. Harris passed her, and held up his hand as he sidled up to the door at the end of the corridor. There was a glass panel, and he peered through.

She hurried to him, keeping to the side to prevent from being seen from the other side. "What's going on?" she whispered.

Harris winced. "You're not going to like it." He moved so that she could peer through the glass. Her jaw dropped, and her inner beast roared in rage.

She didn't wait for Harris to find the right key. She grasped the doorknob, her knuckles white, and she used the combined anger of her and her beast to lend her strength. Her eyes heating, muscles bunching, she growled as she jerked on the door.

Metal groaned and grated as the door buckled, and sparks flew as the panel was pulled out of its frame.

She stepped inside the room, her body thrumming with cold fury. Candles were lit around the room, and a pot of some sort of foul-smelling liquid simmered on a stove. A woman recoiled from the table, the candle she held in her hand wavering, then dropping, the light winking out. Vivianne looked down at the babe on the table, recognizing the blue blanket he lay upon.

A shadowy figure stepped forward to scoop up the baby, and she met the man's eyes, clearly showing the red of her own eyes.

"What the hell have you done, Father?"

Zane peered through the binoculars, eyeing the vampires walking along the perimeter fence. The GPS signal from Vivianne's phone was weak, but Matthias had some wicked tech, and they'd managed to trace it to this site near the mouth of the Kingfisher River. It was well-hidden, nestled up to the base of a mountain, with the stone and glass architecture blending into and reflecting the surrounds. "This place is well-guarded. I count seven on the roof, eighteen on the ground." The facility had been built in the shape of a triangle, three stories high—and that didn't factor any possible levels below the surface.

"This place is huge. How the hell did he do this in such a short time?"

"He didn't," Dave said. "He had help. This place would have taken nearly a year to build, at least. Someone's done most of the build before Marchetta officially purchased the land, and then masked it."

Zane frowned. "Who? This place is completely off-grid."

Matthias nodded. "He's right. Not even Reform satellite imagery shows this place exists."

"Someone with deep pockets, and who wouldn't mind starting a war between vampires and werewolves," Dave muttered.

"A human?" Zane suggested.

Dave shook his head. "A witch."

Matthias looked at Zane, then at Dave. "You never mentioned we were going up against some master witch."

"You're not. You're going up against one of her elders."

"Oh, well, that's reassuring," Zane muttered. You didn't mess with witches if you didn't have to. In this case, though, Vivianne was inside there, so he had to. But an elder? They were powerful.

"I'll take care of the witch. You," he said, pointing to Matthias, "take care of the vamps. You," he said, pointing to Zane, "go in there and rescue your vampy little girlfriend, your friend, and the scion babe." Dave rubbed his hands together as he rose from behind the fallen tree log. "Right. That's the plan."

Zane's hand was quick as he grasped Dave's shoulder and pulled him back down. "Yeah, we need more than that for the plan to work."

Matthias nodded, then looked over his shoulder. Below were gathered some Alpine, Woodland and River guardians, all of whom were itching to spill some vampire blood. He signaled one of the Woodland guardians, Dion, as well as Caleb, alpha prime of River Pack. Dion moved through the forest like a shadow until he could hunker down next to his alpha prime. He slapped a hand on Zane's shoulder. Caleb joined them shortly, and Matthias introduced him to Zane.

"Heard you were back from the dead," Dion murmured. "Good to see you."

Zane smiled. When Dion and he had first met, they had been guardians of warring packs. Battling against Rafe Woodland had created a mutual respect that he still valued today. "Thanks."

Dave held up his hand. "No chick flick moments. Let's get this done."

Vampire strongholds were known as icebergs. What you saw above ground was roughly ten percent of what you were dealing with. After several minutes of harsh whispering, they all nodded in accord. Each pack had valued members inside, but it was Caleb's daughter who'd been captured, and they all conceded that nothing should stand in the way of a father rescuing his daughter, so River Pack were going in first.

"You're sure you don't want any backup in the tunnel?" Caleb asked Zane.

Zane shook his head. "No. Keep your guys out of there."

Caleb frowned. "But you don't know how many blood-suckers will be there. Let me send five of my men—"

"No." Zane's voice was quiet, emphatic. He was here for Nate, for J.J., and the other werewolves, but he wasn't sure what kind of control he'd have in battle once blood was spilled, and he didn't want the werewolves anywhere near him.

"Let him go," Matthias said, placing his hand on Caleb's arm. The russet-haired alpha prime gave him a look of disbelief, and Matthias grinned. "He's spoiling for a fight. Give him room."

Zane knew Nate had spoken to Matthias about him. This was Matthias's way of covering for him, but also ensuring the safety of the other lycans, and Zane gave him a slight nod of gratitude.

"I'll go with him," Dave said, jerking his thumb in Zane's direction. Zane frowned. *Uh, hell no.* He shook his head,

opening his mouth to argue. The witch leaned over and
placed his hand on Zane's arm. "You and I know each other
very well. You do your thing, I'll do mine."

Zane's frown deepened as he met his own reflection in
Dave's sunglasses. The witch's eyebrows rose as he stared
at him meaningfully. Did Dave mean he *knew*, knew? Like,
*everything*? The man nodded, just once.

Great. Did the witch read minds as well? Dave winked behind his sunglasses, and Zane looked away. Dave read minds.

Caleb shrugged. "Okay, if that's how you want to do
it—"

"That's how I want to do it," Zane said. "Let's go."


"A baby, Dad? That's low, even for you." Vivianne glared
at her father as he held J.J. The baby was shrieking, his little
limbs trembling with outrage.

Vincent eyed his daughter. "I see you didn't stick to the
guided tour. You always were too damn curious for your
own good."

"Give me the baby." Vivianne held her arms out. J.J.'s
cries were loud, such a fierce little scream from the baby
boy, the noise was breaking her heart.

Her father's eyebrows rose. "This baby? Do you know
how fortunate we were to get him? He's a scion, Vivianne.
The son of not just one, but two alpha primes."

Her blood iced a little in her veins at his words. "Where is
his mother?" What had he done to Samantha? She couldn't
see how the alpha prime would just leave her son in the
arms of the enemy—and her father most definitely was this
boy's mortal enemy.

Her father shrugged. "I don't know. She wasn't travel-
ing with him—otherwise I'd have an alpha prime to test,
as well. No, this one was travelling with a guardian. He's
currently cooling his heels."

Nate. He had to mean Nate. Vivianne couldn't see Samantha entrusting anyone other than the guardian prime with her son's life. Zane must be going out of his mind. Samantha must be, too. Her own beast was reacting, and she shivered with disgust. This time her father had gone too far.

"Give me the baby," she repeated.

Vincent smiled. "Have I introduced you to my colleague?" he said, lifting his chin in the direction of the middle-aged woman who was now holding out a small sprig of something that made Vivianne frown. Verbena. Toxic to vampires. "Meet Angelica Mendez, my resident witch."

The woman muttered something, a chant in a different language, and then crushed the sprig in her hands, uncurled her fist, and blew on her palm, sending particles of the plant toward Vivianne.

Vivianne's throat started to swell, and her eyes widened as she struggled to catch her breath. Her eyes were burning, and she blinked furiously, doubling over as the plant's effects hit her. Her vision went blurry and gray, and she fell to her knees, her hand catching on the table to brace herself. Verbena was toxic to vampires. Tears formed, and through her blurry vision she saw her father use another door.

Leaving her to…die?

Her beast howled with rage, arching inside her, and she gave into the instinct, just as she heard a dull thunk, and a clatter. She reached for her beast, releasing her, and the shift into her werewolf form was seamless. She rolled to her feet, shaking off the effects of the verbena. Werewolves weren't affected by the plant—a bonus she now discovered that worked in her favor. She turned to growl at the woman.

The witch lay on the floor unconscious, the pot from the saucepan upended over the stove, creating a harsh, astringent smell in the small room.

Harris dropped the fire extinguisher, his eyes wide as

he held his hands up, backing toward the doorway he'd just entered. "Holy shit."

Vivianne glanced up at Harris, who stared at her in awe. "Holy friggin' crap." He nodded calmly. "Nice Vivianne."

She turned back to the door her father had used. She couldn't believe he'd not only used a witch, but used the witch against his own daughter, leaving her to a harsh, painful death. Her beast whimpered at the pain that sparked, but she squelched it. She could wallow in that misery later—she had an eternity to do that. On the other hand, J.J. didn't. Her father valued his quest for vengeance against the lycans over family. He was prepared to harm a baby. She shook her head. Those were not the actions of the loving father she remembered from her childhood. No, these were the actions of a man twisted by hate and bitterness, and prepared to risk his family to serve his own interests. And now he had J.J.

She may never be a mother, but there was no mistaking the protective, almost maternal need that now drove her. She had to save J.J. Vivianne turned at the table, and sniffed at the blue blanket. So many notes. Talcum powder. Milk. A hint of evergreen that was all J.J.

She lifted her nose, smelling the air carefully, until she could find his evergreen scent, and followed it. She padded through that second doorway, nose to the ground, and bounded along the hallway, hesitating once when the hall ended in a T-intersection. She stepped down the left corridor, but the scent faded, so turned and raced down the right corridor, heart beating in her need to rescue the baby.

She howled, a cry that was long and mournful, full of her rage and grief. It seemed to set off a cacophony of howls from the captured lycans, until the complex reverberated with the sound of outraged werewolves.

# Chapter 20

Zane hunkered down behind a boulder, waiting for the guard to make his pass across the mouth of the tunnel. His phone vibrated, and he frowned, checking to see if it was a message from Matthias Dave Carter, who was a few meters back, ready to sweep through behind him.

The vampire passed. Zane reared up silently and snapped the man's neck, lowering him to the ground behind the boulder. There was a shout from within the tunnel, and Zane grimaced. *Here comes the 90 percent.* He held up his hand to Dave, telling him silently to hold his position, then ran into the tunnel. He could see the dark shadows running toward him, and the red haze rose again, bringing everything into crystal clarity. His incisors lengthened, and he roared as he encountered the first vampire guardian.

He grasped the man by the shoulders, saw the momentary shock as the vampire looked at his face, and then threw the man back against the rock wall. He heard the snap of the man's spine. Quickly, he grasped the man's chin and twisted it to the side, breaking his neck. The man would rejuvenate, but at least he'd be out cold and didn't have to go through the pain of his spine knitting back into place.

A howl echoed along the tunnel. Angry, righteous, with a hint of sadness. The pitch, the tone, the emotion—all merged in a sound wave that he recognized instinctively.

*Vivianne.*

His mate was pissed, and upset. She needed him.

Vampire guardians ran up to him, and he plowed through them like a bowling ball smashing through ninepins. Every time he was grasped he reacted, twisting, turning, crushing, throwing—it was as though everyone else was moving in slow motion as he darted between, behind and beyond vampires. He made sure each of them suffered a broken neck—some of them may have been Nightwing, and therefore were Vivianne's colony. They may be just following the wrong prime's orders—or they may actually want to be doing this. Either way, that wasn't his judgment call. He just needed to get them out of his way.

He reached the inner door, and glared at it, panting. It was one of those steel doors that had a wheel lock. He grasped a spoke and pushed, gritting his teeth as he put all of his strength into turning the wheel. Anger fueled his strength, along with his need to get to his mate, and ensure her safety. His vision grew dark red, and his pulse thumped in his ears. For a moment nothing happened, and then the steel in his hands started to shift. Metal grated, screeched, and the lock began to turn, getting easier and easier the farther he pushed it around.

There was a loud clang as the lock disengaged, and he pulled, swinging the massive door open. The damn thing would withstand a bomb blast.

"Okay, some might think that's impressive," a man said behind him.

Zane whipped around, incisors bared, until he realized it was Dave.

The witch stood there, hands on hips, his leather jacket parted to reveal a black T-shirt. There was a damp, shiny patch on the front of his ribs, and Zane's nostrils flared.

Blood.

Zane shuddered, sucking in a breath, but that only increased the bloodlust as the scent of the witch's blood filled his nose, and his teeth ached. The damn fool. Dave had an open wound that was fresh and tempting.

Zane took another deep breath, held it and turned away, his fists clenched as he battled the need to strike—to bite. He focused on his heartbeat, consciously slowing it down.

He ruthlessly pushed back his thirst, quelling the fire of want. The red in his vision slowly dissipated, and his incisors retracted back into his gums. He took a deep, calming breath.

A big hand thudded down on his shoulder. "Well done," Dave murmured. "Now, *that's* impressive. But I'll take it from here."

Zane shook his head. Perspiration beaded his forehead, and trickled down his neck and back. He unclenched his fists and looked down at his palms, surprised to see them rock-steady. He could have killed the man, damn it.

"But you didn't," Dave murmured, turning his head briefly.

Zane frowned. "Damn it, get out of my head."

Dave lifted his hand off his shoulder. "Easy, fang-buster. I'm out. But just for the record, you did good."

Zane watched as the witch preceded him into the facility. He turned around. Twisted bodies lay strewn along the tunnel, but each one of them would recover—in time.

He turned and hurried after Dave. "Was this—was this some kind of test?" he snapped in a low voice.

Dave winked, then held his finger to his lips, and Zane quietened, listening. He could hear howls and roars in the distance, and there was one, louder, angrier, mightier than the others.

Nate.

He and Dave jogged along the corridor, sliding along the walls as they came to corners, and peeking around the bends. A trio of guardians was waiting for them at one such corner, and Zane growled, his fangs extending, fists clenching as he prepared to fight.

Dave muttered words in a language Zane couldn't understand, then brought his hands together in a loud clap. The three men's heads cracked against each other, knocking each other senseless. All three guardians slumped to the ground, unconscious. Zane's eyebrows rose as he turned to Dave.

"You're not so bad, yourself."

Dave grinned, and they continued down the hall, gradually picking up speed into a flat-out run. They arrived at a fork, and Zane glanced up one corridor, and then the other. He cocked his head. The howls were louder, and he could hear clanging, like metal on concrete. He couldn't hear Vivianne, though, and his heart thudded in his chest.

Dave put his hands out and touched the walls, bowing his head as though concentrating on…his feet? Zane couldn't figure what the hell the witch was doing, but Dave lifted his head.

"Your lycans are down that one," he said, pointing to the corridor to the right. "My witch, she's down—"

Dave grunted as he bounced back against a wall. Zane glanced down the left corridor. A middle-aged woman with dark hair and eyes that looked milky white was walking toward them, muttering something, hand outstretched toward Dave. She had a blue bruise darkening one temple.

Zane reached for Dave, who shook his head. "No, go get your friends." He turned to the witch advancing toward them. "This one's mine."

Zane hesitated, but Dave pushed himself up, using the wall as support, his teeth gritted. The scent of blood was stronger. His wound was bleeding again.

"Dave—" Zane began, concerned for the witch.

Dave ignored him, chanting more of those indistinguishable words. He reached a hand toward the woman who was still advancing toward him. Zane glanced between the witches. Dave was up against an elder, a witch who'd gained power each time she'd passed her trials to become an elder. What chance Dave had against the woman, Zane didn't—

The woman gasped, clutching at her throat. Her eyes widened, and a thin trail of blood dripped down from her nose and the inner corners of her eyes. She coughed, her fingers curling up into twisted digits, and she fell to her knees, stunned surprise crossing her face fleetingly. Dave kept murmuring as he advanced, and the woman slumped forward, her hands curving inward as she tried to crawl toward him, her face twisted in anger.

Zane realized his mouth was hanging open, and he snapped it shut. Okay. Apparently Dave stood a pretty good chance against the elder.

A howl rent the air, full of anger and harsh warning. Zane bolted down the right corridor.

*Vivianne.*

Vivianne bounded around the corner and skidded to a halt when she saw her father with the squirming babe. He was hurrying down the hall, his long dark coat flapping behind him. She raised her head and howled.

Her father whirled, then stopped when he saw the dark wolf behind him. His teeth bared, and he held the baby in front of him. "Stop, or I will kill him."

Vivianne shifted, rising to her feet, feeling the cold air of the subterranean corridor against her naked skin.

Her father's face turned ashen when he recognized her, and for a moment, his incisors retracted.

"Vivianne."

He set J.J. on the ground and stepped toward her slowly. "What have they done to you?" he whispered. Then his face became mottled. *"What have they done to you?"* he repeated, this time in a roar.

She lifted her chin. *"They* haven't done anything, Father. Consider this a by-product of surviving a lycan's bite." She felt calm. Balanced. Her worst nightmare was coming true—her father was discovering her secret—yet she'd never felt more confident, or stronger.

She took a step forward, her eyes on her father, but her attention was on poor J.J., who was even now rolling onto his stomach and screaming his lungs out as his skin rubbed against the cold concrete floor.

Vincent's lip curled in disgust. "You had the audacity to question my methods, and you are living proof of why we have to stop them."

Vivianne shook her head. "No, Dad. We can learn from them. They have such a strong family bond, so much loyalty among themselves…" Her lips tightened. "For so long, you had us believe they were not our equals, that they were of less value." She folded her arms. "I've yet to hear of a werewolf killing their young."

Vincent frowned. "Are you still angry about that? For

God's sake, Vivianne, it's been nine hundred years. Get over it."

She stalked up to her father, furious. "You don't get it, do you? Can you seriously be that selfish, that self-serving? You killed me, Dad. You. *Killed*. Me."

"I gave you a better life," he snarled at her.

"No, you *stole* my life," she yelled at him. "You never once asked me if I wanted to become a vampire. You just did it. You didn't want to live your immortal life alone, so you killed us. Mom. Lucien. Me. Tell me, what makes you any better than the people who murdered Mom?"

Vincent's eyes widened, and his hand flashed, catching Vivianne on her cheek, and her face whipped to the left with the impact. She took a deep breath at the sting, and the muscles tightened in her jaw as she clenched her teeth. She pushed the pain, the anger, down and then turned to face her father again.

"I wanted children. A family. Just like you did—just like you *had*. But you stole that from me," she said to him, her voice low, but calm. "You've lost Mom. You've lost Lucien." She nodded toward J.J. on the ground. "After this, you've lost me. You have no family. How does it feel, Dad?"

"You are not my daughter," he growled at her. "You're a monster. A freak. Your mother would turn in her grave if—"

"Mom would not approve of this," she whispered, and stepped around him to walk toward J.J. "She loved children. All children. Guess what? So do I. I'm shutting you down, Dad. We're done, here."

Her father grasped her arm, twisting it around her back in a viselike grip. His hand grasped her chin, pulling her head painfully to one side. "I don't think so. I believe your blood would make an interesting addition to our program, here."

Vivianne's eyes widened as she realized her father's intent. With her arm twisted behind her back, she was in a dangerously vulnerable position. She closed her eyes, sucked in a breath and turned, feeling her upper arm crack as her strength matched his. She surrendered to the pain, just as she did before shifting. She clenched her other hand into a fist and raised it over her shoulder, hearing her father's nose break with the impact. Her father's grip slackened, and she turned to face him, glaring at him with contempt.

He stared at her with a surprise tinged with disbelief and horror. She straightened her arm, feeling the bone click back into place, feeling the warm rush of rejuvenation. She smiled grimly. "One thing I've learned with becoming part-lycan is that bones may break, but bones also heal."

Her father's eyes blazed red, and she flashed her own bloodlust at him. J.J. cried out again, and her father's gaze swiveled to the baby. Vivianne's eyes widened, and she dived just as he launched himself at J.J.

# Chapter 21

Zane skidded as he rounded a bend, emerging into an antechamber. A pot lay overturned on a stove, its contents foul and smoking. A baby's blanket lay on a table, and the roar of lycans echoed from the corridor beyond.

He stepped beyond the chamber and paused at what he saw. A long hallway stretched toward a door that was now shut, a fire extinguisher wedged between the handle to prevent it being opened from the other side. Vampires were pounding on the door, yelling, but as yet, the door held.

Harris leaned against a cell door, blood streaming down his face from a cut above his eye, and his arm badly broken.

At his feet lay three vampire guardians, necks twisted at awkward angles. Harris lifted his gaze, and recognition flared when he saw Zane.

Zane didn't hide his confusion. Harris shrugged, then winced, holding his arm. "They came to kill the prisoners."

Zane's eyes widened. Harris had stopped his own kind

from killing werewolves. He shook his head, still confused. "Why?" Why did this vampire guardian stand—at his own peril—between his own kind and the lycans?

Harris smiled weakly. "My grandmother was a redhead. A sweet little old lady. She made great cakes." He wiped at the blood on his forehead, and it took Zane a moment to realize he hadn't reacted to the sight or scent of blood. "She was also a lycan." Harris moved his head in the direction of the door he leaned against. "They wanted to start with her."

He moved a little so that Zane could peer through the slide window. A young woman with hair that looked like it could have been a burnished red-brown underneath the grime and oil was chained against a wall. She lifted her head, a familiar set of green eyes stared back at him. Caleb's daughter.

"She's a scion," Zane said. He reached for the door handle, then hesitated. He was going to free her. Her and the rest of the werewolves in here. As soon as they saw a vampire, though, all hell would break loose, and after what Harris had done, he didn't deserve to die.

Harris sighed, resigned, as he realized his intent. "You know, this is becoming a habit. Wait," he said, as Zane reached for him. "Give the girl my jacke—"

Zane snapped his neck before he could finish the sentence, and he gently lowered Harris to the ground. He pulled Harris's jacket off him, grimacing at the fluidity of the broken arm in the sleeve, and then yanked the door open, breaking the lock.

"You're Caleb's daughter," he said, to put her at ease as he strode in and pulled the chains from the wall. He slid Harris's jacket over the girl's trembling shoulders.

She nodded. "Rory—Aurora."

He smiled. "Your dad's here. Help me release the others, then you can find him."

She nodded, then stepped toward the door. She stepped over Harris, then turned to look down at the unconscious vampire. "He saved me," she whispered, her brows drawn together in confusion.

Zane nodded. "Yes, he did. You remind him of his grandmother."

Her eyebrows rose as he urged her toward the next door. "You start there. Let's free these people."

He broke the lock on the next door and walked in to break open the chains that bound the lycans. The muscles in his cheek flexed. These people were hurt, damaged. Some were bleeding, but he felt no compulsion to feed off them. Instead, he felt the need to help them.

He peered in the last door, and his shoulders sagged. Nate was inside, his arms chained to the wall, his ankles chained to the floor. His body showed the fight he'd put up, and the abuse he'd taken. His friend lifted his head. One eye was swollen shut, but the other showed his relief when he saw Zane.

Zane pulled the door off its hinges and quickly dispensed with the chains. He caught Nate as he fell, and pulled his arm over his shoulder. Nate's clothes hung from him in rags, torn and bloodied.

"J.J.," Nate said, his voice rough.

Zane nodded. "Let's go find J.J."

He turned to the lycans who gathered in the hallway. The vampires at the door realized the werewolves were freed and began to back away. Zane saw the anger, the pain in the lycans' faces.

"Do what you think is a fair thing," he told them.

Rory walked resolutely toward the fire extinguisher as the others shifted, and suddenly there was a hallway of wolves ready to be let loose.

Zane turned away. Despite these being Vivianne's people, they came down here intending to kill lycans. They deserved whatever punishment the lycans dished out. He didn't look back when he heard the extinguisher clang on the floor, or when he heard the creak of the hinges as Rory opened the door.

He half walked, half carried Nate into the hallway, when a pained screech echoed down another hallway that led off the antechamber, and a baby's cries accompanied it.

"J.J.," Nate rasped.

"Vivianne," Zane said at the same time. They both looked at each other, and then they started running down the hallway, Zane supporting his friend as they went.

Vivianne shifted, bones snapping and reforming, as she wrapped her beast's body around the baby. She felt her father's teeth sink into her shoulder and screeched with the pain. She could feel the blood seep from the wound. She recoiled, twisting around to face her father, teeth bared as she growled a warning at the man who looked like her father, but was indeed a monster.

Vincent Marchetta snapped his teeth at her, and she dodged him, but still kept her body between him and J.J. She growled again, trying to warn her father.

Back. Off.

Fury, hurt, anger, sadness, all the emotions rolled across her in waves, and she didn't know which to go with. Her father was prepared to kill her. Or use her for testing—she wasn't sure which was worse. She couldn't stand it. He was going to kill her—again.

The first time, the realization had almost done the job of the toxin he'd fed her, bringing with it a debilitating pain that almost killed her. He'd coldly, ruthlessly planned her murder, along with her brother's. There was nothing so crushing, so eviscerating, as the realization that your father, one of the people you thought you could trust with your life, was intentionally killing you.

Unless he tried to do it again. Then that *really* hurt.

She lashed out with a claw, catching him on the cheek. She should kill him. After all, he was prepared to kill her. And when he did that, he'd kill J.J. She couldn't let that happen.

She snapped at him, and he recoiled, narrowly avoiding her teeth. Tears formed in her eyes. That had been close. So close, that she realized with all her anger and cold rage, all the resentment that had built up over nine centuries, she couldn't do to him what he had done to her.

She would fight him, but in that minuscule moment, she realized she couldn't kill her father, and from the satisfaction on his face, he must have realized it, too.

He was going to kill her, and then J.J.

She lowered her head and let out a long, rumbling growl. Not without one hell of a fight.

Vincent reached for her, and she barked at him, rising up on her hind legs to hit at him with her front claws. He moved fast, dodging to the side, then twisted to punch her in the gut, winding her. She fell to all fours, wheezing. Of course he'd go for a sucker punch. Even against his daughter, her father fought dirty.

His eyes blazed red, his teeth extended and smiled— *smiled*—at her. "You should have minded your own business, Vivianne." He raised both fists and ran at her.

Zane saw Vivianne in her wolf form, standing over J.J., using her body as a shield between the baby and her father. Then he saw her recoil when Vincent struck her in her stomach, saw her legs shake as she stood guard over the baby. She'd never looked more magnificent, and he'd never feared for her more. He let go of Nate, and when Vincent jumped,

Zane sprang forward, striking the vampire in the jaw with such force, a white tooth flew out and hit the wall opposite.

Vincent rolled along the floor, thumping into the wall. He looked dazed for a moment, and then looked up.

Zane stood in front of Vivianne and J.J., teeth bared, eyes blazing, and he growled at the Reform senator. Vincent bled from one side of his mouth—he'd lost an incisor. Zane rounded his shoulders, clenched his fists, bent his knees—and then a mass of brown fury barreled past him.

The wolf was a moving wall of intensity as he attacked Vincent Marchetta. The senator tried to fight him off, but the wolf was big—and pissed off. Snarling, biting, clawing… Vincent Marchetta didn't stand a chance, and Zane straightened as Nate morphed into his human form once again. He spat out a mouthful of blood, his face an expression of disgust, as he glared down on the now very dead Reform senator.

"You go after our young, we go after you," Nate said in a rough voice. He turned to Zane and paused. Then Nate stretched out his hand, a lycan symbol of shared respect and admiration. Zane clasped his hand briefly, then they both turned.

J.J. was crying, arms raised toward Nate. The dark wolf with deep burgundy highlights stood for a moment guarding him, then moved aside, shakily. Zane caught her as Nate scooped up the baby, clutching him to his chest and saying soft, soothing words that were in such strong contrast to the enraged beast of just a moment before.

Zane dropped to the ground. He felt Vivianne shift in his arm, and held the woman gently to him. Nate startled, his jaw dropping.

"Oh. My. God."

Vivianne shook in his arms, and Zane realized she was crying. "Hey, shh, it's okay," he murmured, stroking her hair back from her forehead. He sat up for a moment to shrug out of his jacket and place it around her shoulders, being extra gentle with the bite wound on her right shoulder. "It's okay," he repeated, scooping her up gently.

She shook her head. "No, I couldn't kill him," she gasped, the tears running down her face as she looked up at him. "He was going after J.J., and I couldn't kill him."

Zane sighed as he rose, holding her in his arms. "It's okay," he whispered. He tilted her head back so her tortured brown gaze met his. "A true werewolf will risk her life to save the young," he said quietly. "You did good."

Nate stepped forward, and Zane met his friend's eyes. Nate's green gaze was somber as he turned to look at the miserable she-wolf in his arms. "And a true werewolf wouldn't—couldn't kill her kin." He cuddled J.J. closer to him. The baby's cries had softened, and now the little boy hiccupped against Nate's chest. "You did good," he said, repeating Zane's words.

Vivianne pulled Zane's jacket around her. It smelled of him. Myrtle. Cedarwood. A hint of almond. She trudged along beside him. She'd insisted she could walk, even though she was so tempted to let Zane carry her. She felt bruised and battered, both physically and emotionally, and just wanted to go home and curl up into a ball under her bed.

Her father was dead.

She knew she'd feel sorrow, and grief, and sadness—at the moment, though, she was numb. Zane said it was shock.

Marchettas didn't succumb to shock, though. She straightened her shoulders, then looked over at Nate. He was carrying a now sleeping J.J. in his arms, but every now and then his gaze darted to both her and Zane, and she could see the conflict in his eyes.

Zane halted, his arm across her body, and she realized belatedly that the battle wasn't over.

Screams, yells, grunts, growls—they could be heard faintly down the hall. More vampires, more werewolves, and all of them sounded like they were at war. Zane looked over at Nate and the baby. "Stay here," he said, and Nate nodded.

Vivianne met Zane's gaze. He arched an eyebrow. "Are you up for this?"

"That depends what 'this' is," she replied simply.

"Our folks are fighting among themselves," he said. "We should stop them."

Our folks. Not lycans versus werewolves, but "our folks." She realized he'd accepted his vampirism, and considered the vampires as relevant, as respect-worthy, as his lycans. After going up against her father, and wanting to look after J.J., she could relate. She nodded.

They both stepped into the antechamber, and for a moment, all was chaos.

Zane growled, a sound so loud, so intense, a couple of broken doors fell completely off their hinges. And frankly, it made Vivianne step back and look at the man who seemed to become the alpha of all alphas when she wasn't looking.

Everyone froze, then slowly turned their attention to the two figures at the end of the room.

"Cease," Zane rumbled, his voice deeper than anything she'd ever heard before. His eyes were red with warning, his fangs were out. He was the embodiment of all the strength and nobility of both races. In that moment, everything coalesced into one crystal, sharp realization.

Zane was her mate. Her true life mate. He was strong enough to let her take her independence and do with it what she will, and strong enough to assert himself with both lycans and vampires, and in that moment, she loved him.

One of the vampires shifted, and she growled in warning, her own eyes flashing as she bared her teeth. He fell back, his face encased in shock.

She glared at everyone in the room. "All Nightwing vampires, stand down," she said, her voice carrying along the hallway. "Vincent Marchetta is dead. If you are Nightwing, stand down. If you are Marchetta, step forward." All of the vampires shifted back, and she nodded.

"All lycans, stand down," Zane growled.

She recognized Caleb, alpha prime of River Pack, as he stepped forward. "They stole our young. Why the hell should we stand down?" He glared at her.

"Because this was engineered. Everyone here has been manipulated," Zane responded. "By fighting, you give the puppeteers exactly what they want." He grinned. "And we're a perverse lot."

"Be assured," Vivianne spoke up, "what happened here—Nightwing were lied to just as much as you. We accept responsibility for our actions, though, and I will discuss reparation with all parties." She looked meaningfully at Caleb. "I, for one, am truly sorry for what has happened here," she said softly. Any father who would fight to keep his daughter *alive* had her full attention and respect. "And I intend to make sure it never happens again."

Caleb's eyes narrowed, but a young woman draped in a large coat stepped forward to tug on his arm. He frowned at the girl, but whatever she said to her father made him nod reluctantly.

A slight shuffling noise echoed down the hallway, and she turned to see Dave Carter, the witch, emerge. Behind him was a troupe of about a dozen people, all of whom she couldn't quite get a read on. Vampire? Werewolf? Human? Witch?

Dave looked about the room. He clutched his side but otherwise looked strong and healthy. His expression showed disappointment. "Did I miss the fight?" he asked, surprised. Vivianne glanced around the room. Everyone was quiet, somber, but at least the blood zest had been taken out of the situation. She nodded.

Dave swore, then, "Well, at least tell me I'm in time for the beers?"

Zane reluctantly smiled at the comment as the were-wolves cheered. The vampires nodded, then retreated quietly, picking up their dead and injured as they went.

Dave crossed over to them, and newcomers followed closely behind. The witch smiled as he looked at Zane and Vivianne. "Well, aren't you two a surprise?"

"Did you know?" Vivianne asked him. "Did you know we were...changing?"

Dave moved his hand from side to side. "Sort of. I got a weird reading off both of you." He sobered. "I had to see whether you could handle the change, or whether it was a mistake I had to rectify."

Vivianne's eyebrows rose. By rectify, she assumed...kill.

"And you think we can handle it, then?" she asked quietly.

Dave looked at Zane and nodded. "Yeah, I do," he said. "So much so that I think you can help these folks." He indicated the group behind him. "These people were under your father's home when Natalie was captured," he murmured.

Vivianne's eyes widened. Natalie's blood had saved her, turned her—and by association, Zane—into something... different. And these people were just like her and Zane... different.

Zane nodded. "We can help them," he said, eyeing the group. He nodded once more. "Yeah. Definitely."

# Epilogue

Four months later, Vivianne walked into the building she now called home. She yawned. The house had been built on the rise above the site that had once been her father's facility. That had been demolished, and while there were still things that needed to be completed, the large house had a roof, a floor and walls, and indoor plumbing. Zane and the rest of the group were currently working on the final touches. Like carpet. She was so looking forward to carpet. She'd discovered a new affiliation for all things tactile in the past few months.

Vivianne clutched her stomach as a wave of nausea rolled over her. *Ugh*. She'd been dealing with the side effects of the mating bond since the night her father died. She'd expected it to dissipate, but it must take a little longer. She and Zane still couldn't seem to get enough of each other, and she still sensed him, just as he sensed her—Zane had told her that wouldn't change.

She'd expected the perspiration and butterflies in her stomach to go, though, and was trying to be patient.

Her engagement ring sparkled in the sunlight. That had been another shock, and one Lucien had finally told her to test. Having the Lycanism traits, she'd discovered she was now a Daywalker—as was her brother, the sneaky bastard. She shook her head. She still found it hard to believe her life at the moment. Once she had negotiated reparation with River, Alpine and Woodland Packs, she'd stepped down from the Vampire Prime position. Harris now ruled the colony, and while he had his own internal squabbles to deal with, he was establishing control with an ease that made her both surprised and proud.

The facility had been demolished. Completely. As had any records that had been created during the time of its operation. Lucien had transferred the Vale property to her personally, and Zane and she were working with all those affected by her father's first round of medical experiments. Each of them manifested the combined traits slightly differently, and she was surprised and impressed by Zane's patience as he worked with each of them. He was a master of control—as he'd proven in their bed time and delicious time again—and had earned the respect and loyalty of each of the "experimentals," as they were called. So much so that the group had petitioned Reform council, and just two weeks ago they were formally recognized as the Vale Pack, a hybrid breed with the same rights and privileges as the other breeds. The pack voted unanimously, and Zane was now the proud alpha prime of Vale Pack.

She trotted up the stairs and into the master bedroom, and halted when she saw Zane putting the mattress on their new, oversize bed. On carpet.

"Oh, it's beautiful," she said, dropping down to run her hands over the charcoal-gray plush fibers. It was soft and silky to the touch, and the smell of new carpet and timber filled her nose. She closed her eyes. "Thank you."

Zane chuckled as he knelt down next to her. "You like it, huh? Maybe we should christen it?" He cupped her cheek, leaning forward to kiss her gently, and she sighed as she closed her eyes and leaned into him. He winked, then twisted, laying her gently onto the carpet, and followed her down with a scorching kiss. He made her head swim.

Her eyes flicked open. Like, literally. Oh, God. She pushed him off her and sat bolt upright to keep the contents of her stomach exactly where they should be—in her stomach.

"Oh, ugh, I'm so sorry," she said, covering her hands with her face.

"Hey, it's okay, it's fine," Zane assured her as he rubbed her back soothingly.

"No, it's not okay," she said, pouting as she peered through her fingers at him. "I thought once I accepted the mating bond, all this sick stuff would go away. The perspiration, the nausea—it's getting worse, not better."

Zane bit his lip as he sat up next to her. "Uh, this isn't the mating bond," he told her gently.

She lowered her hands. "It isn't? What the hell is it, then?"

Zane hesitated, then slid his hand under the bed. "I need to show you something." He pulled out a gift box. "This is for you," he said, his voice all husky.

She accepted the box, but her brows dipped slightly. "A present?"

"Open it. It might explain a few things," he told her softly.

She gave him a sulky look that made him bite his lip harder and lifted up the lid. Inside was a swathe of blue fabric. She lifted it out of the box, frowning in confusion—Oh, it was so lovely and soft, but, seriously?

"A baby blanket? I don't get it. Why do we need a—" She stopped talking, her eyes widening. "Noooo," she gasped.

Zane nodded. "Yessss," he whispered.

She shook her head, tears forming in her eyes. "But I can't… Vampires…"

He smiled, his brown eyes warm with those beautiful hazel-green highlights. "You're not just a vampire, anymore," he told her softly. He took her hand and placed it on her stomach. "Listen."

She stopped breathing, petrified to believe him.

And there it was, a faint but strong, *thump-thump-thump* in rapid succession. A little heartbeat.

She lifted her gaze in wonder at Zane, and his smile broadened. "A baby?" she squeaked.

He nodded. "A baby."

She threw herself into his arms, and he laughed as they toppled back on the carpet. He caught her lips in a passionate kiss, and she responded, wrapping her arms and legs around him. He rolled them gently, bearing his weight on his arms as he pulled back to gaze down at her.

"You are the only woman who can truly drive me crazy, but you're also my sanity," he said softly, his voice low and deep. "I love you." His face became serious. "You brought out the alpha in me, and gave me a pack." He sighed. "I'm a better man because of you."

She smiled up at him, tears streaming down her face. "You were always my alpha." She hugged him. "And you gave me a happy-ever-after, and now…a real family of my own," she whimpered, then started kissing him all over his face. "I love you, I love you, I love you."

He made a noise, a rumble that reverberated through his chest, as he kissed her back. Her beast responded to his. She felt joy, she felt love, and those same emotions were feeding back to her from him. She pulled back and gave him a mock frown. "Annoying?"

He nodded. "Oh, very annoying. But for some reason I find that very sexy." He lowered his head and kissed her thoroughly. She relaxed beneath him, sighing as that same, ever-present passion awoke inside her.

"Sexy, huh?"

"Uh-huh." He started to unbutton her silk blouse as he kissed his way down her neck.

"How sexy?" she asked breathlessly, arching against him.

"Let me show you."

And show her, he did.

\* \* \* \* \*

**Deborah LeBlanc** is an award-winning, bestselling author from Lafayette, Louisiana. She is also a licensed death scene investigator, a private investigator and has been a paranormal investigator for over twenty years. Deborah is currently the house "clairsendium" (clairvoyant/sensitive/medium) for the upcoming paranormal investigation television show *Through the Veil*.

In 2007, Deborah founded Literacy Inc., a nonprofit organization dedicated to fighting illiteracy in America's teens.

For more information, visit deborahleblanc.com and literacyinc.com.

### Books by Deborah LeBlanc

#### Harlequin Nocturne

*The Wolven*
*The Fright Before Christmas*
*Witch's Hunger*
*The Witch's Thirst*
*Witch's Fury*

# WITCH'S FURY

Deborah LeBlanc

To my family for their love and patience.

# Chapter 1

Over the past three weeks, Gilly François and her sisters, Vivienne and Evette, had been living a nightmare that the triplets couldn't seem to wake from. The sisters, known as the Triad—a special set of witches—were at a loss over all of the strange and unusual events that had been occurring lately. Each sister was responsible for otherworldly creatures known as the Originals, the first of their breed. Gilly took care of the Chenilles, the original zombies, Viv the Loup-Garous, the original werewolves, and Evee the Nosferatu, the original vampires. Lately, however, no one seemed capable of taking care of anything or anyone.

Chenilles had been slaughtered, just like Loup-Garous and Nosferatu. Even worse, many of the members of their Originals factions had simply disappeared, leaving the safe haven created by the Triad years ago.

Although the sisters had cast additional protection and boundary spells over their assigned territories, more times than not, the spells appeared ineffective. The killings continued.

Feeling at a loss and hopeless, the Triad were nearing their wits' end when four men showed up on their doorstep: Nikoli, Lucien, Ronan and Gavril Hyland. They'd said they were cousins, known as Benders, and had been sent to New Orleans to help the Triad. Whatever they were, there was no denying they were all tall, muscular and drop-dead gorgeous.

Along with their arrival, the cousins brought unsettling news. They revealed that the local deaths of the Triad's Originals were not due to infighting among the factions as the Triad had first suspected. According to the cousins, the deaths were coming by way of creatures known as Cartesians—massive, monstrous creatures with long, razor-sharp talons and teeth. Their bodies were protected by inch-thick scales that hid behind a heavy matting of fur. Their job as Benders, a special generational group of men ordained by the Church centuries ago, was to destroy the Cartesians.

Gilly and her sisters had heard of the Cartesians before but only in folkloric tales. According to legend, Cartesians were an invisible lot, only revealing themselves occasionally. They fed on other-worldly creatures, anything whose life force exceeded that of an average human, which, of course, included the Triad.

Although it had taken some time for the Hylands to convince Gilly and her sisters that the men weren't a few cards short of a deck, the Triad was eventually convinced. So much so that they'd decided to split up into three groups with the Benders to cover more territory in search of their missing Originals. Viv worked with Nikoli, Gilly with Gavril and Evee with both Lucien and Ronan.

Sadly, in the midst of a surprise attack on Evee, Ronan, whom Evee knew had a crush on her, had rushed over to save her and had been gored in the head by a Cartesian's massive talons. The Cartesian had then disappeared with Ronan into another dimension. Evee and Lucien had witnessed it all; Nikoli had contacted the family back home and notified them of Ronan's death.

Gilly had been sure that after that horrid event, the Benders would be off to their homeland to help console their family and help with Ronan's memorial service. Instead, they'd chosen to stay in New Orleans. It was evident to Gilly that the Benders met their commitments and finished their missions, no matter what.

The Triad had even set up an elaborate feeding system in Algiers, across the river from New Orleans, using cattle as their feeding stock, so the Originals were always satiated: the Nosferatu fed on the blood, the Loup-Garous on the meat and the Chenilles on the bone marrow. But despite the appearance of the Benders and their offer to help, things had started to take a turn for the worse, and quickly. Word from the Triad's Elders was that some of the missing Originals had already moved out of New Orleans proper and murdered two people.

In the midst of all the chaos, the Triad met with their Elders—Arabella, Taka and Vanessa—to ask for their advice, help and understanding.

Unfortunately, not only were the Triad's powers beginning to wane, but the Elders' powers were, as well. Everything from binding to comehither spells worked, didn't work, or barely worked. The last two symptoms became more dominant each day. The only advice the Elders had to offer was to possibly speak to the three sorcerers who lived in New Orleans, in hopes they might be able to break through this spell malaise.

While meeting with the Elders, it was discovered that Viv and Evee had already been intimate with their Benders—more than once. The revelation came by way of the Triad's familiars, all three of which snitched on their mistress for what they thought to be the greater good. Appalled, the Elders demanded that they no longer have any intimate contact with the Benders. Triad members were forbidden to marry or live intimately with humans. If so, they'd lose their powers completely, and the Originals they were there to protect would run amuck, killing humans at will.

Evee and Viv tried to deny that they had been romantically involved with the Benders. But to the Elders, what else explained why things had taken such a severe turn for the worse? It had to be because Gilly's two sisters had sex with their search partners, and the reason their powers were waning Although Gilly had spoken to her sisters about that hypothesis and they had agreed that it might be a possibility, neither Evee nor Viv seemed to regret their actions.

So far, Gilly was the only member of her Triad who hadn't had sex with a Bender, and it wasn't for lack of desire. Every time Gilly saw Gavril, the only thing that crossed her mind, no matter what else might be going on, was kissing his full bottom lip. She wanted to stare into his violet eyes and run her fingers through his collar-length, ginger-colored hair. She could have wrapped up her emotions in one huge, lust-filled package, but it didn't explain why her heart ached when he wasn't near. As much as she longed for him, she supposed guilt played a part in allowing it to go any further. After the Elders had found out that Viv and Evee had been intimate with their Benders, they'd confessed their senses of guilt to Gilly. They worried about the role their intimacy played in making things worse. But despite worry and guilt, however, they both declared that the drive, need and love for their men kept them going back for more.

"Fifty bucks for your thoughts," Gavril said, as they

walked to St. Louis I cemetery to check on the remaining Chenilles.

She gave him a sideways grin. "Isn't it, 'a penny for your thoughts'?" The Benders had been with the Triad for a little over two weeks now, and the longer they stayed, the more Gavril tugged on her heart strings. His looks were one thing, but she so admired his drive and determination, his caring, thoughtful manner, and his do or die attitude when it came to accomplishing any task.

Gilly and Gavril had been searching incessantly for her missing Chenilles. By last count, twenty-five had gone missing. If her brood wasn't found before feeding time, chances were extremely high that they would start attacking humans for food. The police were getting involved, and that scared Gilly to death.

The last thing Gilly would admit to anyone, however— especially her sisters—was how badly she wanted Gavril. So badly, in fact, that it wasn't unusual for her to have wet dreams about him. She felt a bit guilty about that. Viv's entire troupe of Loup-Garous had vanished, as had Evee's lot of Nosferatu. She should be thinking of them, of helping them, while keeping track of her own Originals.

She and her sisters had spent their lives working hard to fit into the social day to day of New Orleans so as not to draw suspicion that they were witches. They were also ultra-careful in tending to their Originals, keeping them out of the way, in safe zones, so humans wouldn't find them. They lived in the Garden District and made sure to play nice with the neighbors at all times.

"So I'm a big spender. Besides, you haven't said three words to me since we left Evee's café to come to the cemetery. You looked so lost in thought, at times, I was sure you'd run headlong into a lamppost." Gavril stopped walking and took hold of her arm gently, stopping her movement and turning her toward him. "I know things are crazy right now, but aside from that, are you okay?"

Gilly sighed. "Yes and no. I wish I could be more help to my sisters, but I know I have my own Originals to look after."

When she stopped speaking, Gavril studied her face. His eyes pierced hers, looking for more answers than what she'd just given him.

Gilly bit the corner of her mouth, unable to resist the questions in his eyes. "And I'm scared. So much has gotten out of control that I don't know if we'll ever know normalcy again."

Gavril ran his hand up and down her arm with a soothing touch. "All we can do is the best we can do. You can't explain why some of you and your sisters' spells aren't working, or if you know you haven't told me about it, and I have no idea why the scabior canopies are failing. I mean, this has never been done before, not to my knowledge, but it should react similar to our scabiors, which never just go out."

The Benders had assured the sisters that the Cartesians were not fictional creatures but real, vicious monstrosities that were determined to be the sole power in the netherworld, a three-dimensional place that held vampires, elves, djinn and other supernatural creatures. They had also dispelled the myth that Cartesians moved under the cloak of invisibility. It only appeared that way because Cartesians were able to slip in and out of physical dimensions in the blink of an eye.

The Hylands were able to track Cartesians by their scent, which was a noxious odor of sulfur and clove. They'd been taught, as were their fathers and grandfathers before them, how to battle the giant hellions in order to protect those who lived in the underworld. They did so by using a special weapon called a scabior—a six-inch rod of steel with a bloodstone attached to one end—which was handed down from generation to generation.

Not long after the Benders had arrived, in order for them to find the missing Originals and keep the ones they had safe, they'd created a scabior canopy, an electrical shelter that hovered over each safe zone. No Cartesian would be able to drop in through that crisscrossed electrical current.

"But they did go out. One of them, anyway—Evee's, the one Lucien set up in the catacombs for the Nosferatu. Remember? He told us he'd had to recharge the current. Then, before we knew it, it was completely out, and all of the Nosferatu that were inside disappeared."

"I know."

"How could that happen?"

Gavril frowned and shrugged. "It's as much a mystery to me as it is to you. What's stranger still is that the canopy was still intact over the north compound, where Viv kept her Loup-Garous, yet all of them disappeared."

"Yeah," Gilly said. "Explain that one."

"I wish I could, but I have no answers. The canopies were something that had never been done before, just a brainstorming idea that seemed to make sense, so we really don't know their power or capabilities. As for the Loup-Garous going missing with the shield over the compound still operational, it's beyond me. The only thing I can figure is that they purposely chose to leave."

Gilly shook her head. "That doesn't make any sense. Their food is there. Safety is there."

"That may be, but if they've never known anything else but the safe zones, they have no way of knowing what they face once they escape it."

Gilly lowered her head reluctantly. She didn't want to break eye contact with Gavril. His gaze consumed her, no matter the topic of conversation. The rest of him was nothing shy of downright hulk, bulk and sexuality. He exuded all three.

Although Gilly had never asked his age, Gavril appeared to be in his mid-thirties. He stood at least six foot four and had a body and face built for *GQ*—wide shoulders, biceps that looked like he could lift an elephant one-handed and, even from the black T-shirt he wore, the ripples in his abs were evident. His violet eyes were accented by a short, red beard, an aquiline nose and a cleft chin. His hair, the same color as his beard, sat just below shoulder length. His lips were always something Gilly worked hard to avoid looking at. Average upper, thick bottom, a mouth made for kissing. For deep, passionate kisses, not only on her own lips but all over her body.

When she looked back up at him, his eyes were still on her face. "Right now, our best move is to make sure your Chenilles are okay in their safe zone and lead them to their feeding. Once that's done, you bring them back here, and we keep hunting for the ones that're missing."

Gilly watched his lips as he spoke, feeling warmth spread through her body. She had to concentrate hard on his words as they were damn near lost to her need for him. So much of this felt odd, yet wonderful to her. It had been at least a year and a half since she'd dated. Since a committed human relationship was forbidden, she'd kept her dates limited, never with the same man twice.

With a feeling of reluctance, Gilly felt Gavril release her arm. "We're almost at the cemetery. I'll wait across the street near the voodoo shop, where it's darkest. Once you have them on their way to the docks, I'll follow but at a distance."

Gilly nodded. "No heroics, okay? Remember, the Chenilles are going to be ravenous by this time. If they see you before I can get them on the ferry and across to the compound, we'll be the ones contacting your family about your death." Gilly regretted her words the moment they came out of her mouth. A cloud of sorrow and depression crossed Gavril's face, and she was sure he was thinking of Ronan. What an insensitive ass she was.

"I mean—"

"I know what you mean," Gavril said, the light returning to his eyes. "No worries. I'll be careful."

Knowing that the François family ferry was waiting at the dock for her Chenilles, Gilly signaled Gavril to go into the shadows. Then she went into the cemetery to round up her brood.

As the Chenilles exited the cemetery—following Gilly's lead Chenille, Patrick—Gilly stood by the cemetery gates and took count as they went by. Ten more short than the last count, and as best she could tell, the scabior dome was still intact and operational. Being led by Patrick, the Chenilles followed in pairs. Their tall, thin figures bent over at the waist slightly, their beautiful faces intent on the Chenille before it. It was feeding time, and every Chenille knew it, which was what kept them from breaking formation and made it easy to walk them through the shadows and alleys to the dock.

Not having time to stop and give Gavril the news, she hurried over to Patrick's side and led her Originals to the docks, winding through side alleys and behind buildings to remain undetected.

Once they were loaded onto the ferry, Gilly got on. As the boat began to move, Gavril came out of the shadows and watched her, and she watched him. With the distance between them growing, Gilly could have sworn she saw Gavril give her the smallest wave goodbye and then lay his hand over his heart. If she was right and hadn't mistaken the gesture for some odd shadow, the thought of him making that heart tap made her heart feel full to the point of bursting. It took a lot of will power for her not to return the gesture. But what if she'd been mistaken in what she thought she saw? What would he think? That she was having a heart attack and attempt to get to her? Or would he see it for what it was and think she was making a move on him?

Deciding to play it safe, Gilly faced forward, glancing occasionally at the water lapping on either side of the ferry, and forced her mind to focus on business.

With Viv's Loup-Garous and Evee's Nosferatu both missing, her clan would have to use their screw-like incisors to drill down hide and meat to get to the bone. Marrow fed them, and they were used to having fresh bone to suck from when brought in for a feeding. Usually the Nosferatu had drained the cattle of blood, and the Loup-Garous had eaten the meat from the same. This left only the bone for the Chenilles to deal with. Now that wouldn't be the case, however. She didn't have any idea how they'd react to this change.

Viv was waiting for her on the Algiers side of the river, as was Evee.

"The cattle are in the feeding area like always," Viv said loudly so her voice carried over the ferry motor. "Lead them down the feeding shoot like usual. We'll be waiting for you here, behind the trees, over there, while they feed."

Nodding her understanding, Gilly moored the ferry to the dock and saw her sisters in her peripheral vision hurry off behind the grove of trees nearby.

Gilly unlatched the back gate of the ferry, led her troupe down a winding path, and once they came to the front of the feeding shoot, no more direction was needed. The Chenilles took off at a dead run, all of them ravenous and anxious for the food awaiting them.

In the distance, Gilly heard a few Chenilles whine, while

others grumbled, obviously displeased over the fact that they'd have to do so much work to get to marrow. Once all had quieted down, and the only sound she heard was the crunch of bone, Gilly went back to the dock to meet Viv and Evee.

"Any issues?" Viv asked.

"Some whining, a few sounding pissed off," Gilly said. "But at least they're eating."

Evee let out a shaky sigh that sounded very much like she was close to tears. "What are we going to do? We can't keep running around the city looking for our Originals. We've run out of time. With so many Nosferatu and Loup-Garous missing, human deaths are going to become the norm—every day."

"We can't give up," Gilly said. "If we do, we're already defeated."

"I'd call losing an entire troupe of Originals pretty much defeat," Viv said. "I have no idea why my Loups left. The north compound was their home. Why would they just walk away from it?"

"*If* they walked away from it," Gilly said. "We really don't know what's happened to them."

She suddenly looked up and about as if just remembering something. "Where the hell are Nikoli and Lucien? They're supposed to be with you, protecting you. Or did they forget that those ugly sons of bitches determined to kill all of our Originals intend to kill us, as well?"

Viv held up a hand as if to stop Gilly's tirade. "Nikoli's still back at the hotel, dealing with his family about Ronan's death. Lucien went to check on him."

"To check on him?" Gilly huffed. "The man's six-four, if he's an inch, and built like a tank. What's to check on?"

"Emotions," Evee said. "I know you're worried about us, Gilly, but you can't forget that these men, no matter their size, have hearts. And right now they're mourning the loss of a close cousin."

"Yeah, whatever," Gilly said. "So is that the excuse I use if one of you gets chewed up by those sky assholes?"

"Chill, okay," Viv said. "We're fine. We'll leave here as soon as you get the Chenilles back city side, and the ferry makes it back here."

"I don't like it," Gilly said. "You're too out in the open. If something happens to one of you…well, it ain't gonna be pretty for Nikoli and Lucien. That's all I've gotta say."

With small shakes of their heads, Viv and Evee cocked an ear toward the feeding area.

"Sounds like they're about done," Gilly said. "Patrick will lead them back here, so go hide behind a tree or something, will you? The last thing I want is for one of my own to get to either of you."

Doing as they were asked, Viv and Evee ducked into a grove of trees just as Patrick led the now satiated Chenilles back to the ferry. They boarded lethargically, all of them seemingly overfed.

Once everyone was on board, Gilly closed the back gate of the ferry, kicked the motor on and steered the ferry to city side, where she knew Gavril would be waiting. She wished the ferry had a throttle, wanting it to go faster. All she cared about right now was seeing his face and getting her sisters back from the compound safely. But there was no throttle, so she had to tolerate the chug-chug of the engine and snail crawl of motion until they reached the other side.

After unlocking the back gate, Gilly motioned for Patrick to take her troupe back to the cemetery and make sure they were hidden in old crypts that had been busted open by vandals or in between any open mausoleum slots.

Patrick nodded and, with a grunt, motioned for the other Chenilles to follow him, which they did. Their steps were lumbering, as if trying to balance oversized bellies as they walked.

When they were well out of sight, Gilly uttered an incantation that sent the ferry back to Algiers for Viv and Evee to board. She waited at the water's edge, nervously biting her nails, her insides shaking. Her nerves were already shot with all that had been going on, but thinking that her sisters might get hurt by a stalking Cartesian en route made her nerves so bad, she thought she'd vomit.

"They'll be fine," a man's voice said behind her. And it took a nanosecond for Gilly to recognize it as Gavril's. He put his hands on her shoulders and leaned closer to her ear. "I promise. They'll be fine. And as soon as they return, they'll have Nikoli and Lucien at their sides at all times. That I assure you."

"But what if—"

"You can 'what if' until the cows come home," Gavril whispered into her ear. "But the key is to think positive. Visualize them back here safe and sound. Nothing will happen to them."

Gilly turned toward him, Gavril's hands still on her shoulders. "Nobody can know for sure. Crap happens, you know?"

Gavril let out a chuckle. "That's one thing I like about you, Ms. François. You do speak your mind, no matter what crosses it."

"It's not funny," Gilly said. "They're alone out there and—"

"Look," Gavril whispered and turned Gilly around. There in the distance was the ferry, already headed city side. From the light of the moon, Gilly easily made out Viv and Evee, both standing near the landing gate. She let out a breath of relief she didn't even realize she'd been holding.

Instinctively, Gilly reached up and covered one of

Gavril's hands with her own. The spark of electricity that went through her when they touched shocked her, and Gilly quickly removed her hand. She thought of the Elders' warning not to be intimate with the Benders, as doing so might be their undoing. Yet she couldn't help but think of Evee and Viv. Both had received the same warning but continued their relationships with Lucien and Nikoli.

Gilly helped maneuver the ferry into its slip and hugged each of her sisters as they walked off the ferry.

"What's with the mushy stuff?" Viv asked with a laugh. "We only saw you a few minutes ago. You're acting like you haven't seen us in a year."

"Mushy stuff, huh?" Gilly huffed. "Just glad both of you are safely here."

"Me, too," Evee said, with a worried expression on her face. "Me, too."

Gavril watched as Gilly greeted her sisters, and felt his heart swell. As tough and independent as Gilly might have come across to the rest of the world, Gavril had been fortunate to see more. He'd seen how hard she could love, how deep her loyalties ran, her tenderness when the moment called for it.

Simply watching her interact with her sisters now, Gavril could not deny the fact that he was falling for Gilly and falling hard. This filled his heart and took him aback at the same time.

Gavril had dated more than his share of women over the years, but not one of them had affected him the way Gilly did. This had him walking in unfamiliar territory, which made him a bit nervous. He didn't want to move too fast or too slow, and knowing either with Gilly was a hard call. Aside from that, he had to keep his mind on the matter that had brought him here in the first place—the Cartesians.

Worrying about how to approach Gilly with his feelings had to come second. His first order of business had to be protecting the Triad and the remaining Originals from the Cartesians. The problem was, every time Gavril saw Gilly, his mind took a hard left without permission, and all he could see or concentrate on was her.

Regardless of how he felt, he had to gain control over his emotions and focus on protection. He'd tried comforting Gilly earlier by telling her to focus on Evee and Viv returning on the ferry safe and sound. The whole time he'd been trying to convince her that they would return safely, he'd been worried about their safety. Both Evee and Viv had been out alone without a Bender to protect them from Cartesians. And having a Triad member out alone when the Cartesians were after them along with their Originals was like teasing a catfish with a fat, juicy worm.

He was just as grateful to see them return safely as Gilly had been. Now, however, things had to change. No more outings without a Bender in tow. And no matter what it took to make that happen, even when it came to feeding the Originals, Gavril would make sure it did.

## Chapter 2

"What now?" Gilly asked as she, Gavril, Viv and Evee walked away from the docks.

"More hunting," Gavril said. They crossed a broken piece of sidewalk, and Gavril placed a hand on the small of Gilly's back to maneuver her around it.

"Our hunting skills suck," Gilly said.

"Yeah," Viv said. "All we've gotten out of hunting for our missing Originals is more missing Originals. There has to be a better way to tackle this."

"I think it's time to hit our Grimoires," Evee said, referring to their book of spells. "Read through them to see if there's not a spell we've missed or one we can alter slightly that might help us."

"You can't just alter a spell," Gilly said gruffly. "You change it, and it changes the outcome."

Evee frowned. "It was just a thought."

"And a good one," Viv said. She gave Gilly a warning

scowl, and then she laid a hand on Evee's shoulder, trying to reassure her. "It wouldn't hurt for us to look at our Grimoires. I vote we go through them…just to be sure."

"Well, if that's the case," Gavril said. "I'll walk the three of you home, then go to the hotel and meet up with Nikoli and Lucien to make sure the arrangements are set up for Ronan. Knowing Nikoli, the details have already been set in stone, though."

"Then why go?" Gilly said and then felt embarrassed for asking.

"Support," Gavril said. "Everyone can use some from time to time. The three of you look through your books, and we'll go back to the hotel and wrap up a few things regarding Ronan with our families. Let's say the six of us meet up in front of St. John's Cathedral in a couple hours."

"Sounds good," Viv said.

"Fine. Two hours," Gilly said, and the she turned on her heels and started for home. She made sure she stayed at the lead as she didn't want Gavril to see the disappointment on her face. She didn't like the fact that he was leaving—for any amount of time.

"Slow down, will you?" Evee said as they neared the Garden District. "We're not running a marathon."

Gilly tsked and glanced over her shoulder at Evee. "No, but the sooner we're off the streets, the better."

When they finally reached home, Gilly unlocked the front door and marched into the foyer. She heard Viv reiterate to Gavril that they'd meet in front of the cathedral in two hours. After closing the door behind her, Viv turned on Gilly.

"What the heck's wrong with you? He only offered to walk us home, and you'd have sworn he carried a contagion the way you stormed ahead."

Gilly pulled off her T-shirt in the middle of the kitchen

and started making her way to the stairs in order to shower and dress. "I wasn't storming ahead," she declared. "Just because I walk faster than you, it doesn't mean anything else."

Gilly heard Evee let out a giggle, and she stopped and glared at her sister. "What's with that? I don't find any of it funny."

"I know why you were acting weird coming home," Evee said.

"Oh, yeah, Smarty? Why?"

"Because you like him," Evee said. "You didn't want Gavril to leave."

"Aw, that's bull-crap," Gilly proclaimed, and she walked into the foyer and started stomping up the stairs to her room.

"No, it's not," Evee said. "Admit it, Abigail François. You like Gavril Hyland."

"Stop acting like a pubescent teen," Gilly shouted down at her. She hated when anyone used her full first name. It made her sound like a wuss. "I'm going to shower."

By the time Gilly made it to her bedroom, Elvis, her albino ferret familiar, was stretched on her bed. He greeted her with a big yawn.

"She's right, you know," Elvis said.

"About what?" Gilly asked, stripping out of the rest of her clothes.

"You liking that Hyland guy."

"Oh, for the love of peace, would you stop already? I'm getting enough crap from Evee about that, and it just isn't true."

"But it—"

Naked, Gilly spun about on her heels and faced Elvis. "One more word out of you, and I'll dunk you in cold water, got it?" Elvis hated to have his body immersed in water, much less cold, which Gilly had done to him by accident a year ago. She'd been holding Elvis while filling a tub with water. Before the water temperature had crawled to warm, as it often took the time to do in their big old house, she'd tripped and accidentally dropped Elvis into the tub. He'd howled and shrieked and sprang up on all fours out of the tub, then ran out of the bathroom into hiding. He'd stayed angry with her about the incident for weeks.

Elvis lay his head down and covered it with his front paws.

Once in the shower, and away from Elvis' badgering and Evee's teasing, Gilly relaxed under the hot spray and thought about Gavril. It wasn't so much how he looked that tantalized her, although his Adonis-like handsomeness was nothing to spit at, it was who he was that intrigued her. It was the intensity with which he tackled any project he put his hand to, his gentleness when he touched her and the caring he showed for his family, which seemed as strong as what she felt for her own. She had a strong sense that Gavril felt for her the same way she felt for him. The way his eyes gazed into hers, how they never moved away from her face when she spoke, as if every word uttered held an importance that needed to be understood. Not once had he ever spoken over her. And the most beautiful thing about him, to her, anyway, was the way he seemed to be able to read her mind. To comfort her without her asking. To give her space without prompting. He accepted her for who and what she was. Never showing a hint of disgust or frustration. Not even when she dropped an F-bomb on occasion. In all of her adult years, Gilly had yet to meet a man with all those wonderful qualities.

Oh, and the way he smelled. An earthy scent, a manly scent with the slightest hint of cinnamon. It made her feel like a starving woman ready, needing, to consume all he had to offer.

It was easy to find one or two of these qualities in men,

Gilly knew, but she had never known one man to possess them all. It was that and so much more that kept Gavril at the front of her thoughts. How would she ever find another man whom she felt had been so perfectly designed for her? She could only wish and hope he felt the same.

With his looks, Gilly was sure that he could have any woman he desired. All he'd have to do was look her way and smile, and any woman would melt like cream on a hot sidewalk at his feet. The thought of that jumbled Gilly's belly with jealousy, and seemed to turn the water about ten degrees colder.

Scrubbing her face with her hands, Gilly let the thought of other women go down the drain with the dirty water she washed from her body. If anything, she'd discovered in the few days she'd known him that Gavril was as loyal as they came. And jealousy was not her strong suit, anyway, which was another piece of the puzzle that made their match perfect.

Only one square peg refused to complete the picture. That peg was the one the Elders had thrown in their lap by demanding that the Triad have nothing more to do with the Benders. They'd reminded the Triad that having relationships with the Benders would be their undoing, which in turn and in the end, would be the destruction of the world.

As Gilly stepped out of the shower and dried her body, she repeated what the Elders had said verbatim in her mind. Although she easily remembered their remarks word for word, she found them unfair and questionable. If having a relationship with a Bender would be the end of them, then what about Viv and Evee? Both had sex with their Benders but were still around, their powers on par with her own. She was the only one who hadn't experienced hers. She wanted desperately to change that, but what if the Elders had been right? What if more intimacy with the Benders meant more destruction, more discord and more deaths among the Originals and humans in the city? Was she willing to take the chance and find out? The more she thought about it, though, the less sense it made. If the Elders' words of warning were to be taken verbatim, then Viv and Evee would be useless as witches right now. Gilly couldn't help but wonder if after all the centuries of interpretation, their Elders might have gotten something wrong or out of context.

After throwing Elvis a warning glance to keep his mouth shut, Gilly went to her closet, chose a pair of light blue linen pants and a short-waisted white cotton pullover. She pulled on a pair of ankle socks, shoved her feet into a pair of white sneakers and hurried out of the room. She was about to head down the stairs, when she heard Elvis' voice.

"Don't say I didn't warn you!"

"Pfft," she proclaimed and hurried down the stairs.

She found Evee in the kitchen, steeping a cup of tea.

"Where's Viv?" Gilly asked.

"She left," Evee said. "Said she had to discuss something with Nikoli before we all got together, so she headed for his hotel."

A prickle of worry stung the back of Gilly's neck. "She shouldn't be out alone. Maybe we should go and find her. Walk her over there."

Evee glanced at the clock on the wall. "Too much time has passed. She's surely already there, safe and in one piece. We still have an hour before we're supposed to meet up with the guys in front of the cathedral. Whatever Viv and Nikoli have to talk about, I think we should give them that privacy." She held up her cup. "Want some tea?"

"No, thanks," Gilly said and found herself starting to pace the kitchen. "It's still very dark outside. Suppose she gets jumped by some freakazoid."

Evee smiled. "She brought a flashlight with her and the

bat we keep in the laundry room. If anyone tries to attack her, I pity them more than anything."

Evee's smile and words usually comforted Gilly, but right now, they did little more than piss her off. They made her feel like she was being treated like a child.

"Look," Gilly said. "I doubt if the Hyland cousins are going to give a rat's ass if we show up at their hotel early instead of meeting them at the cathedral at a precise time. I really think we need to go and check on Viv—make sure she got there okay."

"Okay, okay," Evee finally agreed. "But I'd like to finish up this chamomile tea first, if you don't mind."

Gilly wrinkled her nose. "Chamomile? That crap tastes awful. You just as soon be drinking horse vomit. Why chamomile?"

"It relaxes me. Gets rid of anxiety so I can focus."

"Peppermint tea does the same thing, but at least it tastes good. Besides, chamomile wires me up."

"Yes, but—"

Gilly waved a hand to cut off her words. "Drink whatever you like, but just drink it. I'd like to get going sooner than later."

"What're you so worried about? She'll be with the Benders."

"If she made it there."

Evee gulped down the rest of her tea, smacked her lips and then placed the cup and saucer into the kitchen sink. "Viv's a big girl. She can handle herself."

"You mean like she had to handle herself when a Cartesian attacked and Lucien had to perform a flying tackle to get her out of the way, and Ronan ended up dead?"

"Geez, you don't have to be so brash," Evee said. "I'm done with the tea, so let's go already. Anything to ease that wild-stallion brain of yours."

Satisfied that they were finally on their way, Gilly grabbed a flashlight from the utility room and hurried to the kitchen door to lead the way to the hotel.

"Shall I find another bat?" Evee asked with a grin.

"Don't be stupid," Gilly said. "We only had one. Maybe bring a butcher knife or something like that. Anything to protect us if we need it."

Evee let out a sigh of exasperation. "I will not run around the city with a butcher's knife. Should, and I do mean *should*, something come up, remember we are witches. We'll turn the attacker into a toad or a rabbit."

"I prefer a pile of dung, myself," Gilly said, walking out of the back door with Evee in tow.

"That's because you've got the class of a hyena, sister. You know, everyone claims we're triplets, but really, you could have been adopted."

"Oh, shu…hush up. You're just upset with me because I'm a little wired about Viv."

"A little wired? Abigail, darling, you could light up half the state with your worry wires. She's fine. I'm sure of it. I'll bet you ten to one she's with Nikoli at the hotel, sitting nice and cozy beside him."

It was earlier than they'd originally planned to meet at the cathedral; more than likely, Nikoli and Lucien were still talking to family members about Ronan's death. Gilly knew she should have given them the space they needed to make their family calls, but Viv's heading out there alone made decent protocol appear stupid. She had to make sure her sister was safe with her Bender.

With dawn breaking, and the trolleys still not up and running, Gilly and Evee had to foot it from the Garden District to Royal Street in the French Quarter, where the Hotel Monteleone was located.

Gilly speed-walked the entire way, with Evee occasionally stopping to work out a stitch in her side.

"Slow down, will you?" Evee said to Gilly. "At this pace, you're going to give me a heart attack."

"Witches don't have heart attacks."

"Okay, then my lungs are going to burst. You're faster than I am, so slow it down a notch. Why are you all but running there? We agreed to go to the hotel to make sure Viv was okay, and we're doing that, but you didn't mention speed-walking like a gazelle to do it."

Gilly slowed slightly, allowing her sister to catch up. "Something's wrong," she said suddenly. "I feel it in my gut. That's what's making me so anxious to get there as quickly as possible."

Evee came to an abrupt stop. "What's wrong? Cartesians? Are they around here? Did one of them get Viv?"

Taking her sister's hand, Gilly pulled her forward, not wanting to stop their progress to the hotel.

"I can't quite put my finger on it. It just feels like a fur ball growing in the pit of my stomach. I'm not sure who or what's causing it. The only thing I know is it isn't good."

Evee tugged on Gilly's hand, attempting to slow her down even more. "Is it a Bender? Did we lose another one like we lost Ronan?"

"I already told you, I'm not sure what or who is causing me to feel this way, but there's only one way to find out—get our asses to the hotel and find out."

That bit of information seemed to add new energy to Evee's step. Gilly pushed her speed up a notch. She really wasn't sure how many more catastrophes she'd be able to manage without losing her mind. She might be a witch, but she was still human, filled with emotions and yearnings. Being a witch didn't stop that from happening.

When they finally reached the Monteleone, Evee led

Gilly to the elevator bank near the Carousel Bar. She remembered the room number from before and figured it best to go directly there instead of heading to the reception desk first.

Having reached the appropriate floor, Evee led Gilly to the suite shared by the three remaining Benders and then knocked on the door.

Within seconds, Nikoli opened the door and seemed surprised to see them. His eyes were slightly red-rimmed, as if he'd been crying. Gilly couldn't blame him. Had he not shown some emotion over the loss of his cousin while telling his family, she'd have considered him an asshole of the highest order.

"Are we late?" Nikoli asked, glancing at his watch. Evidently seeing that they were in fact a half hour early, he asked, frowning, "Is there a problem?"

"Is Viv here?" Gilly asked.

Nikoli looked surprised. "No, she hasn't been here since we arrived at the hotel earlier. Why?"

"She was supposed to be on her way here to discuss something with you," Evee said. "At least, that's what she told me."

Nikoli invited them inside and motioned for them to have a seat on the couch in the living area. When they were seated, Nikoli stroked his beard, worry etching his face. "She said she was coming here?"

"Yes," Evee said.

"You mean to tell me she's not shown up here at all this morning?" Gilly asked, getting to her feet.

"I haven't seen her since the feedings," Nikoli said.

"I told you," Gilly said to Evee. "I told you something was wrong."

"What are you talking about?" Nikoli asked.

About that time, Gavril appeared, freshly showered,

barefoot, dressed in jeans and a cobalt-blue button-down shirt.

His eyes went wide when he saw Gilly and Evee, and then narrowed. "Is there a problem?"

"I'd say so," Evee said.

"What is it?" Gavril asked.

"The girls are saying that Viv was on her way here to talk to me about something, but she never showed," Nikoli said, nearly shouting. Dressed in jeans and a forest-green pullover, he went over to the desk in the living area, grabbed his scabior and attached it to his belt. Gilly noticed his hands shaking slightly.

Gilly stared at Evee and said, "She's gone missing. Heaven and all the elementals, our sister has gone missing!"

Instead of answering, Evee suddenly burst into tears. "We have to find her! We have to!"

"She's got to be our first priority," Gilly said. "Screw the missing Originals and those damn Cartesians. We want our sister back—now!"

After Lucien belted his scabior to his jeans, they all but ran out of the hotel en masse.

To the patrons of the hotel, they must have looked like lunatics, running down hallways, across the foyer, and all but crashing through the front doors of the hotel.

Gilly had no idea where to start looking. She feared most of all that somehow the same thing that had happened to Ronan had happened to her sister. The only thing that abated her fear was an innate knowledge that all three sisters carried. One knew when the other was hurt. It only made sense that Gilly would know in her heart of hearts if Viv was dead. And she didn't feel that was the case.

Not dead, but in grave danger.

## Chapter 3

Seeing the worry and pain in Gilly's eyes over her missing sister felt like a dagger in Gavril's heart. He would have done anything to remove the pain from her and make her world normal again.

The problem was no matter how hard the Benders had tried to help the triplets, their situation seemed to be getting worse than better. Yes, they'd managed to get rid of more than their share of Cartesians since they'd arrived in New Orleans. But that hadn't stopped Ronan's death, or the death of some of Viv's Loup-Garous, Evee's Nosferatu and Gilly's Chenilles. It was as if all of the Cartesians ever created from centuries ago had zeroed in on this place and were bound and determined to take out every last Original, along with the Triad.

The Benders had traveled the world, fighting groups of Cartesians whenever they appeared to destroy a sect of the netherworld. From Africa to Alaska, England to New Zea-

land, they'd fought and won each battle they'd been confronted with. Never, however, had any of the Benders faced
a situation like this. The more they battled, the worse things
seemed to become, and for the life of him, Gavril couldn't
figure out why. Certainly it had something to do with the
Cartesians discovering the Originals here, but usually, after
a battle or two or three, they'd move on to easier territory.
This definitely wasn't the case here and now.

Now Gilly and Evee were standing in their hotel room,
claiming Viv was missing. She'd told Evee she was coming
to the hotel to talk to Nikoli, who knew nothing about the
impromptu meeting, but regardless, Viv had never showed
up.

Gavril saw the pain in Nikoli's eyes and how quickly
his expression went haggard. Viv had been paired with
him. His job was to protect her and her Originals, and for
all intents and purposes, judging by what he'd seen when
Viv and Nikoli were together, it had taken on a whole new
course. His cousin was in love with the woman who was
now missing, and nothing short of death would stop him
from finding her.

So far, all that had happened was the disappearance of
all of Viv's Loup-Garous, and now the woman he not only
was supposed to protect, but cared for in a deeper way than
they were allowed, was missing. Gavril could only imagine how deep the wounds were inside of him. Not only had
Nikoli been the one to contact the family about Ronan's
death, recounting the tragic tale again and again to various
family members, but now he had to deal with Viv's disappearance. How much pain could a man bear without breaking? Gavril could only imagine, for if Gilly had been the
one to go missing, he'd have already cracked wide open.

Everyone seemed frozen in place, unsure of what their
next move should be. If by some horrid chance a Cartesian

had gotten to Viv, they'd never find her. She'd be dead, hidden away in another dimension, just like Ronan. Only there'd be no family to contact, save for the Elders, as Viv's entire family members were her sisters, who were already here.

As if reading his mind, Gilly said, "She'd not dead. I'd know it if she was. But she's hurt."

"What do you feel, either of you?" Gavril asked.

"Danger," Evee said.

"Yes," Gilly confirmed. "It's all around her. I get the sense that she's trapped somewhere and has to stay hidden to stay alive. Wherever she is, she was chased there, coerced there, hurt there. The Cartesians are waiting for her to come out of hiding in order to pounce on her again. They're counting on her doing just that."

"Viv's too smart to let that happen," Gavril said. "If she knows they're waiting for her to come out of hiding, she'll nest herself right where she is until we can get to her."

"I know," Gilly said. "But how long will that be? How hurt is she? She's a prisoner for all intents and purposes. That's no way to live—or die."

"We'll find her," Gavril said. "It may be a good idea to start from the beginning. Nikoli, since feeding is over and all the Loups are missing, anyway, go to the north compound and see if Viv's there. Evee and Lucien, you take the Bon Appétit Café first, and then the two of you head back to your house in case Viv doubled back and wound up being there. I'll take Gilly and head for the St. Louis I Cemetery, just in case she decided to go there to help check on Gilly's Chenilles. After that, if we don't find her at the cemetery, then we'll head to the Elders in case she went there, looking for help."

"Not the Elders," Gilly said adamantly. "I'm certain she

wouldn't be there, and telling them she's missing will only freak them out even more."

Gavril laid a hand on the small of Gilly's back. He wanted to wrap his arms around her and never let go. Take her away from this place, from its dangers and heartaches. "We can't leave any stone unturned. From what you've told me, news travels fast among the Circle of Sisters. With all of those witches in your group focused on this, I wouldn't be surprised if the Elders already know she's missing. They might even have a clue as to where she might be."

"You're giving them too much credit."

"They're Elders. We have to allow for all possibilities."

Reluctantly, Gilly gave him a half-hearted nod. "Yeah, no stone unturned."

With everyone assigned a location, they paired together, save for Nikoli, and parted ways, each seemingly carrying the weight of the world on his or her shoulders. They agreed to meet back at the hotel in an hour.

When Gavril and Gilly finally made it to the cemetery, Gavril stayed behind the locked gates, as instructed by Gilly, while she went inside. He hoped against hope she'd find some sign that Viv had been there. He'd never seen Gilly so distraught before, even after all they'd been through so far. He imagined, however, with the Triad being triplets, when one got lost and alone, all of them felt it. He'd heard twins and triplets often felt what their other siblings felt, and he assumed this was no different. Even during their occasional squabbles, it was easy to see how much the sisters adored one another.

By the time Gilly made it back to the cemetery gates, her cheeks were streaked with tears. As soon as she closed and locked the gates, she began to sob. "She's not there. Hasn't been anywhere near here, according to Patrick, her head Chenille. He came up to the gates to find out what I wanted. I hated to tell him because I didn't want him worrying, but I had no choice."

Then, out of nowhere, Gilly's sobs grew louder, and she suddenly pressed a hand to Gavril's chest. He stood fast, placing a hand over hers. Simply by touch he could feel the anger roiling through her. Not anger toward him, but the situation, for the loss of her sister.

Gavril didn't budge when Gilly released her hand from his chest, turned and punched a light post. He knew all too well how she was feeling, since he'd just recently lost his Ronan, who'd been as close to him as a brother.

As Gilly sobbed, Gavril all but carried her to a side alley off Rampart Street so she could have the privacy he knew she needed to let go completely.

Once there, he pulled Gilly close, attempting to comfort her. She struggled against the gesture, evidently not wanting to give in to the over-the-top emotions she felt.

It didn't take long for her to lose that battle, however. Before Gavril knew it, Gilly finally pressed herself against him and laid her head on his chest. He gently rubbed her back with a hand, whispering comforting words in her ear. "We'll find her, I promise."

Gavril had no idea who moved first, but suddenly his lips were locked with Gilly's, and she was kissing him with the same fierceness she felt regarding Viv's disappearance.

Gavril struggled to maintain control over the kiss, not wanting their intimacy to go further than it already had. He didn't want her to hold regrets for something she did out of sheer emotional upheaval. But her kiss kept his head spinning, his body humming with a hunger he'd never felt before.

Obviously frustrated, and still in tears, Gilly took Gavril's hands and brought them to her breasts. In that moment, it seemed she could have cared less whether the alley was dark or brightly lit. He felt she needed the pain inside of her to go somewhere else, and without question, he knew that the somewhere else was having Gavril deep inside her. He carried the same need for her.

As Gavril tried to hold her back, soothe her with his words, Gilly all but threw him down on a grass mound in the alley. She ripped his shirt open, and then her own. She pressed her breasts against his chest and Gavril groaned, quickly losing resolve.

He felt himself hard against her. She'd obviously felt it, too, because it seemed to make something in her mind click into overdrive. Gilly pressed a hand to his chest, yanked open his belt and unzipped his pants. Gavril opened his mouth to protest, but his body defied all he meant to say. He needed her as desperately as she needed him.

Meanwhile, Gilly worked her slacks and panties off with one hand and, without preamble, settled her wet, swollen self over his hardness.

With a groan, Gavril pulled her toward him, yet Gilly kept her hand on his chest and rode him like her life depended on it.

Gavril felt pain in his groin as he fought to maintain control, but the second Gilly flooded him with her hot, soaking juices, he exploded inside of her like a non-stop geyser that dared defy the laws of physics.

With both of them satiated for now, Gilly lay her head on his chest, and he cupped her head and pressed her closer. The fact that they were out in a public place crept into the edges of his mind, but for now he shoved the thought back. He needed to feel her this way. Needing him, satiated.

Finally, Gilly lifted her head and whispered, "We have to find her, Gavril. She's part of me. If something happens to Viv, part of me will die, too. We have to find her."

Aside from an ultra-explosive orgasm, there was nothing that could make a man go as flaccid as the words she'd just spoken.

Gilly rolled off Gavril, her cheeks suddenly red with embarrassment. She quickly pulled her shirt over her breasts and scurried back into her pants. "I—I'm sorry."

"For what?" Gavril asked, although he suspected the reason.

"For…for acting like this. My sister's missing, we have dead Originals with two sectors completely missing, and all I can think about is having sex with you." She scrambled to her feet, her cheeks still bright pink.

Gavril zipped up his pants and closed his shirt over his chest. He couldn't button it because Gilly had ripped every button from its hole when she'd wanted to get to his bare chest. This brought a gentle smile to his face. He got to his feet and reached for her. She took a step back from him, and the movement pierced his heart.

"Listen to me," Gavril said. "You're a wounded woman who needed something real and alive to keep your world in balance. Sex does that and quite well. Believe me, if I'd have thought there was any other intention, you wouldn't have reached first base. I may be a guy, but I do have control over my senses and anything below my belt."

"Oh, that you do," Gilly said shyly.

"I wanted you, Gilly, from the first moment I saw you. Not just to have sex with you, but the whole of you. Your spitfire attitude, your willingness to say what's on your mind, even if it involves an expletive or two. Your loyalty to your Originals and to your sisters. Even the way you carry yourself and the way you look. Your pixie cut, beautiful eyes, your tiny nose. It's all of you, Gilly. All of you."

Gilly stood staring at him silently, and for a moment, Gavril feared he had revealed too much too fast. There was no question in his mind that he'd fallen hard for this woman, but she'd yet to voice how she felt about him. Sex was one thing. Feeling another. Matters of the heart went much further, much deeper than sex. He resented the fact that the Elders had lit into the Triad about having relations with the Benders, but he understood. Every group had their rules. Even Benders. While on a mission they were to keep one head in their pants and the other on the task they'd been assigned. So far they'd blown that one out of the water big-time. The last thing he felt about that, however, was regret.

Letting out a deep breath, Gilly said, "We need to head out. It's a decent hike back to the Elders. We'll probably wind up back at the hotel a bit early, but if Evee shows up first, I don't want her worrying about where I am, as well."

Feeling a stabbing pain in his heart that Gilly hadn't even acknowledged all he'd shared with her, Gavril simply nodded, and both of them headed back to the Monteleone.

By now the trolleys were running, and it would have been easier to hop one and take it down to Canal Street, which crossed Royal, where the hotel was located. But Gavril hoped the walk might give Gilly time to absorb all he'd said and respond in some way.

They'd just crossed Iberville and took a right on Royal, when out of the blue, Gilly reached for Gavril's hand and held it tightly. His heart soared. Her palms were sweaty, so he knew that she was nervous. She probably had no idea how to respond. Although she might not have had the words to respond to him, her taking his hand said more to Gavril than a thousand words would have. Even better, seconds after taking hold of his hand, Gilly moved closer to him. To anyone watching, the two of them must have looked like a couple in love, enjoying each other's company. But sometimes words weren't necessary. Actions spoke more openly and loudly than a thousand syllables strung together.

When they finally reached the hotel and entered, Gilly let go of Gavril's hand and headed to the bank of elevators.

Gavril silently followed, unable to take his eyes off her. He'd known many women in his life, but none so beautiful inside and out as Gilly François. He tried to harden his heart and mind to keep things in perspective, but neither would harden. If only she'd say something about how she felt, aside from holding his hand, he'd be more certain of the direction to head in with her.

Gavril knew of the Triad curse, which mandated that they not marry a human or live intimately with one. Like he needed something else to add to his ever-growing list of things to do—protect the safe zone of the Chenilles, find the missing ones before they attacked humans. And now, everything they'd been working so hard for came to a screeching halt because Viv was missing, and she was a priority. This was something Gavril completely understood.

But somewhere in the middle of fixing this, fighting that, he set it in his mind to find out a way to break the curse that bound the Triad, even if he had to visit their Elders himself. Surely there had to be a loophole; all laws had them. He assumed curses were the same. No one, not even a witch, could remember everything that might cover generations of Triads to follow. Not as far back as the 1500s.

Times and situations changed over the years. Unless the Elders who'd issued the curse were able to see far into the future, they had been only dealing with then, with the times, situations and customs that affected that time period. He seriously doubted they had seen so far into the future. Maybe they had only assumed that the curse they'd set upon the first Triad would hold forever. Or maybe not.

Gavril thought of the Elders who watched over the Triad now. They were like mother hens to those three women. Even in anger, he couldn't see them implementing a curse that had no end, with no out clause. Anger was indeed anger, and punishment was punishment, but didn't love trump them all? Surely the original Elders had felt some sort of compassion for the first Triad and left a door open that no one had found yet.

*Yet.* That was the key word.

Once that curse was broken, and if he ever got Gilly to speak her mind as far as he was concerned, his intent was to have her for the rest of her life. Having traveled the world many times over, Gavril had yet to meet anyone as unique, smart, caring and beautiful as Gilly. A man didn't place the largest diamond found in any mine on a shelf, and then leave, hoping it might still be there once he returned. Gilly was his rough-cut diamond, and if it took his entire lifetime, he'd look for a loophole in the curse for the simple purpose of making her his own.

These were words Gavril kept to himself; if Gilly heard them, she'd take off running like a wild rabbit, thinking him mad. What business did a human, who had no concept of the magic they generated, have in messing in witches' business?

And she'd have been right.

But the one thing he did do well was investigate. He'd developed his investigation skills over the years while hunting Cartesians. If somehow he had the chance to read the document that sealed the Triad curse, he'd pick it apart until he found a loophole that worked for them. They'd be free at last, something he knew the Triad had never experienced before.

He wanted, more than anything, to be Gilly's hero.

# Chapter 4

"I knew something like this was going to happen," Arabella, the head of the Elders, said when Gilly told them about Viv going missing.

"Well, if you knew, why didn't you warn us about it?" Gilly asked. The last thing she'd wanted to do was come back to the Elders, especially after they'd been royally reamed out during their last visit. The Elders lived only a couple of blocks from the Triad in the Garden District, but coming here again felt like they'd walked the green mile. They'd had no choice. Not with Viv missing. No matter what the consequences might be, they had to let the Elders know.

"Oh, she did," Vanessa said.

"She did not," Gilly insisted.

"Uh-huh," Taka, the third, said. "Remember the whole thing about Viv and Evee being intimate with their Benders, how it needed to stop. Well, it obviously didn't stop, because now we've got another catastrophe on our hands. They should have listened—that's all I've got to say."

"I wish," Vanessa said.

"Wish what?" Taka asked, frowning.

"That that was all you had to say."

Taka tsked loudly, and then looked at Gavril and said, "No offense meant, Mr. Bender, but witches have rules to live by. If we don't live by them, then all kinds of havoc occur, like now. There are reasons we have leaders, Elders. It's not like the Triad is out there on their own. They have us to bounce things off of."

"So, you're saying that you're blaming Evee and Viv's intimacy with Nikoli and Lucien for all this chaos?" Gavril said.

"I am," Taka said.

"This isn't the time to go into your rant about the Triad members having relations with the Benders," Gilly said. "Viv is missing and that's what matters most. Besides, I think all three of you have this relationship thing wrong or twisted sideways somehow. It doesn't connect or make sense."

"It makes complete sense," Arabella said. "As it was part of the curse set on the Triads since the 1500s. Nothing has changed to refute it. The intimacy you've obviously taken course with regarding these young men has caused nothing but disaster."

"No disrespect meant, ma'am," Gavril said, "but that's baloney. My cousins and I have tracked these Cartesians around the world. Have been to places where they've taken out an entire species from the netherworld in a city. Humans died, more Cartesians showed themselves. But not once did it have anything to do with me or my cousins being intimate with any female. Witch or no witch."

"But if the Triad doesn't listen, there isn't much we can do about controlling what happens," Taka said.

"Oh, there's plenty we can do about it," Arabella said.

"Like what?" Vanessa said.

"Leave them to their chaos. They asked for advice, we gave it, they ignored it, and now they have to live with it."

"I'd appreciate it if you'd stop speaking about us as though we weren't in the room," Gilly said angrily.

"Hello?" Gavril said. "Did any of you hear what I said earlier?"

"Yes, of course," Arabella said.

"How can you say that when Viv's gone?" Taka said to Arabella. "Mr. Bender said they've been trying to help. Surely you won't attempt to stop them from doing that."

"Please call me Gavril," Gavril said. And Taka gave him a shy smile. "And please give my words some consideration. None of what's been happening was caused by the Triad. The blame goes to the Cartesians."

"Where was the last place you saw her?" Arabella asked Gilly, ignoring Gavril.

"At home. Evee told me she was headed to the hotel to talk over something with Nikoli, her Bender. The problem was that she never showed up at the hotel."

"For the love of stupidity," Vanessa said. "Ever since you three were little girls, your heads were harder than brick and mortar. Now that you're thirty, that doesn't seem to have changed one bit. Arabella told you to stay away from the Benders, and what do you do? Show up at their hotel."

"Talking to someone is no crime," Gilly said. "Especially when we're trying to find Viv. Going to somebody's hotel room doesn't mean sex is involved, Vanessa. People do meet up and talk in those rooms."

"I disagree," Taka said with a smirk. "There are beds in hotel rooms, and where there are beds, there's sex."

"Oh, get a grip," Vanessa snapped at Taka.

Arabella gave Gilly a slow nod. She eyed Gavril, and then looked back at Gilly. "You're right. There's no crime in talking, that's for sure, but let me ask you something." This time she looked Gavril right in the eye before asking Gilly. "Have the two of you been intimate? After I warned you to stay away, did you disobey? Have you been intimate with this man despite our warning?"

"Nothing was her fault," Gavril said. "When she heard about Viv—"

"My question wasn't directed at you, young man," Arabella said. "It was meant for Gilly."

Taka huffed. "You did it, didn't you, Gilly? Was it at the hotel?"

Vanessa shook her head. "A Triad slut brigade, that's what we have on our hands, sisters. They're going to do what they want to regardless of our warnings. How does an Elder combat that? We try and we try to lead them down the straight and narrow, and look, they take the first fork in the road they come to."

"We'll deal with it by allowing the Triad to handle the consequences of their actions," Arabella said.

"Wait a minute," Gilly said angrily. "You're speculating that I've been intimate with Gavril, and because of that, you won't give me any help in finding Viv? What kind of Elders are you? Ever since the beginning, every Triad had Elders who helped them with problems."

"Not all of them," Arabella said. "Or have you forgotten the first Triad? Their Elders didn't change the monstrosities they'd created back to humans. Instead, they punished the Triad."

"So is this what this is?" Gilly asked. "Punishment? You won't help us because of some warped assumption you're making? It begs the same question—what kind of Elders are you?"

"We have tried to help," Arabella said. "Repeatedly. We've even contact the rest of our sisters and asked for help. Something or someone seems to be blocking all of our spells. My only assumption as to why that might be is, once again, your intimacy with the Benders. Part of the Triad curse in action."

"And we're smart Elders," Taka said. "I think." They'd been sitting around the kitchen table, and Taka suddenly got to her feet, seemingly flustered. "Anybody want crumpets and tea?"

"Sit down, Taka," Vanessa said. "Now isn't the time to extend hospitality. We've got to get to the bottom of this."

"But I'm hungry," Taka whined.

Arabella gave Taka a stern look, which sent her back into her seat with a pout. "It was just tea and crumpets."

"You claim your intimacy with your Bender is our speculation, an assumption," Arabella said to Gilly. "Is it an assumption? Or did it happen?" She looked first at Gavril, and then she allowed her eyes to settle on Gilly. "I want the truth."

Gilly sighed heavily. "Yeah, we were intimate," she finally said, and saw Gavril shift uncomfortably in his seat. She didn't blame him. He was sitting at a table of witches, any of whom could have turned him into a frog or turtle with a kindergartner's spell.

"Mr. Bender," Vanessa said, "as you can see, this conversation is getting quite personal. I think it best if you leave us to deal with Abigail, who obviously decided to not heed our advice."

"He doesn't have to go," Taka said.

"It's best he does," Arabella said.

"But he's cute," Taka said. "Easy on the eyes. And besides, we're not going to be saying anything he hasn't already heard or known about. If they were intimate, they were intimate. He already knows that. You think we're revealing a secret?"

"I'd prefer to stay if it's all the same to you," Gavril said. "Gilly is not alone in this. And if I may respectfully add, we came here of our own volition. Vivienne has gone missing, and we wanted to see if you'd seen her or possibly know where she might have gone."

"I haven't seen her," Taka said.

"Me either," Vanessa said.

"Nor have I," Arabella added. "Have you tried the compound where Viv kept her Loup-Garous?"

"Yes," Gilly said. "Her Bender is there looking for her now."

"You sent a human Bender into the compound?" Arabella said with shock. "Did you purposely want this man dead?"

"He'll be mauled like ground beef," Taka said, her brows knitting together. "Surely he's not alone there, right?"

"Haven't you heard?" Gilly said. "All of the Loup-Garous are missing."

"What?" Arabella, Vanessa and Taka said in unison.

Gilly nodded. "They were there one morning, and by the afternoon, not one of them remained on the compound."

"Oh, Mother Earth and every worm beneath her," Taka said. "Does that mean they're all loose in the city?"

"I have no idea," Gilly said. "We've each been taking care of our own. I still have Chenilles in their safe zone, but have about fifteen missing. Evee lost all of her Nosferatu. Same thing with Viv's. One minute they're where they're supposed to be, the next, they've vanished."

Arabella got up from the table and began to pace. "You know what this means, don't you?"

"That we're in deep doodoo," Taka said.

"You're not kidding," Gilly said. "With them missing, it means more humans are in danger."

"If more humans start dying at the hands of the Originals, you know what that means, right?" Vanessa said.

"Well, duh," Taka said. "It means those humans will be dead."

"Stop being an idiot," Vanessa told her. She looked over at Arabella. "It means more cops at our door."

"Why are police coming here?" Gavril asked. "How do they know about you and the Originals?"

"I suspect a leak," Arabella said. "And I'm almost certain it's one of the sorcerers."

"I don't understand," Gavril said.

"I'll explain later," Gilly said. "We've got to stay on task with Viv. She's got to be our main focus right now."

"Oh, heck, that's right about the cops," Taka said suddenly. "What do we tell the cops when they come back here to talk to us? Do we not answer the door like before? Ignore them?"

Arabella shook her head. "Not this time. Too much has gotten out of hand. We've got to let the police know about the Loup-Garous and the Nosferatu. If we don't, the entire city will soon be overrun with dead bodies when those Originals get hungry and need to feed."

"What good will the cops be if they know?" Vanessa asked.

"We'll have to give them information—information we've never given any other human," Arabella said solemnly. "We'll have to tell them how to kill them."

"Have you lost your marbles?" Taka asked. "That means, if they see any Original, attacking a human or not, they'll kill it."

"I know what it means," Arabella said. "But with so

many Originals loose, it's come down to a choice. Their lives or the lives of humans."

"We can't let them all be killed," Vanessa cried. "The Triad needs to find them and regain control."

"I wish it was that easy," Gavril said. "But you have no idea what trauma and drama we've gone through with the Cartesians over the last week just trying to find the Originals."

"To hell with the Originals," Gilly said. "What about Viv? We've got to find her. Do you have any idea where she might be? Do you have any spells that might give us some direction as to where she might be hiding?"

"You know we don't use crystal balls," Arabella said with a huff as if Gilly had used a foul expletive. "Our spells are innate, herbs and elemental. But you already know that. What I don't understand is why you've come here to ask us about finding Viv when you and Evee both have natural talents that can help find her. Haven't you thought of doing something with them?"

Gilly looked at her quizzically. "I don't understand."

Taka rested her elbows on the table. "Sure you do. You know how Evee can talk to the dead? Channel them? If she can contact one of the Loup-Garous, Chenilles or Nosferatu, like Pierre, one of them who's already died, they might be able to give her some valuable information. Once she gets that information, you can use your astral projection thing that you do and bring your energy to whatever place the dead might see Viv. Then you'll know if she's there. The dead see more than we do, you know. They're not stuck with two feet on the ground like we are."

"For once, I think Airhead over here is right," Vanessa said, referring to Taka.

"Who you calling an airhead?" Taka asked. "I'm the

one who came up with the idea, while you were over there checking for chips in your fingernail polish."

"I was not," Vanessa claimed. "I was listening closely. Just because I'm not looking at your mug doesn't mean I wasn't paying attention."

"Both of you stop bickering," Arabella said. She looked over at Gilly. "Taka speaks the truth. You and Evee have natural talents that don't involve spells that may or may not work. Has Evee tried to communicate with the dead? Have you tried astral projection, since that's your specialty?"

"No, neither," Gilly said. "But…the idea has some promise to it."

"It certainly does," Gavril said. "Not only in finding Viv but locating the missing Originals, as well. I say we give it a shot."

Arabella scowled at him. "It's not your business to say whether or not they attempt to use their powers this way."

Gavril cocked his head to one side and eyed Arabella. "Ever since I walked through that door, you've treated me like I have lice. All I've done since coming here is try to protect the Originals and the Triad. We've managed to destroy many Cartesians while here. What problem do you have with me?"

Arabella held up a defiant chin. "Although we do appreciate what you have done to help the Originals and the Triad, I'm afraid that the attraction you Benders have for the Triad has caused more problems than anything. This entire situation might be solved right now if you would have kept certain parts of your body in check."

"Arabella!" Gilly said, appalled that her Elder had confronted Gavril that way. She got up from the table and signaled Gavril to follow her.

"Taka, thank you for your advice," Gilly said. "We'll certainly give it a try. Arabella, if I were you, I'd do a conscience check. You might be my Elder, but when I see you headed in the wrong direction, as a witch, I have an obligation to let you know. You're way off here. Gavril and the other Benders have been nothing but gentlemen. And, if you remember, you're the one who wanted to get the sorcerers involved, which would have been a far bigger disaster than what we're dealing with now."

"I didn't say the sorcerers weren't getting involved," Arabella confessed.

"You...you didn't go to Cottle with any of this," Gilly said. "Tell me you didn't."

"Cottle? No. But I have spoken to Gunner Stern about it. If you remember, Taka was the one who got him involved in the first place. I simply followed through."

Gilly glared at her. "And?"

"There is no 'and.' He's doing some snooping around. Seeing if there's anything he can do to help."

Gilly shook her head. "Look, as much as we warned you about getting the sorcerers involved, you did as you pleased anyway. You know the sorcerers have always thought us to be an inferior, bothersome species. I'd call that even when it comes to your accusations regarding the Benders. If anything, we owe them our gratitude. You have no idea how hard they've been fighting for us."

With that, Gilly walked out of the kitchen and headed for the front door, Gavril by her side. When they'd made it outside, Gavril grinned. "Really. Do you always talk to your Elders that way?" he asked.

"Only when they're going way off track."

They walked a ways, heading down to the French Quarter to meet up with the others as promised. Luckily a trolley came to a stop fifty feet away, and they were able to hop a ride on it all the way down Canal. They then got off where it intersected with Royal.

Gavril got off the trolley and held out a hand to help Gilly down the metal steps. She took his hand and made her way to ground level.

As they walked to the hotel, Gavril kept turning to look at her.

"What?" Gilly finally asked. "Why are you looking at me that way?"

"Just think it's cute."

"What is?"

"The set of balls you have is undeniable. You say what you mean and mean what you say. Elder or no Elder. Hell, it could have been the President of the US, and I think you'd have shot him down the same way."

Gilly shrugged. "I get a bit carried away sometimes."

"I'd say," Gavril said. "But I love it. Wouldn't want it any other way."

Gilly gave him a strange, shy look, and it was then that Gavril realized he'd used the *L* word. Although he hadn't actually said the words *I love you*, it had been close enough to give her pause.

"Good," Gilly finally said. "I'm glad you like it. 'Cause I only come in one color."

"What's that mean?"

She stopped and gave him a long, soulful look. "It means, Mr. Gavril Hyland, that when it comes to me, what you see is what you get."

"And that's supposed to be a bad thing?"

"It's been known to get me into trouble from time to time."

"Good," Gavril said with a chuckle. "A woman after my own heart."

## Chapter 5

When they reached the Benders' suite at the Monteleone, everyone was waiting for them as expected.

"You're late," Evee said.

Gavril glanced at his watch. "Only by five minutes."

"Still, it had me worried sick," Evee said. "I feared something had happened to the two of you."

"Well, worries over. I'm here," Gilly said. "I take it, since all of you are here, except for Viv, that none of you had any luck locating her."

"Nothing," Lucien said. "Evee and I searched our assigned territory and more. Not even a sign that she'd been around."

Gilly turned to Nikoli, who sat on the edge of the bed, just outside of the living room area of the suite. It looked as if he'd purposely distanced himself from everyone in the room. His face looked haggard, his eyes dull.

By the look on his face, Gilly felt stupid for asking, but she had to know. "Nikoli?"

He looked over at her.

"Anything?"

"No," he said, his voice hoarse. "Not even a clue. What about you and Gavril?"

Gavril went over to Nikoli, sat on the edge of the bed beside him and put an arm around his shoulder. "We'll find her, cuz. Somehow, someway, we'll find her."

Nikoli turned to him, a faraway look in his eyes that could be seen by everyone in the room. "She was under my watch," he said. "I screwed up, Nik. She was under my watch."

Gilly went over to Nikoli and placed a hand on his shoulder. "She might have been under your watch, but the bottom line is, stuff happens. I pray to the universe that we find her. I know she's still alive. I can feel her. I just can't feel where she is. If she were dead, there'd be a hole in my heart the size of this planet, and thankfully I don't feel that."

Nikoli looked up at Gilly hopefully. "Did either of you have luck with the Elders?"

"Well, yes and no," Gavril said.

"What's that mean?" Lucien asked, joining them in the bedroom.

"It's either yes or no, right?" Evee asked, joining them. "How can it be both? You either got some info or you didn't." She looked at Gilly. "Well?"

"No, we didn't find her," Gilly said, "but the Elders came up with an idea that might be useful."

"The Elders?" Evee said. "All they've done since this started is perform spells that don't work and contact the entire clan of Circle of Sisters for intercession spells, which didn't work either."

"Yeah, I know, I know," Gilly said.

"What possible idea could they have come up with that made you pay attention?" Evee asked.

Gilly looked at Gavril and he gave her the slightest nod of encouragement.

After clearing her throat, Gilly said, "They brought up the fact that you and I have innate talents that don't involve spells that could be used to locate Viv."

Evee looked at her questioningly. "Huh?"

"You have the ability to contact and hear from the dead. I can astral project. The Elders suggested that you focus on one of the Originals that's already dead and see if he has a better view behind the death veil than we do here, stuck as humans. Witches but humans. Once you lock onto one of the Originals, I can attempt to follow its voice and your trance, and astral project to the location it's seeing and attempting to describe."

"Hmm," Lucien said. "Can the two of you do what the Elders claim?"

"Duh," Gilly said.

"Sorry, I didn't mean to question you or them. Habit to confirm, is all," Lucien said, looking Gilly in the eye.

For a moment, Gilly felt like a stupid schoolgirl. *Duh? Where in the hell had that come from?*

"No need to apologize," Gilly said. "Yes, Evee can contact and speak to people and the Originals that have passed on."

"*If* they're willing to talk," Evee said. "The way it seems to work is, if they crossed over to wherever we cross over to after death, it's less likely they'll communicate. If their spirits are still hanging around on earth, for whatever reason, they're much easier to contact."

"And what's with the astral projection?" Gavril asked Gilly. "Do you just zap yourself to some other location?"

"Not physically," Gilly explained. "My mind goes there,

and although my physical body is still in the place where I began, I see myself in my mind's eye when I'm in the place I'm tracking."

Gavril, Nikoli and Lucien frowned simultaneously.

"Think of it like daydreaming," Gilly said, trying to give them a clearer explanation. "In your mind's eye you see whatever it is you're daydreaming about. With astral projection, it's more specific. I can focus that so-called daydream to wherever I want. Only in that situation, I have a *dream* body that goes along with it. I may still be here, but I can see, hear, react, feel in that astral projection state. The only thing I can't do is alter what I see. The best shot we have is if I pick something up while Evee talks to whatever or whomever she connects with. Astral projection will give us more details, so we'll at least know what direction to head in. Make sense?"

"Got it," Gavril said.

"I'm up for it if you are," Evee said to Gilly. "Anything to find Viv."

Gilly nodded and asked Nikoli, Lucien and Gavril to step away so she and Evee had room to concentrate. Too much energy from too many people in one area would tone down what Evee needed to hear.

The men did as they were told, moving to the doorway that separated the bedroom from the living room suite.

Gilly sat close beside Evee and took both her hands into her own. "Ready?"

"As I'll ever be. I'm just not sure who to try and contact."

"Try Chank, since he was a Nosferatu and one of your own. Even in death, given that he hasn't crossed over somewhere unreachable, he should still recognize and respond to his mistress' voice."

Evee nodded and closed her eyes. Gilly concentrated on

her sister's face and watched her lips move silently, until she felt she was inside Evee.

After about a half hour, Evee opened her eyes and looked at Gilly woefully. "I'm not picking up anything from Chank. Not one word. I can't even feel him around me."

Giving her head a slight shake to disconnect from Evee's mind, Gilly said, "I didn't pick up anything either. It was like your mind was nothing but a black hole."

"That scares me," Evee said. "Not knowing where he is, I mean."

"I know, honey, but we've got to keep trying, for Viv's sake. What about any of her Loup-Garous, the ones who died in the first massacre? Were you familiar with any of them? Can you bring any one of them to mind?"

Evee stared at her sister, but Gilly knew she wasn't seeing her. She was concentrating on the Loup-Garous that had belonged to Viv.

"I remember Moose," Evee finally said. "A big Loup. Kind of slow, though. You know, in the head. He wasn't at all aggressive like the rest of the pack. He had a gentle spirit about him."

"Okay, then try Moose," Gilly said. "Focus on what he looked like. See if he comes to you."

Still holding on to Gilly's hands, Evee closed her eyes once more. Her lips began to move just as they had before. Only this time, Gilly noticed her eyes moving behind her lids, like she'd entered into some sort of REM sleep.

Gilly concentrated on her sister's face, felt something move in the pit of her stomach. Evee had evidently connected with Moose; only, for some reason, when Gilly tried to connect to their conversation, all she saw was the Mississippi River, wide and winding near the city. She couldn't make sense of it.

With her eyes still closed, Evee said, "Big heads. Lots of big heads. Color, too. Fun colors."

Gilly felt herself frown. What she saw when trying to connect with Evee and Moose didn't make sense. It was like she'd entered a carnival, and they were standing, talking in the middle of a midway. She heard warped music, saw clowns with big heads, and, of course, every color of the rainbow decorated the rides that made up the carnival.

"People walking, talking," Evee continued, eyes still closed and moving beneath her lids. "Surprised voices. Excited voices. Wheels. Lotsa wheels and big heads."

Still seeing the same setting, Gilly opened her eyes, frustrated. She let go of Evee's hands, which immediately broke the trance her sister had been in.

"Anything?" Evee asked hopefully.

"Nothing that made a damn lick of sense," Gilly said. "Moose kept saying big heads, colors, surprised voices and something about wheels. The only thing I saw when attempting to connect to you and his voice was a carnival. You know, midway, rides, clowns, the whole bit."

From the doorway, Nikoli asked, "Are there any carnivals in town right now?"

"Not that I know of," Gilly said. "But that's not something I'd usually track. If anyone would know about a carnival being in or around town, it would be Taka. She goes to all of them. Sort of like a big kid. Rides all the rides, eats cotton candy until she pukes. The whole ball of wax."

"Then we should ask her if she knows of any," Evee said.

Gilly groaned. "I've had my row with the Elders already today."

"What?" Evee asked. "Did you get into an argument with them?"

"Kinda," Gilly said. "I told Arabella off."

"Gilly!"

"Well, she'd asked for it. They all did, except for Taka, I guess. She was on the fence during the argument, like always."

"What was the argument about?" Lucien asked from the doorway.

"Nothing that means anything right now," Gilly said and shot a quick look at Gavril, who lifted a brow.

"Abigail François," Evee said with a look of incredulity. "You didn't."

Gilly gave her an innocent look. "Didn't what?"

"You know what. The last time we were all together with the Elders, they reamed Viv and me for being intimate, sexually or otherwise, with our Benders. They warned us that the intimacy might very well be the cause of all the catastrophes we've been experiencing."

"Yeah, and?"

"Don't *and* me," Evee said. She looked from Gavril to Gilly. "The two of you had sex, didn't you?"

Gilly turned away from her sister and threw Gavril a look that said, *No confession necessary.*

"Gilly?" Evee said. "I need to know the truth. It might have something to do with Viv going missing. The Elders warned us that if we didn't back away from having sex or deep relationships with our Benders that things might get worse. Having one of our sisters go missing is about the second worst thing that could happen."

"What's the first?" Nikoli asked from the doorway.

"Viv's death."

Nikoli took a step away from the doorway and ran his hands through his hair. "I should have kept her in my sights. It's my fault. She'd asked me to wait near the feeding shoot, just in case any of her Loups showed up while she went inside the compound."

"And you let her in there, knowing the scabior canopy was no longer operational?" Gavril asked.

"Yeah," Nikoli said. "Dumb-ass move, I know, but Viv can be strong headed when she sets her mind to something. And I really don't need you kicking my ass about it. Believe me, I'm doing enough kicking on my own. But it turned out okay— she came out. Then we parted ways. I walked her home, then came to the hotel. I shouldn't have let her out of my sight. Ever."

"Is there anyone else you can try to connect with besides Moose?" Gilly asked Evee. "What about the female Viv told us about who was in heat and causing all the ruckus in the compound?"

Evee shook her head. "I don't have a visual to work with. Aside from Moose, most of the Loups looked the same to me."

"Damn," Gilly said. "I refuse to hit a brick wall. Let's try Moose again, ask him questions. Maybe we can get clearer answers that way."

Evee shrugged. "It's worth a try."

Gilly took Evee's hands back into her own and held tight. When she saw Evee's lips start moving silently, Gilly closed her own eyes and focused on the energy coming from her sister. She felt Evee's hands grow hot and begin to tremble.

"Big heads," Evee said, her voice low as if it had become male. "Lots of color. Laughing. So much laughing. Some scary, too. Clowns. Clowns are scary. Dragons, too."

"Where are the big heads?" Evee asked in her own voice. "Moose, can you see where the big heads and colors are? The clowns and the dragons?"

Still unable to pick up anything but a carnival setting, Gilly opened her eyes, but kept her hands locked onto Evee's.

"The colors are safe." Moose's voice carried through Evee. "The scary clowns are, too. The wheels don't move, though. Not now—it's not time."

"When is the time?" Evee asked, her voice back to its own timbre. "Do you know?" Evee's voice grew deeper.

"When it gets noisy. Lots of people. Big heads, lotsa color. Scary faces. Happy faces. Sick people."

Evee opened her eyes and released her hands from Gilly's. "The only thing that comes to mind with his gibberish is some kind of carnival."

"There's only one way to find out," Gavril said from the doorway. "We'll pile up in our rental car and head out to check it out."

"There's got to be an easier way," Lucien said, standing beside Gavril. "If Taka's a carnival fanatic like you say she is, she'd know about all the ones in town, and probably knows about any outside of the city."

"I've already told you," Gilly said. "We had a bit of a tiff. I'm not comfortable going back there right now."

"So we'll go," Gavril said.

"And get your head chopped off!" Gilly proclaimed. "You guys are the reason they believe we're in so much crap."

"Talking about crap," Evee sad to Gilly. "You never answered my question."

Gilly frowned. "What question?"

"You said we're the reason the Elders believe we're in so much crap. Well, were you intimate with Gavril?" Evee looked over at Gavril, who was looking down at his boots.

"None of your business," Gilly said.

"It sure as hell is my business," Evee said. "If you were, it could be the reason Viv's gone missing. So give it up. Were you intimate with your Bender?"

Gilly looked over at Gavril and rolled her eyes. When she turned back to Evee, she felt sparks of anger flying toward her sister. "Yeah, we were intimate. Satisfied? It's not like you've been Mother Teresa, you know. You can't blame Viv's disappearance on me. You and Viv gave it up to your Benders as well as I did. For all we know, it could be a collective thing, not just something I did. Besides, my escapade with Gavril happened after the fact. Viv was already missing. I didn't cause it."

"The Elders warned us, yet you went ahead and did what they strictly prohibited us from doing. Is it any wonder Viv's missing? You were the last of the three of us to push the lever over too far. You purposely disobeyed the Elders."

"Oh, get a grip," Gilly said, growing angrier by the moment. "Instead of pointing fingers and placing blame, we need to find Viv and fast. Remember the Cartesians? If she's out there alone, she's a moving target for those bastards."

"Viv's not stupid," Nikoli chimed in. "I don't think she's lost. I think she's hiding out somewhere so she doesn't get captured by the Cartesians."

"So how do we find her to help?" Lucien asked. He pointed his chin at Gilly, and then at Evee. "The two of you didn't seem to get very far with Moose. All we have is what he said. We'll have to try and decipher it."

"We've got to find a carnival," Gilly said. "That's what I saw when Evee was communicating with him."

"Fine," Gavril said. "Instead of beating this up to death, let's set up a plan and make it happen. Gilly, since I was with you at the Elders' earlier and didn't exactly earn any brownie points with them, you and I will take the rental car and head to Chalmette. See if any carnivals are up and running in or around the town. Evee, you, Nikoli and Lucien go and talk to Taka. Find out all she knows about any carnival in a hundred-mile radius."

"A hundred miles?" Lucien asked. "Isn't that a bit far?"

"Not if some of the Originals already infiltrated Chalmette. They could be anywhere. And wherever they are, you can bet the Cartesians are on the prowl. No telling how many Originals we've lost since they went missing."

"I don't know about this talking to Taka thing," Lucien said. "The other two Elders sound like quite a piece of work. For all we know, they might get mega pissed because we're there and turn us into turtles or ants or something."

Evee grinned. "They're tough at times, but not stupid. Nobody's going to turn you into anything. Especially when they know you're only trying to help and find Viv. It'll be a good thing that Gavril and Gilly won't be around. They were their last two targets, so at least you'll have a fairly decent shot at getting their attention, instead of making their anger flare up."

With that plan agreed upon, the troupe left the hotel room. Gavril and Gilly jumped into the rental car, and Lucien, Evee and Nikoli headed for the trolley. It was the fastest way for them to get to the Garden District, where the Elders lived.

As soon as Gavril took off in the rental, Gilly gave him directions to Chalmette.

"What do you think our chances are there?" Gavril asked.

"Finding Viv, you mean?"

"Yeah."

"Slim to none. Just a gut feeling I have. Not that I haven't been wrong before, but I just don't *feel* her there."

"Maybe it's not about feeling her so much as it is getting information that'll lead us to her," Gavril offered.

Gilly stared through the windshield. "I hope that's the case."

She turned to face Gavril. "I didn't want to say anything in front of Evee and Nikoli because I didn't want to freak them out. But from somewhere deep in my gut, I feel Viv's life force draining."

Gavril shot her a quick look before bringing his attention back to the windshield and his driving. "You mean like you feel her dying?"

Gilly took in a deep breath. "That or something like it. All I know is we have to find her and find her fast. Otherwise, we'll be dealing with another funeral."

# *Chapter 6*

Frustrated with the bumper-to-bumper traffic leading out of New Orleans, Gavril did his best to swerve from lane to lane, but most of the time, he was barely able to push ten miles an hour. Drivers had little mercy. Nobody wanted to wait a moment longer than they had to.

"This is stupid," Gilly said. "At this rate, it'll take hours to get there. Maybe we should have taken a different route."

"We'll make it just fine," Gavril assured her. "This is the fastest. Must be construction holding things up. Once we get past it, I'll push some juice, and we'll be there in no time. We're almost in Arabi, anyway. Chalmette's only ten minutes or so from there."

"Feels like we've been on the road for hours," Gilly said, gazing out of the passenger window. She turned to Gavril. "Do you think we'll find her? Any gut feelings?"

Holding the steering wheel with his left hand, Gavril laid his right hand on Gilly's cheek. "I'm not like you and Evee.

I can't pick up signals from the dead or transport myself metaphysically to other places. But I can tell you, I have hope. If you say you still feel her alive, I trust in that. She's still alive." He hoped his words brought her some peace. He'd do anything to take the worry from her eyes, the pain from her heart.

Gilly pressed her hand against Gavril's. "Thanks for the encouragement. Sadly though, like I said earlier, I feel her energy waning."

"Does that mean you think she's been hurt?"

Gilly nodded. "Hurt enough to possibly kill her if we don't find her fast enough."

Gavril grit his teeth, angry that anyone, especially the Cartesians, would hurt someone so innocent. As long as he'd known the Triad, which was but a couple of weeks, all he'd seen was them trying to help, either each other or their Originals.

Anger rushed through Gavril like someone had turned a gas burner up to high heat. To make all of this go away, to protect the Triad, the rest of the Originals, those who made up the rest of the netherworld, he had to find out who the Cartesians' leader was and locate him or it. Cut off the head of the dog, and the rest of the body dies.

The problem was, he didn't have the slightest idea as to where to locate him. In fact, he had no idea what he even looked like. Did he have the same huge body, talons and razor-sharp incisors that his band of Cartesians had? Or did he...or she—he couldn't leave anything on the table by assuming the leader was male—look like a human, hiding among the rest without a care in the world except to accomplish this mission?

Knowing the Benders had to get to the leader to stop the massacres gave him nightmares. It was all he thought about. In his dreams, he'd see an elusive shadow darting in and around corners of buildings, inside houses, and the harder Gavril tried to chase him down, the more elusive the creature became. The dreams were always worse when he felt himself only inches away from seeing the face of the creature, even in shadow. Then it would turn into a huge puff of smoke and disappear right before Gavril had a chance to lock in on him.

With both hands on the steering wheel now, Gavril gripped it so tightly, his knuckles turned white. The traffic had come to a complete stop, all three lanes locked up bumper to bumper.

Gilly laid a hand on his right thigh. "I can feel you deep in thought. Aside from how frustrating this traffic is, care to share what you're thinking? Anything's better than this absolute silence. I'm jittery enough that it's taking us so long to get to Chalmette. Talking might help."

Gavril laid a hand over Gilly's. "Just thinking about the leader of the Cartesians. I've got to find the bastard. Was thinking that you chop off the head of the dog, the rest of it dies. The problem is I have no idea if he looks like a Cartesian or disguises himself as a human. For all we know, he could be walking around New Orleans like any Tom, Dick or Harry, and we'd never know. He could own a tobacco shop on Canal, disguise himself as any nationality, and we'd never get a bead on him. The only way we have to track him is by going through one Cartesian at a time, and hope that one is him." Gavril squeezed Gilly's hand, and then moved her hand back to her own lap.

Gilly looked at him quizzically.

"Even with all we're facing right now, so much seemingly impossible, your hand on my thigh creates a huge distraction. Hard to concentrate with a woody."

Gavril glanced over at Gilly, who now had her hands folded in her lap; her cheeks were bright red.

"I didn't mean to offend," Gavril told her. "It's just, you have that effect on me. Even having you in the same car makes my mind start to wonder from time to time."

"I—I'm sorry. I didn't mean—"

"Stop," Gavril said with a shake of his head. "I know you didn't mean to create the distraction, but let's face it, Gilly, I'm over-the-top attracted to you. Your touch drives me crazy. It makes me crave more. Armageddon could be in full swing right now, and I'd feel your touch, and in my mind, Armageddon become a secondary issue. Don't you get it?"

She cocked her head, eyeing him questioningly. "What am I supposed to get?"

"I'm beyond attracted to you. All of you. So when you touch me, I don't just feel your hand—I feel all of you, and I crave it more than I do food and water."

Gavril saw Gilly do an abrupt about-face so she faced the windshield. Her cheeks were now fire-engine red. He wanted to kiss them.

"Does that offend you?" Gavril asked.

"No," Gilly said, finally looking him in the eye, as his attention went from her face to the road ahead, where cars were still at a standstill.

"I'm not offended because I feel the same way," Gilly said. "It makes me feel guilty, though. With all that's been going on with the Nosferatu and Loup-Garous missing, and now Viv up and gone, you'd think that was the only thing that'd be on my mind."

"It isn't," Gavril said. "Is it?"

Gilly shook her head. "No. I feel the same way you do. I'm going to put myself on a line here, something I've never done before. You can either accept it or crush it. I'm a big girl and can take either."

"What is it?"

"Every time I see your face, I need you. When you touch me, even we're talking about the direst situations, my body races to white hot, and if I had my way, I'd take you then and there." She sighed and stared back at the windshield. "Sounds ridiculous, even to me. Makes me sound like a slut. My sister's missing, and I'm talking about how much I always need you."

Gavril took advantage of the two inches of space between him and the car in front of him, and then turned to Gilly. "Look, I know you don't like to be told what to do. You're independent and often hardheaded—in a good way. You're more woman than any man could possibly think of handling, except me. I see you. I hear you. I understand you. And I want to see just how far you can tolerate me before you kick me to the curb."

"The curb?"

"You know, shove me out of your life because I'm too much for you."

"That'll be the day," Gilly said with a smirk.

"Accident," Gavril suddenly said, jerking his chin toward the fast lane a half mile ahead. "Cops everywhere. That's what caused the slow down. Shouldn't take us long once we get past them."

"Rubberneckers," Gilly said. "That's the slow down. People in the standard lane slowing to a crawl to see the carnage." Suddenly her voice hitched and tears rimmed her eyes.

It didn't go unnoticed by Gavril. "What's wrong? Surely you've seen an accident before."

"It's not that," Gilly said, and then she quickly wiped away a tear that had slid down her cheek. "It's when I said 'carnage.' I hope to all that's in the universe that isn't what we find when we locate Viv."

Gavril didn't comment. He knew that although Gilly

could feel if her sister was alive or dead, he had to let her feel, period. He remembered all too well how it felt when they'd lost Ronan. Yes, there'd been a job to do in protecting the Originals and Triad from the Cartesians, but it was difficult to stay focused on a responsibility when your feelings were swamped with grief.

Traffic broke up about ten minutes later, and it took Gavril another fifteen to get to Chalmette. He drove through the center of town, looking for any sign of a carnival. All he saw, however, were people going about their daily jobs. No signs, no banners, no indication that a carnival had been or would be coming to town.

He saw a Denny's up ahead and turned to Gilly. "Hungry?"

"Not really," she said, still staring straight ahead.

Gavril knew she hadn't eaten that day, since they'd been together for most of it. "Tell you what. I'll go in and grab us a couple of burgers. We can eat them while we drive around town and check things out."

Not looking at him, Gilly nodded, and Gavril had the feeling that he could have said anything and she would have nodded the same way.

Gavril went into the restaurant, intending to get more than a couple of burgers. If anyone knew about a carnival being in town, it would be a waitress. Carnivals meant hungry people, so it only made sense that the restaurant would fill up more than normal.

"How ya doin', hon?" an elderly woman with short grey hair and a yellow uniform said when he walked inside. The name tag over her left breast pocket read Reba. "Place is pretty empty right now, so help yourself to whatever seat you'd like."

"Thanks," Gavril said, "but if you don't mind, I'd like a couple of burgers and two Cokes to go."

"No problem," Reba said. She then wrote up his order and stuck it on a spinning rack for the short-order cook.

"Heard traffic was tied up real bad out there," Reba said. "Construction or accident?"

"Accident, unfortunately."

Reba tsked. "Everybody tryin' to get somewhere too fast, that's the problem. That and textin' on those doggone phones instead of watchin' the road."

Gavril nodded in agreement, and then figured it was as good a time as any to hold Reba's attention.

"I heard you guys had a carnival in town," Gavril said. "Is it still up and running, or did they already break down and head out?"

Reba frowned. "Hon, I don't know who told you about any carnival, but I ain't seen one around this town for nearin' ten years."

"So no carnival or circuses, nothing like that, huh?"

She shook her head. "The only clowns we got around here are some of our regulars. Now I wouldn't tell them that to their face, you hear what I'm sayin'?" She twirled a finger near her right temple, indicating someone with a screw loose in the head. "But it ain't hard to tell they ain't quite right. As for real clowns, like in a circus, no, hon. Same as with the carnivals. Ain't seen one around in more years than I can count."

"What about in a town near you, like Arabi, places like that?"

Reba raised one of her penciled-on eyebrows. "No. Not there either. You know, you're mighty curious about carnivals, circuses and the like for a man your age. Wanna tell me what you're really looking for?"

At about that time, a bell rang, and the cook behind the counter all but shouted, "Order up."

"Aw, well, ain't my business no how," Reba said. "Your

burgers are ready." She grabbed the bag of burgers, brought it to Gavril, and then took two Coke cans out of a glass fridge and placed them in a plastic bag. "Here ya go, hon. That'll be twelve ninety-five."

Gavril grabbed his wallet out of his back pocket, pulled out a twenty and gave it to Reba. "Keep the change," he said with a smile. Then with burgers and Cokes in hand, Gavril hurried out of the restaurant before Reba could ask any more questions.

When he reached the black Camaro Nikoli had chosen as their rental, he noticed the passenger door was open and no Gilly.

Gavril tossed the food and drinks into the car, fear causing his heart to pound against his ribs so hard it hurt.

"Gilly?" he called.

No answer.

Gavril all but raced around the gas pumps, hoping she was standing on the other side of one. Nobody around but an elderly bald man filling up a battered blue pickup.

"Gilly!" Gavril called louder, turning in circles, hoping to get sight of her.

"You looking for that pretty, black-haired woman who was in your car?" the elderly man asked.

Gavril sucked in a breath. "Yes. You've seen her?"

"Sure. Don't see how you didn't. She walked right into the restaurant not long after you did. Figured she was either going to pay for gas or had to go to the john."

"Thank you," Gavril said, and took off at a near run, back to the restaurant. Just as he opened the door, he almost collided with Gilly.

"Jesus!" Gavril said, feeling like he could breathe for the first time in minutes.

"What's wrong?" Gilly asked. "Did you find out anything? Did you talk to anyone? Anybody that might have seen Viv?"

Gavril took Gilly by the shoulders, pulled her toward him until the doors to the restaurant closed behind them, and then pulled her close. "I couldn't find you," he said softly. "I thought I'd lost you."

Gilly pulled away slightly so she could look him in the eyes. "A girl's gotta pee sometime."

Gavril shook his head and grinned with solid relief.

"Any word on a carnival?" Gilly asked. "I saw you talking to that waitress. I was hoping she might have known something."

"Nothing," Gavril said. He let go of Gilly's shoulder, took her hand and led her to the car. "Burgers and Coke in the front seat."

"Nothing as she didn't see anyone who looked like Viv, or nothing on a carnival?"

"No carnival. In fact, the waitress claimed there hadn't been a carnival or circus in this area or the surrounding towns in quite a number of years."

Gilly grabbed the bags of food and slid into the passenger seat.

When Gavril settled into the driver's seat, instead of turning the engine over, he simply sat and gazed out the window.

"What now?" Gilly asked. "What the hell do we do?"

Gavril didn't look at her for a moment, thinking. Finally he glanced over at Gilly and said, "You know how you and your sisters have special sounds you make when it's time to change Originals at feeding time? You know, take out the Nosferatu and bring in the Loup-Garous?"

"Yeah."

"Have you tried calling Viv like that? You and Evee, I mean. Maybe if the two of you try, she might hear you, or more importantly, you might hear her."

"It doesn't work that way. What we do is not a mating or come-hither call," Gilly explained. "It's just an animal noise we copy to let the others know it's their turn."

Gavril chewed on his upper lip for a second, almost fearing the repercussion that might come with his next question. "Have you and Evee tried doing a come-hither spell? Do you even have one of those?"

Gilly frowned at him, anger flashing in her eyes. "Of course we do, but it's for those we command or for something we need. It's not used to call one another. It wouldn't work."

"Have you ever tried it before?"

Gilly narrowed her eyes, and then turned to look at the dashboard. "Actually...no."

"Then how do you know it wouldn't work?"

Taking a deep breath, Gilly sat back in her seat. "Fine, I'll talk to Evee, see what she has to say about it."

Gavril turned the engine over and headed out of the parking lot. "Don't be angry with me," he said. "I'm just trying to think of anything, everything possible we can do to try and find Viv. Even if it means using a spell that's never been used for that purpose before."

"Easy for you to say," Gilly said. "You're not a witch. Things can go wrong if you use spells that aren't used for a specific purpose. Every spell has one. And every spell has a consequence tied to it."

"So you think it might put Viv in even more danger since you've never done it before?"

"Hell, I don't know," Gilly said and slapped the dashboard. "Just get us back to New Orleans. I'll talk to Evee. If it's a go for her, I'm game. If she refuses, it's a no go. We'll have to try something else."

"Like what?" Gavril asked.

"Praying."

# Chapter 7

Instead of following Highway 46 back to New Orleans, Gilly insisted that they head east, in order to check out the smaller towns near Chalmette. Since they were out this far, anyway, she didn't want to miss the chance that some carnival had gone through a small town, even if only for a weekend.

Along the way, they made stops at cafés, dollar stores and gas stations. Sometimes, depending on the location, Gavril would get out and ask about carnivals in town. Other times, Gilly had been the one to leave Gavril in the car while she questioned clerks or waitresses. They drove from Chalmette to Meraux, and then to Poydras, where Gilly got out of the car and went into an old convenience store, its shelves nearly bare. She thought about grabbing a bag of chips for a snack, but then checked the expiration date. April of last year. Knowing she was being watched by the clerk behind the counter, she held back an "Ugh!" She then went over to the small man with dark skin and eyes. Not once did a smile light his face.

"Excuse me," Gilly said, trying to act nonchalant. "We heard there was some kind of carnival or circus in this area. Have you heard of it? Do you know where it might be?"

"You buy something?" the clerk asked frowning.

Gilly grabbed a pack of Juicy Fruit gum near a display case by the register. "Just this," she said.

"One dollar, forty-two cents," the clerk said.

Gilly gave him a double take. "A dollar and forty-two cents for one pack of gum?"

He nodded. "You pay or put it back, please. I keep my store very clean, as you see. Everything must have its place."

Infuriated by the price gouging, Gilly pulled two bucks out of her pocket and tossed it on the counter. She waited while he slowly counted out her change.

"So do you know of a carnival or circus around here?" Gilly said.

The clerk handed Gilly her change, made sure she'd only taken one pack of gum, and then shook his head. "No. We have no such thing here. You want party, you go to New Orleans. They always have party in that city. We have party only one time a year."

Gilly's ears perked up. "When?"

"What do they call Fat Tuesday here?"

"Mardi Gras?"

"Yes, that would be the party. It's chaos, I tell you. People fill up all the towns near here. They steal from my store. I know this to be fact. Last year, I found boy with a beer can in his pants. He tried to leave the store, but I caught him. Caught him and called the police. He must go to jail, I tell the police. He must go to jail."

Gilly's expectation bubble deflated. Mardi Gras was still five months away. No carnival. No circus.

"Anything?" Gavril asked when Gilly returned to the car with the pack of gum, which she abruptly threw out the window. For all she knew, it might have had an expiration date of May 5, 1909.

"Nothing but some pain-in-the-butt guy. Wouldn't even give me information until I bought something from his damn store."

"You talking about the gum you just pitched out the window?"

"Yeah. Everything in that place was so old, the gum probably carried botulism."

"So, I take it, gum or no gum, he doesn't know of any carnivals or circuses."

Gilly shook her head. "The guy said the only party they had in town was during Mardi Gras, and that's five to six months away."

Gavril laid a hand over the steering wheel and sighed. Gilly laid her head back on the seat, closed her eyes for a few seconds, and then she opened them and stared at nothing.

"I just can't figure it," Gavril said. "Why would Moose talk about things that sound like they're from a carnival, yet we can't find one that's happened around here for months?"

"Hell if I know," Gilly said, looking straight ahead.

"What now?" Gavril said as he shoved the gear into drive. "Hmm, other than rain."

As if waking from a dream, Gilly looked over at him, and then followed his gaze to the windshield. Black thunderheads had rolled in, and beyond them lay a heavy sheet of gray. The wind had already started to pick up, threatening to rock the Camaro from one lane to another.

By the time they hit Meraux again, the windshield wipers were going at full speed, but were seemingly as useless as a rosary in a Baptist church. Gilly couldn't see car lights in front of her.

"Can you see anything?" Gilly asked. "Car lights? Flashers?"

Gavril, who was white-knuckling the steering wheel, shook his head. They were barely managing a five-mile-per-hour crawl. "We're going to have to pull off somewhere until this calms down," he said. "The last thing we need is to rear-end somebody or have someone rear-end us. The eighteen wheelers aren't helping either. They're producing so much spray that, even with mud flaps, it's like driving through twice the amount of rain."

Gilly agreed, putting a hand on the dashboard when a set of break lights suddenly appeared in front of them, less than a foot away. She resisted an instinct to put a protective hand out toward Gavril, like a loving mother would a child. He was definitely not a child, and she was no one's mother. But loving was what made her hand want to shoot out to protect him. That she felt to her core.

Gavril inched the Camaro along until they came up to a gravel road about two-hundred feet ahead. Lightning sizzled through the sky, and thunder boomed seemingly from every direction.

"What is that?" Gilly asked, pointing to a large, dull red building nearly five-hundred feet or so off the main road. It had no front door, just an open space in front of the building, wide enough to drive a tractor—or a car—through.

"Looks like a barn. See any houses near it?"

"Hell, I can barely see it," Gilly said. She scooted up to the edge of her seat to get a better look through the windshield and pressed her face against the passenger side window. "Don't see anything but the barn. No houses. No cars or trucks. Just that old building."

"Good," Gavril said, and before Gilly knew it, he squeezed the Camaro through the front opening of the building and drove until they reached a solid-wall cattle gate.

Rain pinged off the tin roof, but it was nothing compared to the sound of driving through gushing water.

Gilly got out of the car, closed the passenger door and stretched her arms and legs. "Man, oh, man, I don't remember the last time I've seen a gully washer like this one."

Gavril followed her out of the car. He did a quick survey of the place. Stables, but no horses or cows. Above them was a semi-circle second floor with bales of hay piled on top of one another.

"You were right about the hay," Gilly said, motioning overhead. "I wonder why there're no cattle here."

"Farmer might be grazing them in another pasture. Hopefully he's taken the hay he's needed for the day."

"But wouldn't he bring the animals in because of the rain?" Gilly asked.

"Cows and horses, unless you're talking high-bred stock, are used to the weather. It can be raining buckets, and they'll either be lying under a tree or still grazing grass. Wet doesn't seem to bother them much."

Gilly walked toward the open end of the barn, wanting to get closer to see if the rain appeared to be slacking. A bolt of lightning struck just outside, and thunder made the ground rumble beneath her feet. The rain had not only slacked, it had intensified, blowing sheets of rain drops the size of raisins.

She crossed her arms over her chest, lowered her head, and walked to the back wall of the building, thinking…thinking. Only there wasn't a damn thing to think about. She'd always known Moose to be a little slow in the brain department, but at least he had brains. She wasn't able to look past what Moose saw to get a handle on the location of these intense colors. The only thing that made sense was a carnival or circus, only she hadn't been able to see that to make it a fact.

Aside from attempting a come-hither call as she'd promised Gavril that she'd try with Evee, the only other option that came to mind was trying to contact Moose again to find out if one of the other dead Loups was with him—one that might be able to give them clearer directions.

Suddenly, Gilly sneezed. She was surprised to find herself shivering. It was too early in the fall for it to be cold, but the rain, together with the wind, made it feel like she'd been dunked in thirty-degree water.

Evidently, seeing her react to the cold, Gavril took off his shirt and wrapped it around her shoulders.

"But you'll freeze," Gilly protested. "You need to put it back on, or you'll wind up with a cold or pneumonia." Gilly felt slightly embarrassed because the entire time she addressed him, she hadn't been able to take her eyes off his chest, his ripped abs and his huge biceps.

Gilly took off his shirt and handed it back to him. "Please, for me. I'll be worried sick that you'll catch your death, and then what will we do without you?"

Gavril gave her a slow shake of his head and put his shirt back on. "I'll wear it," he said, "but we need to find a warmer place before I wind up having to take care of you in a hospital."

Gilly held her hands out. "Unless we sit in the car, we're kind of limited."

"Not at all," Gavril said, and held out his right hand. She took it without hesitation and followed him to a tall ladder that stretched from the bottom floor to the hayloft overhead.

"If we lay between the bales of hay, you'll warm up quickly," he assured her. As they made it up the ladder, Gavril said, "We're talking about a hayloft now, so don't expect the Ritz."

When they made it to the top of the hayloft, Gilly said, "You're right, it's not the Ritz. More like a Holiday Inn."

He smiled, and then started moving bales around.

"How are we going to know when the rain slacks off enough for us to drive out of here if we're stuck between bales of hay?" A crack of lightning, and then a roll of thunder, had Gavril raise both eyebrows.

"Whenever it will be, it certainly isn't right now." He motioned her between two rows of hay stacked three bales high. "And we've got that," Gavril said, and motioned to a small set of wooden doors at the north end of the loft.

"Funny place for doors, don't you think?" Gilly said.

"Not really. Instead of hoisting bales of hay down that ladder when needed, all the farmer has to do is toss however many bales he needs through the window. They land on the ground, and then he loads them into the back of his truck."

"And all we have to do is open those hay doors to check on the weather," Gilly said.

"You've got it."

Rain pummeled the metal roof of the barn, and thunder rolled continuously around them.

Gilly lay between the two rows of hay and immediately felt the difference in temperature. She wasn't shaking anymore. The problem was, she didn't know if it was the change of environment that had relieved her shivers, or if it was Gavril taking control of the situation and taking care of her, the way a man does for his woman.

Thinking of that made her nervous and excited at the same time. To stave off both feelings, she turned on her right side, put an arm under her head and said, "If I drift off, promise you'll wake me when the weather lets us?"

Gavril gave her a little salute. "Yes, ma'am. Immediately."

A few seconds of silence passed, and then Gilly said. "Gavril?"

"Yes?"

"Suppose the weather stays like this for hours? I don't want to be stuck here that long. We've got to find Viv."

"We'll find her, baby. I promise we'll find her." He squatted down, sat on his haunches and rubbed her pant leg gently.

Gilly gave him a soft smile and watched his eyes light up despite another hold up on their mission. She noticed how his attitude wasn't one of frustration and angst, but calm and certainty. He was sure of himself. Sure of how to care for her. For all of them.

Out of nowhere, Gilly suddenly sat up and leaned over so her face was right beside his. She held his face between her hands and said softly, "No matter how chaotic things have become, how we seem to conquer one thing and four more new ones pop up, I—I can't thank you enough for all you do. For all you and your cousins have done for the Triad, for our Originals. I know missing two entire groups of them was not in any Bender's plan, but despite how hopeless it makes everything seem, you never give up. You're always thinking of new ideas, ready to search longer, farther, regardless of how little sleep and food you've had. I didn't want you to think any of what you do goes unnoticed. I do notice and appreciate you more than I can express."

Seemingly left wordless, Gavril sat back, silent for a moment. "You give me far too much credit. You and your sisters have been right along with us on the fight. My cousins have worked and fought just as hard, so much so that it cost one his life. Thank you for the compliment, but don't forget we're all in this together. It isn't just me."

Suddenly Gavril's stomach grumbled, and a look of embarrassment crossed his face. "Well, that was a fine set of manners if I ever heard one," he said with a grin.

"You're hungry. I mean, geez, how long has it been since you've eaten?"

Gavril shrugged. "Not something I keep track of."

"We still have those burgers and Cokes in the car. Would you like me to run over and get them for you?"

"No, thank you, but I can get them for you," he said.

Instead of answering, Gilly reached for Gavril's face with both hands and pulled him close. She kissed him lightly at first, just to taste his lips. "I am hungry," she whispered. "But not for burgers." She wrapped her hands around his neck and pulled him down to her and kept pulling until he lay right beside her.

"Gilly," he whispered, a worried look on his face. "What the Elders told you. All that's happening... I don't want you to feel—"

In response, Gilly lifted her body and kissed Gavril gently on the lips. As if it meant to orchestrate a romantic play, rain pinged heavier on the roof top, lightning cracked like an expert with a bullwhip and wind whistled through the cracks in the building.

When his lips left hers reluctantly, Gavril said, "I am starved, too, but not for food."

Feeling the same, and shoving all thoughts of chaos and heartaches to the farthest reaches of her mind, Gilly pulled Gavril down so his body rested upon hers. He put his hands on either side of her to lift some of his weight off her, and then leaned in to devour her mouth.

Gilly moaned reflexively. His lips were the softest, sexiest ones on the planet, and she couldn't get enough of them. Not only did it start a fire burning inside her, it caused something that felt like an electromagnetic field inside of her body that worked at pulling them closer, closer, so close that she wanted them to fuse together. His kisses were to die for, but if she didn't have the rest of him, she felt like she'd implode.

Gavril broke their kiss for a second and looked into her eyes. "Gilly, I—"

She wrapped her fingers in his hair and took his mouth as a ravenous woman would take a seven-course meal. She simply couldn't get enough of him. Not now. Not ever.

Silently, except for the rapid growth of his breathing, Gavril ran his mouth along the side of Gilly's throat, nipping at it, licking it, kissing her below the earlobe.

Unable to bear the heat of her own body anymore, and despite the itchy twigs of hay that had broken loose from its bale, Gilly reached down and pulled off her shirt. Unable to wait for him to reach other parts of her body, she stripped off her bra, moved him aside for only a moment, and in a flash, was out of her pants and underwear.

Gilly lay back down between the bales of hay, her arms stretched over her head, her legs crossed at the ankles. She saw Gavril's eyes travel hungrily over her and heard his sharp intact of breath. She could almost hear his thoughts... *I want all of her now! Where on earth do I start? Control, man. Control.*

And control he did. With Gilly's arms above her head, her breasts rode high, her nipples rigid, pointing upward, calling to him.

But Gavril accepted the challenge of control. He leaned over Gilly and kissed the opposite side of her neck, sucking and nipping on it, his lips moving across her throat, just below her jaw, and then suddenly moving up and taking her mouth, his tongue plunging in to meet hers. She sucked on it as if she were sucking on the hardest part of his manhood right now, and he had to form an algebraic formula in his head to keep from exploding then and there.

He released his tongue from her grip and teased her mouth, shoving his tongue in and out...in...out, licking as he soon planned to do with the wettest part of her womanhood.

As his tongue and mouth teased her to a white-hot pitch, he cupped her breasts in his hands and smoothed his hands down from her breastbone to her nipples, where he finally caught them between a thumb and forefinger and squeezed. Gently at first, until he heard her groan. Once more, with his tongue still working her mouth, he slid his hands gently up and across her chest until he reached her nipples, which he then locked between a thumb and forefinger. He tugged at both, twisted slightly until she moaned, tugged and twisted more until she cried out his name with need.

Gilly tangled her fingers into his hair and pulled him down lower, lower, until she felt his breath on her right breast. She arched her back, wanting desperately for him to touch her, taste her.

Gavril's tongue flicked ever so gently over her right breast, and she moaned from a need so deep inside of her it sounded animalistic.

"More… More, Gavril, more."

The sound of his name seemed to throw Gavril into a feeding frenzy he had little control over. He licked her right breast while he fondled her left, suckled her nipples, moving from one to the other. Taking them between his teeth and nipping them gently, wanting, needing her to cry out his name, which she did again and again.

Gilly heard her breath go from rapid to almost nonexistent. Gavril had her so wrapped in need, she forgot to breathe.

Soon his lips and tongue moved lower, down to her stomach, his hands never leaving her breasts until he had reached the triangle of her thighs. Then his hands moved down, and he parted her thighs ever so slightly.

"Oh, Gilly…" The sound of her name from his lips sent her back into a high arch. There was no mistaking what she wanted or needed.

Even from where she lay, Gilly felt the heat from between her legs grow furnace hot. She felt warm, fresh juices run out of her slit that was so swollen and desperate for him, and she hadn't even had an orgasm yet.

Gavril spread her legs apart as far as the bales of hay would allow on either side of her, and then placed one finger gently against her wetness. He pressed slightly but didn't enter, causing Gilly to cry out his name.

"Gavril…"

He glanced up at her, his mouth swollen and full from their kisses. "What, baby? Tell me what you want. Tell me what you need."

Gilly arched her back higher, threw her head back, all inhibition lost to this man. "I—I need to feel your tongue there. Your fingers…all of you." She knew how hard he was when he lay atop her. The length and girth of his cock made her all the more anxious to have him inside. She'd beg if she had to. Something she'd never thought she'd be capable of doing in her entire life.

"Tell me, baby," Gavril said. "You want to feel…this?" And he moved a finger slowly inside of her, only to the depth of one knuckle.

The sound that escaped Gilly was guttural.

"Or did you mean this…" And with those words, Gavril placed his mouth over the nodule that he knew would cause her to erupt, to drain every ounce of the sexual juices her body had been holding on to for so long. He licked and sucked and shoved his finger in deeper, widening her enough so a second would slide in easily.

With two fingers inside her, and his tongue over the mound that ruled her, Gavril sucked, licked and shoved his fingers in fast and deep. He pushed them into the farthest parts of her, where he knew that secret button would release more than Gilly had ever felt before.

So much was pent up inside Gilly that she opened her mouth to speak, but nothing would come out. She didn't want to lessen what was about to flood her with words. It boiled inside her like a pressure cooker that was set was on high and didn't a relief valve.

Gavril must have felt what was happening with her body

because he took her clitoris between her legs, used the fingers of his free hand to spread the skin that hooded it as far back and away as it would go, and then he placed his mouth over it, working it back and forth, side to side with his tongue.

Gavril felt his fingers reach way inside of her and touch a place that had no words to describe the way it made her feel. Feeling or being sexual was one thing, but he touched what *was* the peak of her sexual drive. Relentlessly, he worked his fingers on that spot, holding his hand in place, stretching the top of his finger so that it reached it, touched it just so.

All Gilly felt was a tsunami swelling, swelling, ready to crash over her. She tried to tell him, to warn him, but before she could, come squirted from her into his mouth, all over his hand and his chest. It wasn't like Gilly was a prude. She'd had sex before, but nothing as intense as this. Nothing that made her insides feel like they'd just exploded all over him.

Gavril ever so slowly removed his mouth and fingers from her body. He lay beside her, smoothing her tousled hair that had landed across her eyes.

She looked at him, felt her body more at ease and peaceful than she'd known it to be in a long time. And her heart fuller than she'd ever thought possible.

Gavril kissed her on the forehead and was about to get to his feet when Gilly grabbed his hand. "But you…" she said.

"There'll be time for me, believe me," Gavril said. "But listen for a moment and tell me what you hear."

Gilly lay back, closed her eyes and listened carefully. Something occasionally falling on the tin roof…the meow of a cat who'd found its shelter in the same place they had. Suddenly, Gilly sat up. "The storm's passed," she said, becoming excited.

Gavril nodded. "It sure has." He held out a hand to help Gilly to her feet. "Come on, sweet thing. Let's go find your sister."

## Chapter 8

When Gilly and Gavril returned to the François home, she found herself shocked into silence by what she saw. Sitting in the living room was Evee, Lucien, Taka, Arabella and Gunner Stern, one of the three true sorcerers who lived in New Orleans.

"What are you doing here?" Gilly asked Gunner.

"Gilly!" Evee said, reprimand in her voice. "There's no need to be so rude. Arabella and Taka asked him to meet us here, and he was kind enough to do so."

Infuriated that a sorcerer sat in her living room, Gilly glanced about. "Where's Vanessa?" she asked.

"Oh, she didn't want any part of this," Taka said. She took a ladyfinger cookie and napkin from a small silver tray that sat on a glass and mahogany coffee table. Beside that sat yet another tray, this one holding a small teapot and china teacups to match.

"Well, it seems like one of you made sense," Gilly said.

"Gilly, why don't you and Gavril have a seat, and we'll explain all we've been discussing," Arabella said.

"I don't have time for chit-chat," Gilly said. "I'm going to take a shower, and then go and look for Viv. The rest of you can eat cookies and drink tea until you choke on it. Whatever floats your boat."

Gavril lightly took Gilly by the arm and led her to the small couch that was across from the divan where Evee and Lucien sat. Near them, Taka and Arabella sat on the couch closest to the fireplace, while Gunner was in a wingback chair between the divan and one of the couches.

"Just listen to what they have to say," Gavril whispered in Gilly's ear.

She jerked her arm away from his grasp and dropped down with a plop in an overstuffed chair. "Okay, say what you've got to say, but I can't believe we're just spending all this time gabbing away while Viv's out there. Heaven only knows where she is, and in what kind of danger."

"I understand that," Arabella said. "Don't you think we're worried about her, as well? That's why I got Gunner involved. We've been working as hard as we can to try to get the Originals back and into their normal states. We've lost many of them along the way. I spoke with Gunner because I trust him, and I think he may be able to help, if not with finding the missing Originals, then helping us at least find Viv. She's the most important issue we have to concentrate on right now."

"I agree," Evee said.

Lucien nodded his head in agreement.

Gilly stared at Gunner. "You know what the issue between sorcerers and witches has been for generations, right?"

Gunner nodded and offered her the smallest of smiles. "I

can understand why you feel the way that you feel. There's been animosity between witches and sorcerers for centuries."

"No, you don't understand," Gilly said. "I don't like Trey Cottle or his sidekick, Shandor Black. I guess they're in an occupation that suits their sleazy personalities, being attorneys and all. But attorneys or not, I don't trust them. I don't trust what they say. They're only out to help themselves. I've never seen them reach out to help anyone in this community, and I don't mean to sound crass, Mr. Stern, but you're with them an awful lot. Why should I trust you when all I see is you with Trey Cottle and his brownnoser?"

"That would probably be my sentiment exactly," Gunner said. "The truth of the matter is that the three of us are sorcerers. Sometimes we talk shop, but most of the time, believe it or not, I'm with Trey and Shandor just to keep an ear to the ground, so to speak. To hear and see what Shandor and Trey are up to. You're right. Most of what they do with spells or potions has to do with suiting themselves, benefiting themselves. How does that saying go? 'Keep your friends close, but your enemies closer.' I'm not saying that Cottle or Black are my enemies, but I don't exactly see them as tried-and-true Boy Scouts type. I don't agree with a lot of what they do."

Gilly scowled. "What does that matter if you allow them to gain over the community by their spells and their potions? A little potion here to get a city ordinance passed in their favor, a small spell there to get a judge to lean in their direction. Just stepping back doesn't do anything. Why don't you stop them?"

"Once they've issued a spell or used a potion," Gunner said, "I can't stop it. I can put a protection spell, which I've done many times, over the person or city council they're trying to take advantage of. Like you, I want these people's decisions to be their own and not something that's been generated by Cottle or Black."

Gilly blew out a frustrated breath. "If you can't reverse their spells, what makes you think you can help us find Viv? We're sitting here with what? You've got four witches and none of us are able to contact my own sister. What makes you think you can make a difference? You can't even go against your own. What makes you think you can conjure up something that'll allow us to find Viv?"

"I'm not saying that I can," Gunner said. "But I'm here to help in any way that I can."

"And what way is that?" Evee asked.

"I can offer a come-hither spell," Gunner said. "It may work, it may not—because she doesn't know my voice— but it's at least worth a try. You never know, because it's not a voice she recognizes, it may call to her, and she may appear. She may be able to untangle herself from whatever's deterring her so that she can come home."

"That makes sense," Taka said. "You know, if I heard a man's voice calling me, I'd come. But we've already tried that spell. It didn't work."

"Any man?" Gilly asked her. "Even if you don't know who he is? Especially with all that's been going on with the Cartesians and missing Originals?"

Taka took another bite of cookie, chewed for a second, and then said, "Yeah. 'Cause a Cartesian can't talk. They just make loud growling, grunting sounds from what you've told me. So, if it was a man's voice, and he could call to me like that, I'd at least go check it out. That doesn't mean I'd go running and bow at his feet, but I'd sure check him out. You never know, he could be good looking. Might be worth the chance."

"Oh, for the love of the universe, Taka," Arabella said.

"We're not talking about a man for Viv. We're talking about Viv listening to a man's voice."

"I know," Taka said with a pout. "I'm not stupid. I understand exactly what you're saying."

"Just eat your cookies and have some tea, dear," Arabella said. "Let's finish this conversation so we can go about finding Viv."

"I'm scared, Gilly," Evee said. "Viv has never been away like this. She would never just disappear and not tell us where she was going." Evee's lips started to tremble. "I'm afraid something's happened to her, and if it takes Gunner coming here to try and call so that she hears a new voice and comes to it, I'm all for it." A tear slid down Evee's cheek, and Lucien put an arm around her and patted her shoulder to comfort her. "I just want her back."

"I want her back, too," Gilly said. "I want her back in one piece." Gilly turned to Gunner. "Mr. Stern, do you have any idea what a Cartesian is?"

"Yes," Gunner said. "Unfortunately, I do."

"And how is it that you know of them?"

"We have known about Cartesians for many generations. For centuries. I've not seen one for myself or had to deal with any, but I know that they are monstrous creatures, and they are out for blood, for death. They want all who exist in the netherworld. To kill them and make their powers their own."

"That's right," Gilly said. "And what do you think they would do if they captured a Triad?"

Gunner nodded again. "I know the Originals are in danger with the Cartesians, but so is the Triad. Believe me, I've had nightmares about it. That's why I have been so insistent about offering to help. Thankfully, Arabella allowed me to at least talk to you."

"And just what is it that you propose, Mr. Stern?" Evee asked.

"Please, call me Gunner."

"Fine," Gilly said.

"Have you tried a come-hither spell?" Gunner asked.

"I have," Taka said. "I did it the other day. The only thing that came, though, was a sparrow. It came and flew right into the window. Smashed its head and fell to the ground."

"We were just talking about this," Gavril said conspiratorially to Gilly.

Gilly shot him an "I know" look, and then turned back to Gunner. "Fine. So let's do it. Do you need potions, herbs, crystals?"

"No," Gunner said. "All I ask is that we join hands and form a circle. I'll stand in the middle of it and issue the command."

"Let's do it then," Gilly said impatiently.

Everyone got to their feet. Evee, Lucien, Taka, Arabella, Gilly and Gavril. They held hands as instructed by Gunner, breaking rank only to allow him into the middle of the circle.

Gunner closed his eyes, and Gilly could only assume he was visualizing Viv. He'd have no problem bringing her to mind, since he'd known the Triad for years. After a long moment, he held out his hands, palms up, and said,

*Come hither, Triad.*
*One so true.*
*Although my voice be male and new.*
*Let not my command hinder thee.*
*But break all bonds.*
*And come to me.*
*I bind all bonds.*
*That hinder thee.*
*So come hither now.*

*To thine family.*

After issuing the incantation, Gunner stood silently with his arms held out. Everyone listened intently, but heard nothing but the ticking of the grandfather clock at the end of the foyer.

"Well, so much for that," Gilly said. "Seems like you have the same effect that—"

Suddenly Gilly heard a loud bang at the front door.

Taka jumped and slapped a hand to her chest. "For the love of cheese and crackers, that almost gave me a heart attack! Who is that? Maybe it's Viv!"

Gilly released her grip on Gavril's and Evee's hands. She went over to the front door and peered through the security peephole. "I don't see anyone."

Taka marched up to the front door. "Probably some of those kids who live a few houses down from here. They bang on your door, then take off running. I'll catch those little boogers."

Taka yanked the door open, and Gavril yelled, "Shut the door, Taka. Now! Shut the door." Taka turned and looked at him, confusion on her face.

It was then Gilly caught the scent of cloves and sulfur. She shoved her Elder out of the way and slammed the door shut. When she looked through the peephole again, Gilly saw a Cartesian's long black talons. Had Taka stayed at the doorway a second longer, it would have gotten her.

"Goddamn," Gilly said to Gavril. "They know where we are." She felt her hands start to shake as she pointed to the door. Soon her entire body began to tremble. "Th-they... they're out there. They know where we are!"

Gavril hurried to her side and put an arm around her. "It's okay," he said.

"It's not okay, Gavril. They found us. Where we live. How are we ever going to get out of here if they're out there

waiting, watching? Gunner's come hither spell didn't work
either. If they took Viv, they're waiting to get Evee and me
and the Elders. First the Originals. Remember? You said
that they wanted the Originals, the Triad and the Elders for
our powers. How are we going to leave this place? How are
we going to find Viv?"

"Oh, we'll leave," Gavril said. "Now listen carefully.
When I give you the signal, I want you to swing the door
open wide, then take off for your kitchen and go up the back
stairs to the second floor and wait there. Taka, you and Arabella, Evee and Gunner do the same." He turned to Lucien
"You've got your scabior on you, right?"

"Of course, cuz," Lucien said and patted the sheath attached to his belt.

"Good, because I think we've got a bit of a skirmish
ahead of us."

"But you can't just leave us here," Arabella said. "We've
got to fight together."

Gunner took Arabella's hand, and then grabbed hold of
Taka's. "Let's just do what they've told us to. We have no
experience fighting these Cartesians. But these men do.
I'm going to lead you up the stairs, and I'll stay there with
you until they call us back down. Don't argue over this one.
These men know what they're doing. Let them do their job."

"I'm not going anywhere," Gilly said fiercely. "Gavril,
if you're staying to fight, I'm here with you."

"Same with me and Lucien," Evee said.

"The two of you are going to go in the other room,"
Gavril said loudly. "Just like we said." He looked deeply
into Gilly's eyes. "The last thing I want is to lose you."

Lucien took Evee by the shoulders and, in front of everyone, kissed her. "And I don't want to lose you. Please just go
to the other room. We'll get you out of here. Don't worry."

Reluctantly, Gilly took hold of Evee's arm and they went into the foyer.

"On the count of three," Gilly told Evee. She held tight to her sister's arm, and then she yanked the door open and took off with Evee to the kitchen, across the foyer. "Go upstairs. I'll be there in a minute."

Evee scowled. "Promise?"

"Yeah."

"Gilly, please don't do anything stupid. We need you."

"Just get upstairs. Hurry. I'll be up in a few."

As Evee hurried up the stairs to the second floor, Gilly planted herself against the kitchen wall closest to the foyer. She wanted to, needed to hear if Gavril or Lucien called for help. Not that she'd know what to do in the help department, but at least she'd be there. Everything inside of her wouldn't allow her to desert Gavril, even at his command.

From where she stood, Gilly saw Gavril and Lucien rush outside, scabiors in hand. She took a chance and went to the window closest to the front door and looked out. She saw Lucien and Gavril aiming their scabiors up at the sky. From where she stood, Gilly saw rift after rift, large black slits overhead with Cartesians hanging from them, reaching for Lucien and Gavril. Long talons, slicing air, wanting to destroy, to kill.

Gavril and Lucien aimed and fired again and again, pushing the Cartesians farther into a different dimension. From his back pocket, Gilly saw Gavril pull out a second scabior, which she could only assume had been Ronan's.

Gavril activated the second scabior with his left hand and used it. He had perfect aim with his right hand, but his left was off center. He obviously had to concentrate on one Cartesian at a time in order to push it back.

Without thinking, Gilly ran to the door, wanting to, needing to, help Gavril. She heard Evee call to her, crying for her from the top of the stairs. "Gilly, stop. Don't, don't go out there. I can't lose you, too. Gilly, stop!"

Blocking her sister's cries from her mind, Gilly ran outside and grabbed the scabior that was already activated out of Gavril's left hand.

"What the—" Gavril said, shocked and motionless.

Ignoring him, Gilly pointed the scabior she'd taken from him at one of the rifts, and the Cartesian that hung from it, and aimed. She heard a loud pop, and the Cartesian flew back. She aimed again into a black hole, seeing the Cartesian's talons still trying to clutch and hang on to its present dimension. She shot again and again and yet again, pushing the Cartesian back as far as she could, until the rift closed up.

But then, three more rifts began to open up, just when they thought they had everything under control.

Gavril looked at Gilly and shook his head. They each took aim at a rift, and at the Cartesian hanging from it. Surprisingly, Gilly was the one that got her Cartesian sent back five dimensions, whereas Gavril and Lucien had managed only three. Regardless of the number, at least the rifts were closed and the Cartesians were gone.

Gilly turned to face Gavril and found both him and Lucien staring at her. She didn't know how long they'd been fighting the Cartesians but if she looked half as exhausted as they did, it had been a while.

Suddenly Gavril seemed to come to life again and wrenched the scabior out of Gilly's hand. "What on earth were you thinking coming out here like that? You've never operated a scabior before. For all you know, it could have blown up in your hand. It could have electrocuted you. We've never had anyone not trained use a scabior before."

"Well, obviously, I didn't blow up," Gilly said, "And you're more than welcome for the help." She spun about on

her heels and marched back into the house. She stood by
the grandfather clock at the end of the foyer and crossed
her arms over her chest defiantly. She felt cheated from a
win and angry at having been scolded.

Gavril and Lucien came back inside and put their scabiors back into their sheaths.

"We've got to get the Elders back to their homes," Lucien
said. "And we've got to get you and Evee out of here now
that the Cartesians know where you are. They're going to
test their ground, hover over this place. They're going to
stay near here now that they know where you are. There's
no way we can stay in hiding and find Viv, much less the
missing Originals."

"I have the Camaro," Gavril said. "We can use it to get
everyone out of here."

"And I have my Buick," Gunner said. "I'll be more than
happy to take the Elders home."

"Wait a minute," Evee said. "Talking about the Camaro,
where is Nikoli?"

"He's still out looking for Viv," Lucien said.

"Where is he looking for her?" Gilly asked.

"I have no idea," Gavril said.

"Can't you take that watch thing you wear with the GPS
on it and find him? Summon him?" Gilly asked. "Tell him
it's an emergency or something so we can get his help here?
You would think, with Viv missing, he'd be right in the middle of the conversation we had before the Cartesian attack."

"He's doing exactly what I'd expect him to do," Gavril
said. "Hunt for Viv."

"Can you at least find out where he is? If he found her?"

Without answering, Gavril activated the watch he wore
on his left wrist and signaled for Nikoli.

"We're going to take the Camaro and bring the Elders

home, then we'll come back here for you," Gavril said. "Nikoli should be here by the time we get back."

After herding Taka, Arabella and Gunner into one place, Gavril went outside, double checked to make sure there were no longer any rifts around the house or anywhere close to it. Then he corralled the three of them into the Camaro and drove off.

"That was such a stupid thing you did, Gilly," Evee said. "You could have gotten yourself killed."

"That's true," Lucien said. "You shouldn't have gone out there." Then his eyes brightened. "But Evee, you should have seen her. She handled that scabior like she'd been born with it. She aimed and shot those Cartesians without a flinch. Even got the last one and pushed it back farther than Gavril and me put together. She's quite the shot."

"Don't make her head swell any more than it already has," Evee said. "Gilly had no business messing with the Cartesians."

"My head's far from swollen, thank you very much," Gilly said, knowing full well that there was a small bit of truth to it. She was just glad to have been acknowledged for her help with the Cartesians.

Evee turned to her sibling. "You have to promise me that you'll never do anything like that again. We have to find Viv, and I need your help to do it. I don't want to lose you, too, so please, promise me you won't ever attempt something like that again."

Gilly gave her sister a weary look and sighed. "Yeah, yeah, okay, I promise I won't attempt anything like that again," she said…with her fingers crossed behind her back.

# Chapter 9

Once Gunner dropped the Elders off, he left in his silver Buick, heading to his own home to review his spell book.

Arabella could tell how disappointed he was that his come-hither spell had no effect whatsoever on bringing Viv home. She had been as disappointed, certain that, as powerful and stern as his voice had been, there would have been some kind of response from Viv.

Once they entered the house, Vanessa was full of questions. Arabella waved her off and said, "I'm going to take a quick shower. Taka will fill you in."

As Vanessa hammered Taka with questions, Taka took her time, made herself a cup of coffee and added some Irish whiskey to it. Then she sat at the kitchen table, and Vanessa scurried to sit across from her.

"So what happened?" Vanessa said.

Taka took a sip of coffee-laced whiskey and sighed. "It was horrible. Those monsters are bigger than anything I've ever seen, even in horror movies. They had claws that were like talons of a hawk, only four inches long and black, and the tips curled inward. They were sweeping those talons out from a slit in the sky, trying to catch us. Anything they would've touched, they would've stabbed or skewered. We'd have been dead immediately."

"What did you do?" Vanessa asked, wide-eyed. "Wait, before you tell me, I want to get every detail." Vanessa got up from the table, hurried over to the stove, poured herself a cup of coffee and added a little more whiskey to hers than Taka had.

She hurried back to the table and sat across from Taka. "Okay, start from the beginning."

"Well," Taka said, "we got there, and Gunner did a come-hither spell."

"What happened with his spell? Did it work?"

"Do you see Viv here?"

"You don't have to be so snippy about it," Vanessa said. "Did anything happen?"

Taka took a sip of coffee and smacked her lips.

"Crickets," Arabella said, coming into the kitchen. She was dressed in blue linen pants and a white button-down blouse.

"Why are you so dressed up?" Vanessa asked.

"Because Gunner's coming back this way," Taka said. "She's gotta look good for her honey."

"Stop that nonsense, will you?" Arabella said.

"I was just asking Taka what happened," Vanessa said. "She told me those things were huge and monstrous. That they had long black talons."

"She wouldn't know," Arabella said. "She didn't even get a chance to see one."

Vanessa glared at Taka. "You mean you lied to me?"

"No, I didn't lie. I saw them through the window."

"How could you see them through the window?" Arabella asked. "You were hiding behind me the entire time the Benders were fighting."

"Yeah, but I could see through the window from where I stood behind you. I saw their talons come sweeping down. They were huge. They would've killed anything the moment they would've touched it. They were so sharp and pointed and curved."

Arabella shivered. She hadn't seen the talons. She'd only known to try to catch her breath to keep herself from having a heart attack when Gilly ran out to help Gavril and Lucien fight the Cartesians that had shown up over their home.

"Did all of that happen after Gunner did his come-hither spell?" Vanessa asked.

"Yes," Arabella said. "Unfortunately, his spell produced no results. Like I said…crickets."

"There weren't any crickets," Taka said. "I didn't hear one, and you know how it is when a cricket gets loose in a room and makes that aggravating noise. It drives you crazy. If there'd been crickets, we'd have hunted them down, caught them and tossed them outside."

"I wasn't talking about real crickets, Taka," Arabella said with a sigh. "It's a figure of speech. It means nothing happened."

"Viv didn't show up. Not a word came from anywhere." Arabella swiped a loose strand of hair away from her forehead. "His spell didn't work. That's why he's going to look over his book now to see if there's not something stronger that he can use to beckon her to us."

"You trust him that much?" Vanessa asked. "Viv didn't show up but those Cartesians surely did. What about that? Maybe his spell had something to do with it."

"I heard every word of that spell," Arabella said. "It was a come hither specifically targeting Viv, and that's it."

"You're actually going to let a sorcerer use his spell book instead of the Triad using their Grimoires?" Vanessa asked. " By the way, have they even gone through them to see if there's something in there that might help bring their sister back?"

"Oh, yes, they've gone through their Grimoires many times, from what they told me," Arabella said. "But no matter what they've tried, nothing seems to work. The biggest problem we have now…not the only one, but the biggest one…is that the Cartesians now know where the Triad lives. We're going to have major issues with them even getting out of their own home and moving about to search for the missing Originals. Now that the Cartesians know where they are, they'll never give them a moment's peace."

"Talking about Originals," Vanessa said. "I don't know if either of you have heard yet, but we lost five more humans earlier in Slidell."

Arabella plopped down on a kitchen chair. "I hadn't heard."

"Yep," Vanessa said. "Word got to me pretty quickly from Trishmia, one of the sisters from the Circle who lives in Mississippi. Police are all over it. From what I understand, there was a Nosferatu and two Loup-Garous. How or why they didn't kill each other first, I've no idea. But they did get the humans."

"Damn," Taka said.

"Please mind the cursing," Arabella said.

"I didn't curse," Taka said. "'Damn' is just a word. A figure of speech. Anyway, so what do we do now? The Cartesians know where the Triad lives. The Originals are out killing humans. We tried Gunner's spell to bring back a missing Triad, and it didn't work. What now?"

Arabella put her elbows on the table and placed her head in her hands. After a moment or two, she rubbed her forehead and looked up. "I thought about calling everyone in the Circle of Sisters here for an emergency meeting. We may not have been able to get a spell to work since they are at such distances, but what if we got everyone together in one place and did the same spell, hands linked? You know—" she looked at Taka "—the way we did when we did the come-hither spell with Gunner."

"It sounds like a great idea," Vanessa said. "I mean, we'll have to wait because some of them will be coming from other countries, but it might be worth a try. That would sure be a lot of power concentrated in one place."

Arabella let out a frustrated breath. "That's the problem. Concentrated in one place. If the Cartesians know where the Triad lives, and I call all of the Circle of Sisters to one place, we could be talking about the annihilation of an entire breed of witches. I just can't take that chance. They don't know what they'll be facing. We don't know if our spell will work. There's too much that I don't know that I fear to call and bring all of them here."

"Did Gunner say anything about getting Trey and Shandor involved in this?" Vanessa asked, her eyes growing dark.

"No," Arabella said. "He didn't mention either of them in regards to this."

"He didn't mention it to you," Taka said, "but he told me to stay away from Trey Cottle's apartment. Remember that time I went over to Trey's house, trying to find out where Gunner lived? Gunner told me over the phone to make sure to stay away from there. That's gotta be some kind of sign. And he did mention while we were at the Triad's that they weren't exactly the best of friends. Him, Cottle and Black,

I mean. He likes to keep an eye on them, so he knows what they're up to. That's what he claimed, anyway."

"We already know that," Arabella said, "Trey Cottle is always up to something, and with Shandor, his brownnoser, always doing and saying whatever Cottle wants, it's no wonder Gunner always keeps an ear out for what they're up to. Maybe he's stopped more chaos from happening than we can even imagine."

"Maybe so, but if it was chaos he stopped, it had nothing to do with Cartesians, the missing Originals or the Triad. He's been useless," Vanessa said. "Why is he even bothering with looking for another spell? We have all of the spells ever known to the Circle of Sisters written down in three Grimoires. There isn't any reason why we can't get them from the Triad and go through them ourselves."

"Yes, there is," Arabella said. "They belong to the Triad, and it's their responsibility to find something that will work. You know how this works. I don't have to remind you. That's the way it's been designed since the 1500s. Working with the Grimoires is the sole responsibility of the Triad."

Just then they heard a knock on the front door. Arabella got up and looked through the peephole.

"It's Gunner."

"You sure it's not the cops?" Taka asked. "They could be hiding on either side of him, waiting for us to open the door so they can bust in. We've gotta hide. They're probably here because of those dead humans in Slidell!"

Arabella looked through the peephole again. "It's Gunner. And he's alone."

"Ah, your long-lost boyfriend," Vanessa said.

"Would you please stop saying that?" Arabella said in a stage whisper. She opened the door a couple of inches to verify that Gunner was alone, and then motioned him inside.

Arabella couldn't help but notice how his blue eyes sparkled like the finest-cut sapphires when he caught sight of her.

He hurried inside, and Arabella closed the door and locked it behind him. "You have a lovely home," Gunner said, glancing around the foyer and into the kitchen. "Thank you for inviting me here."

"My pleasure," Arabella said. She lowered her eyes and felt her cheeks grow warm.

"Hey, we're over here," Taka said, waving a hand from the kitchen.

"Would you care for something to drink?" Arabella asked as she and Gunner headed for the kitchen. "Tea, maybe?"

"We're having coffee with a splash of Irish whiskey in it," Vanessa said. "How about some of that? That should get your guns moving."

Instead of taking offense to what she said, Gunner grinned and said, "I think I will join you in that drink. But just a half shot of whiskey, please."

Arabella motioned him to the last seat at the table, where they all sat.

"Have you any further news?" he asked, looking at Arabella.

"Vanessa told us when we got back that there've been more humans killed. This time in Slidell."

Gunner gawked at Vanessa. "How did they die?"

"A Nosferatu and two Loup-Garous, from what I was told. I didn't witness it, but the source is trustworthy," Vanessa said. When she said the word *trustworthy*, she gave him a small grimace as if not completely certain about her trustworthy source.

Gunner sighed. "You're in quite the predicament. Now that the Cartesians know where the Triad lives, it'll be all but impossible for them to go out and look for the missing

Originals. They're going to have free rein over the humans around here. Many more are going to die."

"We know," Taka said. "We're not dummies."

Arabella scowled at Taka, silencing her with a look.

"What about you?" Arabella asked Gunner. "Did you find anything in your spell book?"

Gunner rubbed his chin and gave her a reluctant nod. "I did, but the spell is dangerous. It causes a person to move against his or her will. Not by following the sound of my voice because they want to, but because they have no choice."

"Well, then we should do that," Taka said. "No matter where Viv is. Just as long as we can get her back."

Gunner lowered his head for a moment, and then looked up at Taka. "I know how badly all of you want her back. The problem is, if Viv is hurt in any way, and I use this spell to force her to come here, she could die. It's dangerous."

"But we don't know if she's hurt," Vanessa said. "We don't know where she is."

"I have to think of the worst when using a spell like this," Gunner said. "It's the most responsible thing I can do. If she's hurt, and we force her here, she truly can die. She's not immortal. She's human, just as we all are. She can die."

"Then forget it," Arabella said. "I don't want to take that chance." Something in the pit of her stomach warned her to leave things alone, not to get involved in Gunner's spell, or they'd risk losing Viv forever.

"I don't understand why the come-hither spell didn't work," Gunner said.

"That's not all that didn't work," Arabella said. "I was told that Evee called on Moose, one of the dead Loup-Ga-rous she was very familiar with, and one of Viv's Originals. Evee was able to connect with Moose, and at the same time, Gilly was to astral project to the sound of his voice so she'd be in the same location he was, seeing what he was seeing. But the message we got from Moose was so garbled, Gilly couldn't get a fix on his location."

"What did he say?" Gunner asked.

"Something about big heads, clowns and wheels," Arabella said. "Nothing that made sense. He just kept talking about the big clown heads and a devil head."

Gunner frowned. "That is perplexing. I can't think of any place around here that would have such things. No circus or carnival, nothing that he was referencing."

"We're left in the same predicament," Arabella said.

"Have the three of you, as the Elders of the Triad, tried a come-hither spell?" Gunner asked.

Arabella looked at Taka and Vanessa and wanted to slap her hand against her forehead. "No, we've not."

"That's the most brilliant idea we've heard yet," Taka said. "Why haven't we tried a come-hither spell on Viv? We know it. It's different than what you do, Gunner, but we're her Elders. Certainly she'd come to the sound of our voices if she can. And it wouldn't be forcing her to come if she was injured. It wouldn't be going against her will. She'd come because she could and wanted to."

"Then let's try it right now," Arabella said. "See if we can reach her."

"Can I help?" Gunner asked.

"You can help form the circle," Arabella said. "I'll do the call. Let's go into the sitting room, where we'll have more space."

Arabella led the way, followed by Taka, Vanessa and Gunner. When they stood in the middle of the sitting room, Taka, Vanessa and Gunner joined hands, forming a circle around Arabella.

"Now concentrate hard on Viv's face," Arabella said.

"Concentrate on what she looked like the last time you saw her. Concentrate on her eyes, on all that she is."

Gunner, Taka and Vanessa closed their eyes, and soon they were swaying from side to side. Arabella held her arms up at her sides, hands open, palms up and said in a loud voice,

*Come hither, Triad.*
*Your Elders call.*
*Let nothing cause you.*
*To stop or stall.*
*Come to us now.*
*One so tried and true.*
*Let not our voices hinder you.*
*Come hither, Triad.*
*Your Elders call.*

No sooner than Arabella had finished the spell, a loud moan, like one from someone in severe pain, echoed through the house so loudly, it seemed to shake the walls and cause the floor to vibrate beneath their feet.

There was no question in Arabella's mind that they'd just heard Viv's voice. Everyone opened their eyes, and Arabella looked from one to the other. She felt her hands start to shake, her heart thudding painfully in her chest from fear.

"That was Viv," Arabella said. "She's injured. Somewhere. Seriously injured. And if we don't find her soon, she'll die."

"Then it's like we've been saying all along," Taka said. "Finding Viv has to be our top priority. I don't know how we're going to get past the Cartesians, but I'd rather die trying than not look for Viv at all."

"Agreed," Arabella said. She felt nauseous, having heard Viv's pain and knowing they'd have to tell Evee and Gilly.

"I'll help," Gunner said. "Just let me know what you need me to do."

"If you have a spell that can keep her alive," Arabella said, "use it. I'm afraid she doesn't have much time left."

# *Chapter 10*

If he could've danced a jig without looking like a jackass in front of his army of Cartesians, he would have. He'd accomplished so much in such a short period of time. He managed to free the Nosferatu, all the while keeping his army from killing them. He wanted them alive so New Orleans would be filled with much chaos and death.

He'd done the same with the Loup-Garous. They certainly hadn't wasted any time attacking the humans. Such a sight to see. Large, wolf-like animals with claws and teeth made for shredding, tearing…and death. He loved watching each time an opportunity afforded itself.

He was aiming for the Chenilles next, when luck fell upon him, and he'd discovered where the Triad lived. Not only that, he'd actually captured one, it had been far easier than he'd expected. All he'd done was change the pitch of his voice to sound like one of the other Triad members, and Vivienne came running to her aide. One of his Cartesians simply scooped her up, as ordered, before she'd even had a chance to blink, much less yell for help or fight back.

It had taken every ounce of power he possessed to keep the Cartesian that had captured her from killing her. He wanted to use Vivienne François as bait. It would be too sweet to do away with the Triad as one unit, for all three of them together carried more power than just one alone. Vivienne had been a relatively easy catch. Why he hadn't thought of mimicking her sister's voice earlier was beyond him. It was something that he should have thought of from the very beginning. But his thoughts had been elsewhere—in growing his army to its present size. And his plan was to double it.

Unfortunately, in its enthusiasm, that Cartesian had injured her, as well. He could only hope she'd survive until he was able to get her two sisters, too. Then he would take them all and didn't care who died.

He had suspected that the sorcerer who was involved with them now would join their troupe. He was such a weak man, a sorcerer with few innate talents and little backbone. His spells were only as effective as the wind was in making leaves sway on trees.

He, on the other hand, had it all. The Loup-Garous and Nosferatu he'd freed had already murdered five more humans from the last count, and there were more soon to follow. Feeding time was still hours away, but when that time came, and there was no Triad to manage them and corral them to the compound, they would find their own meal. That meant more human deaths, many more. They would be stacking the dead one atop the other in the morgues. They'd lose count of the number of deaths per day. All of it was exactly what he hoped for. What he wanted. What he needed.

Not only were the Nosferatu and the Loup-Garous feeding on humans, but he allowed a Cartesian to have one of the Originals and bring its power to him. He'd felt such a surge of power when he took the Original from his minion that he grew heady and drunk with its power.

And now that he had one of the Triad in his possession, hidden away, waiting for her sisters to find her, which would only be a matter of time, the strength growing inside him felt like he could take Mount Everest and toss it to one side with a hand slap.

His mental capacity felt just as strong. He felt as though he could call upon the water that filled the oceans and have it evaporate into the sky, killing every form of ocean life. As though he could cause, just with a thought, volcanoes to erupt and earthquakes to split entire states in half. Fire to consume large cities, where the blazes would be so intense, all the firefighters in the area would fail to extinguish it. And he wanted more. If one Original could make him feel this way, he could only imagine what it would be like to take all the Originals and the Triad. He'd be invincible. He'd finally get payback for all the many, many years he'd suffered. Having such great power would make it all worth while, and his eternity would finally be directed by his own hand.

But feeling one way about a task and having the ability to do it were two separate things. And he knew he needed the rest of Triad in order to accomplish all that he longed for.

Whenever he felt his power begin to wane, he gave his Cartesians the permission to kill one of the Nosferatu, a Loup-Garou or a wayward Chenille. There was a Chenille that had stood too close to the gates of St. Louis I Cemetery, far enough away from the Benders' stupid electronic canopy that it was no longer under its protection. That was a rare catch. So he kept his mind focused on simpler tasks.

It didn't make sense to fight for something that was so elusive, like confined Chenilles. He needed to keep it simple. What would the Chenilles do once he had all the Triad?

When that happened, they'd be on their own, anyway, without a leader to protect them, feed them. In time, the electric dome that protected them would collapse, and they would free themselves, knocking through the gates of the cemetery and running through the city, looking for marrow to eat. They would be his for the taking.

He couldn't have been happier. His plan to capture Vivienne had gone better than he'd hoped. It had been so easy to mimic Evee's voice because she sounded, to his ear, like a little child calling, "Viv, I need your help. Please, I need your help!" And just as he'd suspected, Vivienne had taken off without a second thought to help her sister, and that's when he had one of his minions capture her.

The Benders were proving to be as useless as the sorcerer they'd added to their troupe. Yes, he had lost some of his Cartesians due to their stupid little toy wands. He was more than a little surprised during the last encounter he'd had with the Benders that one of the Triad had used a wand as effectively as any of the Benders since they'd arrived in the city.

But the toy didn't belong to her. Yet he still had to count on there being four, not three left to attack his army. But he didn't fear four any more than he did three. They could only push the Cartesians back into other dimensions for so long. If he allowed rift upon rift upon rift to open up into the sky, his Cartesians would annihilate anything and everything in their path. Which was not something he was ready to do just yet. He wanted to make his plan work. He had much left to do.

First, he needed the remaining Triad members, and not by a happenstance death either. He wanted them all fearful, he wanted them together, he wanted them as one, joining together, so that he would have their ultimate power. Even when the Triad members were children, their combined power was greater than any one witch, even the oldest in the Circle of Sisters. He knew this because he'd been there, watching, always watching them. That's the kind of power he wanted flowing through him.

The Originals that the Triad ancestors had created had many powers of their own, but that Triad would give him charge over the universe. Every element they were linked to, he'd possess: fire, water, earth... And with that power he'd be able to control air on his own and so many things on this earth that humans would fear him. They'd bow down to him.

With that kind of power, he could eliminate human interference. The president of the United States. The Vice President. Even in this small city, he'd take on the mayor, the city council, whatever it took to get them out of the way. In order to get down to the common man so there'd be no power left greater than his. No laws to fear but his own. No one left to bow to but him. Oh, how they'd fear his superiority.

That's what he was after. First this place, and then the world, and all on it would bow at his feet. Eventually, his army of Cartesians would be so large, he'd be able to manipulate the very universe itself. The placement of the stars and planets. The shadowing of the moon and sun. And he could make it all happen with nothing but a thought. All he needed was that supreme power. Oh, and he'd get it. Yes, indeed, he'd get it.

In the meantime, as his plan began to unfold, he allowed his Cartesians to pick from the netherworld. A fae here, a leprechaun there, a vampire, a werewolf, anything with an ounce of supernatural power. He allowed them to take those, for they were nothing but baubles attached to a string of invaluable pearls. Baubles, yes, but each bauble added a dash of power here, a pinch there—small, but there nonetheless. They still added to his greatness, and he needed all of the strength he could get.

For, to master the universe, one needed to be the most powerful being alive. One needed to be a god.

# Chapter 11

"We're going to have to figure out a way to split up," Gilly said. "I know we only have the Camaro, but I want to go and check the north compound. If Nikoli knows anything about Viv, that's where he'll be looking for her. One man covering five-hundred acres is a lot. If that's where he is, he's definitely going to need some help."

"We should know soon," Gavril said. "Nikoli should be here any moment. He's been summoned, which means, unless he's in dire straits, that he must show up."

"How long do we wait?" Gilly asked.

"If he's at the north compound as you think, I'd give him twenty minutes to a half hour to get here," Gavril said.

"That's a long time," Gilly said.

"Well, it's not like he can fly here," Evee said. "Give the man a break."

"Fine. Good. We'll give the man a break," Gilly said a hint of sarcasm in her voice. "Sorry, didn't mean to come across like a bitch. I just hate being trapped in here. Hate that the Cartesians know where we live. Our Originals have become secondary now. Viv is our priority, and above all else, we have to find her. And here we are stuck like geese in an oven."

"Would you mind going over to St. Louis I Cemetery with Lucien and check on my Chenilles, while I go to the compound and hunt for Viv? Make sure Nikoli's okay, too," Gilly asked Evee. "I know they're my responsibility, but I don't want to put you out in the open at the compound. You and Lucien can take the Camaro and check the cemetery. At least the car will offer some type of protection."

"Sure," Evee said. "But how are you and Gavril going to get to the compound? You can't do it on foot. That'll leave both of you too exposed."

"Hell, we could be too exposed by simply walking out the door," Gilly said. "But we've got to do something. I'm going stir crazy here. I can't just sit in here and do nothing."

"I agree," Evee said.

"We'll wait here for Nikoli," Gavril said. "Then wait for you to get back with the Camaro. Once you return it, we'll take the car to the dock and put it on the ferry. That should minimize our exposure. We'll figure out the rest once we've made it to the compound."

"There's nothing to figure out," Gilly said. "It's easy. Viv keeps an old blue pickup truck hidden in a grove of oak trees and willows. It's almost impossible to see unless you know where to look for it. If Nikoli or Viv haven't taken it, we can use the truck to get to the compound. Viv always kept a spare truck key under the driver's side visor."

"I guess that's the part we'll have to figure out," Gavril said. "Whether the truck's there or not."

"I'm hoping it is, then hoping it's not," Gilly said. "The truck, I mean. If it's not there, then that means Viv's taken it, which means she's got to be somewhere on the compound. Oh, and remember, Viv's got ranch hands out on the southern end of the compound. They take care of the cattle that go through the feeding shoot, so make sure when we go out there, we don't get them involved in any way. We stay in the north compound. That's five-hundred acres. A lot of land to look for Viv. The other part of it is if the truck is there, Viv either decided to investigate the compound on foot, or...she's not there."

"Maybe Nikoli will have some good news for us," Gavril said. "We can only keep our fingers crossed."

"It all sounds like a decent plan," Lucien said. "If it works out in that order. You know how often we've been surprised by the Cartesians, so watch your back when you're at the compound, cuz."

"Always," Gavril said with a short nod.

Lucien turned to Evee. "I'll get the Camaro and pull it up to the front door. Evee, you keep an eye out for me at the side windows by the door. When you see me pull up, unless I signal you otherwise, just come running out and jump into the car. I'll have the passenger door open and waiting for you. We'll hurry over to the cemetery, check on the Chenilles, then get back here, so Gavril and Gilly can use the car to get to the ferry."

"I'm with you," Evee said.

When Evee and Lucien took off for the cemetery, Gilly went to the fridge and made a couple of ham sandwiches. She handed one to Gavril. "It's not much, but I have no idea when we'll get another chance to eat."

"Thanks," he said, and then he wolfed down the sandwich in four bites.

"Want another?"

"If you don't mind," Gavril said. "I don't mean to sound like a pig, but I didn't have breakfast or lunch today. Didn't realize how hungry I was until I all but swallowed that ham sandwich whole."

"No problem," Gilly said.

She was in the middle of making Gavril two more sandwiches, when she heard a knock on the front door.

Gilly and Gavril exchanged glances, and then Gilly went to the front door with him in tow. She looked through the security peephole and was surprised to see Trey Cottle and Shandor Black standing on the other side of the door.

"What the hell do they want?"

"Who is it?" Gavril asked.

"Cottle and Black. The other two sorcerers who live in New Orleans. They own a law firm off of Canal. I don't trust either of them, though. Neither do my sisters or the Elders."

"Then don't let them in."

Gilly chewed on a fingernail for a few seconds. "I have to. I don't know how, but they might have news about the Originals."

Having said that, Gilly yanked the door open. "May I help you?" she asked, her voice hard and not the least bit welcoming.

Trey smiled, and Shandor nodded his head like a manipulated marionette.

"Come in," Gilly said, not out of kindness but because she didn't want to leave the door open and take the chance that a Cartesian might see her and attack.

Trey and Shandor walked into the house. Gilly left them standing in the foyer, not offering them a seat in the kitchen or sitting room.

"How may I help you gentlemen?" she asked.

"We're looking for Gunner," Trey said. "Word has it that he was over here helping you with a spell or something. We thought we might be able to help."

"What word?" Gilly asked. "Who told you he was here?"

"Oh, just word," Trey said. "We were supposed to meet with him for a game of poker, then dinner, but he never showed. We went over to his apartment, and he wasn't there."

"So what? Some homeless guy off the street sent you this way?"

Trey laughed, a phlegm-filled, gurgling sound. "Of course not. If I'm not mistaken, it may have been one of his neighbors or someone in the Quarter. I can't recall at the moment."

"Yeah, right," Gilly said.

"As I said," Trey said, looking a bit hurt and forlorn, all of it an act, that Gilly knew for sure,

"We've come all this way to offer our help. I'm not completely sure what the problem is, but you have our help if needed."

"There is nothing that we need from you, Trey or Shandor," Gilly said.

"So Gunner was here?" Trey said.

"What if he was? What business is that of yours?"

"I was only asking. You know, with everything that's been going on in the city. I don't know if you've heard or not, but there was a group of people in a bar down on Bourbon. Some of the Originals got to them. The Loup-Garous killed ten to twelve people. The police are all over the place. I thought if Gunner was out here trying to give you a hand, you might need some backup. It's ugly out there now, but it's going to get a hell of a lot worse. If that many people were killed right on Bourbon, can you imagine how many more might be killed in the surrounding suburbs, where there's not so much action and noise?"

"What a minute. What's this about the cops? How would they tie us to the Originals?" Gilly asked. "We've never let it out to the public that we were Triad, nor that we were responsible for the Originals, nor that the Originals even existed. We've kept that very hush-hush for generations."

"Oh, well," Trey said, shrugging his shoulders slightly, "word does get around."

"Hold on," Gilly said, fury boiling in her veins. "Did you tell them we took care of the Originals?"

Trey sighed. "Well, you know, when the police asked me, I couldn't exactly lie. That would have implicated me in the situation."

"Why, you son of a bitch! You put me in danger, along with my sisters and the Elders. We have enough problems to deal with. And now we have to worry about the police coming and banging on our door, asking about the humans that were taken by the Nosferatu or the Loup-Garous, or whichever one of the Originals killed those people? We don't even know where the Originals are. What kind of sick asshole are you?"

"We could tell you," Shandor said. "We can tell you. We could tell you because we saw them at the bar. We saw the carnage at the bar. There was blood everywhere. They ripped those people up. The bodies were ripped to shreds. It was really bad, wasn't it, Trey?"

"Shut up," Trey said to Shandor, "until you can talk like you've got some sense."

"Do you mind if we have a seat?" Trey asked Gilly.

"Yes, I do mind," Gilly said. She had to work hard to stay focused, her mind wandering and heart hurting over the humans who'd been killed. "I'd prefer that you not be here at all. If your mouth is big enough to tell the police that we're caretakers for the Originals, especially the ones who murdered those people in the bar, I don't want to have anything to do with you. I've always known you were not to be trusted. And Shandor, my feelings for you are exactly the same. You keep your nose stuck so far up Trey's ass, I don't know how you breathe."

Shandor looked down at the floor, his pale cheeks turning dark pink.

Trey balled his hands into fists and held them at his side.

It was then that Gavril appeared alongside Gilly. "Gentlemen, the lady's asked you to leave. She's been quite clear that she doesn't need or want your help. I would take her advice and leave immediately."

"What do you have to do with any of this?" Trey asked. "You're not a sorcerer or a witch. This is between us and the people who live in this city. I'm concerned about them. I don't know what Gunner did to try to help, but evidently it didn't work, which makes sense because Gunner, in and of himself, is relatively useless. He's too weak."

"And you think you can make things better?" Gavril said with a sneer. "From the looks of things, the only thing you make better is trouble. You and Shandor think you can simply walk in here and make the whole ugliness of this disappear."

"Oh, I know I can," Trey said. "I'm quite confident of it."

"Well, I don't care what you're confident in," Gilly said. "I don't want anything to do with you. The farther you are away from us, the better. I don't want you at this house ever again."

"I'll be glad to come and be a spokesperson for Trey if you'd like," Shandor said.

"I said shut up, Shandor," Trey demanded. "I'm the one with the power here. If you need to call the Originals back, then you need me. If you need to find your sister, you need me. Shandor alone, much less Gunner, is useless."

Gilly held up a hand and felt her heart start beating triple time. "Wait a damn minute. How did you know one of my sisters was missing?"

Trey lifted a brow. "Word gets around, little girl. I told you that once before. There's not much that gets by me. Ever. I always keep my ear to the ground. There's a lot that goes on in this city, and it's my responsibility to stay on top of it. I have to know what's going on at all times so that we're always protected."

Gilly glared at him. "Since you know one of my sisters is missing, do you know where she is?"

Trey shrugged. "Maybe. Maybe not."

"What are you talking about? What's with this maybe, maybe not bull. You either do or you don't."

Gavril suddenly grabbed Trey by the lapels of his jacket. "You need to listen up, little man. If you know where Vivienne François is and don't tell us right this minute, I'll send you flying across the lawn so fast, you won't know what hit you. I'll make sure your head hits concrete so it splatters like a water balloon."

"If you're smart, you'll take your hands off of me," Trey said to Gavril. "You forget. I'm a sorcerer. You're just a commoner." And with that, Trey waved a hand, and Gavril's hands suddenly released Trey's lapel, and his arms fell limp at his side.

Gavril looked over at Gilly, dumbstruck.

"You think you've come over here to save the day," Trey said to Gavril, "but all you've done is stir up more trouble."

"That's right," Shandor said. "That's right. More trouble. All trouble. Look at all the humans that are dead and all of the Originals that are missing. You caused the trouble. You are the trouble."

"Shut up, Shandor," Trey said, his voice harsh. "You're just talking to hear yourself talk."

Shandor lowered his head.

Trey gave Gilly a stern look. "Now you either want my help or you don't."

Gilly stepped closer to Trey, until she was almost nose to nose with him. "I asked you a question. I don't want an ambiguous answer. Do you know where my sister is?"

"And my answer, once again, is the same. Maybe, maybe not," Trey said.

"I don't understand what you mean by that," Gilly said.

"If I issue a spell to find her, we will find her," Trey said. "But you have to be willing to accept my help."

"Mine, too," Shandor said. "Because I'm with Trey, so mine, too. I can do spells, too. I can do a lot of spells."

Trey gave Shandor a hard look that made the sorcerer quickly shut his mouth.

"I don't know what you and the elders have been trying but it's obviously been useless. Things have gotten far worse. Because I am always alert, always aware of what goes on around me, I have the spells that are needed to bring back the Originals and find your sister. I can make all this ugliness disappear."

Something in Gilly's gut began to churn and made her nauseous. "You're lying, Trey. I wouldn't believe you if you were standing right next to Buddha and introduced him for who he was. You're conniving. You're a liar, and you always do things in your own best interest."

"So you're going to stand there and tell me that you're just going to deny our help? You're going to leave your sister alone to die?" Trey asked.

Goose bumps spread up Gilly's arms. "What do you mean, to die? You said you may or may not know where she is. Is she ill? Has she been hurt?"

"Maybe, maybe not," Trey said again.

Gilly let out a small growl. "I want you out of here. I can't take this anymore. You're driving me insane. I don't want to get caught in your trap, owing you for anything. You're nothing but a snake. So take yourself, Mr. Snake, and get

the hell out of this house. You're not needed or wanted. If
you know where Viv is, then get her and bring her home.
And do it simply from the kindness of your heart, Trey. If
you have a heart, which I seriously doubt, because if you'd
really cared about my sister and knew where she was, that's
what you would've done in the first place, brought her home.
As for Gunner, you already know where he is. There's nothing here that you've questioned me about that you didn't already know the answer to. That's why I don't trust a thing
you say, and I have nothing more to say to you. Now either
step back and step out or we'll see whose spell works better. Yours or mine, when I turn your face into a goat's."

Gilly opened the door and ushered them out quickly. "I
don't ever want to see the two of you back here again. Understand? No matter what information you think you have,
the things you don't have are integrity, truth or hope. So get
your asses back to the snake pits they came from."

And with that, Gilly slammed the door in their faces.

Then she turned to Gavril and laid her head on his chest,
exhausted.

After a moment, she lifted her head and said to him, "I'm
scared. Suppose Cottle was right. Suppose Viv is in serious
danger, near death even."

"I'm with you on not trusting that dude," Gavril said,
holding her close. "I think ninety percent of him is bullshit."

"But what if—"

"Shhh, baby, no worries. I promise you that we'll find
Viv if it's the last thing I do on this earth."

# Chapter 12

As they sat in the kitchen waiting for Lucien and Evee to return with the car, Gavril said, "Remind me next time never to piss you off." He gave her a halfhearted grin. "You handled those bastards, Cottle and Black, just right. I was thoroughly impressed."

"You were, huh?"

"Heck, yeah. You blasted them with words, which was the way to go. Me? I'd have knocked Cottle's front teeth out. No worries about Black. That form of dentistry would have sent him running home to mama or daddy."

"You've got that pegged right. Black is Cottle's yes man, no man, anything-you-want man. You saw the two of them in action. At any time, did you see Cottle allow Black to take charge of the conversation?"

Gavril chuckled. "Take charge? Black could barely get a cohesive sentence out."

"Exactly. I've heard Black talk before in a different

venue, and he's articulate enough, but when Cottle's got him shaking in his boots, his brain seems to revert back to a nine-year-old's."

"Have they always been that way?"

Gilly nodded. "As long as I've known them, which, unfortunately, has been most of my life. For the most part, we've stayed out of one another's business. Everyone in town, witch or human, knows that Cottle is a slimebucket. How he keeps clients is beyond me. Well, no, rephrase. He uses spells to generate clients. Definitely not his Humpty-Dumpty looks or charming personality. Pretty pathetic when the only clients you can get are the ones you conjure up, forcing them to you."

"To overcome looks and lack of charm, he must have to go through the entire day spouting spells."

"Wouldn't surprise me," Gilly said. "I just hate that those sons of bitches even had the nerve to come over here, acting like they wanted to help. Cottle does that 'I'm innocent' look so well, and, of course, Shandor follows suite. A leader like Cottle always has a follower. It makes their balls grow."

"Not to question what you did, but are you sure that they really can't offer you some kind of help?" Gavril asked. "I mean, I trust you implicitly. I don't know these men at all."

"You can trust that there is something in this that they're after, and they're going to do whatever it takes to get it. I don't have the slightest idea what it is. But whenever Cottle is after something, it usually has money or power tied to it. They're not out to help us. They could care less about saving anyone but themselves."

"How could anyone stand doing business with a guy like that, human or otherwise?"

"Like I said," Gilly said. "The only thing he could use to have anyone tolerate him are spells. Desire spells, hope spells, desperation spells. You name it, I'm sure he's got a bag full of them."

"Then why doesn't he use them on you?" Gavril asked. "Make you want him to help?"

"Because we're witches. The spell would wind up bouncing back on him."

"Does he hide the fact that he's a sorcerer to humans the way you do about being a witch?"

"As far as I know, yes."

"Then why in the hell would he talk to the cops about you? Wouldn't that lead them right to him, being a sorcerer and all?"

"Because, in truth, he's a greedy, manipulative dumbass who oftentimes doesn't think past his nose. Believe me, I'm not going to be surprised if the police suddenly show up here looking for us because Trey pointed them in our direction. I can't believe he told the cops where we lived, all the while knowing that could implicate him, as well."

"Then we need to get out of here and not give the police the chance to find you."

"But how do we get out of here?" Gilly asked. "Evee and Lucien still have the car. The only other way for us to make it to the docks is on foot."

"I don't want to take that chance with you," Gavril said.

"We'd be safe enough, I think," Gilly said. "You've seen me use a scabior before. You wouldn't be taking a chance with me, because I can fight Cartesians right alongside you. I'm pretty good at it, if I say so myself. Not as good as you, Lucien or Nikoli, but good enough." Gavril's eyes suddenly went wide.

"What's wrong?" Gilly asked.

"You just reminded me about Nikoli. He should have been here by now."

They stood up simultaneously, both fidgeting nervously.

"Why do you think he isn't here yet?" Gilly asked. "Do you think… Could he be in trouble?" She grabbed Gavril by the arms, barely able to put her hands around his huge biceps. She squeezed his arms. "Could he be where Viv is? Could he be trapped? In trouble?"

"I don't have the slightest idea, because I don't know where Viv is." Gavril swiped a hand through his hair. "This is getting weirder by the minute."

"Doesn't Nikoli have a watch like you? You know, the one with the GPS thing on it that lets him locate you?"

"Not if he's been stripped of it. Then he'd have no idea we're trying to contact him, and he'd have no way to let us know where he is."

Gilly swiped a hand over her face. "Gavril, we've got to find them. We can't leave anything to chance. Someone somewhere knows where they are. But who?"

"I have no idea. And, yeah, I know about Nikoli. For him not to show up is a pretty serious matter. It's a code of honor thing with Benders. A code of ethics. When a Bender, especially two of us, me and Lucien, contacted Nikoli, he should have dropped what he was doing and come to us right away. The only reason he wouldn't is if he was in danger himself, and that's what I'm afraid of."

"So how in the hell do we get to the docks?" Gilly asked. "That's the most logical place for us to start looking for him and Viv."

"Unfortunately, I think you're right. I don't know what's taking Lucien and Evee so long, but we can't wait here any longer," Gavril said. "Especially with Nikoli not responding. And now we have the police to worry about."

"I'll be right there with you," Gilly said. "And I think, if we run headlong into some Cartesians, all you have to do is charge Ronan's scabior, and I'll use it and fight with you side-by-side. Cartesians or not, we'll get to the ferry and cross over. That's the only logical place that they could be. It's a lot of land, a lot to cover. We can't take a vehicle into the feeding area, anyway, because it's thick with trees and brush. No vehicle has ever gone past the front gate. Viv used her truck just to check the perimeter of the acreage, make sure the fencing was secure.

At least the tree coverage in the feeding area, if that's where they are, will give them some kind of protection."

"I don't want you using the scabior again," Gavril said. "I still can't believe you yanked the second one out of my hand."

"But I got the Cartesian, right?"

Gavril's brow knitted together.

"Come on, you've got to at least give me that. I got the Cartesian without your or Lucien's help, right?"

"Yeah, okay, I'll give you that. But that doesn't mean it'll happen again."

"Just give me a chance," Gilly pleaded. "I've done it once. I can easily do it again. I've got a great aim. Look, I can't just sit in this house. Not with Trey having alerted the police. I'll either have to face the police or a Cartesian. I'd rather it be a Cartesian. At least I can do something about one. If the police catch me, they can hold me for questioning for hours."

"True," Gavril said, worry etched on his face.

"All we have to do is get through the Garden District, grab the trolley, take it to the Riverwalk, then we'll only be a couple hundred feet from the ferry."

"I don't want to take that chance with you," Gavril said, suddenly pulling her close. He held the back of her head, pressed a hand at the small of her back. "Don't you understand?" he whispered. "I don't want to be without you. I can't lose you and can't take the chance that something might happen to you. I can't chance that a Cartesian might get you, even a trainee with a scabior. And now we have Cottle and Shandor on our ass, and the police. God, what do we do if we see the police while trying to make the ferry? If they see us while we're out there running to the ferry like we've got something to hide—because we do have something to hide—"

"For universal sake," Gilly said, "for all we know, they could have wanted posters out for me by now." She wanted to say much more, to let him know she couldn't live without him either. But she held her tongue, fearing the Triad curse would bring those words to naught.

"You're right about the questioning part," Gavril said. "Only you'd probably be manhandled and put under arrest if for nothing but questioning. They'd probably put you in a holding cell until they were good and ready to interrogate you. You know how the cops are around here. Act now, question later. We simply have to figure out a different way."

Gilly pushed away from him. "Then the only other choice we have is using the Camaro as soon as Evee and Lucien get back. Can you at least try contacting Lucien with your GPS, find out if they're okay, if they're on their way back? They were just going to do a head count and make sure those Chenilles were still protected."

Gavril did as she asked, pressing buttons and knobs on his watch. Then they waited, holding their breath, listening for the slightest sound.

Gilly's ferret, Elvis, came into the room and slithered between and around her legs. She shooed him away. "I want you upstairs. I don't want you to be in the middle of this. You can't follow me."

"But you mustn't go," Elvis said. "It's dangerous in more ways than one. You're an idiot for even considering half of what you're thinking of doing."

Although Gilly knew that Gavril couldn't understand what Elvis' squawks and squeaks really meant, she had to talk to her familiar and convince him to stay, even if it meant Gavril thought her to be crazier than a loon.

"I'm going to be fine," Gilly said to Elvis. "Remain here with the other familiars, and that's an order. I'll be safe. I promise I'll come back to you."

"You can promise all you want," Elvis said. "But you can't control everything. Suppose whatever has Viv in danger gets a hold of you. Then what? You still going to fulfill your promise to return?"

"Now you're just being a smartass."

"At least it's better than being a dumbass," Elvis said. He looked at Gavril, and his beady eyes grew darker. Then he slowly turned about and took off for the stairs, squeaking and chittering the entire way up.

"That was your familiar, wasn't it?" Gavril asked.

"Yes."

"And you talk to him that way? I mean, in English, and he understands what you're saying?"

"Of course."

"Those funny noises he makes, I take it you understand what he's saying to you?"

"Yes. To me, those sounds are as easy to understand as English. The only ones who can understand the familiars are their mistresses and the Elders."

"What does he think about all of this?" Gavril asked.

"He doesn't want me to go, of course. He thinks I'm stupid for attempting it and wants me to stay here and out of danger."

Just then Gilly heard the sound of squealing tires coming from the front of the house. Gavril must have heard it, too, because they both took off for the front door at the same time.

Before they reached it, Evee burst through the front door, her face white and eyes large. Lucien was right behind her.

"What's wrong? Are you okay?" Evee asked Gilly.

"I'm fine. But you look anything but. What's wrong?" Gilly asked.

"When Lucien's beeper thingy went off, I thought you were in danger...and that was after we discovered that all of the Chenilles are gone."

"What?" Gilly said, taking a step back. "What do you mean, they're gone? Did you check the old tombstones? The open grave slots?"

Evee nodded. "We checked everywhere. Not one Chenille in sight. The electronic dome that had been set up in the cemetery to protect them was dead. Nothing. No power."

Gilly began to pace, feeling like she might lose her balance at any moment. Panic and fear were inching their way up to her heart by way of her spine.

"I don't know what we're going to do," Evee said. "We can't find them all, Gilly. We have no more Nosferatu, no more Loup-Garous and, now, no more Chenilles. They're all gone, and only the universe knows where they are. When it comes to feeding time, every human on the street will be in danger unless we do something."

Gilly took a deep breath, holding back tears. "The most important thing we have to do first and foremost is find Viv. I hate to say it, but the humans in the city and the suburbs surrounding it are going to have to fend for themselves. Viv is our priority. She's part of us, Evee. Like a kidney, heart and lungs make a body function. As a Triad and sisters, without Viv, we're only two-thirds of a whole."

Evee stood silent, tears streaming down her face.

To stop her tears, Gilly decided to give her news that she knew would piss her off. "By the way, Trey Cottle and Shandor Black came here while y'all were gone."

Evee wiped the tears from her cheeks, and her eyes grew fierce. "What the hell were Trey and Shandor doing here?"

Gilly gave her sister and Lucien the rundown of their confrontation with Cottle and Black. "The police could show up here at any time. We have to stay away from them, as well, or we'll get locked up for hours under questioning. Right now, Gavril and I will take the Camaro over to the docks so we can head to the north compound."

"We can come with you," Evee said. "We can help you look."

"What I want you to do," Gilly said, "is to go into the workshop behind the house where all of our crystals and herbs are. See if you can put something together with the herbs and crystals that might help. Whether or not you find something, the two of you hunker down there. If you hear anyone knocking on the door, don't answer it. The workshop isn't in view from the front or sides of the house, so no one will know to look for it. Stay there until we get back."

"But—" Evee said, her face drawn.

"It's like you told me earlier," Gilly said to her. "I don't want to lose you either, Evee. Gavril and I will take care of the north compound. I will come back for you, whether I have Viv or not. If I don't, we'll figure out what to do from there."

Evee nodded reluctantly. "I'm sorry about your Chenilles. I know what it feels like to lose your entire brood."

Gilly closed her eyes for a second, envisioning her Chenilles, and felt the hole in her heart from their loss grow wider. She shook her head to clear her thoughts. "Viv first, okay?"

Evee nodded. "Viv first."

"Nikoli, too," Gavril said.

"What do you mean?" Lucien asked.

"We signaled for him, but he never showed."

"He never showed?" Gavril said. "That can only mean one thing."

Lucien's expression grew hard. "He's in danger. I wonder if he's with Viv. Maybe they're in the same place."

"Evee, take Lucien to the workshop. Check your Grimoire. See if there's anything in there we might have missed. We've been focused on spells, but maybe there's an herb-crystal combination that might be effective. Gavril and I will head to the docks. We'll find them. Viv and Nikoli. We'll find them. I'll get back to you as quickly as I can."

"Promise?" Evee said.

"I promise, sister, with all of my heart. I will get back to you. And somehow, someway, the three of us will be together again. You, me and Viv. It's the way it's supposed to be. I still feel her life force, which is a positive thing. And I promise you'll always feel mine."

## Chapter 13

The ferry seemed to move slower than ever before. Gilly grew so frustrated, she told Gavril she had to keep herself from jumping into the river and swimming to the other side. She felt she would have gotten there faster.

When they finally made it across the river to Algiers, Gavril parked the Camaro behind some brush and went hunting for Viv's blue truck. Gilly was right behind him.

"It's here," Gilly said, her voice low and trembling. She pointed to a grove of oak and willow trees about two-hundred feet away. The look she gave Gavril tore a hole in his heart.

"If her truck is here," Gilly said, "chances are she isn't. Nikoli either. She would have taken it to the compound. If it's still there, that means there's a good chance she never made it here. She'd not stupid. Viv would have never tried going out that far on foot."

"Nikoli either. I'm not ready to jump to conclusions, though," Gavril said. "Both could have left the truck to keep from drawing attention to themselves and simply dodged in and around trees to get to the feeding area. Nikoli would have chosen that way for sure."

Gavril jumped into the blue truck, and Gilly scrambled onto the bench seat beside him.

"Keys?" Gavril asked.

"Check the visor," Gilly said. "She usually kept an extra set there."

Gavril pulled down the driver's side visor and a set of keys dropped into his lap. "Good call."

With that, he shoved the key into the ignition, revved up the engine and drove as quickly as he could down a dirt path that sat beneath a huge canopy of large oak trees.

When they reached a fork in the road, Gilly pointed right. "That way."

Gavril had to slow the truck down due to an overgrowth of trees. Their thick, long branches scraped, scratched and screeched against the roof of the truck. Dusk was setting in, and with the heavy foliage, which darkened things even more, he had a hard time staying in the center, on the dirt road.

He didn't want to turn the truck lights on for fear of being noticed. Gilly had mentioned the ranch hands that lived on the south side of the compound and how she didn't want to get them involved. If they noticed headlights bouncing around back here, one or more of them might be tempted to come out this way and make sure it wasn't someone who shouldn't be there.

They finally reached a clearing.

"Stop the truck here," Gilly said. "The inside of the compound is worse than what we just drove through."

"Crap."

"There is no vehicle access in the compound. Viv used the truck only around the perimeter to maintain the fencing.

If we're going to go into those five-hundred acres, we're going to have to walk it."

"And leave you exposed to the Cartesians? No way," Gavril said. "You know how I feel about that. Scabior or not."

"Well, I guess you'd better charge the other scabior and let me hang on to it, because it'll be the only chance I have if we run into any of those ugly bastards," Gilly said. "Especially if they show up in bulk."

Gavril shook his head. He was about to say something, but Gilly beat him to the punch.

"You know that I'm right," she said. "You've seen me use it. I'm good with it, almost as good as you."

Gavril sat in silence for a moment. He then finally blew out a breath and got out of the truck. Gilly followed him.

He took the second scabior out from behind his back, where he'd tucked it into his jeans. With one last look at Gilly, he flicked his wrist, then twirled the scabior between his fingers lightning fast, which charged it. He handed the scabior to her. "You know, you've got to be one of the most hardheaded women I've ever known."

"And that's why you love me the way you do, isn't it?"

Gavril looked at her, felt his expression soften, his heart wanting. He opened his mouth to affirm her statement, but then thought better of it. He didn't want to share his whole heart with her now. Not when they were in the middle of hunting for Nikoli and Viv. It felt like the wrong time and the wrong place to bring up such matters.

"Keep your eyes on the sky and be careful with the scabior," Gavril said. "We're going to have to call out for Viv and Nikoli, which means nothing is going to be quiet about this. Call Viv as loud as you can. I'll call for Nikoli, but we're going to stick together through this."

"But we can cover more ground if we separate," Gilly said.

"We're not separating," Gavril said sternly. "Period.

We'll start at the west side and work our way east until we get back to the truck. If they're not here, we head back to the ferry. We can't afford to keep running in circles, staying out in the open this way. We're taking a big chance as it is, tree coverage or not."

"Agreed," Gilly said. She opened the large gates as she'd seen Viv do a hundred times, and they stepped inside the compound.

Gilly held out the scabior, kept an eye on the skies and started calling for her sister. "Vivienne! Viv! Answer me!"

At the same time, Gavril shouted for Nikoli. "Answer me, Nikoli. Where are you?" Every couple hundred feet they walked, Gilly would call out for her sister, and Gavril for his cousin.

The only response either of them received was the sound of leaves rustling in the trees. The whine of insects. The croak of frogs. No howling from any Loup Garou, no human answer to be had.

They walked for what seemed like hours before they finally made it to the back of the compound and started heading east.

Suddenly, Gilly said, "Up there, look!" She pointed to a rift opening up in the sky and a second one below it. A third one suddenly appeared on top of the first.

"You aim for the one at the bottom," Gavril said. "I'll get the one in the middle and the one at the top."

The second the Cartesian laid a claw outside of the bottom rift, the maw not yet having opened wide enough for it to stick out its grotesque head, Gilly aimed her scabior at the third rift and shot. It pushed the Cartesian back, but didn't close the rift.

All the while, Gavril aimed his scabior for the middle Cartesian, and then the one above it.

Miraculously, they closed all three rifts in less than ten minutes.

"That was too quick," Gavril said. "Not one of them put up a fight or tried to push out of the rift."

"What do you mean?" Gilly asked.

"I don't know. Something just doesn't feel right. It's like they gave up too easily. Usually they struggle to get out, head, talons, leaning over the rift at the waist. Those three barely had their talons out and disappeared too quickly."

"But isn't that a good thing?" Gilly asked.

"Yes and no. It feels too much like a setup. They could be setting up for a takeover."

"A takeover? Of what? Who? Is it us? Are they trying to take us over? Is that their plan?"

"I think so. Like letting out ten to twenty Cartesians at once. We need to get out of here before we get slammed. Just in case."

Gavril took Gilly by the hand, and they took off at a run, still calling for Viv and Nikoli.

"Viv, where are you?" Gilly shouted. "We need you! Where are you?"

"Nikoli, answer me," Gavril yelled.

By the time they made it back to Viv's pickup truck, there were no other rifts that had opened up in the sky as Gavril had suspected.

Out of breath, Gavril opened the passenger door for Gilly, and once she was safely settled inside, he hurried to the driver's side and jumped behind the wheel of the truck.

Gilly handed Gavril the scabior she'd been using, and he disarmed it, as he did his own, and sheathed his and stuck the second in the back of his jeans.

Gavril started the engine, peeled out of the compound and headed down the dirt road again toward the dock.

Once they tucked the truck back under its haven of overgrown oaks and willows, Gilly leaned her head back against the seat, trying to catch her breath.

Gavril did the same. "I thought for sure the Cartesians were going to push back a second time," he said. "It just doesn't make sense. It's not like them to give up so easily."

"I'm just glad they did," Gilly said.

Gavril sat upright. "You know, I wonder if it may have had something to do with you."

"Me? Yeah, like I'm a big, bad Bender. How do you figure?"

"They're used to Benders fighting them, but never a Triad. Maybe that confused them."

"Well, if they're confused about me using a scabior, that's pretty dumb," Gilly said. "I might weigh a hundred fifteen pounds soaking wet, and they have to know that I don't have the experience with a scabior the way you do. So, you're right. It is weird that they didn't come back and try to attack us again."

"They are pretty dumb creatures. They follow the orders of a leader."

"Who's this leader? Have you ever tried to capture him? Kill him?"

"In all our travels, we've yet to figure that out. It doesn't show itself. Only allows its minions to do its dirty work. As for the Cartesians, sometimes it seems they get this leader's orders right, and other times, it seems like they're simply winging it and screw up."

Gilly yawned. "Like I said…dumbasses."

Gavril grinned, watching Gilly's eyes slowly close.

"I don't think I've ever yelled so much or run so fast in my entire life," Gilly said, her voice growing hoarser the more she spoke.

Gavril locked the truck doors. "Come here," he said. He pulled her close to him, put her head on his shoulder and smoothed her short black hair with a hand, comforting her. He did this until he felt her breathing grow slower, easier, and then he leaned over and kissed the top of her head.

Then he kissed her again.

Suddenly, as if waking from a deep sleep, Gilly grabbed hold of Gavril's shirt, pulled him close and kissed him back on the lips with the same fervor she did everything. All or nothing. Fierce, hungry and determined.

Gavril couldn't help but react to her kiss, to her desire. They were here to hunt for Viv and Nikoli. Had Cartesians appear, and then suddenly disappear. How could his mind be on anything else?

Making love to Gilly was an experience he'd never known with any other woman. There was no mandatory cuddling. Tender moments were short. A touch on the cheek, a kiss on the lips, but even those wound up becoming hungry and fierce. She emptied his mind of everything but her, which only served to fill his heart all the more.

As if to prove the point he was thinking, Gilly put her mouth on his neck and bit down, tasting the essence of him. He did the same to her, nipping at her neck softly, and then harder, until she groaned with desire.

Then, just as fast as they'd run the last half of the compound, they began to rip off clothing. He couldn't get to her skin fast enough.

In a matter of seconds, he had her breasts in his hands, her nipples in his mouth, sucking, rolling his tongue over them, so hungry for them. She had her hands wrapped in his hair, pulling him closer. He kissed her, sucked on her, flicked her nipples with his tongue until she moaned and cried out.

"More, goddammit, more!"

Suddenly, without any indication from him, Gilly quickly unbuttoned, and then unzipped her trousers and slid them off along with her bikini panties. Then she turned to undo his pants, his belt and zipper.

Gavril took hold of her hand, moved it away from his pants and unfastened them himself.

He was hard, had been hard since the first time they'd kissed.

"Gavril..." Gilly uttered his name hoarsely, and before Gavril knew it, Gilly maneuvered herself from the passenger seat and straddled him. She lowered herself onto him until the tip of his hardness touched her wet opening.

So much heat emanated from her, it felt like a furnace. That alone had Gavril biting the inside of his cheek to keep from coming right then and there.

Gilly lowered herself slowly, slowly. An inch here, and half an inch more, teasing him. The expression on her face was one of determination and utter desire. Her eyes never left his.

Then, without warning, Gilly slammed her body down the length of him. She took his face in her hands and kissed him with all the ferocity that she had as she rode him up and down...up...down.

Because of their position, and closeness of the steering wheel, as much as Gavril wanted to match her move for move, he had a hard time doing so.

Somehow, though, he knew that was exactly what Gilly wanted. He knew her well enough to know that if she'd needed it any other way, she would have positioned it so. But she rode him hard, wanting more, and before long, Gilly bit into Gavril's shoulder, and then threw her head back and howled as her body shuddered with a powerful orgasm. She contracted against him over and over, and he could feel her wetness leaking down the length of him.

The power of her orgasm had been so strong that Gavril thought it had satiated her. He couldn't have been more wrong.

Gilly continued to ride him like she was a starving

woman without enough to eat. He allowed her to pummel him, and he tried matching her movements, albeit slightly because of his position.

He wanted to turn his leg sideways so that he could penetrate deeper, but when he attempted to do so, she bit into his neck, stuck her fingernails into his back, scratched him, pulled him toward her and held him tight.

Gilly pulled his hair, pushed his head back, kissed his mouth, his chin and rode him even faster until he could stand it no more.

She lowered her head and bit into his shoulder hard once more, and then he heard her cry out, felt her contracting over her him again and again, and her orgasm spilling out of her, soaking him.

Gavril felt himself unable to control his body any longer, and he exploded inside of her, throbbing as if there were such a well of come inside him that could never be completely emptied.

As he felt his hardness continue to throb inside her, she sat up on him, and contracted around him, sucking him with her body, milking him dry.

Gavril knew this was exactly what Gilly wanted. The control. Wanted to own him for that moment. Wanted to own him every time she touched him. He knew this was her way of giving herself emotionally, fully to him during a time when most women would have been huddled in a heap in a corner, refusing to face the danger and problems muddying their lives.

The problem was she not only owned him now, she owned him for the rest of his life.

She just didn't know it yet.

# Chapter 14

"Did you find anything?" Gilly asked Evee when she and Gavril returned home.

"Nothing that even came close to a come-hither spell," Evee said. "I've been through the Grimoire twice, felt through the crystals and herbs. Nothing."

Gilly leaned against Gavril, not concerned about letting her attention to him show in front of Evee or Lucien. She already knew those two were a couple. Despite the warnings the Triad had been given by the Elders to stay away from the Benders in order to stay safe, Gilly didn't feel one ounce of guilt for having been with Gavril. She'd been close to him body and mind, and the soul part was growing closer every day.

As they sat around the dining room table, Gilly gave Evee and Lucien the run down on what had occurred— except for the sex—while they hunted the compound.

"The place is so deserted, it's creepy," Gilly said. "I've

never seen it that way before. I mean, I've never been inside the compound because of the Loup-Garous, but inside or out, you barely heard bugs chittering. It was as if the universe had simply deserted the place as part of the planet. Like it no longer existed. Just dirt and trees."

"That's how I felt while going over the Grimoire, crystals and herbs," Evee said. "It felt like something was blocking me from seeing something that should have been right in my face."

"Is there anything else we can try?" Gavril said.

"It doesn't make sense for us to go out hunting for the Originals right now," Lucien said. "Viv and Nikoli trump the Originals by far."

Gilly nodded.

"What if I try connecting with another dead Original, someone other than Moose?" Evee said. "Then, if we get a decent connection, you can astral project and see things from their eyes."

"I'm open to anything," Gilly said, "but who do we summon this time? Who can you picture well enough in your mind's eye to summon them, attempt to communicate with them?"

"Maybe Chank," Evee said. "You know, the Nosferatu that Pierre had to put down. I remember what he looked like because of his red hair when he was human."

Gilly frowned. "I don't know. Chank was a bit like Moose—a bit wobbly in the brain. How about if we try to connect with Pierre? He was sharp, responsible."

"Yes, but if he's not dead, there's no way I can connect with him," Evee said.

"Let's try him, anyway. If he doesn't come through, we'll work on Chank," Gilly said.

Evee nodded. "I'll channel anyone to get Viv back."

"Great," Gilly said and got up from the table. "Let's go

into the sitting room, where we'll have more room to form
a circle."

Evee, Lucien and Gavril followed Gilly, and when they
reached the center of the sitting room, they held hands as
they had done before, leaving Evee in the middle to call
upon the Nosferatu.

"Instead of just focusing on them and repeating what
you see or hear, try a spell to go along with it," Gilly said.
"Maybe that'll throw more power at it."

Evee sighed, closed her eyes and spread her arms out
wide, while the three remaining encircled her.

*Come hither, mine Nosferatu.*
*Your mistress calls.*
*Pierre, tune thine ear.*
*To mine voice; that is all.*
*If death has claimed thee.*
*Rise above its chains.*
*Open thine eyes and speak to me.*

Everyone held their breath, waiting and watching Evee
as she stood stock still, her arms still outstretched. After a
moment or two, she opened her eyes. "Pierre must still be
alive. I hear and see nothing from him."

"Try Moose again with a spell. That might help him
speak more clearly," Gilly said.

Evee pursed her lips, looking unsure. Then she closed
her eyes and lifted her head slightly.

*Come hither, Moose.*
*With clear head and mind.*
*Tell me, show me.*
*What I seek to find.*
*Let thine words be strong.*
*And they direction true.*
*Show me now that I may follow you.*

With her eyes still closed, Evee cocked her head to one

side as if to listen more closely. Blindly, she held out a hand in Gilly's direction, and her sister immediately broke the circle and held Evee's hand.

"A lot of water all around," Evee said. "Tall building. Giant heads with bright colors. Clowns, devils, animals. The heads don't move. The heads don't talk. They're simply there."

Holding tightly to Evee's hand, Gilly closed her eyes and followed the sound of her sister's voice with her mind's eye. She felt her body lighten as if it was filled with air instead of blood and bone. Soon she found herself standing near the shore of the Mississippi River, overlooking it. Nothing in sight but water and faraway bridges.

The sound of Evee's voice made her want to turn around and face the opposite direction, but for some odd reason, she wasn't able to move. Gilly knew in her heart of hearts that if she could only turn around, they'd have the answer to where Viv was. But her feet felt sealed in concrete, her body stiffened by rods of steel, her head like that of a concrete statue. She felt molded, held, imprisoned in place. She strained to hear sound, anything that might give some indication as to what lay behind her. All she heard, however, was the lapping of water as it hit the shore. Seagulls cawing.

Then, from somewhere far away, she heard a tapping sound, like someone knocking on a door. It came from behind her, though, and no matter how hard she struggled, she couldn't turn around to investigate what might have been making the sound.

Frustrated, she let go of Evee's hand and opened her eyes.

Evee's eyes were already open.

"I saw water," Gilly said. "It was the Mississippi River— I know that for sure. But all I heard were seagulls, the lapping of water and a tapping sound like someone knocking on a door."

"Could you make out where the tapping was coming from?" Gavril asked.

"No. I was frigging stuck in place. Really stuck. I couldn't twist my body around, not even my head."

"I didn't get much more than the first time," Evee said. "He kept talking about big heads with a lot of color. Clown heads, devil heads, animal heads. He did mention the water, though, which is what you picked up on, I guess. I don't know why you couldn't see the rest of what he was talking about."

Gilly started pacing the sitting room, thought about Trey Cottle and Shandor Black. "Because some son of a bitch doesn't want you to get too clear a picture by words and doesn't want me to see it at all."

"You're talking about Cottle and Black, aren't you?" Lucien said.

"Damn right I am," Gilly said. "We pissed them off by denying their help, so they're going to make it as hard as they can for us to do this on our own. They *want* us to call them for help." Gilly kicked the leg of a chair. "I'll lay eggs before that happens!"

"Can they actually stop you from seeing when you astral project? Or keep Evee from hearing clearly when she contacts Moose?" Gavril said.

"With the right spell, and Cottle knows plenty, they can do just about anything. I'd bet anything that they're involved in this."

"Can't you do a protective spell or some kind of binding spell to keep them from affecting you?" Gavril asked.

"Of course we can," Gilly said. "But it would be like children shooting at each other with water guns. We do a binding spell or protection spell, they'll come up with something stronger to make our lives and our efforts more difficult."

"Even if they don't know you're putting a spell on them to stop their antics?" Lucien asked.

"That's right," Gilly said. She saw the question still in Lucien's eyes. "Look, I'll show you."

*I bind thee now.*
*Enemy of mine.*
*Powerless unto your kind.*
*Powerless unto mine.*
*So—*

Gilly felt her lips still moving but heard no words coming from her mouth.

"Why didn't you finish it?" Gavril asked.

"Because they shut me down before I could finish," Gilly said, satisfied that she'd proven her point.

"Holy crap," Lucien said.

"Can they hear everything you say?" Gavril asked.

"Only spells directed at them. Then again, where Cottle is concerned, it's hard to tell. He may have a spell that allows him to eavesdrop on us from anywhere."

Evee shook her head, rubbing her temples with the tips of her fingers. "We need help, Gilly. Big-time. I just don't know where to get it."

"Since we're dealing with the sorcerers, I think we need to get the Elders involved again," Gilly said. "Arabella was the one so set on getting Gunner involved in this mess. Maybe he let something slip to Cottle or Black. Maybe that's what led them here. I mean, I seriously doubt they pulled it out of their ass. Visiting us, I mean."

"Didn't they claim they heard word on the street about all those humans dying on Bourbon, and that's what sent them here?" Evee said.

"Yeah, but when have you ever known Cottle to tell the truth?"

Evee shrugged. "Problem is, I don't deal with him

enough to know when he's lying either. We confirmed the deaths, so that's a given. It's the part about him and Black coming here that's the question. It makes more sense to me that those two would have been celebrating all the chaos we're dealing with instead of offering to help."

"My point exactly."

Gilly looked at Gavril for confirmation.

Gavril frowned. "All I know is what I saw when he was here. In that brief visit, I wouldn't trust the guy with his own mother. But I could be wrong. This witch-sorcerer animosity has gone on for generations, from what you told me. If that's the case, then the cards do seem stacked against them."

"I think getting the Elders here is a good idea," Lucien said. "Maybe they can help with your mediumship, Evee, and Gilly with your astral projection. I don't think the sorcerers would think the Elders would get involved at this point, unless Gunner told them different, so having them here helping might just take them by surprise."

"It might be easier for us to go to them," Evee said. "You know how long it takes the Elders to get dressed just to go to the supermarket."

"Yeah, but if we go to them, we could very well be leading the Cartesians to them, as well," Gilly said. "At least we can bring them here in the Camaro, then get them back. The entire time the Cartesians will know we're here. They wouldn't have a reason to track the Elders. Not now, anyway. I'm sure once we're out of the way, they'll be the next target, but until then, we should try to keep them as safe as possible."

"I don't know," Evee said. "The Cartesians have sprung more than one surprise on us. I'd hate to see any of the Elders taken. Even if we bring them here, what's to keep the Cartesians from following the Camaro back to their house and seeing where they live?"

"Because the Cartesians are single-minded," Gavril said. "If their leader wants them to get the Triad, that's where their focus is going to be twenty-four-seven, especially now that they know where you live."

"That's why we bring the Elders here," Lucien said. "If we all piled into the car and headed to the Elders, the Cartesians might follow simply because you're in the car."

Gilly let out a long, frustrated breath.

"What keeps them from breaking into our home?" Evee asked. "If they know we're in here, why don't they just crash the place and take us?"

"Remember, they only come out of their rifts up to the waist," Gavril said. "I'm not sure what would happen if one fell out and wound up on the ground in full sight. Rumor has it, and those rumors come from other Benders, that they'd lose some of their strength because their legs can't hold the bulk of their bodies and heads."

"Well, that's pretty friggin' stupid," Gilly said. "Whoever created those creatures sure didn't think past his ass if he or she created the Cartesians to be limited to the waist."

Lucien shrugged. "Stupid, sure, but it's in our favor. Can you imagine what would happen if they were able to fully drop out of those rifts and start chasing whatever or whomever they were after?"

"True," Gilly said.

"Who exactly created the Cartesians?" Evee asked.

"From what we've been told," Gavril said, "one man was turned into a Cartesian for having defiled a witch's secret meeting. Once it turned, from what I understand, anyway, it figured out that killing anything from the netherworld gave it more power and allowed it to create more Cartesians."

"How?" Gilly asked.

Gavril shrugged. "Stories vary too much on that account. I really don't know. I haven't seen it happen. Something about the power a Cartesian brings to its leader strengthens the leader, and it is able to birth another Cartesian due to that additional power."

"You mean birth, as in a baby?" Evee asked.

"Birth as in waving a hand and another Cartesian appears—at least, that's the best I can put together from the stories I've heard," Gavril said. "No Bender has actually seen it happen, so we're all working on hearsay."

Gilly frowned. "So are Cartesians kind of like the Originals, only they have to eat from the netherworld in order to survive?"

"Yes," Lucien said. "But before they can consume it, they must bring the essence of that netherworld creature to the leader so it can drain it of its power. Then the Cartesian is allowed to feed on the rest of it."

Gilly started pacing the sitting room again. "In order to destroy the Cartesians and be done with them, we have to get to the leader."

"You're absolutely right," Gavril said. "The only problem is, no Bender has been able to detect where it hides. Its minions do the work. The leader only oversees their work, but from where, we don't have a clue."

Gilly suddenly stopped dead in her tracks and looked at Evee. "We've wasted a few Cartesians since the Benders have been here. I don't know what happens to them when they're pushed back to other dimensions, but what if you try to communicate with one, and I'll astral project to where its voice is coming from?"

"Absolutely not!" Gavril said. "I don't know what happens to the Cartesians that are pushed back to far dimensions, but I do know, if you attempt to astral project to whatever one you wind up communicating with, you'll get stuck in that dimension, as well. And we wouldn't have a clue as to how to get you back or if we could ever get you back. Out of the question."

"What about if I just try to communicate with one," Evee said, "and Gilly doesn't astral project? Would that be safe enough?"

Lucien chewed his lower lip and threw a glance Gavril's way. "I honestly don't know. I would think communicating with them wouldn't put you in harm's way, but the problem is, no one has ever tried it. Suppose you do wind up communicating with one, and someone, while you're talking with it, winds up pulling you into the dimension it's stuck in."

"Since you're not a hundred-percent sure," Evee said, "I'd take the chance. Especially if it can identify the Cartesians' leader."

"That's going to be the key," Gavril said. "*If* it identifies the leader. For all we know, all Cartesians could have sworn some kind of destructive oath never to reveal who their leader is."

"Another thing," Gilly said. "I've never heard a Cartesian talk. They only make growling, grunting, howling sounds. How would you understand what any one of them would be saying, Evee?"

"Just a feeling," Evee said. "Their grunting and growling is their language. I might be able to interpret it. I might not. But don't you think it's at least worth a try?"

"Not if it puts you in danger," Gilly said. "If you start communicating with one and you suddenly start disappearing piece by piece into some other dimension, what am I supposed to do? Tackle you?"

Evee rubbed a hand across her forehead, and then suddenly looked up. "Hey, what if I try to communicate with one and use an illusion spell? That way, they'll see multiple images of me and not know which one to go after."

Gilly stared at her, contemplating. She had to admit,

her sister could be right. "That might work, but we need a fallback position if it doesn't and they wind up with the real you."

"Oh, that's easy," Evee said. "I can have all the images of me speaking at the same time, while the real me is hiding away somewhere. Either upstairs or in a closet. They'd be expecting me to be one of my illusions that's standing out in the open."

Lucien glanced at Gavril, who looked at Evee and then Gilly.

"Could that really work?" Lucien asked. "Would that help keep Evee out of danger?"

Gilly squinted her eyes, thinking the plan through. Finally she nodded. "I think it has some potential. We have a lot to gain by finding out who the leader is, but I have more to lose if something happens to my sister. So all I ask is that Lucien and Gavril be on standby with their scabiors. Since we're only going to be dealing with a voice and not a body, I'd say, aim an ear for their voice if one happens to come upon the real Evee."

"No problem," Gavril said.

"You've got it," Lucien agreed.

"Wait," Gilly said suddenly. "Before we attempt this, I think we need to get the Elders here. If we're going to do this, find their leader, I mean, then we should gather all the power we can to make it happen."

"Good idea," Evee said.

"I'll contact them," Gilly said. "Lucien, would you mind going to the Elders, picking them up, bring them here?"

"Not at all, if you think it will help."

"I'm not sure of anything," Gilly said. "Only that, the more power we can throw at this, the better."

# Chapter 15

A couple of hours later, when Lucien arrived with the Elders, they seemed harried and nervous as he all but shoved them through the front door.

"What's going on?" Arabella said. "Lucien came rushing over and said you needed us right away."

"We do," Gilly said.

"Yeah, Lucien came pounding on our door," Taka said. "We thought it was the cops at first. Arabella checked the peephole, saw it was Lucien and let him in. He all but grabbed us and shoved us into the car like we were convicts or something. Then, when we got here, he did the same thing."

"Sorry," Lucien said. "We've had some major issues with the Cartesians, and I didn't want any of you endangered in any way."

"Cartesians?" Vanessa asked. "Where?"

"Had I not rushed you into the Triad house as quickly

as I did, you would have seen them overhead. They've figured out that the Triad lives here, and I think they're bound and determined to wait them out so they can catch them. Kill them."

Taka slapped a hand to her heart. "Why would they want to kill them?"

"Because they're Triad, and the Cartesians' leader wants their power, just like he wants the power from every Original. And I fear, once they've accomplished that, they'll come after the three of you, as well."

"Not if I've got anything to say about it," Taka said, hefting her purse so it hung in the crook of her arm. "How do we help?"

"We want to try something," Evee said. "I want to channel one of the Cartesians and see if we can find out who their leader is. It stays well hidden. No one, not even a Bender, has seen it. Maybe if I can connect with one of the Cartesians, I can get him to talk."

"That's dangerous territory," Arabella said. "You have no idea what kind of power they possess. Suppose you summon one and it suddenly drags you into the dimension where it's stuck?"

"We've thought of that," Evee said. "That's why we wanted you here. I'd like you to do a protection spell over us. Then we'll do an illusion spell. The Cartesian will hear me, but twenty or thirty of me, and won't know which is real. In the meantime, I'll be hiding in the closet beneath the stairs."

Taka blew out a breath. "I don't know. You're talking about some dangerous crap here. We can't afford to lose you, too."

"Talking about being lost, have the three of you tried to contact one of the Originals to see if they have any idea where Viv might be?" Arabella asked.

Evee nodded. "Twice. The first was Moose, one of Viv's Loup-Garous, and the second was Chank, one of my Nosferatu."

"And?"

"They're communicating back with me, but what they're saying makes no sense."

"Like what?" Vanessa said.

Everyone had been standing in the sitting room as if on high alert. Evee motioned for them to have a seat.

Once everyone was settled, Evee stayed standing and said, "Moose keeps talking about big heads, clown heads, devil heads and bright colors. Chank keeps talking about water and big heads."

Arabella frowned. "Instead of going for a Chenille first, let's circle and see if we can get Moose or Chank again. Maybe one of us can make sense out of what they're saying."

Evee shrugged. "I'm game for anything where Viv's concerned."

Everyone stood back up and held hands, forming a circle around Evee.

Evee held out her arms as before; only this time, Arabella did the incantation.

*Come hither, Moose.*
*With clear head and mind.*
*Tell me, show me.*
*What I seek to find.*
*Let thine words be strong.*
*Thy direction clear.*
*Show me now if Viv's far or near.*

As Evee kept her arms stretched out, her eyes rolled up in her head and a male voice came from her mouth.

"She is far, but not too far. She is where the big heads live. The clowns, the devils, the animals. So many colors, it hurts your eyes."

"What else do you see?" Arabella demanded.

"Large, huge boxes with wheels. And blood. I see lots of blood."

"That's the clearest he's been," Gilly whispered. "Keep him talking. I'm going to astral project to him, to where he's seeing all of this."

Arabella nodded but didn't take her eyes off Evee. "What else, Moose? What else is there?"

"Things that make music, but the music isn't playing. The music is dead."

"Is Viv dead?" Arabella asked, her voice trembling.

"Not yet, but not long now. They got her. The bad man got her."

"What bad man?"

"The one with the black fur. The big head with the black fur. Bad, evil eyes, bigger than saucers. He caught her. Hid her."

"Where did he hide her, Moose?" Arabella asked.

"With the big heads."

"Where are the big heads?"

"I don't know. Never been there. Never saw this place before."

Gilly had her eyes closed, concentrating on every word Moose spoke. Images started flashing in her mind's eye. Row after row after row of large papier-mâché heads. Clowns, demons, jesters, princesses, dragons, trailers with ten-foot walls on each side.

"Mardi Gras!" Gilly suddenly shouted.

Evee's eyes rolled back into place, and she lowered her arms.

Everyone turned to look at Gilly.

"Moose is talking about Mardi Gras. I saw the scenes, just like they were in a parade," Gilly said excitedly.

"But Mardi Gras is months away," Taka said. "That can't

be it. Maybe it's a circus. I don't know of any going on in town, but maybe nearby. We could check. Look it up on-line."

"Computer's down," Gilly said. "But it sounds like he was talking about something bigger than a circus. It sounded like Mardi Gras. Where do they store the floats when it's off-season?" Gilly asked.

Evee, Arabella, Taka and Vanessa looked at each other, and then all four of them shrugged.

"We've no idea," Arabella said.

"Who would know?" Gilly asked.

"Someone on the city council, probably," Arabella said.

"Fine." Gilly headed for a house phone, and then turned on her heels. "Sorry, ladies. I just remembered, it's past five. The City Council building closes at four."

"What about the police department?" Taka said.

"Well, that's a bird in a bush if I ever heard of one," Arabella said.

"Huh?"

"We could call the police to find out where they keep the Mardi Gras floats stored, but they've been beating our door down, trying to get to us," Arabella said. "Bad call."

"Then who?" Taka asked. "How about the Office of Tourism? I bet they'd know. Or we could Goggle it."

"Google," Vanessa said.

"Can't," Evee said. "Computer crashed two months ago. Tourism sounds like a good idea, though."

Arabella suddenly lifted a brow. "I bet Gunner would know."

"Whoa," Evee and Gilly said simultaneously. "No sorcerers."

Arabella looked deflated. "What now? He's helped us in the past."

"That may be," Gilly said, "but it could have been a setup."

"What are you talking about?" Arabella asked.

Gilly filled her in on Trey and Shandor's visit to their home and how secretive they'd been about who told them where they lived.

"The only one I can think of who knew and would have told them is Gunner."

"No way he would have done that," Arabella said adamantly. "He knows Cottle and Black are snakes in the grass. There's no way he would have given out that information."

"Then who did?" Gilly asked.

"For heaven's sake, child, remember who they are," Arabella said. "Cottle and Black are sorcerers. It would have been easy for them to get a handle on your location."

Everyone stood silent for a moment.

"Fine," Gilly suddenly said angrily. "Call your boyfriend, Gunner. If that's the only option we have to find out where this Mardi Gras warehouse is, we'll just have to take our chances."

"He's not my boyfriend," Arabella insisted.

"Yeah, okay, whatever," Gilly said. "The house phone's in the kitchen. You can call him from there."

As Arabella hurried off to make her call, Evee shook her head and began to pace. "I think getting Gunner involved is a big mistake. He did help us before, sure, but it's like you said, Gilly—it could have been to use us for info." Her voice shook with worry.

"The two of you need to breathe for a moment," Gavril said. "If anything goes south with this Gunner dude, Lucien and me will take care of him."

"But he's a sorcerer," Evee said to Lucien. "You're not."

"He might be a sorcerer," Lucien said, "but he's twice my age and moves slower. Before he gets any mumbo jumbo curse out of his mouth, I'll have smashed his teeth in. End of story."

"To hell with 'end of story,'" Gavril said. "Not until I knock his balls up into his belly button."

Gilly grinned at Evee. There was enough testosterone flying around the room to rebuild a third man. She felt something warm growing in her stomach, over her heart, as she watched Gavril—his protectiveness, his strength and determination. As hard as she'd tried to keep herself for the sake of the disasters she and her sisters faced, just looking at Gavril always managed to soften her insides and quiet her mind.

Arabella came into the sitting room.

"Any luck?"

"Yes," Arabella said, eyes shining. "I told you Gunner was a good guy and just wanted to help us. The Mardi Gras warehouse is a giant metal building just off the New Orleans pier."

Gavril whistled through his teeth. "Good distance away."

"Doesn't matter if it's in Nebraska. We've gotta go find her," Gilly said.

"What about the leader?" Gavril asked. "Remember the reason you wanted the Elders here in the first place?"

"But Viv's our priority," Gilly said. "We can deal with the leader crap later."

"But what if he sends his entire troupe to follow you to the warehouse? At least if we know what we're looking for, we can take him out and kill two birds with one stone."

"Fine, fine," Gilly said impatiently. She turned to Arabella. "We're trying to reach one of the Cartesians. I can't astral project because I don't know if it'll have the power to pull me into another dimension. So to protect Evee while she channels one, we wanted your help with a protection spell, then an illusion spell. Like she said earlier. She'll be hiding in the crawl space beneath the stairs."

"Then let's get to it," Arabella said. "Join hands—everyone except Evee. You're in the middle of the circle, like before."

As everyone stood and held hands, encircling Evee, Arabella said,

*Oh, enemy mine.*
*Keep thy anger at bay.*
*And leave us here.*
*Among thine fray.*
*Thy shall not touch.*
*A person here.*
*But shall run instead.*
*In voluminous fear.*

Arabella nodded, and Evee began her chant.

*Come hither now,*
*Enemy of mine.*
*Tell me words.*
*That have kept me blind.*

A booming male voice suddenly came from Evee's mouth.

"What do you want from me, you slimy bitch?"

"In what dimension do you reside?" Evee asked.

"None of your business."

"I demand that you tell me by the will and power of all the elementals on this earth. In what dimension do you reside?"

"S-sixth. Happy now, bitch witch? If you want to talk to me, keep your childish spells to yourself."

"I will do as I please, for it is I who commands you now," Evee said.

A loud, bellowing laugh filled the room.

"You control no one," the voice said. "You can't even

control your own. You're a weakling, and you're attempting to play games with one who will be master of the universe."

Evee frowned but kept her eyes closed. "And would that be you? The one who will master the universe?"

"No, you imbecile. The master will soon have enough power to take over this planet you call earth and the entire universe that surrounds it."

"And just who is this master of yours."

"None of your damn business."

Evee pursed her lips for a moment. "If it's none of my business, then why are you making it my business? Why are you after my sisters and me?"

"Are you that dense, witch? Because my master desires your powers. All three of you. Why do you think we've been wasting so much time on the Originals, on the lower echelon, like vampires, elves and such? It's all for the master, and it all leads up to taking the three…well, actually, the six of you down."

"What do you mean six?"

"Well, we certainly can't leave your Elders out of the mix," the voice said. "Wouldn't want them to feel neglected."

"You know, I'm tired of you blowing smoke up my ass," Evee said. "I already know who your master is."

Another boisterous, booming laugh. "And whom do you think it is, Miss Pollyanna?"

Evee held silent for a couple of seconds, letting her mind disconnect from the Cartesian. Then she blurted out, "Your leader is a sorcerer."

Silence filled the room. No booming laugh, no sarcastic remarks. Silence. This set every nerve in Gilly's body on edge.

After a moment or two, the voice said, "You think I'm that stupid that you can trick me by throwing out the first thing that comes to your mind?"

"Oh, it wasn't just something that first came to mind. I know it to be a fact," Evee said.

Gilly knew Evee's proclamation was a ruse but she kept silent.

A roar that sounded like the jet engine of a plane sounded throughout the house, shook the walls.

"Who is the one who told you?" the voice demanded.

"None of your damn business. All that matters is that I know."

Another moment of silence.

"And has your source identified which sorcerer?"

"Of course." Evee tilted her head, taunting it.

"Well, speak, woman!" the voice shouted. "Who is your source?"

"The man himself."

"What man?"

"Your master, ass-wipe."

Another thunder blast shook the walls of the house.

"You want to play games, little bitch witch, then let's play." At that, a crash sounded in the foyer, and long black talons reached through the broken window. Seconds later, another shattered, this one in the sitting room.

"Now," Arabella said.

Evee took off for the crawl space beneath the staircase, while Arabella shouted an illusion spell.

*Double, thrice, by tens shall ye see.*
*No longer one to be seen by thee.*
*Thine eyes shall fully confuse thine mind.*
*Making all evil intentions blind.*
*Blunder thee blunder now.*
*I call upon thee Poseidon, Tiamat and Apsu.*
*To bring strength to my command.*
*So it is said.*
*So shall it be.*

Gilly gritted her teeth as for more than a half hour, windows throughout the house shattered, and talons reached for an Evee they only perceived existed. Arabella's spell had copied Evee's likeness so it appeared that twenty Evees ran through the house, purposely moving from window to window.

When nearly every pane in the house had been destroyed, Arabella called back Evee's lookalikes, and almost immediately, the crashing, banging, howling and screeching stopped.

Gilly went to the storage cabinet beneath the stairs and found Evee inside, sitting with her legs drawn up to her chin and trembling.

"It looks like they've gone," Gilly said. She reached out and took Evee's hand, helping her out of the storage area. Seeing her visibly shaken, Gilly wrapped an arm around Evee and held her close. "We'll get through this, sis," Gilly whispered in Evee's ear. "I promise."

Everyone looked around at all of the broken glass strewn about the house.

"I'll have that taken care of right away," Lucien said. "I'll contact a repair company and throw them a little extra for emergency, after-hours service. Either way, you won't be without windows tonight."

"Th-Thank you," Evee said, her voice shaky.

"Well, the house might look like crap right now, but at least we found out something," Taka said. "Something to work with, anyway. The master of those hideous creatures is one of the sorcerers here in the city."

Arabella nodded. "You made a good choice twisting your words around, Evee. It finally got him to admit that the master was a sorcerer."

Gilly ran her hands through her hair, staring at all the broken glass in the sitting room, the foyer. "Yeah...but which sorcerer is it?"

## Chapter 16

Taka yawned expansively. It seemed contagious, as Arabella immediately hid a small yawn behind her hand. Gillly understood their exhaustion. Everyone had been carrying a boatload of worry and running around the city looking for or protecting the Originals and fighting Cartesians.

"Lucien, would you mind bringing us home?" Arabella asked.

"But aren't you going to come and help us look for Viv?" Gilly asked.

"Of course we are, dear," Arabella said. "But we can't all fit into that Camaro."

"So how do we all get there?" Gilly asked.

"No worries," Arabella said. "I'll get us a ride, and we'll follow each other."

Gilly's eyes narrowed. "Where do you plan on getting this ride?"

"I'm going to call Gunner. He's got quite a fine vehicle.

A Buick, I believe. Plenty of room. That way, if we do find Viv, and she is in dire straits, we can take her straight to the hospital."

"What do you mean, take her to a hospital?" Evee said. "We can heal her right then and there."

"That's right," Gilly said. "And you heard the whole thing that Evee was talking about when she connected with that Cartesian. One of the sorcerers is their leader. How do you know it's not Gunner?"

Arabella shrugged. "I don't know what else to tell you except that I just know. You're going to have to trust me on this one. I just know."

Lucien looked from Gilly to Evee, and then back to the Elders. "Of course I'll give you a ride home. But when you do get that ride, we'll follow each other closely so we can keep an eye on you. It's either that, or you stay here."

"Oh, we'll follow. Not to worry," Arabella said. "I have no idea how to get to the warehouse, anyway. I'm hoping that GPS thing you're wearing on your wrist will get us to the location as quickly as possible."

Lucien nodded. "You know the one thing we didn't ask about was Nikoli and where he might be."

"I have a feeling," Gilly said, "that wherever Viv is, Nikoli's with her." She prayed that was the case. The thought of her sister being alone and injured, seriously injured, made her nauseous. She'd give her life for either of her sisters.

"So, for all intents and purposes, they could both be hurt and in danger," Lucien said. "Suppose Nikoli is already dead? Why don't we try to contact him? Evee, can you do that?"

"Instead of wasting our time in attempting another connection that may or may not work, I say that we go to the warehouse and start searching," Arabella said. "We'll find out soon enough whether Nikoli is there and what condition he's in. First thing's first."

Arabella gave Taka and Vanessa a short nod, and then turned to Lucien. "If you don't mind, we should be leaving now."

Taka picked up her purse and held it close to her chest. "I'm ready."

"So am I," Vanessa said.

"I'm going with Lucien," Evee said.

"No," Lucien said. "You need to stay here, where it's safe."

"What's safe?" Evee said. "They've busted damn near every window in the house. If we can fit everybody in the Camaro, I'd want to take Gilly and Gavril with us, too. If I go with you, at least I can help keep an eye on the Elders, especially if they're going to contact Gunner. I can help with some kind of spell if need be."

"Let her come along," Arabella said. "I'll make sure no harm comes to her. She won't be in any danger."

Shaking his head, Lucien went to the front door, peered out to confirm that there were no rifts awaiting them. Evidently seeing that all was clear, he ran out to the Camaro that was parked in front of the house and opened all four doors. He then signaled for the Elders and Evee to hurry to the car.

When everybody was loaded into the car, Lucien slammed the doors shut, jumped into the driver's seat, turned the engine over and took off.

Lucien was headed for the Elders' home when Arabella said, "If you don't mind, Lucien, I need you to make a stop first before we go home."

Lucien looked at Arabella through his rearview mirror. She was sitting in the middle of the back seat. "And where would that stop be?" he asked.

"Trey Cottle's office."

Evee, who was riding shotgun in the front, swung around in her seat to face Arabella. "Are you freaking crazy? The Cartesian told us that their leader was a sorcerer. It's early enough in the evening that all three of them could be together."

"We don't know that for sure," Arabella said. "But I need to find out some information from Trey and find it out now if we're going to help Viv."

"And Nikoli," Lucien added. "This is against everything I believe in, every rule I've ever followed."

"What is?" Arabella asked.

"Sticking your head into the mouth of a lion before you have a surefire way of locking its jaws open."

"Trey doesn't have a lion," Taka said. "I know because I've been in his apartment. I'd have seen a lion if he would have had one. They're too big to hide."

Vanessa tsked. "That's not what he meant, Taka. He's not talking about a real lion."

"Then what is he talking about?"

"If you'd stop yammering about stupid stuff, you'd find out," Vanessa said, and then pursed her lips.

With a loud exhale, Lucien took a left on Iberville and headed toward Trey Cottle's office.

"I know this isn't something you'd do, Lucien," Arabella said. "You're just going to have to trust that we know what we're doing. Remember that we're witches. There are certain things we can see, know and do that you can't."

"It's not that I don't trust you," Lucien said. "I just don't want any harm to come to any of you, especially Evee. She's not going to get involved in this in any way."

"You're talking for me now?" Evee asked Lucien with a raised eyebrow.

"No, he's not," Arabella said. "He's talking for us. We

wouldn't want you to be involved in this in any way. This is a job for me, Taka and Vanessa. It will be over quickly, but there's something that I need to confirm." When they arrived at Cottle's office, the office lights downstairs were off, but the apartment upstairs, were Cottle lived, as Taka pointed out, had the lights on.

After much shuffling of purses and squeezing through the opening of the car, Vanessa, Arabella and Taka got out of the Camaro. They looked up at the lighted windows. The alleyway gate leading to the stairs that reached Cottle's apartment was locked. Standing at the far side of the gate, Arabella caught sight of the three sorcerers sitting at a table near one of the lighted windows. It looked like they were playing some sort of card game.

"They're all together," Arabella said to Taka and Vanessa. She pointed to the window.

"So what do we do?" Taka asked.

"Get this over with," Arabella said firmly.

"But what do you plan to do or say?" Vanessa asked.

"I plan on finding out which one is the leader of the Cartesians," Arabella said.

"Have you lost your mind?" Vanessa said. "We have no more powers than they do. If one of them really is the leader of the Cartesians, what powers do we have to stop him from turning into one of those monstrosities and destroying all three of us? We'll be toast!"

Arabella looked from Taka to Vanessa solemnly. "I know this is dangerous. I'm well aware of that. But if we don't find out who the leader is, the whole world—the very universe—becomes his. I'm determined to figure out a way to stop him. For now, if one of them comes after us, no old-lady business. Get your running shoes on. If you're wearing heels, take them off and run barefoot. That's it. Be prepared to run if it comes down to it."

"I can barely walk up a flight of stairs without limping," Vanessa whined. "How do you expect me to run away from something like that?"

"I just expect you to," Arabella said. "Now put your big-girl panties on, because we're going, and we're going in for blood, if it comes down to it."

By the light of a nearby street lamp, Arabella searched for a service bell or knocker that would notify Cottle he had company. She found nothing.

"If you're looking for a bell," Taka said, "he doesn't have one. The only way to get attention is like I did last time."

With that, Taka scooped up a handful of pebbles from the side of the street. She threw one at the window where they'd seen the three sorcerers. Instead of breaking the glass, Taka managed to get the pebble to simply ping against the glass.

The sound obviously caught Trey's attention, because within seconds, he was peering out of the window. He looked from side to side, spotted them, smiled, said something to the other two sorcerers, and then disappeared from the window.

Before long, his apartment door opened, and he headed down the stairs and over to the gate.

"How lovely to see you, ladies. Shandor, Gunner and I were just in the middle of a poker game. Would you care to join us?"

"We'll pass on the poker," Arabella said, "but we would like to speak to the three of you, if you don't mind."

"Of course," Trey said. "Please, do come in." He unlocked the gate, and then led them down the alley, up the stairs and into his apartment, where he motioned them to a small sitting room.

The room had a card table near the window, a shelf against one wall that was crammed with books of every genre imaginable and a fireplace against the opposite wall with ladder-back chairs flanking it. From the looks of the hearth and cleanliness of the bricks, Arabella had to assume it had never been used.

When Gunner and Shandor saw the three women enter the room, Gunner stood up.

"What a surprise," Gunner said, his eyes on Arabella. "How wonderful to see the three of you."

Shandor stayed seated, and Arabella caught him giving Trey a look that said, *What the hell are they doing here?* His face was pinched as always, his expression one of anger or confusion. Both emotions looked the same on his narrow face.

"We have a couple of questions to ask you gentlemen," Arabella said. "Please—" she motioned to Trey and Gunner "—have a seat. We won't be here long, and I'm sorry we interrupted your game."

"No, not at all. Please, you have a seat," Trey said. "Would you care for tea or coffee?"

"Nothing for me," Arabella said.

"I'll have some water, if you don't mind," Taka said.

Arabella elbowed Taka who quickly said, "Never mind about the water. I'm not really that thirsty. I just thought I was."

"I'm fine," Vanessa said. "Thank you."

Settling back at the card table, Trey asked, "How may we help you?"

Arabella cleared her throat. "We have it on good information that one of the sorcerers in New Orleans is the leader of the Cartesians."

Taka's and Vanessa's mouths fell open, as did Gunner's; all of them were obviously shocked by her abrupt revelation.

Shandor eyes shifted from Cottle to Gunner, and then back to the card table. He shoved his glasses farther up his nose.

As if they were talking about nothing more serious than the weather, Arabella continued in a calm voice. "Since the three of you are the only true sorcerers in the city, we'd like to know which of you happens to be their leader."

Trey let out a hearty, bellowing laugh. "I don't know who your sources are, but they're very, very wrong."

"I don't know," Arabella said. "Our source seemed extremely confident when relaying the information. Anyway, I just wanted to let you know, in case one of the three of you happens to be the Cartesians' leader, that you've already lost the fight. You're not going to control this world or this universe. It belongs to the humans and other beings who have purposely been placed here. You're not going to affect the weather or any of the elementals. In fact, you'll no longer get a taste of any more of the Originals."

Cottle fidgeted in his seat. Shandor kept his eyes on the playing table. Gunner looked up at Arabella.

"I have no idea what you're talking about," Gunner said.

"I know you know what the Cartesians are," Arabella said.

"Of course I do. We all do."

"Well, again, we have a source that has directed us to you. 'You' being one of the three of you, the leader of the Cartesians. The one who's murdered all of the humans by releasing the Originals. The one responsible for killing one of the Benders' cousins, the one responsible for causing our Triad to live in terror. I just want you to know that no matter which one of you it is, that it will be no more. The three of us are involved now."

"The three of you are old hags who don't know a spell big enough to get yourselves out of a paper bag," Trey said, his voice low and angry, his eyes suddenly ablaze with fury.

"You'd be surprised what we know. We're not like you. We don't throw our spells around just for any reason. They always have a purpose, and that purpose is always to help someone. When you utter spells for your own gain, Cottle, the universe has a way of throwing them back in your face, and not in a good way. So if any of you were planning to take over this world, forget it. We've got that covered."

"You don't have anything covered," Trey said. "You don't have the slightest idea what you're talking about. This source that you claimed gave you information was probably drunk or on drugs, and you were stupid enough to believe them."

"Oh, I don't think they were on drugs or drunk," Arabella said calmly.

"And what makes you so sure of that?" Trey asked.

Arabella cleared her throat again. "Because the source who gave us the information was a Cartesian."

Suddenly Trey jumped to his feet and held his hands out at his sides and balled them into fists. "That's not possible! It's not possible that a Cartesian would point a finger at its master. They are trained to serve, not to give out information. They are to receive it and comply. But never, ever to defile the name of its master."

"Really," Arabella said. "Then I think you'd better have a refresher course, Trey."

"Why are you directing that derogatory statement at me?" Trey demanded.

"Because I have a very strong feeling that the Cartesians' leader is you. There are three of us and one of you. You may have thousands of Cartesians at your beck and call, but all it will take to bring all of them down is chopping off the head of the dog. The rest of the body will die without it. As you know, we're from the Circle of Sisters. Within our group are thousands, which we'll call upon and have here to help our cause. To call the leader of the Cartesians out so it can be confronted and destroyed. We will capture your Cartesians. We will torture them, pummel them with questions, until they'll be begging to give us information."

Trey's body began to shake, slowly at first, and then harder, faster, as if he were having a seizure. He shook so hard, his glasses fell off his face, and his jowls jiggled like so much Jell-O.

With a look of shock on his face, Gunner got up from the card table and backed away from it. In that moment, Trey's head became five times the size of a normal man's, and it was instantly covered with black fur. His arms began to swell, until they were at least five to six times the circumference of a normal man's, and his fingers suddenly turned into talons, just like the Cartesians'.

"You will not interfere with any of my plans," the creature who once was Trey Cottle said. It's voice held a low, menacing growl. "You'll die here tonight, and no one will know any different. You are nothing. You are and have never been nothing. It's you and your own from generations ago that caused this to happen. That turned me into what I am. I will have my due. You turned me into this creature. I will take it back. I will use it to take back what should have been mine in the first place!"

The Trey-creature swiped a hand with its talons backward, seemingly ready to swing at Arabella. Instead it caught Shandor, who had scrambled out of his seat when he saw the transformation happening to Cottle and was standing beside him. Cottle's talons dug deep into Shandor's gut.

With a roar, the creature shook Shandor about like a ragdoll, evidently trying to free itself from the man's entrails. There was no question that Shandor was already dead.

"Run!" Gunner shouted at the Elders. "Run!"

The creature continued to roar, shaking, pushing, trying to free itself from Shandor. Its talons seemed to be cemented into the dead sorcerer.

The creature reached out for Arabella with his other hand, but the Elders were already ten steps ahead of him, followed closely by Gunner.

They flew out of Trey's apartment, ran down the back steps and through the alleyway.

"My car's parked around the corner," Gunner said.

By this time, Lucien was standing outside of the Camaro. "What the hell is going on?"

"Get to the warehouse," Arabella yelled toward him. "Hurry!"

The Elders followed Gunner to his Buick. He hit a key fob that unlocked all four doors, and the Elders jumped inside. Gunner hurried over to the driver's side, scrambled behind the wheel and keyed the engine to life.

As Gunner slammed his foot on the accelerator, Lucien revved up the Camaro and followed him until they got to a side street, where he could take the lead.

After taking a hard left on Bienville, Lucien floored the Camaro, and the Buick followed bumper close, both racing off at breakneck speeds.

# Chapter 17

Gilly paced the floor from the kitchen, through the foyer, into the sitting room and back so many times that her feet hurt.

"This waiting is driving me crazy," she said to Gavril. "When are they going to be back?"

"They'll be back soon, I'm sure," Gavril said.

"Can you contact Lucien and find out if they're at least okay?"

"Of course." Gavril hit two buttons on the sides of his watch, and within a matter of seconds, there came a beeping noise.

"That indicates that he's fine," Gavril said. "I don't know how far away they are or where, but at least we know they're all right."

Gilly nodded, stared at the floor, still pacing. "You know, if Viv and Nikoli are really hurt, we need to come up with something more than just a normal healing spell."

"Wouldn't taking them to a hospital be the best course of action?"

"I don't trust doctors and hospitals. We've always healed our own. I'm going to check my Grimoire to see if there's anything in there we can use that's more powerful than the standard healing spell."

"Don't you know that book cover to cover by now?" Gavril asked. "I remember you telling me that the three of you read yours every day."

"Reading it every day doesn't mean I can't recheck it," Gilly said. "Especially if I'm looking for one specific spell. It's a lot easier to go through it focused on finding one than it is reading each one, knowing that you're reading just to read. Make sense?"

"Totally."

Gilly took off for the stairs, and Gavril followed her. She turned when she got to the fourth step and looked back at him.

"Where are you going?" Gilly asked.

"Oh, I'm following you. I'm not leaving you alone in this house. Look at all the windows that are broken. Do you really think I would leave you in any room with Cartesians hanging around outside, just waiting to break through another window and snatch you at any moment? It's not going to happen."

"But no average human has ever seen our Grimoires," Gilly said. "It's not allowed."

"There are a lot of things that aren't allowed that I think we have allowed," Gavril said. "Besides, is that all I am to you? An average human?"

Gilly bit her lower lip and continued up the stairs, knowing that Gavril was right behind her. When she reached her bedroom, she went to her dresser and pulled open the bottom drawer. After moving aside shirts and lingerie, she pulled out a thick wood-covered book with an odd symbol on the front.

"What is that?" Gavril asked.

"It's an *absolutus infinitus*," Gilly said. "The symbol for eternity."

"Ah, I see now," he said as she held the cover up to him.

She nodded. "Triads have carried the symbol on their bodies since the 1500s. Mine's on my ankle." She twisted her foot to show Gavril and noticed that hers had turned from black to gray, just as Viv's and Evee's had after they'd been intimate with Nikoli and Lucien. Right now, she didn't care what color it was. She opened the book and gave the mirror inside the cover only the slightest glance. She didn't care that it still revealed only gray swirls.

Gilly sat on the edge of the bed and started flipping through the pages, and Gavril sat beside her, looking as she turned them. She went farther toward the back of the book, running a finger across faded words written in a language he didn't understand. The words had been written with what appeared to be a quill pen. Some of the letters were fading and had been retouched with a standard pen. Which made sense. If these books had been transferred from one generation to another, without a touch-up here and there, the words would have quickly become illegible.

"This is something that might work," Gilly said, tapping her finger on one page. She nodded, and then closed the Grimoire and laid it on her nightstand. "It just might work."

"What is it?"

"A different healing spell. One that I've never used before. Neither has Evee or Gilly to my knowledge. But there are a lot of spells in these books we've never used before. The one I just found for healing is different… I hope."

Gavril took her by the hand and pulled her up and close so that she stood between his legs. "I'll take care of you through this. You're not alone, Gilly. Neither are your sisters. Lucien and I are going to be right beside you. We'll find Viv and Nikoli, as well. If you can heal Viv, I trust that you can heal Nikoli."

Gilly looked down at him solemnly. "Unless he's dead. I can't bring back the dead."

"That's a given," Gavril said, "but I don't believe he is. I still feel him, the essence of him, if that makes any sense. If he was dead, I'd know it, just like I knew Ronan was gone when the Cartesian first slashed him. There's an empty spot that I carry in my heart because he's gone for good, but I don't have that same sensation when it comes to Nikoli." Gavril pulled Gilly closer, reached up and put a hand behind her head and kissed her. "We'll hope for the best, right? I don't want to do dead family again. Ronan was enough for a lifetime."

"For the best," she said. Then Gilly leaned into him, their mouths parted and their tongues touched ever so gently. Before she knew it, Gilly had pushed Gavril back onto the bed. She straddled him, kissing him as she always did with the ferocity of an animal that hadn't eaten in days. Starving for food, craving, always craving. She kissed him, and then lowered her lips to his throat, licked him, the essence of him—the scent of musk and male and fresh spring soap. As her lips moved over to his Adam's apple, she began to unbutton his shirt and lowered her mouth even farther. She pulled the shirt from the confines of his pants and pushed it away from his chest. She licked his nipples. First the left, which she teased and toyed with using her tongue; she scraped it with her teeth, and then slid her tongue across his chest to his right nipple and did the same. Only this time, she bit down a little harder.

She continued to lower her mouth down the ripples of his stomach muscles, and as she licked there, flicking her

tongue and sucked on his skin, her hands began to work
on his belt and the zipper of his pants. When both were undone, she tucked her hand inside of his pants and freed his
hardness from its confines. Once she had him, she stroked
him once, twice, three times. After the time it took for her
mouth to travel south, she was able to take him into her
mouth. The taste of him was exquisite. It was like tasting
the essence of him, times a thousand. She wanted to consume him right then and there.

Gilly lowered her mouth, for even as big as he was, she
wanted the entire length of him as far back in her throat as
she could get it. She was only able to manage a little over
half before her gag reflex kicked in. She tried to relax and
take more of him. When she reached the deepest point, her
mouth and throat would allow, Gilly raised her head, licking the head of his penis. Then, lowering her mouth again,
she sucked on him. She used her right thumb and forefinger to circle the bottom of his cock that her mouth couldn't
reach and stroked him.

While she licked, and then sucked on him hard, she heard
Gavril groan and moan her name. "Gilly... Oh, Gilly..."

She didn't want to hear what he had to say, only wanted
to feel him in her mouth. She wanted him to come inside her
there so she tasted all of him, all of who he was and more.
She kept her lips moving up and down, lower and higher,
and then moved one of her hands up and across his stomach
to his nipples, teasing first one, and then the other. She used
a thumb and forefinger to pull them, flick them, rub them.

Then Gilly took the hand that had been stroking him and
moved it lower until it covered his balls. She squeezed them
gently, and then released. Squeezed. Released. Just as she
felt them tighten in her hand, heard his breathing grow fast
and shallow, Gavril suddenly grabbed Gilly by the shoulders and pulled her up.

Gilly had only a second to feel confusion when Gavril quickly flipped her over on the bed so she was beneath him. Gilly fought like a cat, wanting to be back in the same position he'd pulled her from. But he had her on the back, and he was too strong for her to flip over. "No... Gavril..."

Gavril held Gilly's hands over her head, pulled off her blouse and bra, so that her breasts were exposed, and this time he was the teaser. He ran his tongue over her left nipple. He bit down on it and pulled until she cried out, and then he did the same with the other. He encircled them with his lips, suckled on them, scraped them between his teeth. Then he lowered his lips down to her stomach, as low as he could manage to go and still hold her hands over her head.

He put her right nipple into his mouth and sucked and licked, all the while working her pants with one hand, pushing them down, along with her panties, until they were at her knees. From there, she worked her clothes off her body with her feet, until she lay naked from the waist down.

Gavril stopped for a moment and looked into her eyes. "If you move your hands away from where they are right now, I'll stop and walk out of this room. Got it?"

"Don't threaten me, big man."

"Oh, it's no threat, my sweet." Gavril grinned. "It's a promise."

Gilly whimpered and nodded, and Gavril lowered his mouth down the length of her body, down to the sweet part of her that was already soaked with her juices. He teased her, nipped her, and then set his mouth and tongue over her mound with its swollen nub, until she screamed his name.

Gilly felt herself tense. She had to move her hands. Had to touch him. Grip him. Gavril must have sensed the same from her, despite the order he'd given her, because he reached up and grabbed her hands once more, holding them over her head. This time he lay atop her, holding his weight up with one hand so her body wouldn't have to bear it. Then he pushed himself inside of her, his hardness deep into her hot, wet slit.

Gilly immediately bucked up against him, matching him thrust for thrust. She wanted it hard. She wanted it fast. She always wanted it that way. But Gavril took his time, driving into her slow and deep, until she thought she'd go insane. She moved with him. Slow and deep. Deeper, slightly faster. Over and over and over, until she exploded around him.

"More," Gavril said. "I want it all. All of you." Then he shoved himself inside of her again, touching a spot she didn't even know existed. It felt like fireworks suddenly went off in her body, and it threatened to take her head with it…into orbit…into Wonderland. And in that second, her body erupted into an even stronger orgasm than her first. This one soaked him, soaked the sheets beneath her, leaked down her thighs. Only then did he allow himself to release inside of her.

Gavril's orgasm had him calling out her name. He held on to her tight.

When Gavril let go of her hands, Gilly wrapped her arms around him, and he laid there, his head nuzzled in the crook of her neck. She shivered, waiting for the throbbing in her body to slow. He shifted his body ever so slightly so he lay beside her and pulled her close. She curled her body against his, and he smoothed her hair with a hand, stroking slowly, softly, over and over. Her eyes closed, and her breathing grew steady and easy.

With her eyes closed, Gilly had never felt so relaxed in all her life. She had to fight sleep. They had to get up and get dressed. Lucien would be back soon. They had to get up…

Just not this second.

# Chapter 18

Gilly lay face up and naked, in a huge vat of whipped cream. She didn't care that it covered her hair or got into her ears. It felt luxurious as it lapped over her body, like a thousand silk ribbons caressing her body. It made her feel relaxed, and she didn't want to leave it. Something in the back of her mind kept niggling at her, though, reminding her that it would be someone else's turn soon, and she'd have to relinquish her little piece of heaven. She pushed the thought away and just allowed herself to float, moving her arms and legs ever so slightly, so that the cream covered her breasts, rolled over her thighs and between her legs. It felt sensual. Glorious. She couldn't remember how she'd gotten into the vat of whipped cream to begin with and really didn't care. All that mattered was she was here.

"They're here." Gilly felt her body suddenly tense when a strange voice seemingly came out of nowhere.

"They're here. You need to get up."

With a start, Gilly realized she'd fallen asleep and had been having one of the best dreams of her life. A place where she floated without trouble, concern or worry. Her eyes blinked open, and she saw Gavril looking down at her.

"I hear them downstairs," he said. "The Elders, Evee and Lucien. They're back. We need to get downstairs and meet them before they come up here looking for us."

Gilly's brain jolted to full consciousness, as did the realization that she'd just had sex with Gavril. She sprang out of bed, straightened her clothes, put on whatever clothes she was missing, and then hurried to her dresser mirror to make sure she looked as normal as possible.

As she panted and fluttered, Gavril buttoned his shirt and tucked it into his pants. He combed his hair with his fingers.

Gilly grabbed a brush from the top of her dresser and ran it through her short crop of hair, which was sticking up and disheveled.

When she was done, she eyed Gavril, gave him a nod, indicating that he looked about as guilty as she did, but they'd done the best they could.

"I'll go down first," Gilly said. "You follow later. If they ask what we were doing, I'll tell the truth. That we were looking through the Grimoire. Evee will give me hell about having you there while I went through the Grimoire, but I'll deal with her about that later."

As Gilly hurried down the stairs, she caught a loud tumble of voices coming from the sitting room. Amid the mayhem, she heard Arabella, Taka, Vanessa, Evee and Lucien talking over one another.

When Gilly made it to the sitting room, she found them all standing near the fireplace, all gibbering at the same time.

"You should have never—"

"—could have gotten killed!"

"I should have let—"

"—you had no choice."

"I can't believe—"

"We were that close."

"We had no business—"

"It was our business, can't—"

"I should have figured right from the—"

"—and you had no way of knowing."

"Well, we know now."

"—that was a stupid move."

"What an ass he was."

Gilly let out a shrill whistle, which stopped their conversation dead, and everyone turned to look at her.

"Oh, Gilly," Evee said. "You're not going to believe this!"

"Where's Gavril?" Lucien asked.

Gilly looked over her shoulder. "Must be in the restroom. I'm sure he'll be here any second."

As if by command, Gavril suddenly appeared at the sitting room doorway. "What's all the hubbub in here?" he asked. "All of you are talking over one another like a gaggle of squawking geese."

"You're not going to believe this," Lucien said to him. "We know who the leader of the Cartesians is."

"What?" Gavril and Gilly said in unison.

"It's Trey Cottle," Lucien said.

"Get out," Gilly said.

"I should have known," Arabella said. "Right from the beginning. There were signs. The way they stayed cloistered, always up each other's behinds. Their evasiveness, then sudden attentiveness. Their eagerness to help when things really started to turn sore."

"What kind of signs?" Taka asked. "Other than him being a jerk like always?"

"You can't blame yourself," Vanessa said to Arabella.

"Wait a sec," Gilly said, holding her hands up. "How did you find out he was the leader?"

Arabella took the lead and told Gilly and Gavril how they'd convinced Lucien to stop at Trey's apartment.

"And you listened to them?" Gavril said to Lucien.

Lucien shrugged. "I know, I know. I've been beating myself up about it since it started."

"Are the three of you out of your minds?" Gilly asked the Elders.

"Do you want to hear the rest of the story, or are the two of you going to bitch and complain the entire time Arabella's trying to tell it?" Taka said.

"No, I'm sorry," Gilly said. "Please continue. But I think I'd better sit down for this one." And she plopped down onto a couch.

When Arabella got to the part of the story where Trey began to mutate into a Cartesian, everyone, including those who'd been with her, seemed to be holding their breath.

"What did Shandor do while all this was going down?" Gilly asked.

"Die," Arabella said.

"Huh?" Gavril said.

"Trey had those long black talons, and he swung back to strike at me," Arabella said, "but when he swung back, Shandor was standing in the wrong place, at the right time. Trey's talons wound up in Shandor's gut. He kept trying to shake him loose, but those hook-like things on the ends must have gotten caught on Shandor's entrails, because every time Cottle tried to shake him loose, Shandor just jiggled around like a ragdoll. No way Shandor survived that."

Gilly swiped a hand through her hair. "Sweet mother earth. Then what?"

Arabella sighed heavily as if saying anything more would lead her into a coma stemming from exhaustion.

"Gunner got us out of there. We took off from Cottle's and jumped into Gunner's Buick. There was more room in there, anyway. We told Lucien and Evee to follow us here. The thing is, we've got to get out of here. Go and find Viv and Nikoli, of course, but we have to leave."

"Yeah," Taka said. "'Cause the first place he's going to come looking for us is our house, then here."

"Where's Gunner now?" Gavril asked.

"After he dropped us off here," Vanessa said, "I heard him say something about going to his house to get tools. He plans on helping us find Nikoli and Viv and figures we might need something to either get into the warehouse or help them out of wherever they're trapped. Things like bolt cutters, screwdrivers, a hammer and heaven only knows what else. He said he'd be back here to pick us up so we can all go to the pier."

"Y'all aren't going to the warehouse," Gilly said. "There's no way. I just have this sick feeling in the pit of my stomach that Viv and Nikoli are at the warehouse, but Cottle, if he is the Cartesians' leader, put them there as bait. He's waiting for us all to go out there and look for them so he can take us out in one fell swoop."

"If you think you're leaving me behind," Taka said, "you're crazy. We're the ones who found out who Cottle really was. We deserve to be there and help."

"We want to find Viv and Nikoli," Vanessa said. "Viv is one of our own. We have every right to be there to look for her. Besides, we'll have you, Gilly, Lucien, Gunner and Gavril there to help protect us. If these creatures come out of rifts from the sky, they can't reach us in the building."

"That may be true," Gavril said, "but you have to get from the car into the building, then back out again. We have no idea what kind of shape Viv or Nikoli will be in, so it may take us some time to get them loaded into the car.

It's putting too many people at risk if we all go. It leaves no one here."

"That's our point," Arabella said. "What good would just one of us being left behind do if the rest of us get destroyed by Cottle? His intention may be to collect us all in one place, but that doesn't mean he's going to win. We just have to keep our wits about us, find Viv and Nikoli and do what we have to do to get out of that place as quickly as possible."

"He's got hundreds, if not thousands, of Cartesians at his command," Gavril said. "If he calls them all to one place, we might as well kiss our asses goodbye. It won't matter how many of you are left. I don't know how we'll get past his army."

"Pretty down-and-out talking for a Bender," Gilly said.

"I'm only being realistic," Gavril said. "You've fought them with us. You know how long it takes to close a rift. Imagine a thousand opened at one time."

"But can all of the Cartesians get to our dimension all at the same time?" Gilly asked.

"For all we know, Cottle could have them waiting in the very next dimension, which would take nothing for them to rip into ours," Lucien said. "All Cottle would have to do is issue the command."

"Well, we'll drive right into that damn warehouse if we have to," Arabella said. "We wouldn't even have to get out of the car. We'd just slam right into the building."

"Uh, you said the D-word," Taka said.

"Oh, get real," Arabella said. "I've got a few more choice words to give this whole issue."

"Hopefully, it won't come to that," Gavril said. "We have no idea how many steel struts hold up that place. We might wind up slamming headlong into one, killing all of us before Cottle gets a chance to. Maybe Gunner's bolt cutters will help us get the job done."

"Wait," Gilly said. "Since Gunner is a sorcerer, Cottle wouldn't harm him, would he?"

"Yeah, I think he'd slice him wide open," Lucien said. "Especially now that he's with us. To Cottle, that means betrayal, and certain death if he gets his hands on him."

"We just need to take one thing at a time," Gilly said. "First we've got to find the frigging warehouse, then—"

"I know where it is," Taka said. "I visited it a few years ago with a group of tourists."

"What do you mean, you know where it is?" Vanessa said. "Why didn't you say something when Evee was channeling Moose and Chank? Did nothing they say ring a bell? I'm ashamed that it took us as long as it did to figure it out, but you'd already seen the place. Couldn't you put two and two together?"

Taka gave her a "pfft."

"None of that matters now," Arabella said. "What's done is done." She turned to Gavril and Lucien. "The biggest worry we're going to have, despite the hundreds or thousands of Cartesians, is Cottle being there. I just know that he'll want to be there for what he'll consider to be the *coup de grâce*. I doubt he's ever been in the middle of any of the other Cartesian attacks before. That would have been beneath him. But this, having the entire Triad and their Elders wiped out in one shot, he'd think himself to be king of the world."

"That's what he's wanting, anyway," Vanessa said. "Remember what he said at the apartment when he started to morph into that horrid creature?"

Arabella nodded. "Oh, yes. This will be a big deal for him. No doubt. And he set it up perfectly, releasing all the Originals without killing them so they'd wreak havoc on the humans in the city. Enough chaos to keep us running from one direction to another, all the while he's planning this coup."

"We have to focus on him," Gavril said. "The other Cartesians are important, ridding ourselves of them, I mean, but Cottle is the one we have to kill. It's just like we've always said—if you cut off the head of the dog, the rest of it will die. The same logic applies here."

"So, the game plan is to have Gilly, Evee and the Elders look for Nikoli and Viv, while we fight Cartesians and find that bastard Cottle?" Lucien said.

"Sounds about right," Gavril said.

"But Gunner will be there," Gilly said. "He can take my place hunting for Viv and Nikoli, and I can help the two of you fight Cartesians. You know I can do it. I already have. Twice."

"No," Gavril said. "If you find Viv and Nikoli, they're going to need all the healing spells the Triad has to offer."

"I get that," Gilly said, "but the two of you alone can't take on hundreds of Cartesians." She balled her hands into fists, released them. Balled them up again. A hundred Benders wouldn't be able to kill hundreds and hundreds of Cartesians. She felt angry that the situation felt so humongous and hopeless.

"Neither can three," Gavril said. "We'll come up with our own strategy to get as many of them out of the way as possible and keep our eyes peeled for Cottle. For all we know, he may show up in human form so he can gloat. Either way, he's going to want to take a lead role."

"That will be his last mistake," Arabella said.

"Most definitely," Gilly said.

At that moment, a knock sounded on the front door. Gavril went to look through the peephole, while everyone else stood stock still, seemingly holding their breath.

"It's Gunner," Gavril said, and then opened the door.

"Sorry it took me a while," Gunner said, a little out of breath. "I had trouble finding my bolt cutters. Thought we might need them if there was a locked gate we had to get through. I brought other tools, too, in case Viv and Nikoli are trapped in some place too difficult for us to access. I have a hammer, a crowbar, a screwdriver, chisel and a flashlight. They're all in the trunk of my car."

"Did you notice anything coming up here?" Gavril asked. "Any rifts in the sky?"

"Not that I could tell. But to be honest, I wasn't looking for any. I was in too big a hurry to get the tools and get back over here. We've got to go and get Viv and Nikoli before it's too late. Before we do, though, I want to apologize to all of you." Sorrow filled his deep blue eyes.

"For what?" Gilly asked.

"Cottle, Shandor. Especially Cottle. Just the fact that I've spent so much time with both of them over the years and had no clue about any of this."

"It's not your fault," Arabella said. "When you don't harbor evil in your own heart, sometimes it's difficult to see it in someone you're close to."

"Back on track for now, guys," Gavril said. "We think Cottle's set up a trap."

"Captured those two just to get all of us over there. Have us all in one place."

Gunner nodded. "You can probably count on it being a trap."

"Have you heard any word on Shandor?" Evee asked. "Is he involved in this? Is he a Cartesian?"

Gunner shook his head. "The last time I saw Shandor was when the Elders came over to Cottle's apartment. From the looks of Cottle's talons jammed in Shandor's gut, I don't think he survived. I know this is going to probably sound pretty cold, but at least we won't have him to worry about.

Because I assure you, if he was alive, he'd be on Cottle's side, fighting to make certain all of you were dead."

"All right," Gavril said. "So how do we split up?"

"You should be able to hold four in the Camaro comfortably," Gunner said. "And I can roll five in my Buick, no problem. We'll make room somehow when we get our hands on Viv and Nikoli."

"Evee and I will take the Camaro," Lucien said. "Gilly and Gavril can ride with us. That'll leave the Elders with you, Gunner. We'll have to follow you there, because the only person here who seems to know where this place is happens to be Taka and Gunner. She'll tell you how to get there. We'll be right behind."

"In case we get separated," Gunner said, "just stay east on River Road. Follow it until the end near the peninsula. You can't miss it."

"Got it," Gavril said. "Now, first things first," "I want to make sure there are no rifts outside this house with Cartesians waiting for us. I'll check out the area. When you hear me give the all clear, hurry to the vehicle you're assigned to and jump in as quickly as you can."

Gilly felt her stomach twist up in a knot. Every nerve ending in her body on alert. She couldn't wait to get to Viv and wasn't looking forward to the battle sure to come once they found her.

Everyone nodded and followed Gavril to the front door.

Gavril opened the door, stepped outside and called for Lucien. Within a matter of seconds, his cousin was at his side.

"There are two rifts—east side. I don't see any Cartesians hanging out of them, though. Still, I think we should close them before we attempt to get to the cars. It wouldn't surprise me if they're just out of sight, waiting for us to come out. Let's blast them. See if we can make anything happen."

"I'm with you, cuz," Lucien said.

Both of them pulled their scabiors from their sheaths, snapped their wrists, twirled the wands between the fingers of their right hands lightning fast, and then aimed them at the rifts.

Although there were no Cartesians in sight, they still heard loud popping sounds—the same sound that occurred whenever a Cartesian was pushed back a dimension. That confirmed that two Cartesians had indeed been hiding within the rifts, waiting for them to come out of the house.

"Keep shooting until the rifts close," Gavril said.

Together, Lucien and Gavril kept their scabiors aimed at the rifts until finally, after what seemed like a lifetime, the gaps finally zipped closed.

"Now!" Gavril shouted to everyone waiting behind him in the house. "Evee and Gilly in the Camaro. Gunner and the Elders in the Buick. Now! Now!"

As Taka, Vanessa and Arabella scurried outside, looking nervously overhead, Gunner opened the doors to the Buick, jumped into the driver's seat and set the engine to roar. He hit the horn on the steering wheel, indicating to the Elders to get a move on. Within seconds, Taka and Vanessa were sitting in the back seat of the Buick, and Arabella rode shotgun next to Gunner.

Gilly, Gavril, Evee and Lucien scrambled into the Camaro. When Lucien turned the engine over, he lowered his window and signaled for Gunner to go.

Gilly felt they were driving the race of a lifetime. As engines roared and tire rubber squealed on the road beneath them, Gilly wanted, needed them, to go faster. She heard her heartbeat thudding loudly in her ear, over the voice in her head that kept crying out, "Please be alive!"

# *Chapter 19*

Trey Cottle did not know what to do with all the blood. After Gunner and the Elders had run out of his apartment, it had taken him quite some time to calm down enough to morph back into a human. Only then did the hooks on the talons release, enabling him to slide his hand out of Shandor's stomach.

Unfortunately, the poor fool had been in the wrong place, at the wrong time. Shandor had been a decent friend, and it certainly hadn't been Cottle's intent to kill him, but he'd gotten in the way, as he so often did. Cottle had meant to get rid of Arabella, that bigmouthed bitch witch who refused to shut the hell up. She'd taunted him, coerced him, angered him until he had no choice but to allow his true nature to emerge. He'd meant to swing back a taloned hand and swipe not only the smirk from Arabella's face, but her head, if possible, from her shoulders. But Shandor had messed up his plans. Evidently frightened by Cottle's transformation,

Shandor had gotten up from the card table and stood behind Cottle's right side. Wrong move.

Cottle had intended to swipe his right arm forward and do away with Arabella. But when he swung his arm back, talons extended, Shandor had been standing too close to Cottle's backswing and wound up stabbed in the gut by Cottle's talons.

Cottle had done everything he could to shake Shandor loose, which only exasperated the problem. If one could exasperate death.

His remorse for Shandor's death lasted all of two minutes. He grew angrier by the second, unable to disconnect from Shandor, all the while watching Arabella escape.

For years, he'd tolerated Shandor Black. The man had always followed him around like a starving puppy, eager for any bone Cottle might throw his way. He was worth the time and effort, though, because no matter what Cottle asked Shandor, he was more than glad to oblige. He could've asked him to piss in a glass and drink it, and the idiot would have done it without question. It saddened him to see such loyalty lost. But now he had much bigger plans.

His true being, his true self had been revealed; the Elders and Gunner, whom he'd planned to destroy, had found out his secret.

Gunner had broken the sorcerers' rule of silence. How dare he side with those witches instead of standing by Cottle's side and helping to take care of Shandor? Cottle had been slightly shocked when Gunner had taken off at a full-out run, like a little girl, leading the Elders out of his apartment. Gunner was a sorcerer. He should have stuck with his own.

Although Cottle had not quite planned to bring things to a head today, sometimes circumstances presented them-

selves that removed all choices. He presumed that today
was one of those days.

Oh, yes, he had captured Vivienne and one of those ridiculous Benders. He'd hurt them badly, and then stashed them
away, using them as bait, knowing full well that somehow
the rest of the Triad and Elders would find them. It would
only be a matter of time, and that time consisted of the remaining Triad members and Benders finding them before
they died from their wounds.

Cottle counted on the former more than the latter. Although he'd injured Vivienne and the Bender, he'd made
sure the wounds were serious but wouldn't cause instanta-
neous death. The only thing that had concerned him was
the possibility that both might bleed out before being found.

As a Cartesian, he didn't exactly have full control of the
talons that he used to catch and kill his prey. Sometimes
they seemed to have a mind of their own, just reaching out,
digging deep, ripping, tearing, stabbing. It had taken quite
the effort to keep the witch's and Bender's injuries to what
he considered to be a minimum. They had been walking
and talking among each other when he caught them by surprise from behind. From the sound of their conversation, the
Bender had been out looking for Vivienne, wanting to protect her, then found her and planned to return her to safety.

Too late. Luckily, there'd been no witnesses around when
he'd sliced Vivienne's stomach open and cut deep into the
Bender's head.

So now the better part of the show was about to begin.
He knew that the Elders, the rest of the Triad and the Benders had been looking for Vivienne and Nikoli. He also knew
that the remaining two of the Triad had the ability to connect with the dead. One by direct communication, the other
by astral projection. Knowing this, he'd stashed the injured
Triad and Bender in a place that would cause confusion, if

in fact, the Triad member with the ability to communicate with the dead latched on to someone, especially an Original, who might have seen where he'd hidden them. Either way, he really didn't give a damn. He just knew that they would eventually find Vivienne and Nikoli alive or dead. And the condition they found them in didn't matter to him either. They were only bait. To that end, he knew the other two Triad members and the Elders would move heaven and earth to find them, even forsaking the hunt for their Originals for a time.

This was going to be his day of glory.

Cottle went into the kitchen and washed Shandor's blood from his hands. He watched the red turn to pink and get swallowed up by the drain.

He contemplated over what to do with Shandor's body. It was not like he could very well go behind the house and bury him in an unmarked grave. The neighbors were too close, too many and too nosy.

To expedite the situation, Cottle decided to take the easy way out. He morphed back into a Cartesian, the largest of them all, the smartest of them all, and began to dismember Shandor with his talons. He sliced and diced the man into small enough pieces so he'd easily fit in a trash bag and the can outside, the one scheduled to be picked up and dumped in the wee hours of morning by a sanitation company.

When he finished, he allowed himself to turn into a human again. He triple-bagged the body and placed it next to the kitchen door. Then he started scrubbing the floor and carpet. So much blood had soaked into the carpet, he didn't know if he could get all the stains removed.

Nothing a little spell couldn't handle, however. Even though he didn't feel up to doing that at the moment, sometimes crap had to be handled pronto. Should someone come looking for Shandor, which he seriously doubted would hap-

468 Witch's Fury

pen, he had to do something with the evidence of blood all over the floor. It had to be handled before he could continue the quest he'd set for the day.

Cottle gave the command, a short spell that caused the blood that had soaked into his carpet to disappear as if it had never been there before. He checked every room for red specks. The sitting room where they'd been playing cards, the hallway, the kitchen, the bathroom. Even his bedroom, although Shandor had never gone into it.

With that task completed, he wiped down every doorknob and piece of furniture that might be carrying Shandor's fingerprints. Only then did he leave his house. He brought the trash bag with Shandor's remains along with him and carried it down three blocks, where he found a large garbage container. It would have been easier, and he could have gone farther, if he'd owned a vehicle, but he'd never had the need for one until now. All of the business he tended to was done in his office downstairs or somewhere within walking distance of the Quarter. He'd never considered that he might need a car for this.

With the evidence in the large garbage bin, all he'd have to do was wait until trash service made its rounds around four thirty in the morning. Their vehicles would hook up to the Dumpster and simply toss its contents inside the garbage truck.

No one was the wiser. Everyone used trash bags. And he had triple-bagged Shandor's remains to make certain no blood leaked out. It was almost as if Shandor Black had never existed. That's how he viewed it, anyway.

Now, with Shandor out of the way, Cottle was free. He had a long way to go to get to the warehouse where he knew the Elders, the Benders and the two remaining Triad members were waiting. Waiting to see if they could rescue Viv and Nikoli. Walking there would take too long, and he didn't want to alert a cab driver by having him drive him to the location that in and of itself could signal trouble.

Left with few choices, Cottle took a trolley as far east as it would take him, and then hiked the rest of the way on foot, determined to meet his fate.

No more waiting. Too many people knew who he was now, what he was. If the city thought it had a catastrophe on its hands when they were confronted with Originals, they had no idea as to what was about to hit them right between the eyes.

The leader, the master, the god of the Cartesians, was ready to reveal himself in all his glory and begin his fight for power. The waiting was over, and it had been worth it. He would've rather that it would have been on his own schedule, and he blamed the Elders for causing him to have to rush about as he had to now. He wanted to be in a Zen state of mind when it came time to destroy the Triad and the Elders, even the Benders. He wanted to make sure that he would absorb every ounce of power they possessed.

His mind was still on Shandor and on the fact that Arabella, simply by her words, had caused him to become so upset that he'd morphed. Cottle wanted to kick himself for that. For now, they would be on the watch, and his surprise attack as he had planned wouldn't go as neatly or as sweetly as he'd hoped. They'd be on the lookout for him, knowing that he was out and about and probably heading to take charge.

Yes, the world would be his. As would the universe. But for now, he would take the city by storm. And with the Triad and Elders out of the way, no one in the city would have anyone to protect them. It would be death upon death upon death, which is exactly what he'd hoped for, what he'd planned for, what he meant to have happen.

With great power came great responsibility, and he was

ready to take on any and all responsibilities thrown his way. Humans would bow at his feet. Those remaining from the netherworld, like vampires and werewolves, would fear him with great trepidation.

Neither human nor remaining netherwordly creature would ever know what to expect from him at any time. With his power, he could easily wipe out every human.

The thought of so much power and control made him feel heady and anxious.

He'd dreamed so many times of all he would do as he moved on to take over the world, and then the universe. With a flick of a finger, he'd be able to create great tsunamis, huge hurricanes, rains of biblical proportions, earthquakes that would destroy whatever territory he chose.

Oh, yes, that much power was heady. And he was impatient.

The Triad had to go.

# Chapter 20

The Mardi Gras warehouse was a much bigger building than Gilly expected. It was a large gray metal structure with six huge bay doors. The landscape behind the building was the banks of the Mississippi River. To the right of the warehouse was a small peninsula.

To the left of the massive warehouse were storage units. In comparison, the Mardi Gras warehouse was square and looked to be the size of one and a half football fields.

Gunner pulled up to the warehouse, and Lucien, who'd been driving the Camaro, backed up, and then went forward so that they were facing driver to driver.

"Okay," Gunner said. "There are locks on the bay doors, but nothing my bolt cutters can't handle. I'll just have to get my cutters out of the trunk. I'll open the bay door closest to the peninsula. I think that'll leave us a little less exposed. What do you think?"

"Decent plan," Lucien said. He stuck his head out of the

window and already saw the rifts forming in the sky. "The rifts are already opening, which means you've probably got one minute after you get the bolt cutters in your hand to get the bay door open. Think you can swing that? I know that Cartesians are nearby. They're already waiting. Do you think you're strong enough to cut through that bolt?"

"All I can do is try," Gunner said.

"Tell you what," Lucien said. "Pop your trunk. I'll get the cutters and give the bolt a try."

"No," Evee said. "If something comes out of those rifts, we're going to need you and your scabior to get rid of them."

"It won't take me long," Lucien promised. "One snip from the cutters, and I'll have that door open in seconds. Then we'll be able to get inside."

He looked at Evee and gave her a half smile. "It'll be all right. Cross my heart. Now I want you to climb over the seat so that you're near Gilly. And let Gavril sit in the front. He's going to be my wingman. I'll cut the lock open, and if any Cartesian tries anything, Gavril will fry his ass."

"But what if all of them decide to come out of those rifts at the same time?" Evee said. "There's no way Gavril can handle all of them alone."

Lucien gave her a somber look. "If that happens, we'll have to abort."

Turning to Gunner, Lucien said, "Pop it."

Gunner reached for a lever on his dash, pressed it and the trunk of his Buick swung open. Lucien jumped out of the Camaro with Evee yelling in the background, "No!"

Gilly tugged on her sister's arm. "Do as Lucien said. We've got to make this easier, not harder. Come back here with me so Gavril can sit up front. At least he'll have a chance to fight off some of the Cartesians long enough for Lucien to get the bay door open."

No sooner had Gilly said that than she saw in the rearview mirror that Lucien already had the bolt cutters in his hand and was working on the lock. The handles looked at least four feet long; the jaws could have fit around the neck of her familiar.

"Get it now, cuz!" Gavril said, aiming his scabior at one of the rifts.

With a loud grunt, Lucien squeezed the handles of the cutters together and sliced through the lock. No sooner did the lock hit the ground than he slid the bay door up and open.

"In the warehouse! Everybody, now!" Lucien shouted.

Everyone sitting in both vehicles began scrambling like mice. The Elders and Gunner out of the Buick, Gilly, Evee and Gavril out of the Camaro. All of them raced for the open door of the warehouse.

Fortunately, Gunner had the forethought to bring a flashlight, because they couldn't find a light switch anywhere near the opening, and it was darker than pitch inside. Not that turning on the lights in the warehouse would have been a smart idea. Might have drawn unwanted attention.

Gunner aimed the flashlight toward the back of the warehouse, and as far back as Gilly could see, there were big heads, most of them as tall as five feet, all made from either papier-mâché or Styrofoam. There were clown heads, devils, voodoo priestesses, snakes, giant bubbles, princesses, kings, animals and cartoon characters. Every theme was so typical for a Mardi Gras celebration in New Orleans. Colors beyond imagination glittered everywhere: red, gold, purple, green, silver, white and blue. The heads sat atop what looked like flatbed trailers with ten-to twelve-foot sidewalls, where, during the parades, riders stood dressed in costumes, tossing beads and trinkets to onlookers.

The walls of the floats were too high to look inside from either end. Behind each, however, were two doors, which

Gilly assumed was the only way the riders had access into or out of the float. She opened one set of back doors and saw a retractable set of steps.

For them to go through every one of these floats, door by door, step by step, to find Viv and Nikoli, would take them nearly a month.

"Viv!" Gilly shouted.

"Nikoli!" Gavril yelled.

Their voices echoed throughout the building.

No voices returned, save for their own.

Gilly heard a skittering sound nearby and caught a mouse running by in her peripheral vision. It was obviously running to safety.

"Great," Gilly said. "Just what we need. Mice."

Although the inside of the building was quiet, the tin structure caught the sounds of traffic two streets away. The rumble of tires, the screech of brakes, the blast of horns.

"There's no way we're going to find them," Gilly said to Lucien. "Not unless we climb into each and every frigging float in this place."

Gilly walked farther inside the warehouse and saw pieces of Styrofoam strewn about the floor near places where mice had chewed off a decorative nose or ear.

"Viv!" Gilly yelled again. She cupped her hands around her mouth to form a haphazard megaphone. "Viv, are you in here?"

Still no response. As hard as Gilly worked at holding back tears, they came anyway, stinging her eyes.

Viv couldn't be dead. She refused to believe it. She still felt her sister deep inside her heart and mind, which told Gilly she was still alive. But the feeling was beginning to wane, flashing on and off like a flashlight with dying batteries.

Gilly knew they didn't have much time to find Viv

or Nikoli. Her own steps were growing slower, her voice weaker, all signs reflective of Viv's condition.

"Nikoli!" Lucien shouted from behind Gilly.

Everybody stood quietly, listening for a few seconds.

"I'm not hearing anything," Taka said. "And we can't just stand here and keep complaining that we'll never find them in all this mess."

"She's right," Arabella said. "Vanessa and Taka, you two come with me. We'll start on the other end of the building and work our way to the middle. Lucien, Evee, Gavril and Gilly can work it from this end until we meet up."

"I'll come with you," Gunner said to Arabella. "It's darker back there. You'll need this flashlight. I'll also be able to get the back doors of the floats open and the stairs down for you."

"Sounds like a plan," Gilly said. "But keep calling Viv and Nikoli. They might hear us, or more importantly, we might hear something from them."

As the crew divided, Gilly jumped toward the first float in her line of sight. It had a princess head, and the trailer it was attached to had been shaped like a pumpkin with many windows. She unlatched the back doors, pulled down the retractable stairs and scrambled up the stairs onto the float. "Viv! Are you here?"

Dusk was pressing in on the sky and pressing into the open bay door. Although Gilly was working the floats near the door, it was getting harder and harder to see anything.

"We've got to find some lights in here," Gavril said. "No matter what attention it may draw. If we don't, we could lose Viv and Nikoli forever. The two of you, keep searching floats. I'm going to look for some kind of light switch."

Somehow, amid the chaos, Gilly found her rhythm. She unlatched the back doors of floats one handed, pulled down retractable stairs, ran up the stairs and throughout the float, calling Viv and Nikoli's name. She didn't bother righting the stairs or closing the back doors of one while she ran off to the next.

"Viv! Nikoli!" Gilly yelled until her throat hurt. She heard the Elders calling the same names from the opposite end of the warehouse.

Gilly saw the flashlight bouncing from one wall to the next and assumed that Gavril had managed to confiscate the light from Gunner, at least until he found the warehouse's light switch.

"Hey, wait, I think I found something!" Gavril yelled. By the beam of the flash, Gilly saw a long metal box with a large lever connected to it, and all of it was attached to a steel pole.

"This is either going to set off an alarm or turn on the lights," Gavril said. "So hold on to your drawers."

"Push it!" Gilly shouted. "Push it up! If it's an alarm, we'll get the hell out. If it's lights, we'll go to church."

Gavril nodded and threw the switch up.

Suddenly, the inside of the warehouse lit up like a football field at game time. It made the colors of all the decorations nearly blinding to the eye.

Gilly saw a devil's head and remembered how, when Evee had connected with him, Moose kept talking about one. She understood now why all he could talk about was big heads, lots of colors.

Gut instinct sent Gilly running to the float with the devil's head. "Viv! Where are you?"

Then suddenly, from somewhere, about a quarter of the way where the Elders were, Gilly heard the softest of moans.

"I heard something!" Gilly shouted. "Arabella, it's not far from you. A moan. I heard someone moan."

"We're going through them as fast as we can," Arabella shouted back. "We're even taking them two at a time."

"Please hurry!" Gilly took off running to the area where she thought she'd heard the moan come from. She remembered how Moose had kept talking about a devil's head. Although there was more than one float with a devil's head, she took off for the biggest one. The one with the red horns, the evil grin set in perpetuity by black glitter.

When Gilly reached the float, she unlatched the back doors, and before the stairs had a chance to unfold all the way to the ground, she scrambled inside.

There, from around the center aisle that gave the float a second tier, she spotted a foot. It took only two more steps for Gilly to confirm it was her Viv. Her pulse quickened and tears immediately stung her eyes.

"She's here! She's here! I found her!"

Within seconds, Lucien jumped onto the float beside Gilly and scanned the inside. He spotted Nikoli at the head of the float.

"Nikoli's here!" Lucien shouted. "He's here!"

"Look at the blood," Gilly cried. She pressed two fingers against Viv's jugular. "She's breathing, but it's shallow. She barely has a pulse."

"Same with Nikoli," Lucien said. "Cuts on his face. His stomach."

In a matter of seconds, the rest of the crew was inside the float, everybody wanting a firsthand view of Viv and Nikoli.

"Oh, mercy," Taka cried. "They're dead. They're both dead."

"Stop your yammering," Vanessa snapped, and then looked over at Gilly. "Is she dead?" She glanced over at Lucien. "Is he dead?"

"Both have lost a lot of blood. Pulses, but barely. Shallow breathing."

"Mercy, mercy, so much blood," Taka said.

"Nikoli," Lucien said. "You can't waste out on me now,

man, you hear? You come back to me. Come back to us. Wake up. Wake up!" Lucien lay his hands, one over the other, and placed them over Nikoli's heart; he pressed five times, and then pinched Nikoli's nose closed and blew air into his mouth. He did that over and over.

Viv's pulse was fading fast.

"They're here," Gilly yelled. But where was here? "They needed help in the worst way. I need your help, please. Their injuries are bad. I don't know if we can save them. We may already be too late."

"Can't you use your spells?" Gavril asked.

"I don't know," Gilly cried. "Look at them. Look at them. We can't bring back the dead. No spell can." If there had been a spell to bring back the dead and it called for the sacrifice of her own life, Gilly would have gladly given up hers for Viv's. Her heart ached that it wasn't that simple.

# Chapter 21

As Gavril held Nikoli's head in his lap, and Gilly held Viv's, Arabella, Vanessa and Taka paced the back end of the float.

"Oh, my goodness. Oh, my goodness," Taka said. "What are we going to do? They're dying, and there's nothing we can do."

"We're going to heal them. That's what we're going to do," Gilly said.

Gilly motioned to Evee to come over to her and said, "I want you to put your hands on her, over her wound. Concentrate on healing her."

In that moment, howling and growling echoed through the building. There was scratching and scraping overhead on the tin roof that sounded like nails on a chalkboard. The howling grew louder, and the scratching and scraping stronger. All of it was so loud, Gilly couldn't hear herself think. Not that she wanted to. She'd have preferred this to be a nightmare she could wake from.

"They're trying to get inside," Vanessa cried. "The Cartesians are trying to get in."

Gilly saw Lucien's face grow beet red with anger. "Gavril, you hold on to Nikoli. I'm going to see what's going on out there."

"Don't go out there by yourself, cuz," Gavril said.

"I have to at least assess what's happening."

"Then I'll check it out," Gavril said.

Gunner stepped forward and said to Gavril, "You stay with them. I'll go out there and see what's going on."

Arabella cried out. "Gunner, no! You have no way to battle those creatures. There're too many of them."

As if to confirm what she said, the howling and growling amplified tenfold. The scratching, ripping, scraping against the tin roof grew louder, as well, adding to the cacophony of horror.

Gilly had never seen a Cartesian, save from the waist up. But Arabella, Taka and Vanessa had when they'd witnessed Cottle's transformation. They'd know what to look for.

"Stay here with Viv," Arabella said to Gilly. "I'm going."

"No, you're not going by yourself," Gilly said. She laid Viv's head gently back on the floor of the float, and then got to her feet.

With everyone on the float yelling for her to stay put, Gilly climbed down the ladder at the back of the float. She was about to hurry for the open bay door at the far end of the warehouse, when she felt a strong pair of arms grab her beneath her arms and pull her back onto the float. It was Gavril.

"You're not going anywhere," he said. "You stay here. I said I was going, and I am."

Before Gilly could protest, Gavril scrambled down the

stairs, folded them back onto the float, and then closed the back door and locked it so she couldn't follow.

"Stay put," Gavril said to Gilly from the other side of the door. "I'm serious. Stay put."

"Open the damn door!" Gilly shouted.

The screeching and scratching that had been deafening on the roof suddenly changed direction. The same sound was now coming from the sides of the warehouse. Gilly wanted to put her hands over her ears for the sounds were so tinny, the scratch-scratch so disturbing, it made her teeth hurt.

When Gavril made it to the bay door, he heard Gilly shout, "What do you see?"

For a second, he didn't answer. The only word that came to his brain was *hell*.

"What do you see?" Gilly repeated.

"Hell," Gavril yelled back. "There are more rifts in the sky than I've ever seen before. Hundreds of them. Thousands of them. It looks like somebody took a giant razor blade to the sky and sliced it a thousand times over."

Gavril hurried back to the float, unlocked the back door and dropped the stairs.

"Well?" Taka asked.

"We're in deep," Gavril said. "There are thousands of rifts out there. So many, I couldn't see them all. Not one Cartesian hanging out of any, though."

Taka pointed with a shaking finger to the back of the warehouse, where the bay door was open. "If there are that many out there, how are we going to get back to the cars? We won't be able to? We're trapped."

"I can help fight them with the extra scabior," Gilly said, and before Gavril had a chance to protest, she turned to Evee. "Did you say your healing spell over Viv?"

"Yes, twice," Evee said. "But it's not working. I need your help."

"Quit being such a wuss," Gilly said angrily. "You've got to concentrate."

"I did!" Evee cried.

"Try again."

Gilly looked from Lucien to Gavril. "We've got to get the rifts that are closest to the opening of the warehouse closed. Give me the extra scabior so I can help."

As Gavril started to object, Gilly reached around him and yanked the extra scabior he kept tucked in the back of his pants.

"Now, you either come with me and charge this damn thing, or I'll go alone and figure it out by myself," Gilly said. "Either way, we've got to get the rifts closest to the warehouse opening closed. There may be hundreds, even thousands, up there, but not all of them can reach this far. They're held at the waist. Not all of them will be able to reach us. I know we can fight the ones closest to us so we can at least get out of here."

A piece of tin overhead ripped open, and they saw a black talon from a Cartesian punch through the roof.

"Are we having fun yet?" a voice called from the back of the warehouse. "Tell me you're having fun. That would make me so very happy."

Gavril and Gilly froze, as did everybody else.

The sound came from the back of the building, low and muted but distinct. It was the voice of Trey Cottle.

## Chapter 22

Gilly's heart was torn in two. She didn't want to leave Gavril and Lucien alone, fighting all of the Cartesians that obviously were preparing to drop from the sky. But her Evee needed her help with Viv, and she couldn't just turn her back on them.

She suddenly thought of a plan. A spell.

Above the howling, growling and scratching sounds echoing through the building at a deafening rate, she yelled at Evee, "Use the elemental spell."

"I can't," Evee said. "Not by myself. You know that. It takes all of us to do that."

Gilly felt like an ass. She did know that.

With a growl of her own, she ran back to the float where Viv and Nikoli lay, seemingly lifeless. Evee was leaning over Viv, her hands on her wounds and covered in blood.

Viv's eyes were closed, her breathing too shallow, her pulse barely there. Gilly had no other choice. Lucien and

Gavril would have to do the best they could with what they had. Her sister had to be her priority right now.

Above the howling and growling, she moved Viv's hands over to her wounds, and then laid hers on top of Viv's, and Evee rested her hands on top of Gilly's.

The Elders stood to one side, whispering to themselves what Gilly could only imagine was a healing spell of their own.

"All right, you start," Gilly said to Evee.

Evee closed her eyes and issued her incantation:

*Oh, king and minions of water be.*
*Ever mindful of my voice to thee.*
*Loose thy healing powers from depths below.*
*So that health through this woman shall flow.*

Gilly quickly followed with her portion of the elemental spell:

*Oh, warriors of fire.*
*Hear my plea.*
*I invoke thy healing powers unto me.*
*That they shall bring healing for all to see.*

Since Viv was unable to complete the incantation, Gilly and Evee said it for her:

*Giant earth thy orbit bound.*
*Release their power from underground.*
*From which fire, water and earth abound.*
*And instant healing shall now be found.*
*Ingus, Hosomus, Faroot—So let it be!*

Gilly opened her eyes and saw that Viv's eyes were still closed, and blood still trickled from her abdominal wounds.

"Again, Evee. We say it again, as loud as you can. Scream it if you have to!"

Evee nodded and yelled:

*Oh, king and minions of water be.*
*Ever mindful of my voice to thee.*

*Loose thy healing powers from depths below.*
*So that health through this woman shall flow!*
Gilly shouted d her part until her throat hurt.
*Oh, warriors of fire.*
*Hear my plea.*
*I invoke they healing powers unto me.*
*That they shall bring healing for all to see!*
Gilly nodded at Evee and both bellowed Viv's part at
the top of their lungs.
*Giant earth thy orbit bound.*
*Release thy power from underground.*
*From which fire, water and earth abound.*
*And instant healing shall now be found.*
*INGUS, HOSOMUS, FAROOT—SO LET IT BE!*
In that moment, Viv's eyes fluttered open.

Gilly removed her hands, as did Evee, and both saw, right
before their eyes, the wounds on Viv's stomach close up as
if they were being sutured from the inside out. No more
blood. Relief tumbled over Gilly's heart in huge waves.
Exhaustion weighed down her shoulders.

Viv looked up at them, confusion on her face. "What are
you two doing here? Where am I?"

"It's a long story, sweetie," Gilly said. "But for now,
we're going to need your help. How are you feeling?"

"Strong as an ox. Feels like I just woke up from a long
nap," Viv said. "What happened?"

"You were hurt pretty bad. We just finished an elemental healing spell on you," Evee said.

Viv sat up as if nothing had ever happened to her. She
got to her feet, wobbled for a second, and then caught her
footing. "Where's Nikoli?"

Gilly frowned. "He's at the front of the float, and he's
not doing so well."

"We've got to get to him now," Viv said.

"For more reasons than you know," Gilly agreed.

As the Elders continued to silently murmur their own spells, Gilly, Viv and Evee went over to Nikoli.

Viv's face turned gray when she saw him, saw the blood pooled around his head.

"We've got this," Gilly reminded her. "No worries. Just concentrate. Same elemental incantation for him that we did for you."

"What?" Viv asked. "What's all that noise? I can barely hear you. Are we on a Mardi Gras float? What the hell?"

"More long stories," Gilly shouted. "Too long to go into now. We've got to help Nikoli. We're going to do the elemental incantation for him, but you're going to have to shout your part as loudly as you can so it'll be heard over all this racket."

Gilly, Viv and Evee placed their hands on Nikoli's wounds, and Gilly started shouting her part. She was quickly followed by Evee, and Viv brought up the rear, saying hers so loudly, she went hoarse at the end.

"What is all that noise, though?" Viv asked. "What's making all that noise?"

Gilly sighed. "Cartesians. Hundreds of them, if not more. And they're trying to get to us."

Viv's face went a shade paler than pale. "Oh, no. No way they're going to get us."

No sooner had Viv finished her confirmation than Nikoli's eyes flickered open, and they saw the wound on his head close almost instantaneously. He blinked, looking similar to Viv when she'd been healed, like he'd just woken from a long nap.

Nikoli pulled himself up, resting on his elbows. "Where are we?"

"We're at the Mardi Gras warehouse," Gilly said. "Both you and Viv were hurt badly and brought here. Used as bait by the leader of the Cartesians to bring us all out here. His intent is to collect us all in one place and kill us all at one time."

"I'll be goddamned if I'm going to let that happen," Nikoli said, getting to his feet. "Where are Gavril and Lucien?"

"They are at the far end of the warehouse, at the last bay door. The one we opened to get in here," Gilly said. "There are hundreds, if not thousands, of rifts out there right now, but not a sign of a Cartesian. I think they're hiding just behind those rifts, awaiting a command from their leader in order to attack."

"Some of them have to be out, though," Evee said. "Look at the one that ripped the hole in the roof."

"Some may have sneaked out," Gilly said. She turned to Nikoli. "Gavril and Lucien are trying to close the rifts closest to the building so we'll have a way to get out."

"Where's my scabior?" Nikoli asked, and then padded the right side of his belt, found his sheath and pulled his scabior from it.

"I know you're itching to go out there and kick ass with your cousins," Gilly said. "But how are you feeling?"

"What do you mean? I'm fine. Like I had a long night's sleep. Hell, I don't even remember how I got here." He turned to Viv. "Are you okay?"

She nodded. "Shaken and a bit out of sorts with all that's going on, but okay. I don't remember how I got here either."

"It's the leader of the Cartesians," Gilly said. "We found out who he was. It's Trey Cottle."

"One of the sorcerers?" Viv said, surprise on her face.

"Yeah, if that's what you want to call him," Gilly said. "He's just waiting to give the command to his Cartesians. His plan was to hurt you and Nikoli, hide you out here and have us scrambling all over hell and back to find you. This place is so secluded, I guess he figured it would be the perfect spot to get rid of us all."

Viv's brow furrowed.

"He used you and Nikoli as bait," Gilly explained. "He knew we'd all come looking for you. Now that we're all in one place, I think his plan is to take all of us out. The Triad, the Elders, even the Benders."

"I'll be damned if I'm going to let that happen," Nikoli said. He got to his feet, blinked his mind back into clarity. "I'm going to help Gavril and Lucien."

"There's a fourth scabior," Gilly said. "Ronan's. If you can charge it, I know how to use it. I used it before. I can help."

"You stay here," Nikoli said. "All of you stay here."

Gunner, standing near the Elders, his eyes closed, his mouth moving as if he were saying his own incantation for safety and protection.

Nikoli's command to stay put went in one of Gilly's ears and out of the other. She appreciated Gunner's efforts because she certainly did not plan to stay put while the Benders fought off all of those Cartesians alone. One more person in the fight might not make that big a difference, considering the number of Cartesians they were dealing with, but it couldn't hurt. For all the right and wrong reasons, Gilly wanted to watch Gavril's back. If any Cartesian came within a hundred feet of him, that ugly bastard would meet its match.

*Chapter 23*

Although she had been told to stay put, Gilly had never been one to follow directions to the letter, much less be told what to do.

She jumped off the float and told Viv, Evee, Gunner and the Elders, "Stay here. I've got to help the Benders. There are four scabiors. Certainly one more helping to fight these Cartesians can't hurt."

"But you can help better here," Arabella said. "We can do an illusion spell so that the Cartesians will see hundreds of Luciens, Nikolis and Gavrils. They won't know which ones are the real Benders. We can do the same with this building, create lots of them so they won't be able to tell which one we're in."

"But there are so many rifts in the sky," Gilly said. "You have no idea. They can easily get one of the Benders accidentally. There are so many of them, and they seem to be multiplying faster than we can count. If we triple the illusion spell and create thousands of Benders and warehouses, that may work…it may."

"All we can do is try," Taka said. "We've got to at least try that. We've got six witches here. We can multiply the illusion spell until infinity if we wanted to."

"Yeah," Vanessa said. "We'll hold hands, meld our energies together and create as much chaos for them out there as they are creating for us in here."

Gunner, who'd been standing off to one side, said, "May I join you? I don't know the illusion spell, but I can certainly add my energy and intent to have that spell come to pass."

"Yes, please join us," Gilly said, and she held out her hand to him. Once she had hold of him, everyone linked hands with them. And the witches began to chant:

*Double, thrice, by thousands shall ye see.*
*No longer one to be seen my thee.*
*Thine eyes shall fully confuse thy mind.*
*Making all evil intentions blind.*
*Blunder thee, blunder now.*
*We call upon Poseidon, Tiamat and Apsu.*
*To bring strength to our command.*
*So it is said.*
*So shall it be.*

Gilly opened her eyes. They still held hands. Everyone else's eyes were closed, intent on the incantation they'd just cast. The scratching and ripping at the roof came to an abrupt halt, and Gilly only heard an occasional scrape on the roof. She was about to take off from the float to the open bay door to see what was happening with Lucien, Gavril and Nikoli, when she heard a voice from the far end of the warehouse.

"Well, well, well, aren't all of you resourceful."

The sound of the voice made Gilly's blood run cold and sent goose bumps running up her arms. The voice belonged to Trey Cottle. The same voice she'd heard earlier. Only this time, she saw him clearly. This wasn't an illusion, a sorcerer's version of ventriloquism. Trey Cottle was indeed here.

Gilly saw him walking slowly up the center aisle, heading toward them. He was in human form, dressed in black slacks and a white button-down shirt. Sweat had beaded up on his bald head and forehead. His glasses sat near the tip of his nose, as usual.

"You think you're smart, don't you?" he said. "All of you. You're not as smart as you think you are. You might have healed Vivienne and that Bender, and you may have confused my Cartesians, but it won't be for long. I just wanted to make sure I got one last look at all of you before your demise."

"Kiss my ass, Cottle," Gilly said.

Cottle screwed up his face as if the thought of kissing her ass nauseated him. "Be as brash as you wish, little girl. But it's my turn now. Your ancestors ruined my life many generations ago, and I've carried that loathing all this time. Today I get my revenge for what they created when they made me. They had no idea that this sorcerer, this leader of the Cartesians, had the ability to take over the world, the universe. All it took was a mind like mine. One that is resourceful, powerful, industrious. Your little illusion spell may have confused some of my Cartesians, but when I issue my command, they'll no longer be confused. They've been trained since their conception as to what to do to you when the time came. And today is that day. All of you are exactly where I want you. The Triad, the Elders. The Benders are only lagniappe. I will get my revenge, and I will gain more power than any human or any being from the netherworld will ever be able to control. I will master this world. Your Originals that I set free to wreak havoc over the city, I will take down one by one. Consume every one of their powers."

"I don't believe you," Gilly shouted. "You're just a big talker."

Cottle paused in mid step. "Really? Then why don't you go to the bay door and tell me what you see happening out there right now? Then, once you've seen it, let's see if your belief system changes."

"I'm not going anywhere near you, you ugly asshole," Gilly said.

Cottle tsked. "Such language from a beautiful mouth. It really doesn't matter. Because all of you will be nothing shortly. And I'll take my time with each of you, savoring every morsel of your powers. What was taken from me, my life, normalcy, I will take it back, and in spades. There will be no more Triad, no more Elders. I'll have run of this city, this state, this country. And it will continue until I have control of the very universe. You see, that's been my plan all along. Someone takes something from me, I take everything back, plus more. There'll be such regret, such mourning, such sorrow that the world itself will not know how to deal with it. And the beauty of it all is that I'll never get caught. Just as it took as long as it did for you to find out that I led the Cartesians, I'll never make that mistake again. I'll have no need to, for my powers will allow me to do as I please, when I please, how I please and from whichever dimension I please. Save for the eleventh, of course, since nothing returns from there. But there is no one on this planet strong enough, powerful enough to send me there. That leaves me in complete control."

"I bind you, you ugly son of a bitch," Viv said. "I bind you from coming any closer to us."

"You bind me?" Cottle laughed. An ugly snort of a laugh. "How droll. Do you think your petty little spells can affect someone of my stature?" He took a step toward them, and then another. "How's that for binding? Do you actually think you can keep me from you? All I have to do is keep the Benders busy outside with the Cartesians—if the Benders survive, that is—and I'll have you all to myself. And that is exactly what I wanted. I don't have to depend on my minions to bring you to me. I have each of you all to myself, and there's not a damn thing you can do about it. For you see, even though I'm a Cartesian, I'm still a sorcerer and can bind all of you little snits to the floor of that contraption that you're standing in now."

"You're giving yourself far too much credit, Cottle," Gilly said. "We may be witches, but we do have our powers."

"Oh, I'll agree with that," Cottle said. "But they're so miniscule in comparison to my powers, it's laughable. I can take you down like a flea, and all the others will be able to do is watch as I suck every ounce of power from you until you're left drained, like an empty plastic bag. Dead, drained, owned by me."

Gilly leaned over to Evee and whispered, "We have to say the 'Marsailla Mon.'"

Evee frowned. "I don't know that spell."

Gilly turned to Viv. "We have to say the 'Marsailla Mon.' The three of us."

Worry marked Viv's face. "The 'Marsailla Mon' is so far back in the Grimoire, I don't know that I can remember how it goes."

"Just repeat after me," Gilly said to Viv and Evee. "I saw it today when I went through my Grimoire. For it to work, though, you have to take all the anger and frustration you feel over all that's happened to us in the last couple of weeks and let it bubble to the surface. Let it rise up until you want nothing more than to knock somebody out. Think of the loved ones we've lost, and let love follow those emotions.

Mix them together, but let those emotions be your power source, not your brain."

"And what could you possibly be whispering about at a time like this, you little pathetic bitch witch?" Cottle said to Gilly. "You think you're going to connive some kind of trick to escape from me? That's a laugh. I can take all of you down in one fell swoop. But I just can't help but be greedy and take one at a time, making the others watch, feeling useless, helpless. I want to savor the look of horror in the eyes of your sisters and Elders while I take you down."

"Leave them alone, Cottle," Gunner said, suddenly appearing. He took a step forward. With a wave of his hand, Cottle sent Gunner flying to the opposite end of the float.

"Stay out of this, pissant, before I turn you into a groundhog," Cottle said. "You're taking the side of witches over your own. I never thought I'd see the day."

"You're not my own," Gunner said, getting to his feet. "I don't know what the hell you are, but I don't want any part of it. I'm a sorcerer, not one of your stupid minions. What you're doing is wrong. As sorcerers, we have a code we live by, and you're certainly not living up to that."

"Screw the code," Cottle said. "I'm making up the codes now, and any to come. That's what leaders of the universe do. As for you, I'll simply take the miniscule powers you have and make them my own. Don't want you to feel left out, right? When was the last spell you cast, Gunner? Two years ago?"

"That's because I don't like taking advantage of people the way you do," Gunner said.

"Shut up!" Cottle said. "You don't have any idea what you're talking about, so the best thing you can do is keep your damn mouth shut." Cottle put his fingers against his lips and moved them from right to left, like he was zippering them shut. Suddenly, Gunner's mouth pinched closed, and he couldn't open it to say anything further.

"Grab my hands now," Gilly said to her sisters. "Take all the anger you feel toward that bastard, all of the passion you have for the ones you love—let that be the catalyst that drives this spell. Now hold your hands up. We're going to say this spell twice to make sure it sticks. We'll have to make it quick before he catches on and comes after us."

Gilly studied the Elders. "I know you want to help, but it has to be just the three of us. I'm not sure why. Just something I know."

Arabella nodded. "We understand more than you know."

"The three of you, please do a support spell," Gilly asked. "So that ours can be the most powerful it can be."

"No problem," Taka said.

"Of course," Vanessa agreed.

Gilly turned to Gunner. "I know you can't speak now, but please, in your mind, say a spell that will give extra powers to ours."

Gunner nodded enthusiastically.

With that, Gilly, Viv and Evee, still holding hands, raised them up high.

"What are you up to now?" Cottle chortled. "Going to play 'Ring Around the Rosie'?"

Gilly felt fury roll through her as she thought of how close she came to losing Viv, her missing Originals and all of the humans who'd lost their lives because of the asshole standing in the middle of the warehouse. All the Benders had sacrificed, even one of their own. In that moment, her mind and heart filled with Gavril, with his bravery and determination. With love for him.

Gilly could tell her sisters were experiencing the same emotions, for their grips tightened on her hands.

"Just repeat after me," Gilly whispered to her sisters. Then said loudly,

*Hochezamo, conja, marsailla mon.*

*Elementals far and wide.*

*Come hither and forgo thy pride.*

"Stop!" Cottle screamed.

*Bind together one to one.*

*And shout into the universal ear.*

*That every power in the cosmos may hear.*

"Shut your mouth before I kill all of you right this minute!" Cottle began to transform into a Cartesian, standing at least ten feet tall, his head five times the size of a human's.

*Combine thy strength and open thee.*

*The folds of time to rid us of our enemy.*

*Hochezamo, conja, marsailla mon.*

*Let it be said.*

*Let it be done.*

*Forever!*

With legs that looked like they belonged on a grizzly bear, Cottle was now on his feet, talons fully extended.

"Again!" Gilly shouted.

Having already gone through it once, the Triad spoke the spell in unison.

*Hochezamo, conja, marsailla mon.*

*Elementals far and wide.*

"Shut up!" Cottle yelled, quickening his pace toward them.

*Come hither and forgo they pride.*

*Bind together—*

"Noooo!" Cottle screamed.

*One to one.*

*And shout into.*

*The universal ear.*

*That every power in the cosmos may hear.*

*Combine they strength and open thee.*
*The folds of time to rid us of our enemy.*

"No! No!" Cottle's voice began to shiver and shake, and he stood in place, his entire body trembling.

*Hochezamo, conja, marsailla mon.*
*Let it be said.*
*Let it be done.*

Then the Triad, the Elders and even Gunner, who was now able to move his mouth, shouted together, "FOR-EVER!"

As they watched, Cottle rose into the air and blipped out of sight, like a soap bubble that had burst. They heard a loud popping sound, and then a second one, a third, a fourth; they were up to ten before all went quiet.

"Oh, hell, no, you bastard. Not the tenth dimension. You're going to the eleventh, where you'll never be able to return," Gilly said. "*Hochezamo, conja, marsailla mon.* Let it be said, Let it be done, *now!*"

And for the first time ever, for a Bender, for any of the Triad or any other being listening, there came one more popping sound. Trey Cottle had been pushed back to the eleventh dimension, from which there'd be no return. To a place where he'd be trapped forever.

In that moment, the scritch-scratching against the building stopped immediately. Gilly took off running for the open bay door, with Evee, Viv, the Elders and Gunner following closely behind.

When they reached the door, Gilly saw Gavril, Nikoli and Lucien standing just outside with their scabiors in hand and a look of shock on their face as they looked upward. Gilly followed their gaze and saw that there was not one rift left behind. The dusky sky was a starlit gray with a quarter moon.

"They just vanished," Gavril said. "We were trying to

close them up, you know, the ones closest to the bay doors, then suddenly, poof—every damn rift just disappeared."

Everyone looked up at the sky. A normal sky. A rift-less sky.

Gilly smiled and looked at Gavril. "It's like you've always said. Chop off the head of the dog, and the rest of it will die. Cottle's gone. In the eleventh dimension. He'll never be back to harm us again."

"How...how did you—"

"We're the Triad," Gilly said with a soft smile. "Had I not looked through the Grimoire earlier, I wouldn't have seen the spell we needed to get rid of him. It saved our lives. The Cartesians are gone. With their leader gone, they've followed him to the eleventh dimension. Like sheep, one runs off a cliff, the rest follow because they're too dumb to think for themselves. I feel it in my heart and soul that we're free of them. We're finally free."

# Chapter 24

"It feels weird, doesn't it?" Viv said, as she and her sisters sat with the Elders at Bon Appetite, Evee's café. They'd decided to meet there for an early breakfast.

"Which part?" Gilly asked.

"Which part what?" Taka asked, and then shoveled down a forkful of scrambled eggs.

Vanessa sipped on some orange juice. "She means, all of it feels weird."

"That's what I'm trying to understand," Taka said.

"Oh, for the love of breakfast, eat your eggs and hush," Vanessa said, and then took a big gulp of juice, emptying her glass.

Gilly did her best to help Taka understand. "Viv is saying that our lives feel weird right now. And I asked which part feels the weirdest."

"Oh," Taka said, dabbing the corners of her mouth with a napkin. "So which part feels the weirdest to you?"

"I don't think there's only one part," Gilly said. "Everything is so different now."

"Right," Evee said and took a sip of coffee. "It got stranger still when the Benders left to tend to Ronan's family."

Viv nodded. "True. But you can't blame them for hurrying out there so quickly. They could have bailed on us right when it happened. Instead, they stuck with us throughout the whole Cartesian ordeal."

"We were very lucky to have them," Arabella said. "If I've ever felt grateful that humans were around, I certainly was for them."

"Well, you'll be seeing more of them," Gilly said. "Gavril told me they'd be back in about a week, as soon as they helped get their uncle's affairs in order."

"Why are they coming back if the Cartesians are gone?" Taka asked.

Vanessa and Arabella gave her a sideways glance that all but said, "You're kidding, right?"

Taka shrugged her shoulders and sopped up the last of her grits with a piece of biscuit. Then she patted her stomach. "I'm so full, I can't even swallow my own spit right now."

"Ugh," Viv said. "Maybe you should have stopped after the half pound of bacon you ate."

"It wasn't a half pound," Taka assured her. "I just asked Margaret, Evee's manager, to triple the order, which should have been only six slices. She put ten. Can I help it if I like bacon and Margaret likes me?"

Gilly chuckled. "Taka, you crack me up."

"But you don't think I'm like…cracked?" Taka asked.

"Oh, for Pete's sake," Vanessa said. "Do you have to fish for compliments? Of course you're not cracked. A little pit-ted in a few places, but not cracked. You were a big help during all we went through, and I'm proud of you."

Everyone sitting at the table stopped in midbite or mid-drink and looked from Vanessa to Taka.

Taka's mouth dropped open, and then she snapped it shut when she realized she'd still been chewing on part of the biscuit. She quickly washed her food down with some water and eyed Vanessa. "You mean that? Like, you didn't even shoot me a comeback. You really meant it?"

"Of course I did," Vanessa said, and patted Taka's hand.

Tears welled up in Taka's eyes. "I'll never forget this day as long as I live," she said.

"I think there are quite a few days we won't forget," Arabella said. "And I've got to throw my two cents in, too. I'm proud of all of you. When things got really tough, not one of you gave up. You simply kept on fighting and hunting like all Circle of Sisters would."

"Well, except for me," Viv said with a smirk. "I evidently decided to take a nap through some of it."

"That's not even funny," Gilly said to her. "You have no idea how hard we searched for you, how worried we were about you. We came so close to losing you." She shook her head. "I don't even like to think about it much less talk about it."

"Then we'll change the subject," Arabella said. "But before I do, I have to admit, and I think Vanessa and Taka will agree. We were wrong about the Benders. I'd hate to think where we'd be now had it not been for them. And anyone who can make the three of you so happy can't be bad certainly." She smiled. "Now, something I've been wanting to know but never found the right time to ask," she said to Gilly, "was, how did it feel to pop one of those suckers back into another dimension?"

Gilly grinned. "Glorious. Once the scabior was charged,

it was pretty easy. All I had to do was aim, and the lightning bolt that came from the bloodstone on top of the scabior just seemed to know what to do."

"Yeah, but you had to have a pretty good aim," Evee said. "It's not like the scabior did it all by itself."

Gilly felt her cheeks grow warm. "Okay, so my aim was decent. Now can we talk about something else?"

"You know what feels pretty weird to me?" Viv said. "It's going to the compound and not having to feed any of the Originals. Turning that entire place into a cattle ranch was a decent idea. We're getting some great stock out of there and selling them for premium. Even better, no more wee hours of the morning. I can work eight to five like a normal person."

"I hear that," Evee and Gilly said in unison.

"Those early mornings were killers," Gilly said. "I'd leave the bar and grill around two in the morning and couldn't even take a nap before I had to start corralling the Chenilles for their feedings."

"Want to know what's better still?" Arabella asked.

All eyes zoomed in on her face.

"It's that the Originals all came back, only as human. We don't have them to feed anymore because they're no longer turning into the creatures they were. And that's because of you three."

"As in me, Viv and Evee?" Gilly asked.

"That's right," Vanessa said.

"It's all because of you," Arabella said. She lowered her voice and glanced around to make sure no one was eavesdropping.

Arabella leaned into the table and lowered her voice. "As the Triad, you've been told the story about how the Nosferatu, Loup-Garous and Chenilles came to be in the first place, remember?"

"Yeah," Gilly said. "The first Triad got pissed off at their boyfriends for cheating on them."

Arabella grinned. "Close enough."

"That first Triad was so angry over the incident, they collectively issued an incantation that they had no business messing with. It turned their betrotheds into the creatures you've been responsible for all these years."

"But why did it have to follow so many generations?" Gilly asked. "We didn't have anything to do with it. Doesn't seem fair, does it?"

"I agree," Taka said, and then burped.

"Although it didn't seem fair," Arabella said after giving Taka a disgusted look, "the creatures would never die, and someone had to watch over them. The Elders at the time simply added to the punishment curse that the ones who'd be responsible for them would be Triad, since they were the ones who created them."

"Well, I'm glad things worked out the way they did," Viv said. "It's only been a couple of weeks since this all came down, but I've seen some of my Nosferatu in town in human form. I don't think I've seen them so happy."

"Same with my Chenille," Gilly said.

"Ditto with my Loups," Viv said.

Arabella wiped the corners of her mouth with a linen napkin and placed it on her plate, indicating she was done with breakfast. "Thanks to you, they're all living normal lives."

"What about them?" Taka asked.

"Them who?" Vanessa asked.

"The Triad, ding-dong. Don't they get to live normal lives?"

Arabella studied Gilly's, Viv's and Evee's faces. "Once a Triad, always a Triad," she said. "That's something that can't ever be changed. You were born witches, and you will die witches. The same goes for me, Taka and Vanessa. It's just part of who we are."

"Being a witch isn't such a bad thing," Vanessa said. "You can always use your powers to help others, and for the love of biscuits, there are a lot of people here who can use your help."

"You most certainly can," a man said from beside them, startling everyone at the table.

Taka slapped a greasy hand to her heart. "Gunner, you almost gave me a heart attack!"

"I'm sorry for startling you," Gunner, dressed in a gray-and-black pin-striped suit with a gray shirt and black tie, said. "I saw all of you sitting here and was hoping you'd have room for one more."

"Of course," Evee said, and then got up and grabbed a chair from one of the other tables. She placed it between her and Arabella. "Please have a seat."

A look of embarrassment crossed Gunner's face. "I hope your conversation wasn't private. If it was, please let me know, and I'll be happy to meet up with all of you some other time."

"Not a conversation you can't be involved in, that's for sure," Gilly said. "We've just been talking about how different things are now that the Originals are all humans. Our lives and sleep have certainly changed because of it. How about you? How've you been?"

Gunner settled himself into the offered seat with a huge smile on his face. "Life hasn't been this good since… I don't remember when."

"I'm so glad to hear that," Arabella said.

"How so?" Taka asked.

"Well, first of all, I don't have to worry about Cottle and Black anymore. Both always gave me a hard time if I didn't spend enough time with them. Now, with so much time on my hands, I've been able to open my own hardware store."

"How wonderful," Vanessa said.

"Oh, it's not a huge place," Gunner said, "but it makes me happy. I've kind of always been handy with tools and such, so helping others find just what they need is right up my alley."

"Do you miss hanging out with the sorcerers?" Taka asked.

"Taka!" Arabella reprimanded.

"It's okay," Gunner assured Arabella, and then turned to Taka. "To be truthful, no. I always make a little time in the evening to go over my spells so I don't get rusty. You know, just in case I need to use one or two. But so far, it's only been me, the hardware store and my handful of spells. Oh, and I've started a vegetable garden. Tomatoes, okra, snap beans—things like that." He blushed. "I'm sorry, I'm sure this is boring the heck out of you."

"Not at all," Arabella said. "You sound very resourceful."

"I don't know about that," Gunner said. "But it's nice to be able to share fresh vegetables with my neighbors. In fact, if any of you ladies are interested, I've got a boon supply of tomatoes this season. I'd be happy to bring some to you if you'd like."

"That'd be great," Arabella said. "I love tomatoes."

"You hate tomatoes," Taka said with a frown. "You said they give you hives."

"Only raw tomatoes, dear," Arabella said, and Gilly could hear the restraint in her voice.

"That's very kind of you, Gunner," Gilly said. "Thank you. And thank you for all you did to help us in our many hours of need. Had it not been for you and your car…well, there's no telling how this might have turned out."

Gunner lowered his head for a moment, and when he

lifted it, his lips were pursed. "If it's the same to you, Miss Gilly, I'd prefer never talking about that again. I'm just getting over nightmares about it now."

"Me, too," Taka said. "I keep dreaming of clown heads and devil heads and—"

"He asked us not to discuss it any longer," Arabella told Taka with a stern look.

"Oh…yeah…sorry," Taka said.

Gunner gave her a small smile. "Well, ladies, if you'll excuse me, I'm off to the store." He turned to Arabella. "I noticed you were here and just wanted to stop in and say hello."

After they shared their goodbyes, Taka leaned over toward Arabella. "I told you he likes you."

"He sure does," Vanessa added.

"Both of you stop it right now," Arabella said. "He's just a nice man and likes all of us."

"Hmm, I don't know," Gilly said. "He looked to be pretty sweet on you."

"Like sugar on a cream cake," Evee said.

"Don't encourage them, please," Arabella said. "They give me a hard enough time as it is."

Viv chuckled. "It's kind of hard to miss, though, Arabella."

"Well, miss it and move on," Arabella said, and then abruptly stood up from the table and headed out the door.

"Hey, you forgot to pay for your breakfast," Taka called after her.

"That's okay," Evee said. "I'll put it on a tab. Tell Margaret she had cream cake with sugar on top."

With that, the entire table of women broke into side-splitting laughter.

# *Epilogue*

*Three months later*

She wanted a candlelit wedding, but since St. John's Cathedral wouldn't allow open flames due to fire marshal laws, the wedding planner had come up with a the idea of putting battery-operated flickering flames in five-foot bronze candle holders that stood at the end of each pew.

The front of the altar was adorned with carnations, roses, lilies and a nervous groom awaiting his bride. The entire congregation fidgeted as they waited for the organist to play the right song.

As the organist began the traditional wedding march, the priest walked to the front of the altar.

Everyone in the church let out a little gasp as the bride entered the church. She was beauty personified.

She wore a slim-fitting, floor-length satin wedding dress with three-quarter-length lace sleeves, a high lace collar, and a row of mother of pearl and sequins that ran from her bodice to the floor, down the middle of the gown. A three-foot satin train flowed behind her, and her veil, the front covering her face, was made of simple tulle that reached her shoulders, with rows of baby's breath forming the crown. She walked with her arm linked through that of a handsome young man, who led her to the altar.

There were no bridesmaids or flower girl. She'd wanted a simple ceremony. The only two thing she'd insisted on were the candles and to have someone walk her down the aisle, both of which the planner had managed to accomplish.

As the ceremony began, sniffles could be heard in the audience. The cathedral was nearly packed to capacity. Neighbors, friends—it seemed like the entire community at large had come to participate and wish the bride and groom the best of luck.

When the priest finally said, "I now pronounce you man and wife. You may kiss the bride," Gunner Stern gently lifted Arabella's veil and kissed her softly on the lips.

The entire congregation went wild with excitement. People whooping and shouting, "Congrats!" and thunderous clapping.

As Gunner and Arabella headed down the center aisle, arm in arm, their expressions couldn't have been happier, or their smiles bigger. The moment they reached the steps of the church, the congregation followed, throwing dry rice at the bride and groom for good luck.

The couple jumped into a waiting limousine and was whisked off into the night.

They'd told no one where they were headed for their honeymoon, and Gilly couldn't blame them. So much had happened over the past three months, ever since they'd gotten rid of Trey Cottle, their lives had become so different. Of the Originals that had gone missing, Gilly had spotted many walking the streets in New Orleans as human. They were no longer tied to the creatures they once were. No more hiding in dark corners. No more hidden feedings. They were now permanently human.

The Triad no longer had Originals to feed, but could still enjoy their company. The Originals had been family to the Triad, and they always would be. Just because they'd become human hadn't changed that at all. It all seemed so gloriously strange.

It took the Elders to make sense of it all. They explained that back in the 1500s, the original Triad had turned the men they were to marry into a Nosferatu, a Loup-Garou and a Chenille. They'd held hands and combined their powers, fed by anger to turn them into the creatures that had lasted for so many generations. When Viv, Evee and Gilly had joined hands and issued the spell to destroy the enemy, they did it with the same amount of fury as the first Triad, only fury for their loved ones that have been lost. Fury over injustice. Fury over the chaos that they had to deal with and for the humans who had died because of it. Fury over Cottle and his manipulative ways and his determination to take over the world and the universe. That same fury that started this all in the beginning broke the curse, for its origin was different. No longer were there any Chenilles or Nosferatu or Loup-Garous. There were still offshoots of the Originals, like vampires, werewolves and the like. Those did not disappear. But they were someone else's worry. No longer that of the Triad.

Lucien, who'd been chosen to walk Arabella down the aisle, was grinning like a kid who ate an entire jar of cookies. He took Evee by the shoulders and hugged her close. "I can't wait."

"Me either," she said.

The city itself, people who'd witnessed some of the Originals killing the humans, went silent. It was almost as if they'd had their memories erased. No one ever brought up the incident again. The police no longer bothered the Elders and, in fact, nodded hello cordially whenever they crossed them on the street.

No longer did they have to worry about relationships with another human. And the proof of that would be solidified by the triple wedding planned in the same Cathedral two months from now. Evee was to marry Lucien, Viv had Nikoli, and Gilly had her precious Gavril. Man and wife. Since the traumatic incident with Cottle, they'd become inseparable, each Triad with her Bender, learning the depths of one another. They lived, laughed, loved and craved more of the same.

Never in a million years would Gilly have thought that possible. The entire time she and Gavril had been intimate, she had feared the repercussions of their actions, thinking that, because of their sexual exploits, they had caused things to become worse. When, all that time, it had been Cottle planning his universal domination.

Man and wife.

Finally, without consequence.

All because of love. All because of the fury of love, the passion of love.

As if to prove what she was thinking, Gavril squeezed Gilly's hand, and she glanced up at him as they walked down the steps of the church and down the Riverwalk.

"I love you," he whispered.

"I love you more," Gilly said aloud, and then smiled, knowing she'd never have to fear those words again. Anger and disdain had caused the curse to be issued so many years ago, and it had taken the fury of unconditional love mixed with determination to break it. Love broke the curse. Love bound her to Gavril. And love gave her a new forever.

\* \* \* \* \*

We hope you enjoyed this story from

Unleash your otherworldly desires.

Discover more stories from
Harlequin® series and continue
to venture where the normal and
paranormal collide.

From passionate, suspenseful
and dramatic love stories
to inspirational or historical...

With different lines to choose from
and new books in each one every month,
Harlequin satisfies the most voracious
romance readers.

# *Love Harlequin romance?*

## DISCOVER.

Be the first to find out about promotions, news and exclusive content!

**f** Facebook.com/HarlequinBooks

**y** Twitter.com/HarlequinBooks

**◎** Instagram.com/HarlequinBooks

**℗** Pinterest.com/HarlequinBooks

ReaderService.com

## EXPLORE.

Sign up for the Harlequin e-newsletter and download a free book from any series at **TryHarlequin.com.**

## CONNECT.

Join our Harlequin community to share your thoughts and connect with other romance readers!
**Facebook.com/groups/HarlequinConnection**

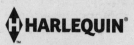

**HARLEQUIN®**

**ROMANCE WHEN YOU NEED IT**

HSOCIAL2018